ENDLESS CHAIN

*Also by Emilie Richards
in Large Print:*

To the One I Love
Wedding Ring

This Large Print Book carries the
Seal of Approval of N.A.V.H.

Endless Chain

Emilie Richards

Thorndike Press • Waterville, Maine

Published in 2005 by arrangement with Harlequin Books S.A.

Thorndike Press® Large Print Core.

The tree indicium is a trademark of Thorndike Press.

The text of this Large Print edition is unabridged.
Other aspects of the book may vary from the original edition.

Set in 16 pt. Plantin by Liana M. Walker.

Printed in the United States on permanent paper.

Library of Congress Cataloging-in-Publication Data

Richards, Emilie, 1948–
    Endless chain / by Emilie Richards.
        p. cm. — (Thorndike Press large print core)
    ISBN 0-7862-8048-4 (lg. print : hc : alk. paper)
    1. Shenandoah River Valley (Va. and W. Va.) — Fiction.
2. Toms Brook (Va.) — Fiction. 3. Guatemalans —
United States — Fiction. 4. Emigration and immigration —
Fiction. 5. Conflict of generations — Fiction. 6. Quiltmakers
— Fiction. 7. Quilting — Fiction. 8. Large type books.
I. Title. II. Thorndike Press large print core series.
PS3568.I31526E53 2005
    813'.54—dc22   2005018327

ENDLESS CHAIN

As the Founder/CEO of NAVH, the only national health agency solely devoted to those who, although not totally blind, have an eye disease which could lead to serious visual impairment, I am pleased to recognize Thorndike Press★ as one of the leading publishers in the large print field.

Founded in 1954 in San Francisco to prepare large print textbooks for partially seeing children, NAVH became the pioneer and standard setting agency in the preparation of large type.

Today, those publishers who meet our standards carry the prestigious "Seal of Approval" indicating high quality large print. We are delighted that Thorndike Press is one of the publishers whose titles meet these standards. We are also pleased to recognize the significant contribution Thorndike Press is making in this important and growing field.

Lorraine H. Marchi, L.H.D.
Founder/CEO
NAVH

★ Thorndike Press encompasses the following imprints: Thorndike, Wheeler, Walker and Large Print Press.

Acknowledgments

Many thanks to the volunteers at La Casa de San Felipe in Elizabeth City, North Carolina, for sharing La Casa and the wonderful work they do there, and for allowing me to participate on my brief visit. Particular thanks to Bev McGee, whose energy and willingness to help are always admirable.

Thanks to Fran Bevis for graciously sharing her knowledge about nursing homes, and the duties and schedules of personnel.

Thanks to Gloria Alvarez and Erica Fuentes for their patient assistance with Spanish phrases and for always understanding so perfectly exactly what I needed.

Thanks to attorney Joshua Berman, who

answered all my questions on federal laws and guidelines.

Thanks as always to my wonderful resident sports consultant, minister and impromptu editor, Michael McGee.

As always, despite all their efforts, any errors in the novel are mine alone.

And finally, thanks to the late Reverend Nick Cardell and many others who have gone to jail to protest the School of the Americas and shared their experiences in interviews, letters and journals. From these the seed for this novel was planted.

Chapter One

*Shenandoah Community Church
Wednesday Morning Quilting Bee
and Social Gathering — August 6th*

The meeting was called to order at 9:00 a.m. in the quilters' beehive. Helen Henry suggested (once again) that we change the name of our group to SCC Bee and be done with it. She insists that reading the heading of the minutes takes most of our business session. To please Helen, who lacks patience, we agreed to drop "Morning" from the written notes, beginning next week.

Cathy Adams brought a quilt top for show and tell in the Chinese Coin pattern, using oriental prints. (Peony

Greenway noted politely that Cathy paid too much for them.) *We will begin quilting the top after Labor Day, when we hope to be finished with a lap quilt of appliqued Autumn Leaves, which will be a gift for Martha Wisner.*

Helen agreed to stay after the bee and help Cathy square up her quilt top so that the finished product won't look like it was quilted by "drunken sailors." Please note the quotation marks. I am only the scribe.

Kate Brogan brought her two youngest children as guests. After Rory jumped on Cathy's quilt top, Chinese Coins will need all the help Helen can give it. The meeting was adjourned soon after, and those bag lunches that survived Rory's karate demonstrations were shared among the quilters who remained.

Sincerely,
Dovey K. Lanning, recording secretary

"So . . ." Anna Mayhew looked up from one of her tiny, even stitches and wiggled her eyebrows to signal what was to come. "I hear Chris-tine Flet-cher —" she punched all the syllables "— is coming for the fund-raiser tonight. What do you suppose she'll wear to the party?"

"The heck with what she wears," Dovey Lanning said. "Let's talk about where she's going to *sleep*."

"There is a child under the quilt frame." For the life of her, Helen Henry couldn't figure out why she had to remind the others. At the moment little Rory Brogan was banging the floor at her feet with a picture book of talking bunnies that his mother had given him to read. Kate Brogan was nothing if not an optimist.

"Rory!" Kate, an attractive thirty-some-thing brunette, vacated her chair and dragged her son out from under the frame. "Go outside and play on the slide. Now."

Rory protested. "I was killing germs. There are a million germs under there!"

"He just learned about germs in pre-school camp," Kate apologized. "Knowledge is a dangerous thing."

"These were ninja germs!" Rory insisted.

"I believe I saw those very same ninja germs escaping into the play yard," Anna told him. "And if you don't stop them there, they might get all the way to the road."

11

Rory's eyes brightened. He had shiny dark hair and eyes that matched. He was a wiry child, one part willfulness, two parts energy, three parts resolve. Today he was wearing a white "gi" and the yellow belt he had earned the previous week in his Tai Kwon Do class.

Helen didn't like children, of course. But she had to admit that this one had spunk.

The silence thrummed once Rory had left for his search-and-destroy mission, and everyone inhaled it gratefully. In the hour since their short business meeting, there had been precious little silence. The "Beehive" in the walkout basement was cramped. Once it had been the nursery, before the church's expanding baby population had been moved into a brand-new wing. Several months ago the quilters had commandeered the tiny room for their own use. It was just wide enough for a quilting frame and several comfortable pieces of furniture along the wall, but it was filled with light from windows overlooking a fenced-in play yard and an expansive parking lot. And it was all theirs.

"I could just stay home," Kate volunteered when they'd all recovered a little. "Until Rory's in school full time."

"Don't you dare." Cathy Adams patted

Kate's shoulder. She was a warmhearted grandmotherly woman, a former insurance agent who was now reaping the benefits of an excellent 401K. Cathy was the least accomplished quilter among them, but she was learning fast.

Peony Greenway cleared her throat. Peony's self-appointed job in the group, and in the church in general, was to smooth out trouble spots. "Rory adds something to the mixture." She paused for effect. "And by the way, on that 'other' subject, I know for a fact Christine will be sleeping at the Inn at Narrow Passage. She has a room reserved through the weekend."

"You called to check?" Dovey asked.

"Of course not!" Peony realized Dovey was teasing and relaxed her spine a millimeter. "Reverend Kinkade mentioned it, that's all. He asked if the inn was a good place for Miss Fletcher to stay."

"So Sam wanted the word to go out that they aren't sleeping together, in case any of us have narrow little minds," Cathy said.

Almost nobody but Peony called the Shenandoah Community Church's present minister Reverend Kinkade. It was hard to imagine their jeans-and-T-shirt-clad pastor with a title that formal.

"Narrow minds, Narrow Passage . . ."

Dovey inclined her head toward the door, which was propped open so Rory and his younger sister Bridget — who was napping in an overstuffed armchair in the corner — could run in and out at will. "Narrowing window of opportunity for gossip."

In the fenced-in play yard, Rory could be heard screeching. Soon he would be back inside to make a full report.

"Sam and Christine *have* been engaged for years," said Anna, ever the amateur psychologist. "To me, this signals major conflicts in their relationship. Why hasn't he married her?"

Helen thought Anna's logic was mostly wishful thinking. Sam was a charismatic charmer who attracted females the way the trumpet vine against her barn attracted hummingbirds. At forty-four, Anna was at least ten years too old to be a contender, but she still had a crush on the minister. Sometimes Helen wondered if Sam's "engagement" was merely a tool to keep young women in the congregation at arm's length.

"He hasn't married Christine because she doesn't like the country, and she doesn't like *us*." Dovey leaned over the quilt, stretched taut on a wooden frame, and squinted at a row of stitches.

Satisfied, she looked up. "Christine

Fletcher is a hothouse gardenia, and we're a wilted bunch of black-eyed Susans. That's a fact."

"As if this church isn't filled with government retirees who have seen most of the world up close and personal." Cathy fumbled under her chair for the water bottle she always carried and uncapped it for a big swig.

"Maybe so, but *those* folks came here for the country life and took right to it. Look at you and that husband of yours. Keeping bees, goats . . . whatever else do you have?"

"Last I heard, Alf was looking for a couple of alpacas." Cathy capped her water bottle. "Pretty soon I'll be scared to go out my own door."

"Was a time not so many years ago in these parts that farming was deadly serious." Helen looked up from her perfect line of stitches. "And *nobody* was from anywhere else."

"Must have been pretty boring," Cathy said.

Helen humphed, but she supposed not all the changes in Toms Brook, Virginia, were bad ones.

"Back . . . to . . . Chris-tine!" Dovey shook her head in disgust. "I swear, this group leaves a subject faster than a hawk

15

swoops off a tree limb."

Peony glared at her. "What else do you want us to say?"

"Is Sam going to make an honest woman out of Christine or not? And if he ever does, will the two of them be leaving for the big city? Because I don't think Miss Chris-tine Flet-cher sees herself as a country pastor's wife."

"Can you see Miss Christine Fletcher playing the organ or teaching Sunday school?" Anna laughed.

"Well, we need a new sexton," Dovey said. "There's dust everywhere. Maybe she scrubs floors?"

Rory chose that moment to streak through the doorway and into the room, skidding to a halt at his mother's side. The accompanying war whoops woke Bridget, whose whimpers escalated with his shouts.

"Ninjas!" He grabbed Kate's arm and tugged. "Ninjas! I saw 'em!"

Kate disengaged herself, then turned and put her hands on her son's shoulders. "You woke up your sister, Rory. How many times have I told you not to shout?"

"Ninjas!" To his credit, the excited little boy tried to lower his voice, but he danced from foot to foot. "A whole truck of ninjas.

16

Two trucks. All dressed in black. They're coming back!"

"The trucks were dressed in black? Or the ninjas?" Cathy teased.

Rory's excitement gave way to a frown. "I don't think I can fight 'em all."

"Just take them one at a time," Helen advised. "Tell the others to wait their turn."

That seemed to make sense to the little boy. He wriggled out of his mother's grasp and turned back to the play yard. In an instant he had disappeared again.

"When he wins the Academy Award, we'll all say we knew him when," Cathy said.

"At least he's never bored." Kate got up to rescue Bridget, who stopped whimpering immediately and rested her curly head against her mother's shoulder. "Maybe I'd better call it a day. I'm not going to get anything else accomplished. Maybe I can get a sitter next week and stay longer."

Helen rose and stretched a moment. At eighty-three, she was too old to sit in one position for long without turning to stone. "Quilt's almost done. Martha will like it. Darn shame her mind is going, but at least she still remembers most of us."

The lap quilt, with appliqued leaves in

autumn colors, was to be a gift for Martha Wisner, who had been the church secretary for many years. She had moved into an assisted living facility several years before and was now in the nursing home wing. Martha's memory was slipping fast, but whatever form of dementia she suffered, she did not seem unhappy. She was always glad to see visitors, whether she remembered them or not. The quilters had chosen the pattern because Martha had loved fall in their Shenandoah Valley. Helen had hand appliqued the top as a reminder of better times.

"If we stay another hour, we can get it finished, then Helen can take it home and bind it," Anna said. "Unless you want me to do that?"

Helen shook her head. Everybody knew Anna had no color sense. Her stitches were even, points matched perfectly, blocks were square. But Anna's fabric choices were legendary. Helen was afraid if Anna picked out a binding, the earth-toned leaves would forever be rimmed in shocking pink.

"No, I'll do it," she said. "You're planning to go to that silly Mexican fiesta tonight, aren't you? I've got nothing but time these days."

"Ninjas!"

This time everybody turned to stare at Rory, who was jumping up and down in the doorway. Before Kate could shush him, there was a crash from the front of the church. The women looked at each other; then, as one, they hurried to the windows overlooking the broad expanse of parking lot that led to Old Miller Road in front of the church.

Teenagers were pouring out of two pickups that were parked within inches of each other. One of the trucks was nose first against an ancient sycamore that anchored the lot. Helen hoped the trucks had collided with each other and not with the tree. As she watched, a group of three boys, dressed in dark jeans and dark T-shirts, started toward the new sign the congregation had erected and blessed that very Sunday, a sign that had already caused its share of controversy within the church community.

One of the boys took a playful swing at the other, dodging and feinting with apparent good spirits. But high spirits or not, Helen didn't think they were up to any good. They were quickly joined by a fourth boy. That one was carrying a sledgehammer.

"We'd better stop them," she said. She

turned and found her path blocked by a small athletic body.

"Nin-jas!" Rory singsonged. "I — told — you!"

Elisa Martinez was as accustomed to walking miles every day as she was to the sound of her new name. Weeks passed when the reality of her present life seemed to be the only reality she had ever known. Her legs were strong, and no matter how far she had to walk, she was seldom winded. The name flowed off her tongue, as if she had been born to it.

This morning, though, she was tired and growing discouraged. The Shenandoah Community Church sat on a country road as muddy as it was long. As she had walked Old Miller's length, she'd skirted so many ditches and puddles she'd probably traveled an extra mile. She had been warned that the previous summer had been dusty and dry, and she should be glad for the rain. She understood rain well enough, but she was learning firsthand the perils of a personal relationship with it.

This morning the air was oppressively humid in preparation for a new storm. The sun was directly overhead, peeking out from coalescing clouds just frequently enough to taunt her. She could see her immediate future. First she would bake, then she would drown. There was little chance she could hike back home from her interview in time to miss the downpour, and she had little protection except a lightweight plastic poncho she carried in a small backpack that doubled as a purse. If the rain started soon, she hoped the church pastor would let her stay inside until the worst of it ended. *If* it ended.

From the top of the last hill she had glimpsed a steeple, and she knew she was nearly at her destination. She had spent most of the walk trying on "Elisas" for this interview. The stakes were too high to give this less than her best. She needed this job. She could not thank a God she no longer believed in for making it available, but she was grateful that coincidence had gone her way. Now if this brief streak of luck would simply hold.

She reviewed her credentials. She was slight, but she was strong. That would be important to show. She must not appear over- or under-qualified. She must seem accessible, but not chatty. Intelligent and resourceful, but not above menial labor. Interested in the church, but never nosy.

She needed to explain that she would

willingly work long or late hours without sounding desperate or pushy.

She needed to tell as much of the truth about herself as she could, so that she would not be tripped up in her own lies.

Old Miller Road curved sharply as she descended the last hill, and when she rounded it she saw the church just a hundred yards in front of her. Like so many of the area churches, it was white, with a tall steeple gracefully in proportion to the building. The roof was dazzling tin; the wings that jutted from either side had been designed to harmonize, not detract. Lovely old trees dotted the grounds; a garden of some sort lay against one side, and as she neared, she saw roses in bloom, despite August's moist heat. Someone cared about those roses — and cared *for* them.

She wondered if gardening would be part of the sexton's job, and she tried to remember when the roses had been pruned at the home she had shared with Gabrio. When had they been fertilized and watered, and how had they been selected? Now she wished she had paid more attention.

She was fifty yards closer before she noticed the two trucks in front of the church, parked beside a white sign. At first she merely noted their presence, but as she drew closer, she saw there was more to note. Much more.

A group of half a dozen boys — high-school age, she thought — were gathering near the sign, which stood about twenty feet to the right of the front door. The boy in the lead, just a few feet ahead of the others, was swinging what looked like an axe. She heard shouts, profanity and forced high-pitched laughter that shattered her preoccupation with the coming interview.

Her pulse sped; her hands grew damp. She stumbled to a stop. This scene was too reminiscent of another in her past, the same high-intensity, testosterone-fueled prequel to violence. For a moment she wondered if she could escape without being seen. Then she read the sign the boys were clearly bent on destroying, and something inside her snapped.

"Stop it!" She was running before she had time to think. Not away, which would have made sense, but directly toward them. *"¡Sinvergüenzas! ¿Qué andan haciendo?"*

Perhaps the boys weren't as brave as they'd thought. Perhaps they were only interested in a new and more personal victim. Whatever their reasons, they stopped and turned to watch her approach. She slowed to a halt just in front of the sign, reaching it before they could.

"What do you think you're doing?" she demanded in English. She glared at them, burying all lingering fears where they could not be seen. She knew these boys, had met them a hundred times in a hundred different places. She was too well acquainted with pack mentality, wolves in jeans or soldiers' uniforms, men and boys who could forget what made them human as long as they stood shoulder to shoulder with others like themselves.

Oh yes, she knew these boys and how dangerous they could be.

The boy in the lead was narrow-shouldered and hipped, with a shock of light brown hair falling over his eyes. He had the soft cheeks of mid-adolescence, a tiny cut on his chin, perhaps from inexperience with shaving. For a moment he looked uncertain, as if he might consider leaving if everyone would just shut their eyes so he could slip away.

Then his expression hardened. "Hey, *chica,* who do you think you are?"

She wondered what B movie he'd watched for that bit of Spanish.

"Get away from there before you get

24

hurt," he said when she didn't move.

"You would hurt me over a sign? A sign in front of God's house? You're not afraid He's watching, waiting for you to make a better choice?"

For a moment fear flickered in his eyes. Her own gaze flicked to the boys behind him, then back to his. "They're not worth it," she said in a softer voice. "They want you to take the risk while they watch. What kind of friends are those?"

"Go back to Mexico, cunt!" one of the boys shouted. "We don't need your kind here."

"Maybe you do," she said, not taking her eyes from the boy with the sledgehammer. She was glad it was not an axe, as she'd first feared. "Maybe you need a reminder this is a welcoming country, that your own grandparents or great-grandparents might have come from somewhere else."

"Just do it!" one of the boys in the back shouted at the leader. "Just smash it and let's get out of here."

"I'm not going to let you," Elisa said, as calmly as she could. "And I've seen you, every one of your faces. If you damage this sign, I will remember and describe you, one by one."

The boy in the lead looked torn. His

thoughts were easy to read. If he was arrested, someone in his life would not be happy about it.

She lowered her voice and hoped what she had to say was just for his ears.

"I have a brother. I know it's hard to stand up for yourself, but you have better instincts than this. I know you do."

"Yeah, Leon," one of the closer boys said. "You have girly man instincts. Even the Mex can see it."

As if propelled by those words, Leon stepped directly in front of her, as if he planned to walk right through her. She put her hands against his shoulders and shoved. He stumbled backward, clearly caught off guard. She took that brief moment to move backward to the sign and stand firmly against it. "You will have to hit me first," she said. "Are you willing?"

"That's enough! What is going on here?"

None of them had noticed the approach of a man dressed in a blue polo shirt and khakis. The boys turned as the man bore down on them, and, as one, they stepped backward. Leon moved away so quickly Elisa could feel a breeze.

"Leon Jenkins." The man moved to stand just in front of the boy and grabbed him by one shoulder. "Let's hear an explanation."

"Get your hand off me."

"When I'm good and ready." The man reached out, twisted the sledgehammer from Leon's hand and tossed it on the ground behind him.

Elisa heard voices and turned her head to see a small group of women approaching from the direction of the parking lot. She slumped against the sign, sure now that she was out of danger.

"Just what is going on?" one of the oldest of the women demanded.

"Some of the local youth were planning to renovate our new sign," the man said. His voice was low and controlled. He still sounded furious.

The other boys looked at each other, then whirled and took off for the pickups.

"Stay out of their way," the man told the women. He didn't take his eyes off Leon, who was squirming and clawing at his hand. Only when the pickups were out of sight did the man's hand fall to his side.

"Exactly why?" he demanded.

The boy backed away, but he didn't run. Where could he go now? Clearly he would be caught and humiliated further if he tried.

Elisa saw the boy's fear and his realization that nothing good could come of this. She was unaccountably moved. Now she saw a boy, just a boy like her brother, and no longer a threat. She stepped forward and rested her fingertips on the man's arm. "He didn't hurt me," she said. "Not even when I pushed him away."

"He might have tried."

"No, it was the sign he wanted." She turned to the sign now and read the words out loud. It was an ordinary church sign, announcing the times of services and the name of the minister. Only the last sentence, in Spanish, was at all unusual. *"Todo el Público es Bienvenido a los Servicios de La Iglesia Comunitaria de Shenandoah."* The Shenandoah Community Church welcomes everyone to its services.

She shook her head. "You welcome everyone. A thoughtful gesture to put the words in Spanish? But controversial because you've targeted the Latino community? There are those who would prefer we go elsewhere?"

"Jesus ran into the same problem," the man said.

Elisa turned back and addressed the boy. "But you're sorry, aren't you? Because I

28

don't think you really feel that way, do you? You just made a mistake today." She lifted a brow and cocked her head to prompt his answer.

The boy shoved his hands in his pockets and thrust back his shoulders. He looked as if he was going to argue; then he slumped. "Yeah. I guess."

"Guess?" the man demanded. "Your father's a deacon in this church, Leon."

"So? He hates the sign worse than I do."

"But you're old enough to begin thinking for yourself." Like the boy's, the man's posture became less defensive. "Shall you tell your father, or shall I?"

"He hates your guts."

A muscle jumped in the man's jaw. "If anything happens to that sign, I'll report this incident to the police. You can tell your friends they'd better stay away, unless they're here to join in church activities. Then they'll be welcome. Otherwise, at the first sign of vandalism anywhere on these grounds, I'll hunt them down and have a little chat with their parents and yours. Understand?"

The boy gave a curt nod.

The man gestured toward the group of women watching on the sidelines. "You've got a long walk. I suggest you get started.

None of these ladies is planning to give you a ride home."

The boy took off at a fast clip along the route that Elisa had just traveled.

Only then did the man turn to her. For the first time she had the opportunity to really take stock of him. He was tall and broad-shouldered. His hair was the color of darkly roasted coffee, his angry eyes a blue so intense they were the most arresting feature in an immensely attractive face.

"Thank you." He held out his hand. "Sam Kinkade. I'm the minister."

She had already guessed that. She extended her hand. "Elisa Martinez. I hope I'll be your new sexton."

They stared at each other longer than politeness called for. In those unexpectedly charged seconds, she warned herself of a hundred different things. The incident with the boys had left her shaken and vulnerable. This man might well be her new employer. She was lonely and worried about getting this job. The talk of police had frightened her. Adrenaline was pumping through her body.

And still, if she subtracted all those things and added in years of hard-earned caution and the fact that she could not afford even the briefest foray into romance, she was still left with a strong attraction to Sam Kinkade.

"Well, go ahead and hire her right now, preacher," one of the women, the oldest, demanded, moving closer. "What other proof do you need that she can do the job? A signed statement from the Almighty?"

Chapter Two

Sam turned to the old woman and managed a smile. His anger was just beginning to fade. He was not easily provoked, but by the same token, he was not easily placated. "Thank you, Helen. I'll take your recommendation into consideration."

"You do that, and don't you try to humor me. I saw the whole thing. We could use somebody around here who takes matters into her own hands. If she's not scared of that gang of teenage thugs, she won't be scared of a little dirt."

Sam walked over and slung his arm around Helen Henry's shoulders, steering her back toward the church, which was not an easy job. She was a big-boned woman in her eighties, but she still knew how to do a day's work. The church had been a far more boring place before she started coming regularly, and before the quilters organized and commandeered the Beehive.

Sometimes he was nostalgic for boredom.

"How's the quilt coming?" He knew this subject would take them all the way inside.

The other women started heading inside. He walked back to Kate Brogan who was standing ten yards behind the others, and he scooped the flailing Rory out of his mother's arms and set him on his hip, leaving Kate with only shy baby Bridget.

Sam paused a moment and turned to Elisa Martinez, who was standing exactly where he had left her. He was struck, as he had been a moment ago, by how gracefully appealing she was. She was average height and slender, wearing a simple white blouse and black pants. She had shining dark hair clipped back in a ponytail that fell past her shoulder blades, creamy toffee-colored skin, and eyes so darkly liquid and expressive that he had felt himself going down for the third time in just the seconds he had stared into them.

He shoved his mind back into gear. "Do you mind following us inside? We'll do the interview in my study."

Cathy Adams, one of the quilters, waited to walk with Elisa. When he saw they were bringing up the rear, he made his way through the lot and the play yard into the Beehive. He deposited Rory in a corner after a brief man-to-man chat about ninjas and sledgehammers, said a few words to each of the women, genuinely admired the quilt stretched out on the frame, and finally motioned for Elisa to follow him upstairs.

He was in marginally better spirits by the time he closed the Beehive door and they started for the steps. Beside him, Elisa was silent.

They were upstairs and on the way to his study before he spoke. "No sign is worth risking your safety for."

"I'm not sure what came over me."

He wondered if that was true, or if she knew very well and wasn't going to acknowledge it. He unlocked his door and ushered her inside, leaving the door open, as he usually did. He did not like enclosed spaces, and today the church secretary, who was usually at the desk in the next office, was out of town for the rest of the week.

"I'm sorry your first visit to our church started that way." Sam motioned to the leather sofa that sat in front of two large windows looking out over the rose garden.

While she seated herself, he noticed that yesterday he had forgotten to put away the wheelbarrow after he dumped a load of compost to be spread. He made a mental note to do it later, then asked himself why he was avoiding looking at Elisa. He was not a man who was uncomfortable with women. His fiancée Christine, with her blatant sex appeal and choke hold on femininity, had never intimidated him in the least.

"I've encountered prejudice before," she said.

"I'm sorry for that." He made himself look down at her. "Under any circumstances there would have been resistance, but as you probably know, there's some troubling evidence that Hispanic gangs have moved into the area. Peaceful, sleepy Shenandoah County." He shrugged. "That's set off a backlash."

She was smiling softly. "Let's find a subject that doesn't make you feel sad. Or guilty."

He relaxed a fraction. "Iced tea."

"Iced tea as a subject?"

"Would you like some?"

"Very much, if it's not too much trouble."

He was grateful for something to do. He

left for the kitchen and returned a few minutes later with two glasses. "The staff goes through gallons of this every week. Whoever drinks the last glass has to make a new pitcher."

She took the glass, then a sip. "I can do that."

He had debated where to sit. She had left him a full half of the large sofa, and there was a table just in front of it with room for his tea. It was the obvious choice.

He sprawled over his half. "So . . ." He considered where to start.

She solved the problem. "Elisa Martinez, thirty-three. Like every Spanish-speaking friend I have made here, I am not a gang member. I am well acquainted with cleaning products, mops and brooms, and the need to clean the men's urinals more often than the ladies' toilets. I've been working the late shift as a nurse's aide at the Shadyside Home in Woodstock, but last week my shifts were cut to two because the aide I replaced is returning from maternity leave. If you hire me, I promise that won't interfere with my work at the church. On those mornings I can start here as soon as I've finished there."

He didn't speak, and she went on. "My supervisor will be glad to write a reference, or she'll be glad to talk to you."

He had already noted that her command of the English language was as good as his own, but there was a trace of an accent, a musical elongation of vowels, the slightest flipping of *r*'s, a trace more formality, that he found charming. As an employer, he had to ask the next question. "Were you born here?"

She shook her head. "Mexico. A little village in the south."

"Are you a citizen?"

She reached in the front pocket of her black slacks and produced a card with her name and photo for him to examine. "A permanent resident. My not-so-green card."

He scanned it, then nodded. She slipped it back into her pocket and waited.

"It's hard work." He sat forward and reached for the tea. "There's a lot of lifting and moving. You'd be required to set up and take down tables and chairs for any meetings or events, and this is a busy church. That would be in addition to heavy cleaning and minor repairs. It's tedious, and the hours are long. The pay isn't great."

"I'll manage just fine. I lift patients in and out of bed, move beds and furniture, push wheelchairs uphill. I'm used to hard work."

Sam thought she must be made entirely of muscle, then, because there wasn't much to her other than the gentle swell of breasts and hips.

"Do you have a car, Elisa?"

She straightened a little, and he knew she had been waiting for this. "I don't own a car, no. But I have two good legs, and friends with cars at the park."

"Park?"

"I live in the Ella Lane Mobile Home Park, near the nursing home. I live with a friend and her two children. Adoncia has a car, and so do others nearby. Much of the time I would have a ride."

He calculated that distance. At least four miles, probably more. He was about to shake his head when she stopped him by raising a hand.

"I walked here today. There was a storm about to break, but I came anyway. I wasn't late, and I wasn't too tired to face down your deacon's son. Wouldn't you rather have a sexton with determination and no car than one with a car and no work ethic?"

He sat back. He sipped his tea and watched her.

She fiddled with her glass — still nearly full — then she leaned forward. "I don't mind long hours, and I don't mind hard work. I don't gossip and I don't complain." She sat back. "I also know when to stop talking. I'm easy to have around."

He thought that last part might be the hardest to deal with. He was acutely aware of this woman already, and they had only just met. He was caught between doing what the law required — in this case choosing the best candidate for an advertised position — or following his best instincts, which told him that temptation was best avoided, no matter how strong or sure he was of his own power to resist it.

"I haven't told you everything," he said, buying time. "We have a new program here, and it might be what set off those boys. The sign is part of it, and it means more work for the sexton."

She took a long sip of her tea. Her self-control had already been noted. He imagined she was thirsty after the long, hot walk. "Tell me about it," she said, when she'd finished.

"I'll show you." He turned and peered out the window. "Normally I'd show you the church first, but it's pretty straightforward. A sanctuary and social hall, classrooms and meeting rooms. We'd better do this now, before the rain begins. Then I'll find you a ride home."

"I —"

He didn't let her finish. "The quilters will be leaving about the time we're done. Someone will be happy to do it."

"Reverend Kinkade, it will not be your job to find transportation for me. Managing that is a small thing, but it will be *my* small thing."

He rose. "It's Sam. Finish your tea or bring it along. It's only a short walk."

Elisa felt the first hesitant drops of rain as they exited the building through the rose garden.

"The roses aren't happy with all this moisture," Sam said. "I use natural sprays to keep them from succumbing to blackspot, but every time I plan to spray, it rains. And when I do spray, a storm comes up the next day and washes it right off."

"You take care of the roses?"

He shot her a smile, a friendlier smile than she'd seen, but one that still maintained a certain distance. If he was setting boundaries now — and that was how she interpreted it — then perhaps he was seriously considering her for the job.

40

"It's not in my job description, but I promised our building and grounds committee if they would help me prepare the plot and plant the bushes, I'd do the maintenance. We use the garden for weddings. This is a very popular spot in June and September, but mostly they're there for me to enjoy every day. Just don't tell anybody I said so."

She was relieved the sexton was not expected to take care of the roses, but it brought up another subject. "Is the sexton expected to do any work outdoors?"

"Marvin — he's our present sexton — starts each morning with a cleanup of the grounds, just trash and such. We use professionals for mowing grass and raking leaves. One of our deacons . . ." He gave a humorless laugh. "Leon Jenkins? The boy with the sledgehammer? His father George has a landscaping business and provides services for us at a reduced rate, which probably means that he pays his men less when they're here, so his own profit isn't affected. The way his crew changes from week to week, it's pretty clear he hires whoever he can find that day and pays them under the table."

"Undocumented workers?"

"That would be my guess. Our board believes it's up to George to stay abreast of the law, and they accept his assurances he's in compliance."

She knew from his tone that he didn't agree with the board's choice. Resolutely, she changed the subject. "Do you mind telling me why Marvin is leaving? Unless it has nothing to do with the job, of course."

"As simple as a better paying job. He's juggling both right now, but the church is suffering. We need someone who can start training right away." He glanced at her. "Could you start immediately?"

"I was hoping to."

She had been paying attention to his words; now she paid attention to their destination and felt excitement build. They were headed toward an old frame farmhouse painted lemon-yellow. It was set back from the church, at least an acre to the northwest. A narrow gravel drive snaked to the front porch from the road, between a grove of oaks and maples that hid the house until visitors were almost on top of it. The house itself sat in a field of Queen Anne's lace and brilliant blue chicory, black-eyed Susans and puff-ball dandelions. The effect was charming.

She had seen the house before, of course, visited it late one night and stood in front of it to imagine its history and the people who once had lived here. On that night several months ago the house had been a sad gray and far more dilapidated. Now it was a proud buttercup blooming in a field of admirers. In front of it was yet another sign.

"*La Casa Amarilla,*" she read. "Good choice for a name. Very definitely a yellow house."

"What do you think? Did we overdo on the paint?"

She stared at the house and thought it was as welcoming as outstretched arms. "It's a happy house. Is that what you hoped for?"

"Exactly." He stood beside her, gazing up at it. "It used to be the parsonage. Don't tell anybody, but I like it better than the one I live in down the road. In the fifties, when the church built mine, a three-bedroom ranch house was every working man's goal. Farmhouses with history and character fell out of favor, and little brick boxes with narrow windows and air-conditioning fell in."

"I'm sure somebody would remove your air conditioner if you complained."

He gave a small laugh. "And I won't."

The raindrops, scattered at first, were

falling a little faster. He put his hand on her arm to nudge her forward. "Let's go in."

The house was narrow, but the porch was deep enough for several old rockers. She imagined former occupants rocking away the twilight here. "You haven't told me what you use it for now."

"Besides experimenting with shades of yellow paint?"

"Besides that, yes."

He pulled a tennis-ball-sized clump of keys from his pocket and used one to open the door, standing back to usher her inside. "Come see."

She stepped in and waited. He left the door open — for fresh air, she supposed — and flipped a series of switches that filled the house with light. The front room just beyond the tiny entryway where they stood was small, but comfortably furnished with sofas and chairs covered by bright red slipcovers.

There were computer desks lining one wall, three of them, each with what looked like a new computer in place. The old wood floor was covered by a bright circular rag rug. Posters in primary colors filled the walls. She saw that each one was a humorously illustrated vocabulary lesson.

"Weather, flags of Europe, telling time . . ." She walked along the wall, looking at each. "Colors . . . seasons, opposites. I like this one." She pointed to a poster with barnyard animals in funny hats. "But won't the children think that a cow is only a cow if it's wearing a baseball cap?"

"I'm hoping that won't be a problem."

She smiled back at him. "*La Casa Amarilla.* You're teaching English lessons to Spanish-speaking children?"

"It's more diverse than that. I'll tell you as we go."

She followed him into the kitchen. The room was large enough for a round pine table flanked by six mismatched chairs. Bright green cushions unified them. The center of the table was taken up by a plastic caddy filled with art supplies. She picked up a felt-tip marker, one of dozens in a variety of colors. "The art room?"

"Also the snack room and the place where we'll teach nutrition basics. Come see the dining room."

The dining room was no longer for dining. Four small tables sat in the middle of the narrow space, and bookshelves lined the walls and stood under two windows. Each table was large enough for four small children. Some of the books looked new; some looked as if they had come from a rummage sale.

Sam stood in the doorway, arms folded across his chest, as Elisa silently scanned the titles. She chose one to leaf through as he spoke.

"One of our members works as a school administrator here in the county. One day we were talking, and he told me what a disadvantage Spanish-speaking children have when they enter the local schools. There are more of them each year. The schools do what they can, but it's not enough. He told me that without extra help, the kids just can't catch up and keep up, and not because they aren't bright. Because they need an extra boost with the language and the culture."

"So you decided to start your own program?"

"We'd been debating what to do with this house. Our former church secretary lived here until a few years ago, but no one has lived here since. It needed too much work to continue as a rental. Some people wanted to tear it down and build a four-unit apartment as extra income for the church. Some wanted to sell the house and property. Of course others thought we should preserve history, not sell or destroy it."

"History?" she asked, curious as to how much he knew.

"It's a very old house. Pre-Civil War, at least the main portion of it. The original family and their descendants lived here until the 1930s, when they sold their farm, and the church was built on what was once their front cornfield."

" She was glad, very glad, that the developers in the congregation had not won out. "You were one who didn't want to tear it down?"

"I convinced our lay leaders that using the building as an outreach program for local children would be the best use of the property."

Judging from the incident with the sign, she was certain that had not been a battle without casualties. But Sam looked like a man strong and determined enough to weather them. "And it has been successful?"

"We open once school opens. We've spoken to the authorities, and they've promised to put us in touch with the parents of all the children who can use our help. The school will bus them here if the parents sign permission slips. We have two donated vans we'll use to take them home at the end of the afternoon. We have a dozen tutors who have signed up to take shifts, a Catholic nun who has agreed to supervise, and a retired Presbyterian minister who is coordinating transportation and communications with parents."

She was impressed. "So many different churches?"

"It's our building, but it's the community's project. You should have seen how many people turned out on the weekend we painted. People on the roof, people clearing away badly overgrown shrubs, people scrubbing floors." He seemed to think better of his enthusiasm. "I'm sorry. It's a subject close to my heart."

"Do the tutors speak Spanish?"

"Unfortunately, no one speaks much. We're hoping that will change as the community gets more involved. I'm working hard on mine. Right now, if any child needs to know where the bathroom is located, I can direct him in his own language. That's about it. For good or for bad, I'm afraid it's an English immersion program."

She spoke before she had time to think. *"Puedo ayudar cuantas veces me necesiten."* She bent and placed the book back on the shelf.

"My Spanish must be better than I thought. You just said you wished I would dye my hair green and hire out my services as a belly dancer."

She laughed. "I said I could help any time I'm needed. I think that's a good example. There will be moments when fractured Spanish and good intentions might not be enough. I would be happy to translate."

"Be careful what you volunteer for. We say yes with alarming frequency."

She straightened. "So it's part of the sexton's job to clean *La Casa*?"

"Just a lick and a promise once a week, which is all we can afford. The volunteers will do some of it. I suspect I'll do some of it, too. But even the little the sexton will do extends the job. And you haven't seen the rest of the church plant. There's a lot of work here, Elisa."

She didn't have the job yet. She knew it and wondered how to convince him. "If I were a man, would you warn me so many times . . . Sam?"

"No."

"Then you shouldn't do it now. I'm capable and willing, and I have excellent references. I hope that's what you remember when you make your decision."

He looked at his watch, then back at her. "Let's go find that ride. In a couple of hours a horde of caterers and volunteers are heading this way. There's a party tonight, a Mexican fiesta to raise money for *La Casa.* It's something of an unfortunate afterthought, which is why it's on a weeknight, and it's going to be chaotic, especially if the rain continues. You'll want to escape all the prep work. I wish I could."

She followed him out, and he locked up. She had said she knew when to be silent, and she did. She didn't speak, and neither did he. She hoped he was using the time to favorably consider her application.

When they approached, the quilters were already coming out to the parking lot. Sam stopped just short of the asphalt.

"Are you working at the nursing home tonight? Or would you be free to come back about seven-thirty to talk to Marvin and shadow him for the rest of the evening?"

"I don't work tonight. But either way, I could be here."

"We'll talk again, after you've had a chance to see everything the job requires and I've had time to organize applications."

For the first time she felt real hope that she was going to be hired. Only a small part of her found her own reaction ironic. The part that was *not* Elisa Martinez seemed to shrivel with every decision she was required to make.

Several yards in front of them, a woman in a blue sundress got out of a car parked near the others. Sam saw her and gestured. "That's Tessa MacRae, Helen's granddaughter. Helen is the woman who insisted I hire you. I'll ask Tessa to give you a ride. She won't mind."

Elisa had made her statement on the subject. Later they would have to deal with his need to take care of her, but for the moment she was not sad to be offered a ride. The rain had stopped, but she was afraid it had only stopped to gather forces.

Sam started across the lot, and she followed, skirting puddles. They stopped beside Helen and her granddaughter, who was admiring the quilt Elisa had seen earlier on the frame.

Sam greeted both women, kissing Tessa on the cheek before he introduced Elisa. "Elisa walked here, and she insists she doesn't need a ride out to the trailer park on Ella Lane, but I'm insisting otherwise. Would you mind?"

51

Elisa spoke up. "Only if it's no trouble. I don't want to inconvenience anyone."

"I'm taking Gram into Woodstock to buy groceries. I'm sure we go right past the turnoff," Tessa said.

Elisa liked Tessa's voice, which was modulated and low. She was an attractive woman, with brown hair as long as Elisa's own and a thin face with wide cheekbones. She looked tired, and as they stood in the lot, she put her palms against her back and swayed, as if to minimize pressure. For the first time Elisa realized she was pregnant. The sundress, which fell from a high yoke, had hidden it.

There was no time to say anything else. A car sped into the parking lot and pulled into a slot several spaces away. Elisa had never been interested in cars, and she was only rarely able to tell one from another. But this was a sports car, low-slung and elegant. The door opened, and a shapely leg appeared, followed by the body to go with it.

The woman who emerged was nearly as tall as Sam, with dark-red curls that fell past her shoulders, a carefully painted megawatt smile, and white shorts that stopped just shy of revealing. As she approached she was preceded by a scent that

Elisa could only recognize as expensive. Nothing about the woman was cheap, although the overall effect flirted with it.

"Sam." She went to him and kissed him. The kiss wasn't long enough to embarrass anyone, but long enough to stake her claim. "I took a taxi to Chevy Chase and borrowed Jenny's Viper so I wouldn't have to rent some old wreck at the airport. You remember Jenny O'Donnell? Senator O'Donnell's daughter? What do you think?"

She didn't give him time to answer. She turned to the others. "I'm Christine Fletcher." She held out her hand to Tessa, then to Helen. "Sam's fiancée."

"We've met," Helen said dryly. "I've lost count how many times."

"I am *so* bad with names and faces," Christine drawled. She turned and thrust her hand at Elisa. "But I know I haven't met you. I would remember that lovely hair. I've wished for hair like that my whole life."

"Elisa Martinez." Elisa put her hand in Christine's and felt the strength of the other woman's grip. She also felt something cutting into her fingers. When Christine withdrew her hand, Elisa noted rings, one on each finger except the little one, each with a different flashy gemstone. Her eyes flicked to Christine's left hand, where a modest diamond resided on the ring finger.

Elisa wondered if the rings were a message of sorts. The English expression "on one hand" seemed to have been coined for the situation. On one hand Christine Fletcher was a woman of obvious wealth. On the other the fiancée of a man of moderate income.

"I'm here for the fiesta." Christine pressed one hand against her chest and lifted the other in the air as she swivelled her hips. "Let the festivities begin."

"Me, I'll be home binding this quilt," Helen said. "Let's get to it, Tessa."

Tessa inclined her head toward Elisa. "Are you ready to go?"

Elisa glanced over to see that Sam was watching her. From the corner of her eye, she noted that Christine was watching him.

Tessa said goodbye for both herself and her grandmother, then took Helen's arm.

Sam spoke. "Elisa, if you have any questions tonight, just find me and ask away."

"I will. Thank you." Elisa followed Tessa and her grandmother, and gratefully escaped.

Chapter Three

"So who's the Mayan goddess, Sam?"

Sam helped Christine out of the tricked-out Dodge Viper, the likes of which the simple brick parsonage had never seen. "Elisa has applied to be our new sexton."

"Sex-ton?" She raised one shapely brow. "Are we getting right to the heart of the matter, honey?"

He pulled her close and kissed her hair. Her body was warm and soft against him, and his reacted accordingly. "It's not like you to be catty."

"Hey, I'm just marking my territory like a good pussycat. She's a head turner. Even the preacher man noticed."

"The preacher man is not immune to a beautiful woman, but he's committed to another one."

Christine lifted her lips for a luxuriant

kiss, then she put her arm around his waist, and he led her up the flagstone walk. "She is beautiful, but I'm not worried. She's not your type."

"You could have fooled me." Sam said it as a joke, but he realized he was still annoyed at his attraction to Elisa and concerned it might get in the way of his decision whether to hire her.

She punched him lightly. "You like a woman with education and plenty of style."

"And you think those are the things that attracted me to you?"

"What else do I have to offer besides sex, and somebody else could deliver that? I'm not good minister's wife material. You know God and I have an understanding. I don't pay Him much attention if He promises to return the favor. We get along, but we're not bosom buddies."

"You're a better person than you think you are."

"And that's why you want to marry me? The strength of my character?"

He didn't have to answer. They had been engaged for almost four years, through better and worse times, the latter of which said enough about her character to impress him. She knew it.

He returned to the subject of Elisa, hoping he could talk his way to a decision. "I've had four applicants for the sexton's job, and we're getting desperate. Two are men with questionable work histories. The other won't take the job unless we raise the salary substantially. Then there's Elisa, with good references and a willingness to work hard. She walked to the interview from her mobile home park, and that's four, maybe even five, miles away. She's determined."

"She lives in a *trailer?*"

He imagined Elisa's home, even new, had not cost as much as the Viper Christine had borrowed so carelessly.

He tried to tamp down a surge of annoyance. "She's poor. So what? That means very little, Christine."

She wrinkled her nose and sniffed. "I smell a sermon coming on."

They had reached the front gate. He had installed a picket fence hoping it would keep Shadrach, Meshach and Abednego in check whenever they escaped through the front door. Shad and Shack, canine mixtures that probably included Irish wolfhound and St. Bernard, sailed over it with enthusiasm. Bed, a tiny rat terrier, simply stood at the gate and barked incessantly.

Now there was a chain link dog run in the back for those rare moments when the dogs weren't under his direct control.

"No sermon," he promised, "and end of subject."

"I don't suppose you've replaced the dogs with something a shade more refined?"

"Like a porcelain cocker spaniel?"

"You know me so well."

"Not as well as I hope to again."

She nudged his hip with hers. "Abstinence makes the heart grow fonder?"

He unlocked the front door. Their sex life, or lack of it, was no longer a subject of real debate. He was a heterosexual male with all the requisite urges. They had been lovers in the days when their wedding date was on the calendar and their invitations at the printer. But now that the date was long past and the invitations interred at a Georgia landfill, they no longer made love.

When he didn't respond she settled her hip firmly against his, brushing it back and forth. "I'm always ready and willing."

He closed his eyes, and for a moment, temptation was the only thing on his mind. His body responded exactly the way she had known it would. She was not as convinced of the need for abstinence as he was. "How can I talk to the youth group about controlling their budding sexuality if I'm not controlling my own?"

"You're an old-fashioned man."

"Who needs an old-fashioned commitment and a wedding date before he takes his woman to bed. And that's pushing liberal as it is."

She moved away, and they were no longer touching. "Just for the record, *I* wasn't intending to lecture your youth group about our sex life. Or lack of it."

It was time to change the subject. "Brace yourself." He opened the door and stood in the opening to fend off his dogs. He thought they were relatively well-behaved for young, slobbering dogs. He loved the three of them unreservedly.

"Nice dogs," Christine told them, screwing up her face. "Nice pen outside?" she asked Sam.

Christine's parents, former Georgia governor and congressman Hiram Fletcher and his wife Nola, had two spoiled shih tzus that Christine adored. Sam was astute enough to recognize the difference.

"I'll be back." He whistled for the dogs, who, having ascertained that Christine did not have food or affection to offer, covered the distance to the kitchen in great leaping strides. Or rather, Shad and Shack did. Bed, who weighed all of thirteen pounds, followed as fast as she could.

He returned a few minutes later to the sound of forlorn howls from the dog pen. The dogs were too well-behaved to continue for long.

Christine had made herself at home in his kitchen, and she flipped on his coffeemaker as he entered. He began to open all the windows. "Have you had lunch?" she asked.

"I'm not even sure I had breakfast."

"I'm starved. I had to be at the airport at dawn. I've been up forever." She opened the refrigerator. "Want an omelet?"

"That's a lot of trouble. I have some leftovers. I did a stir-fry last night."

She peeked over the top of the door. "You made it?"

He tried not to smile. "Uh-huh."

Her eyes widened. "I'll do omelets."

He was perfectly satisfied with his own cooking and never understood why others weren't. There had been a time in his life when the meals he now prepared for himself would have tasted like five-star cuisine.

"I'll do toast," he said.

She considered a moment. He could read her indecision. "Christine, I can toast bread, I promise."

She shrugged and dove back into the contents of his fridge. Sam hoped she wouldn't remove everything inside. From experience, he knew he would have to replace anything she took out, as well as wash and dry every plate, cup and frying pan. Christine liked to cook, but she did not clean up after herself. She had never needed to and couldn't see why she should start now.

He thought of Elisa, who cleaned up after anybody who would let her.

Christine closed the refrigerator door, eggs, milk and cheese cradled in her arms. "I checked in before I came looking for you. I like the inn. Quaint and tasteful. I suppose it will keep people from talking."

Mostly, as they both knew, Christine sleeping somewhere else would keep Sam from succumbing to his fiancée's considerable charms.

"I'm glad you decided to come." He took a loaf of bread from the cupboard, a knife from a drawer and a butter dish from the counter. Then he made himself comfortable at the small kitchen table and started spreading butter from one crust to the other.

"I didn't want to." Christine began

breaking eggs into a bowl. "But I missed you. I don't see why you haven't been able to get away and come home."

He didn't remind her that Atlanta was not his home and probably never would be again. He didn't remind her that he had a job that required his presence on weekends. She knew both and chose to forget them whenever the facts got in the way.

"I'm coming to see you next month," he reminded her. "For Torey's wedding." Against his better instincts, he had agreed to help preside at a ceremony in his former church for one of their friends.

"Well, I'm here now. But the whole time I was packing, I thought about that fundraiser Savior's Church did in the last year of your ministry there. Do you remember?"

He remembered all too clearly. At the time he had been the assistant minister of The Savior's Church, one of Atlanta's oldest and most influential congregations. He had given an invocation that had prompted the wealthiest members to fund a fledgling television ministry. Just two months later, they had begun televising their early-morning service, at which he almost always presided. The church's membership had increased substantially because of it.

In case he didn't remember everything, Christine hit the high points. "City Grill catered the dinner. We had Kobe beef and smoked trout. We flew in the Preservation Hall Jazz Band for entertainment."

He remembered that part too well. The African-American members of the band had been in a distinct minority that night.

She flicked on a burner and reached for his one and only frying pan on a rack above the stove. "I wore an outrageous red dress by Zac Posen. He was brand-new on the runways back then, and I knew he was going places. The air reeked of politics. Daddy introduced you to Sam Nunn during dessert. Daddy told him that one day *you* would be the next Georgia senator named Sam."

He waited until she was clearly done, using that time to slip the bread onto the rack of the tabletop toaster oven. "I suppose the point of this trip down memory lane is to draw a contrast between that night and the one to come?"

She faced him, her back against the stove as the pan heated. "A Mexican fiesta, Sam? In some damp field in the middle of nowhere? To raise money for what? Books and crayons for immigrant kids? It's a noble cause. I hope you get enough money to buy crayons in every color of the rainbow. But this isn't where you belong, and you know it."

"Don't you mean it isn't where *you* belong?"

She didn't deny it. "That, too."

"You didn't have to fly in for this. I didn't expect it."

"Sometimes I want to shake you silly. Are you trying to misunderstand?"

"Chrissy, I may not have left Savior's Church of my own accord, but I have a job here, and I'm grateful after everything that I do."

"And I'm not." She turned back to the stove and poured the beaten egg mixture into the pan. From this angle her wild red hair hid her shoulders, but he knew they were hunched in frustration.

He rose, went to her and put his arms around her, resting them just below her generous breasts. For a moment all he wanted was for things to be the way they once had been.

Elisa appreciated honesty, even if she no longer practiced it. Two minutes into the trip back to the trailer park, she knew she liked Helen Henry. Some people decided late in life that pretense was too much work. They simply said whatever they wanted in the short time that was left them. Elisa suspected this was not the case with Helen. Helen had probably been truthful her entire life and scared away a lot of people in the bargain.

They were only half a mile up Old Miller Road when Helen started expounding on Christine. "Maybe that Christine Fletcher *is* pretty, if you like women who make 'pretty' their life work. She dyes her hair, you know. Nobody's hair is that color." Helen said the last in a tone that brooked no resistance.

Tessa, who was driving, resisted anyway. "No, her hair is natural, and she's stunning. And you were not very nice, Gram. Do you really expect her to remember everybody's name in between trips?"

"I expect her to try. She doesn't like us, and that's a fact. I'm not sure I cotton to Sam Kinkade, you understand, but I did expect better from him."

"You adore Sam, and she seems pleasant enough."

"I won't ask Elisa what she thinks. You can hardly say, can you, girl, when you're hoping to get a job there."

Elisa tried not to laugh. "I have no opinions about anything."

Tessa laughed for her. "We're going to leave poor Elisa out of this."

Helen shook one finger at her granddaughter. "You just mark my words. Either Christine will take Sam away from us, or he'll tell her to hit the road. But there won't be a wife in that parsonage anytime soon, at least not one with dyed red hair."

Tessa changed the subject. "Elisa, have you been in the area long? Are you from the valley?"

"No, I've only been here six months."

"What brings you here?" Helen asked.

For a moment Elisa was stumped. Clearly a job had not brought her. If it had, it was unlikely she would be looking for another so soon. If she claimed the reason had been family, then someday she might be expected to produce them.

"A friend invited me to share her home while I looked for work. I was ready to leave . . . Texas."

"I would imagine so." Helen sounded as if she could not conceive of anyone who wouldn't prefer Virginia.

Tessa slowed at a crossroads, then sped up again. "Do you like it here?"

"I like everything but the rain."

"It's not usually like this. Last summer was dry. This summer is wet. Maybe next summer will be just right."

"Too dry, too wet, just right . . . Sounds like you've been practicing your Three Bears," Helen said. "Getting ready for the baby."

Elisa wanted to slip out of the spotlight. She leaned forward. "I couldn't help but notice there's a baby on the way. Will it be soon?"

"It better not be," Tessa said. Elisa thought there was a touch of anxiety in the reply.

"She's due in January," Helen said. "And she refuses to find out the sex. And she hasn't chosen names because that's bad luck."

"No, we haven't chosen names because there are too many choices."

"Because it's bad luck," Helen repeated.

Tessa sped up some more, as if she hoped to distract or drop off her grandmother quickly. "Do you have children, Elisa?"

"I'm not married. My roommate has two. I enjoy them."

"I never did see the point of babies," Helen said. "Of course, Tessa's will be different." She said this as if Tessa had better make sure of it.

Rain began to fall in earnest, not the

teasing harbinger of a storm but the real thing at last. Tessa snapped on her windshield wipers and slowed to a crawl. "I'm certainly glad you didn't try to walk home in this."

Elisa was glad, too. She was frightened of storms, although she did not let that deter her from going out in them if she had to. She didn't have the luxury of giving in to haunting memories or of forgetting why she was afraid.

"You don't even have an umbrella," Helen chided.

Elisa looked at Helen instead of the storm outside the window. "In a real storm, an umbrella means nothing. And I didn't want to carry anything I didn't need to."

"Well, we're almost to the park," Tessa said. "Isn't that the turnoff just ahead?"

Elisa saw she was right. The trip was so short, so easy, in a car.

Tessa pulled into the drive leading to a village of less than a dozen mobile homes separated by tiny, sloping lots. One home, just off to the side, had a canopy and a sign in front announcing it was the office, although in truth, little business was ever accomplished there. Some of the homes were fronted by awnings adorned with hanging plants; some had storage sheds; some had a rosebush or flower borders. In a field just yards away a chestnut mare grazed on dandelions and crabgrass.

Elisa pointed to the fourth home on the right, which had a metal awning over a small plywood porch. "Right there."

Tessa pulled alongside it. "Will they mind if I park under the canopy by the office for a minute? I'm going to get out and clean some mud off the windshield. My wipers aren't getting it."

"You need new wipers," Helen said. "And that's a fact."

"No one would mind," Elisa said. She thanked Tessa, who assured her again it had been no trouble; then Elisa said goodbye to Helen. She got out and stayed on the porch to wave goodbye as they turned and started toward the office, just across the gravel road.

The door was locked, which surprised her, since she had expected Adoncia to be home. To the drumming of rain on the metal awning, she slipped off her backpack and fumbled through it for her key.

Once the door was open, she started inside, but something made her turn, perhaps a noise that didn't seem to be part of the storm, an instinct. She saw

Tessa, parked now under the office canopy, slumped against the side of the car. Elisa leapt off the porch and sprinted across the road. Helen had emerged by the time she got there, and the two of them caught Tessa before she slid to the ground.

Between them they managed to get her to the steps leading up to the office. She was semiconscious, although Elisa thought she had passed out completely for at least a few seconds.

Gently she nudged Tessa's head toward her knees. "Take a deep breath," she said. "It will pass quickly. Just stay there until you feel better."

Tessa made a noise one degree from a moan. Helen was wide-eyed with alarm. "She's as healthy as a horse. Eats right, does everything right. I don't know what could be wrong with her."

"Has she been having fainting spells?"

"I don't know. She hasn't said a thing to me, and if she'd told her mother, I'd have heard about it, believe me."

"I'm . . . fine." Tessa lifted her head, then rested it on her hands.

Elisa sat beside her and rubbed her back. "Has this happened before?"

"No." Tessa took a deep breath, but she

still sounded frightened. "Something is obviously wrong."

Elisa weighed silence against her own comfort, but she had little choice. "I wouldn't worry too much, not unless a doctor tells you to. It could be several things, all minor."

Tessa looked up. "How do you know?"

"I — I have a sister who had the same thing happen to her." Elisa smiled her reassurance. "She told me exactly what her doctor said. Iron deficiencies or infections of the inner ear may cause fainting in pregnancy, but most likely the baby is just pressing against a nerve or a blood vessel. None of those things are serious. There's no danger to you or the baby, but of course you must go in to be checked as soon as possible."

Tessa looked somewhat relieved. "I thought . . ."

"She thought she was going into labor and losing the baby," Helen said bluntly. "And so did I."

Elisa squeezed Tessa's hand. "Most likely your doctor will tell you to be sure you change positions often when you're sitting. Perhaps he'll point out that since you've had this episode, you shouldn't drive or sit in a car more than necessary."

"It *was* a long drive from Fairfax, and I came right over to get Gram."

"And you weren't out of the car for more than five minutes when you got to the church," Helen said. "That's probably it."

"See?" Elisa stood. In the moment it had taken her to reach Tessa's side, she had gotten soaked. Her shirt clung to her chest. "How do you feel now?"

"Fine. I think."

"Forget the groceries. We'll go straight home, and I'll drive," Helen said. "I still have my license."

"No, I'm fine now. I'll be fine," Tessa said. She stood, as if testing her words. "But I will check with my doctor. Right away."

Elisa nodded. "Stretch and move around a little before you get back in the car. If you feel even the slightest bit dizzy afterward, let your grandmother drive you home."

Tessa turned to her. "You've been very kind."

Elisa considered Tessa's words and the real truth, that this had been more than kindness. She touched Tessa's arm. "I'm glad I could help. At least a little."

Chapter Four

The rain stopped by three, and the fund-raiser committee went to work mowing the wet grass in front of *La Casa Amarilla* and raking it into steaming clumps. A crew came to string colorful plastic lanterns from the aging oaks and maples, none of which had ever seen this kind of festivity in their century or more of life in Virginia. Another crew set up tables and covered them with red-and-blue plastic. Yet another set up a temporary platform for a mariachi band they had hired at a discount.

There was little call for mariachi bands in Shenandoah County.

Christine had promised to find her way to the church about dinnertime, when the fiesta would just be getting into swing. At four Sam rolled up his sleeves, and by six he stepped back and took a long look at what they had accomplished. He loved being outdoors, having open space around him, the fresh breeze tickling his skin. He was going to enjoy the evening.

"I'm impressed," he told the president of his board of deacons, Gayle Fortman, an attractive single mother of three teenaged boys. "Now if the rain just holds off . . ."

"It's supposed to." Gayle's short blond hair stuck out in a hundred directions, and she had a streak of dirt on one cheek. She had been on ladders for hours stringing lights. Two of her sons had helped and were now wheeling clumps of grass to the church compost bin.

"People will have a good time," he promised. "Even if we don't raise a lot of money, this gives everyone a look at what we've done to the house. Good feelings will be worth a lot down the line."

"Not everyone's happy with this project."

He knew she wasn't talking about tonight's fund-raiser. "You've been getting calls?"

"Sam, everything you do pisses off somebody. I need a hotline."

Sam supposed three rambunctious boys taught a mother not to beat around the bush.

"Most of the calls are from perpetual

malcontents who weren't happy we hired you in the first place," she continued, when he didn't defend himself. "I suppose they would call if Jesus was the pastor, too."

"Probably more often. At least I don't turn water into wine."

She had a deep, satisfying laugh. "A lot of people are coming tonight. The summer's ending. This is the final social event before Labor Day. For a last-minute, middle-of-the-week celebration, we did good, huh?"

"It's a testament to the church's well-being that when we decided to hold a fund-raiser, there were few dates not booked for something else."

"You do keep things moving. I'll give you that."

He took that as a compliment, although it was questionable. "I've had four interviews for a new sexton. I'll be choosing by the end of the week."

"Good. Marie Watson called to tell me the women's bathroom was not clean enough to suit her. Twice."

"She's only been to church twice all summer."

"Well, we know where she spent her time when she was here."

One of Gayle's sons called her away, and

she lifted a hand in farewell. "I'm going home for a shower, but I'll be back in half an hour. If the caterer doesn't show up in fifteen minutes, call me?"

He watched her go and wished he had four dozen more just like her in the congregation.

The caterers did arrive, and competently erected grills and serving tables before they began to set out covered bowls of salsas, guacamole and sour cream. The Sunday school superintendent arrived with the largest donkey piñata Sam had ever seen and strung it from an appropriate tree limb far away from where the food would be served.

He slipped home for a quick shower, too, and changed into a colorful shirt and dark pants.

He beat Christine to the party by close to an hour. The mariachi band, dressed in full black-and-gold regalia, was playing a lively version of "La Bamba" when she arrived in an off-the-shoulder white dress cinched at the waist with a wide silver belt.

"The fiesta has begun," she said, kissing his cheek, then wiping off her lipstick. "And they're actually in tune."

She sounded surprised, and he couldn't chide her. Considering what the committee was paying the band, he had expected the men to take turns strumming one guitar. Instead, seven members had arrived, complete with elaborate costumes and expensive instruments.

"They're great," Sam said. "You ought to hear them sing *'Malaguena Salerosa.'*" He hummed a few bars.

"Better them than you."

People began to come forward to be introduced to Christine. He did his part, and watched her chat with his parishioners and those of the surrounding churches who were helping with *La Casa*. He had seen Christine in action a thousand times and knew how much more energy she was capable of expending, if she thought it mattered. She was polite tonight, even friendly, but he knew — even if no one else did — that her heart wasn't in it.

"Fajitas, Sam?" she said, when they were temporarily alone again. "They're serving fajitas?" She gave a low laugh.

"I've eaten four. Come on, I'll load up your plate."

"I'll just take a pass. That's a week's worth of calories on a tortilla. Cheese, sour cream, guacamole." She rolled her lovely green eyes.

"It's a party, Chrissy. Worth a few fat grams."

"Plastic lanterns and piñatas do not a party make, sweetie. There's nothing to drink, is there?"

"Not with children present." He felt a flash of annoyance that she would make a point of that. They had never served liquor at family functions at The Savior's Church, either, a fact she was well aware of, since she was the headmistress of the private school associated with that congregation.

She made a face. "I'll just go see what I can find that's safe to swallow. I'll catch you later."

He didn't volunteer to go with her. Instead, he wandered over to the tree where the donkey piñata hung. Two dozen children stood in a wide circle watching a blindfolded second-grader swing a plastic bat in the donkey's general direction.

He was squatting on the ground, surrounded by four elementary schoolgirls who had just finished explaining what they would do with the bounty if they opened the piñata, when someone spoke above him.

"We can safely say it will take dynamite to crack that facade."

Sam stood to find a cleaner, happier

78

Gayle. "We're preparing them for a life of frustration."

"In ten minutes someone will take a chain saw to that thing and be done with it. The kids won't care, as long as they get the candy and toys."

"I've had a load of compliments on what we've done with the house, and a good number of checks accompanied them."

"Terrific."

"Sam!"

Over the strains of *"Cielito Lindo,"* Sam looked for the source of the shout and finally spied one of the deacons, a man in his late seventies named Early Meeks, coming from the direction of the church. Early was tall and completely bald. He drew attention away from the hair he lacked with brightly colored neckties and suspenders. He was a favorite of the Sunday school children, who appreciated his flair for comedy.

Early looked anything but comic now. Sam excused himself and went to meet him halfway.

"What's up?" Sam asked.

"We have a situation in the social hall."

"Situation?"

"George Jenkins is here."

George's presence surprised Sam.

Jenkins was the member of the board of deacons least likely to go along with any good idea. He had opposed *La Casa Amarilla* from the first, expounding on the need to "pull together" as a congregation, which was George's own code for "keeping outsiders away." He had been overruled on *La Casa*, as he was usually overruled, a fact that made him even more determined to make trouble for Sam. Sam gave silent thanks every time he remembered that George was serving his final months of a five-year term.

"His son was here earlier today," Sam said. "There was another *situation* during that little visit."

"Leon never really struck me as a chip off the old block." Early nodded toward the church. "But you'd better come quick. George is making threats. We're trying to keep him out of sight."

"We?"

As they strode toward the church, Early explained that several partygoers had removed George to the social hall. "I was coming for the party, too. I heard a commotion just inside the front door and went to check. Apparently George doesn't know the party is elsewhere." He hesitated. "Actually, George probably doesn't know much of anything right now. He's had more than a few drinks tonight."

Sam was grateful the men had stopped George before he destroyed the good spirit at the fiesta and made more of a fool of himself in the process.

"Maybe if he has a chance to insult me he'll calm down and we can get him home. How did he get here?"

"His car's in the lot."

"He's lucky he didn't kill somebody on the way over. *They're* lucky."

"We won't let him drive home."

Sam briefly considered calling the sheriff and having George removed from the premises, but the temptation passed quickly. There were better ways to deal with George, both for his sake and that of the church.

They reached the building and entered through a side door. When it closed behind him, Sam could no longer hear the band or the happy squeals of children. They turned down several corridors, ending up in the large room where most social events were held. Sam saw George in the corner by the door, flanked by the other men Early had mentioned. George, in his forties, was not aging well. He had coarse, bulldog features, a perpetual scowl, and a physique that was more out-of-shape wrestler than boxer.

Everyone but George looked uncomfortable. George looked furious.

Sam wasted no time reaching the others. The other men stepped away, leaving him to face the angry man.

"What's going on, George?" Sam kept his tone carefully neutral.

"You're . . . what's goin' on, preacher."

Early had been right. Jenkins was clearly drunk. His words were slurred, his face flushed, and his eyes were not quite focused.

With effort, Sam remained polite. "There's probably a better time and place to explore our differences. Why don't I come to your house tomorrow, and we can talk about this all you want?"

"You . . . 'umiliated my boy! Right in front of . . . of his frien's . . . and those damn quilters. . . ."

Sam had guessed this visit was about Leon. He wondered how much of the story the boy had told his father and what his version had sounded like.

Sam explained. "Leon tried to take a sledgehammer to the new sign. I stopped him and sent him home. That's about it for the facts."

George took a step closer and stuck his finger in the air near Sam's nose. "You had no right!"

"George, I was trying to keep the sheriff out of it."

"I'm gonna get you fired. You see . . . if I don't."

Sam hoped that was all the man needed to say. He saw no point in listening to more. "Why don't you go home now? One of your friends will drive you. We'll talk tomorrow."

Sam started to turn away, a mistake he only realized when he heard George's angry grunt. He whirled back just in time to see a fist coming directly at his face.

Sam was a coal miner's son. He had spent his childhood years in a Pennsylvania coal patch defending a skinny younger brother from the sons of other coal miners. He did what came naturally. Lifting one arm, he blocked George's punch, stepping sideways as he did. George, off balance to begin with, stumbled forward and fell to the floor at Sam's feet.

Everyone stared. George lay as still as a corpse.

"He's breathing," Early said at last.

Sam felt only a touch of remorse. He

had not punched Jenkins, only blocked his poorly aimed attack. He squatted and put his hand on the man's neck. Jenkins' pulse was strong and steady.

"Would that be a new version of turning the other cheek, pastor?" Early asked.

Elisa waved goodbye to the neighbor who had dropped her off at the church for the evening. She had promised to return when Elisa finished, despite Elisa's assurances it wasn't necessary. The Latino families at the park watched out for each other. During her months in residence, Elisa had done her share of favors for some of the young mothers, and the favors had been returned in a number of ways.

The night had turned cooler, and despite the afternoon storm, the humidity seemed to be dropping. She could hear music playing and wondered if her ears deceived her. Someone was singing in Spanish.

"Miss?"

Her head shot up, and she gazed in the direction the voice had come from. A young man — all too familiar — materialized from the deepening shadows at the front of the church.

She took a step backward. "What do you want?"

"Please . . ." He put his hands out, palms up, in supplication. "I — I'm sorry about, you know, that thing with the sign."

"Were you waiting here just to tell me that?"

Leon Jenkins — now she remembered his name — shoved his hands in the pockets of baggy jeans. "I — you've got to help me."

"I doubt I have to do anything." She stepped forward to make up for the ground she'd lost. Anger shot through her as she remembered how vulnerable she'd felt when he'd stood in front of her with a sledgehammer. "And unless you're really not very smart, you realize there are people nearby, yes? People who will come if I scream."

"Don't scream!" He looked around. "I mean, there's no reason to scream. God, that will make things a whole lot worse."

"I doubt your God has a thing to do with this. Maybe you ought to leave."

"But I can't! It's my dad. He's inside. And, well, somebody's got to help me get him outside so I can take him home."

She had no idea what he was talking about, and her expression must have said so.

"My dad, he's, you know, mad at Reverend Sam. Real mad. Furious. I came home all wet and, like, soaked from that walk. And I had to tell him what happened. And I didn't blame anybody. I told him it was just me being stupid."

For the first time she noticed a bruise on his cheek. "He hit you?"

"He never hits me. I . . . tripped."

She would just bet he'd tripped. Right into his father's fist. She was beginning to feel sorry for the boy, and sorrier for falling prey to pity.

"Why does somebody need to get your dad and bring him outside?"

"Because he's drunk, that's why! And if I go in there by myself . . ."

Good old dad would hit him again. She saw the fear, and, worse, she saw the love. The boy was worried about his father's safety.

"Leon — that's your name, yes?"

He nodded.

"I don't see what I can do about this."

"Somebody's got to do something."

"I can go find the minister. Maybe Sam will know what to do."

"No, he hates Reverend Sam. He really hates him. That's why he came. He says he's going to find him and show him what he thinks of him, once and for all."

She wondered if the boy dealt with this problem often. It explained a lot about the way he had behaved that morning.

She debated her role. She had no reason to get involved except one. She liked teen-aged boys, understood them as well as any parent, and unfortunately, this one was tugging at her heartstrings.

"¡No cabe duda que jamás cambiaré! Por mucho que juré no volver a arriesgarme el pellejo por desconocidos, ¡Ahí voy de nuevo!"

"What?"

"Short version? I said I'm a fool. But I'll go in with you and look for your father. What should we say to get him outside?"

"He won't hit a woman. He never did, not even when my mom said she was going to leave him."

"Did she leave?"

He nodded. "A long time ago."

The heartstrings were twanging. Mama had left the young boy to the mercies of an abusive father, and Leon had watched her leave. Considering all this, he was a model of deportment.

"What will he say if I ask him to come outside to look at something in front of the church?" she asked.

"He might come."

"If he does, will you be able to get him in . . ." She stopped. "Do you drive? Are you old enough?"

"I drive. I followed him here in the pickup." He waited. She didn't answer, just lifted a brow expectantly. "I'm fifteen," he admitted. "I just have a learner's permit, but better me driving home than him, right?"

She supposed so. "You'll come with me?"

"If we get him outside, I can get him in the truck."

She muttered in Spanish as she opened the front door. She didn't ask what the boy's father looked like. She hoped there weren't too many angry men in the building to choose from. She wandered a minute or two with Leon just behind her until she heard voices. Following the sound, she stepped into a large room and examined a group standing around a man who was passed out cold in the corner.

"Increible . . ." They were clearly too late, but she started toward the men anyway. Behind her, she could hear Leon breathing hard, as if he was trying not to cry.

For just a moment, Sam watched Elisa

and Leon approach; then he turned to the others. "I think it would be best if you left. He's going to wake up in a minute, and it's going to be worse if he has an audience."

"You're sure?" Early asked. "I mean, we don't want him to take another swing at you." He paused. "Or you at him."

Sam stared at him without comment, and Early finally stepped back. "We'll wait nearby. Just in case."

"It's taken care of," Sam assured him. "But thank you just the same."

The men left by the side door. Sam was fairly sure they would continue to hover there.

Elisa and Leon reached him. Sam spoke before they could. "He took a swing at me, stumbled and fell."

Elisa stooped and put her fingertips against George's throat. Then gently — and what looked like thoroughly — she probed the back of his head, his neck and shoulders, running her hands down his arms, then over his back and legs, in a manner he could only term professional. For a moment Sam had the oddest desire to *be* George, passed out cold on the social hall floor.

She got to her feet. "No obvious injuries. How hard did he hit his head when he fell?"

"He stumbled and pitched forward. He wasn't standing tall. I think he more or less caught himself. Then he just . . . dissolved." He paused. "Where did you learn to do that?"

"What?"

"That kind of examination."

"I worked at a bar in El Paso. There were a lot of fights."

"Is he going to be all right?" Leon asked.

"I think he's going to have *un grandísimo dolor de cabeza.*" She sighed. "One big headache. Mostly from the liquor."

George punctuated her words with a groan. He stirred, and in a moment he tried to push himself off the floor. Elisa bent over him. "Mr. Jenkins, are you all right?"

"What happened?"

She looked up at Sam and motioned for him to step away. He was only too aware that his presence would not be appreciated.

"You poor thing," she said in her musical voice. "You fell and hit your head. But I think you're going to be okay. Let me help you sit up."

"Where the hell . . . am I?"

"Not where you should be," she soothed him. "You need fresh air for that poor head of yours. I bet it hurts, doesn't it?" She smoothed her hand over his cheek.

"It hurts . . . like hell."

"I am sure it does."

He rolled to his side, and she positioned herself to help him sit up. With a minimum of fuss, he was soon sitting with his head in his hands.

"You aren't going to feel any better until we get you some fresh air." She sounded concerned. "It's hot in here, not comfortable at all. You need to be comfortable. You deserve it. Let me help you stand."

He looked up at that point and saw Leon standing a few feet away. Jenkins squinted. "Lee?"

Leon approached tentatively. "Right here, Dad. I'll help you up."

"What . . . r'you doing here?"

"I asked him to help me get you outside where you'll feel better," Elisa said in a voice like gentle rain. "He is a good son. He is right here waiting to help you."

"Always been a good son."

Sam watched as Leon and Elisa positioned themselves on either side of the man and lifted him as if they had always worked together. He felt helpless, but he knew better than to assist. One glance at him and the fight would all come flooding back.

George hobbled toward the door, stopping once, as if nausea was building. Luckily he seemed to recover. They got him through the door and out into the fresh air. Sam followed at a distance. In only minutes they had George inside an old truck with Leon at the wheel.

"You'll be okay?" he heard Elisa ask Leon. "You can drive this home?"

"I drive all the time."

"And you can get him to bed?"

"I've done it before."

"Watch for signs of concussion. Wake him up a few times through the night to be sure. But I think he's going to be fine."

She stepped back and slapped the passenger door in signal. Leon gunned the engine, and in a moment, the pickup was gone.

She was still staring at the road when Sam came to stand beside her. "You seem to know how to defuse every situation," he said.

She faced him. "What is it about this church that there are so many situations to defuse?"

She said it with good humor. He smiled at her, not quite sure how to thank her, not quite sure exactly what he was feeling at that moment.

He didn't have time to worry about either. Early and the others approached and congratulated them both on their handling of the incident. Sam was sure he would hear more about this — and not necessarily congratulations — in the weeks to come.

"Sam?" Christine joined the growing group at the front of the church.

"You're okay?" he asked Elisa, before he faced Christine.

"I'm fine. Now I'll go find Marvin and see what else a good sexton has to do."

"Thank you. I don't know what I would have done without you."

She nodded.

As Sam whisked Christine off to the side, the others were already embellishing the story beyond recognition.

Christine spoke first. "You punched somebody?"

He wasn't sure if she was pleased or embarrassed. He suspected she was just sad she had missed the excitement.

"I didn't punch anybody. I dodged a punch."

"And Miss Mexican Working Girl helped you?"

He told the story quickly. "Elisa managed to convince him to go home. It's not as exciting as it sounds." He changed the subject. "What are you doing out here?"

"I decided to go back to the inn. I'm tired."

"I need to stay around for a while."

"By yourself, I'm afraid. I've done all the good I can here."

He was sorry she wasn't enjoying herself, but what exactly had he expected? That she would fall in love with these people tonight when she hadn't fallen in love with them in the years of his ministry here? That she would fall in love with the valley and the green hills of Virginia when he wasn't certain *he* had?

"Would you like me to go with you to make sure you get back all right?" he asked.

"I'll be fine." She touched his cheek, and her eyes sparkled. "After tonight, you're definitely going to hire that woman, aren't you?"

"Apparently she can handle anything we throw at her."

"I guess she'll be another of your do-gooder projects." She gave an intimate laugh. "That's one of those things I love about you. The way you take little wounded birds under your wing and make them all better."

"Elisa is nobody's wounded bird."

"Of course you look for the best in every person and situation. I love that about you, too."

Sam had known for a long time that Christine did not look for the best. She looked for the most comfortable, the most familiar, the most expedient. Most of the time he was glad of it. She was practical. She kept him on track when he lost his focus.

Still, he knew his intended well. Tonight she was also pointing him along the highway she intended them to travel together and warning against detours into the unfamiliar forests of the soul.

Christine might not see herself as ideal minister's wife material, but she was reminding Sam that someone like Elisa Martinez was even less so.

Chapter Five

Sam did not believe in putting on a show on Sunday mornings, nor did he believe boredom was conducive to spiritual growth. His worship services were high-energy affairs that made use of the arts to emphasize the simple message that God asked us to love our neighbors and treat them the way we wanted to be treated ourselves.

This was at the core of every one of his sermons. He was less interested in proclaiming ironclad answers to life's questions and narrowly interpreting scripture. Those who needed a longer list of *do*s and *don't*s, or weekly promises that their way was the only way, had moved on to other churches. For every family he lost, he gained several more.

On the Sunday after the fiesta, he was donning a colorful liturgical stole woven in

Guatemala to brighten his somber black robe. His early service had been well attended for one so late in the summer, and a peek into the sanctuary a few minutes ago had confirmed that this one would have respectable attendance, too.

He was wiggling the stole into place and matching the edges when Andy, the choir director, stomped in. He was a young man, flamboyant and outspoken, who, despite impressive credentials, had not been able to find a position in a church near his Strasburg home until Sam hired him.

"They're murdering the Spanish on the processional! I've never heard anything like it." He flopped down on Sam's sofa, mock outrage distorting his face. He was a lanky six feet, with a collar-length Prince Valiant haircut colored a stunning orange, and large teeth with a pronounced overbite that made for a spectacular smile. "You're sure you want us to process to that . . . that song *again?*"

Sam was used to Andy's tirades. " *'Des Colores'* is the official song of the United Farm Workers. Did I tell you that?"

"About a million times. You'd better hope there aren't any union members at this next service, or they'll come after you with shovels and hoes. Oh, I got some more rhythm instruments after the last service. Somebody donated them. We'll march with maracas this time."

"Good, that will drown out the bad Spanish. God works in mysterious ways."

"I just can't be-lieve you keep this job!" Andy got to his feet. "Off to see who shows up to sing. You know, I could have gotten a gig in D.C. They wanted me at the Cathedral."

"We'd miss you, Andy."

Andy grinned.

Out in the hallway, Sam was greeted by the dance director in leotards and a tunic adorned with a wide swath of brightly colored fabric. Liturgical dancers were an innovation he had encouraged, and as they headed for the sanctuary, he agreed to smooth out a transition between his sermon and the dancers' entrance to a recording of "Amazing Grace" played on marimbas. The theme of the day was clear. The celebration of *La Casa Amarilla* was still in progress.

At the wide double doors leading into the sanctuary, he stood at his place in front of the choir. The sanctuary was nearly full.

As always, he said a short prayer as the organist concluded the prelude. Then he lifted his head and waited for the opening bars of the processional. He felt his traditional mixture of elation that he'd been blessed to stand in front of these good people and fear that he wasn't worthy.

He realized, as the processional began, that today he didn't feel sadness that he was not walking down a longer and wider center aisle to the music of the one-hundred-voice chancel choir of Savior's Church.

Adoncia Garcia's home was crowded with toys and furniture her mother-in-law had given her. The mother-in-law, and Adoncia's two children, Maria, age three, and Fernando, eighteen months, were the only good things to come from her marriage to Fernando Garcia the first, who now rested permanently under a headstone on which his mother was still making payments.

Fernando had been a bad choice for both Adoncia and the woman in whose bed he'd been shot by a jealous boyfriend. Adoncia, who had been courted by half a dozen faithful, hardworking men in her home city of Guanajuato, had been blinded by Fernando's smile and promises of a better life in the United States. Both the smile and the promises had been lies.

Now she was in Virginia, and her family was in central Mexico. For better or worse, her children were U.S. citizens and her home was here.

"Maria, you put away your toys now, so we can get ready to go." Adoncia demonstrated by dropping Maria's favorite teddy bear in one of three bright plastic tubs along one wall. "You do it like this."

Maria complied. She had her father's smile and her mother's energy. Elisa was certain the little girl would go far.

"Today is an English day," Adoncia told Elisa, who had the day off and was letting it unfold slowly for a change. "Today we speak to the children in English only. Tomorrow, Spanish."

"Does Diego agree to this system?" Diego was Adoncia's boyfriend, a good-natured, intelligent man who was determined to get ahead in the world. He was the polar opposite of Fernando the former.

"Diego will do anything I say." Adoncia made a face. "Almost anything. But he will speak English today, or I will not speak to him."

Elisa dusted the few vacant surfaces as Adoncia moved into the connecting kitchen to do dishes from their late breakfast. She and the children had an outing planned with Diego, something she had looked forward to for days. Adoncia worked five difficult shifts each week at the chicken plant south of Woodstock in Edinburg, while the children stayed with their grandmother. The overly attentive Mrs. Garcia spoiled her grandchildren as badly as she had spoiled her son, but Adoncia made sure they obeyed the rules at home.

Fernando toddled over and raised his arms to be lifted up. Elisa settled the little boy on one hip and finished dusting with the other hand.

"The good thing about a small house is that it takes no time to clean." Adoncia pulled the plug in the sink and let the dishwater drain out. "I should be grateful for poverty, huh?"

"After Diego moves in, you can save enough to buy a little house of your own. As hard as you both work, it shouldn't take too long."

"That's what he says, only he says big house. He wants a big house for all the children."

Wisely, Elisa said nothing.

"Many children." Adoncia began to rinse and dry the dishes she'd washed. "A hundred children."

"Probably only ninety-five."

Adoncia laughed. Whenever she did, the responsibilities that weighed so heavily on her twenty-four-year-old shoulders seemed to disappear. Elisa thought her friend was beautiful. She was too plump by this country's anorexic standards, but she had black hair that curved around her face in shining layers, and warm brown skin she enhanced with bright cosmetics and clothing. It was no surprise to Elisa that Diego Moreno had fallen in love with Adoncia the first time he'd set eyes on her.

"He would keep me pregnant until I'm an old woman, if he had his way. I tell him 'one baby will show the world what a big man you are, Diego,' but he doesn't see it that way."

"You think he's trying to prove his manhood?"

"You know a man who isn't?"

Elisa thought about Sam Kinkade, who twice last Wednesday had been forced to prove his. She doubted he had wanted or relished either experience.

"No," Adoncia continued, "Diego is determined to show everyone he is a big man. In every way," she added slyly.

Elisa laughed. "And you'll be a big woman if you have all those children."

"Bigger." Adoncia pulled the elastic band of her pants away from her waist to illustrate. "Much, much bigger."

Elisa genuinely liked Diego, who often complained of missing his extended family in Mexico, just as Adoncia missed hers. "I don't really think he wants a large family to prove anything. I think he wants a family to love."

"The effect is the same. Me, pregnant. Over and over. And he wants it to happen soon."

This was new information for Elisa. Adoncia had enough stress in her life, and although she was an exemplary mother most of the time, her temper was already too short by the end of the day. "Soon?"

"Marry him, have his baby the next year. No compromise."

"But you have your hands full, Donchita," Elisa said, using her pet name for her friend. "He doesn't see that? Working, taking care of two small children?"

"He says once we're married I can quit my job, that he makes enough money to keep us happy. But I know better. We will struggle. We need a year, two, maybe even three, to make things right, to save for a house, to get Nando out of diapers. Then maybe we could have a baby of our own, even two. But no more."

Elisa was sorry to hear that her friends were locked in disagreement about something so fundamental. "Is birth control the problem, do you think? Because there are ways that the church approves of. Not perfect ways, but better than nothing."

"One of the problems, yes."

"I hope you and Diego can agree about this."

"So do I. He wants to marry just as soon as —" Adoncia stopped. "As soon as we're able," she finished after a moment.

Elisa realized what her friend hadn't said. Until Elisa moved out of the mobile home, there was no room for Diego here. Right now Adoncia shared the master bedroom with her children, while Elisa slept in the tiny second bedroom.

"I'm going to look harder for another place to stay," Elisa promised.

"You are a good friend, and I am in no hurry."

The debate was interrupted by a crash, then a wail, from the corner by the toy baskets. Elisa spun around to see Maria surrounded by shards of the ceramic lamp that had once resided on an end table.

"Don't move, Maria," Elisa commanded,

reaching her in three strides. She scooped the little girl against her vacant hip and away from the broken lamp.

"I'm . . . I'm bleebing!" Maria looked down at her hand.

Elisa whisked her to one of two old armchairs crowded in the corner. Adoncia had reached them, but instead of taking Maria, she lifted Fernando into her arms so that Maria had Elisa all to herself.

"Let me see now." Elisa gently pried the little girl's fingers away from her wounded palm. "Oh, it's not so bad. Just a little scratch."

"It hurts!"

"Well, yes, that's good. If it didn't hurt you might not know you had scratched yourself."

Adoncia had turned her back on them, supposedly to jiggle the whimpering Fernando, but in actuality Elisa knew her friend got queasy at any sign of injury. Once they had seen a dying robin by the roadside, and Adoncia had nearly passed out.

"Let me get the first aid kit," Elisa told Maria. "Then you can help me clean the cut and put on the Band-Aid."

"I'll get it," Adoncia said. She returned from the bedroom she shared with her children and presented it to Elisa, turning her eyes to her daughter's face. "Ah, Maria, you are very brave. A good brave girl."

Maria stopped sniffling.

"How did you break the lamp?" Adoncia asked.

"Don't . . . know."

"I bet she got her foot tangled in the cord," Elisa said. "It would have been easy to do."

Adoncia addressed her daughter. "I will make you an ice cream cone. Would you like that?"

"Choc-late," Maria said.

"And one for Nando, too." Adoncia headed back to the kitchen.

Elisa had the kit open now. She lifted Maria in her arms and carried her to the bathroom to wash her hand with cool running water. Then, back in the living room, she let the little girl guide her as she put antibiotic ointment on the shallow cut and covered it with a glow-in-the-dark SpongeBob Squarepants Band-Aid.

She finished just as Adoncia returned with an ice cream cone in each hand and the broom tucked under her arm. "I will just clean up the mess now."

Someone knocked on the front door before Adoncia could begin. Elisa got to her feet and swung Fernando into the chair beside his sister. Then she went to answer the door, expecting to find Diego.

Sam Kinkade was standing on the porch. He wore dark pants and a gray T-shirt bearing three monkeys and the words: "The only thing necessary for the triumph of evil is for enough good people to do nothing."

"Amnesty International," he said, as she silently read the words. "Once I join enough organizations and buy enough T-shirts, I won't have to give sermons."

For a moment she didn't know what to say, but his warm smile — all too rare when last she'd seen him — made him more approachable. "I like it." She stepped away from the door and motioned him inside. "Please come in."

"I don't want to bother you. I just thought —"

"No, please come in and meet my roommate and her children."

As he stepped inside, she saw the trailer through his eyes. It seemed more cramped, dilapidated, even more crowded with furniture Adoncia thought she could not afford to throw away. The last occupants had knocked a hole in the paneling, which

Adoncia had covered with festive strips of adhesive-backed paper. The curtains had been intended for different sized windows and pinned to fit, since Adoncia had no sewing machine.

Elisa made the introductions and explanations, and Sam gravely examined Maria's hand, despite the fact that it was now sticky with melting ice cream.

"You were obviously a very brave girl," he said.

She thrust out her cone, to give him a friendly lick.

Adoncia blocked the thrust. "Father Kinkade will not want a bite," she told Maria.

"Just call me Sam," he said.

Another knock sounded, and this time Adoncia went to answer it. Diego stepped inside, sweeping Adoncia close for a kiss. He was medium height, with a wide-shouldered square body and muscular arms. His round face was brightened by a shy smile, and his short black hair stood out from his head like burrs on a chestnut.

He released Adoncia and grabbed Fernando, who had run straight for him. He lifted the little boy off his feet, tossing him in the air to the sound of frantic giggles. Rapid-fire Spanish ensued.

"I should go," Sam said. He looked uncomfortable. Elisa wondered what made him feel most out of place. The obvious poverty here? The crowded room? The people who were now chattering eagerly in a language he did not understand?

"I'll introduce you to Diego first." She waited for a break and made the introduction. The two men shook hands; then Sam said goodbye to everyone and started for the door.

Elisa went with him, stepping over the threshold and closing the door behind her. Outside, where it was a little quieter, she let out the breath she hadn't even realized she was holding.

"You must have come for a reason," she said. "Your Sundays are busy. You must have finished with church only a short time ago."

"I wanted to talk to you, but I should have called first. I was just heading back from the nursing home and thought I might find you here."

"Nursing home?"

"I went after church to check your references. I've been too busy to do it before."

"We can talk right here if you'd like." Happy shrieks from inside drowned out the last word.

"Have you had lunch?" he asked.

"No, but we ate a late breakfast."

"Do you have time to get some coffee, then?"

"Plenty of time."

"I can wait if you need to do anything first."

"I'll just tell Adoncia. I won't be a moment."

"They seem very happy together. Already a family."

Elisa thought he sounded wistful, and that surprised her. She thought of the struggles Adoncia and Diego faced, and Sam's words surprised her even more.

"I'll be right back," she said.

He nodded and started toward a mud-splattered SUV parked just in front.

Elisa had expected coffee at Arby's or McDonald's on West Reservoir Road, where nearly all Woodstock's fast food restaurants congregated. Instead, they started back toward the church in Toms Brook.

"I can't think of any place where we won't be constantly interrupted except my house." He glanced at her. "Do you mind? The choir is practicing for a concert, and there are at least three rental groups using the building, or I'd take you to my office."

"You live near the church?" She thought

he'd told her as much.

"Just far enough away that people have to think twice before dropping by for keys or casual conversation. The minister they built the house for made sure of that."

They drove the rest of the way in silence. He pulled up in front of a neat brick house with gray shutters and a matching wooden fence enclosing a shallow front yard. A felt banner in brilliant jewel tones hung from the front door.

"Peace," she read out loud.

"The junior high school group made it for me last Christmas, and I can't bear to take it down."

The front porch was a mass of blooms in different sized and colored pots. "You like to garden."

"Plants don't talk back to me." He got out and came around to open her door, but she had already let herself out.

Sam unlatched the gate and waited for her to precede him. "I'll warn you about my dogs."

She stopped, and he nearly ran into her. "You have dogs?"

He skirted her so he was in front. "A problem?"

"It's just . . ." Her heart was pounding

111

too hard. She took a deep breath. "No, it's just . . ."

"You don't like them."

"No. I —" She shrugged. "I'm a little . . . I was attacked in . . . in my hometown. I had a full course of rabies shots." She made a face. "I'm a little dog shy."

"I would imagine you are." Sympathy was clear in both his face and words. "I can promise these dogs won't attack. They're not exactly well mannered, but they would only love you to death."

"Well, good." She stood a little straighter. "I'll be fine."

"I can put them in the dog run, if you'll just wait here."

"No. I'd like to meet them."

He searched her face, then nodded. "Let me go first, so I can calm them a bit."

She did, waiting until he had unlocked the door and disappeared inside for a minute before she opened the door to join him.

She was met with a blaze of color. She hadn't known what to expect, but she certainly hadn't expected this. The foyer was an extension of a dining area in the middle of the house, with walls painted a warm gold. The living room on her left — a nook more than a room — was a deep sage green. Beyond the dining area was a family room painted a stormy blue. Every wall was covered with photographs, posters and paintings. The mantel on the brick fireplace was crowded with keepsakes.

Sam was kneeling on the floor just in front of a small dining-room table, his arms around two huge dogs. If the breed had a name, the name was mutt. Both dogs had patchy fur, misshapen ears, long pointed snouts. A dog about one-tenth their size was leaping up and down, trying to lick Sam's face.

"I've got the big guys, but you're on your own with the little one. That's Abednego, Bed, for short."

Bed spied her at that moment and ran to greet her. Heart still pounding, Elisa stooped to pet the dog. Bed was white, with large black spots, a stump of a tail and a grin. Elisa fondled her ears, and the dog wagged her entire body in response. "Abednego?"

"From the Old Testament. The Book of Daniel. Shadrach — that's this one. Meshach — this one — and Abednego."

"My Bible skills are rusty."

"They were three Jews who refused to worship the golden idols of King Nebuchadnezzar, so the king had them

113

thrown into a fiery furnace. Later, when he looked into the flames he saw four shapes there. Shadrach, Meshach, Abednego and a mysterious figure. Some say it was their guardian angel, and some say God himself. When the three men emerged, not a hair on their heads had been singed."

"Long important names for dogs. Even large dogs."

He turned his face from a long, licking tongue. "Shad and Shack are brothers. They barely escaped alive from a burning house and were badly singed, unlike their biblical predecessors. I took them when the owners said they couldn't care for them or pay the vet bills, and planned to have them put down. Bed was abused by local boys who had nothing better to do last summer. I barely rescued her in time."

"Lucky dogs, then." She looked up from petting Bed. "Do you rescue everything?"

"It's gotten me in trouble."

She wondered what kind of trouble. She got to her feet, and so did he. One by one he let the dogs go, and they came to her to be petted, too. She ruffled their ears, not even needing to stoop.

"You're okay?" he asked.

"I'm okay." And she was. The dogs were no longer strangers.

"I'll just get coffee going."

She'd had two cups already that morning. She shouldn't have more, but she ignored her own silent advice. "Do you need help?"

"You can keep me company if you'd like."

She followed him into the kitchen, where a gentle breeze rattled the plantation shutters on double windows. The walls were a rich terra-cotta color, but the items on the walls were most interesting. "Lunch boxes?"

He turned from retrieving the coffeemaker from a cabinet. Clearly his addiction to caffeine was not as pronounced as hers. "What lunch boxes?" he asked with a smile.

The one wall in the room that didn't hold cabinets had been covered with shelves. She estimated fifty lunch boxes were on display. "There are more lunch boxes here than in a school cafeteria."

"I have even more."

"More?"

He opened a new can of coffee. She recognized the familiar figures of Juan Valdez and his faithful mule. Even if Sam wasn't much of a coffee drinker, at least he bought Colombian.

"I probably have a hundred lunch boxes." He glanced at her, possibly to see if she was laughing yet.

"It's a slice of popular culture." She walked closer to examine some of the collection. "The Flintstones. Scooby Doo. Superman." She leaned closer to the familiar caped figure. "That one is older than the others."

"One of my favorites."

"They make your kitchen come alive."

"Thank you. I was waiting for you to ask me why I have them."

She cocked her head. "I can only assume you eat lunch often."

He fished through several drawers before he came up with a measuring spoon and began to scoop grounds into the filter.

"My mother and father worked hard for everything they had. There were three children, me, and my brother and sister, Mark and Rachel. We had everything we needed, but if we wanted something our parents saw as a luxury, we never got it. Lunch boxes were a luxury."

He was telling the story without a trace of self-pity. She realized she was smiling.

He went on. "One day, when we were all grown up, Mark, Rachel and I were sitting in a restaurant trying to top each other with terrible stories of our childhood." He went to the sink to fill the pot with water. "There *were* no terrible stories, but there *were* two empty bottles of good Merlot on the table, which made the exercise worthy. I told them my worst memory was the year I had to take my lunch to school wrapped in newspaper, because Mom decided newspaper was cheaper than buying lunch bags."

"And this reminded you to go out and buy a hundred lunch boxes?"

"No, but for Christmas Mark and Rachel each bought me one. In one fell swoop I got Pac-Man and *The Empire Strikes Back.*" He glanced at her and smiled a little. "You have no idea how badly I wanted Pac-Man when I was in first grade."

He poured the water into the coffeemaker and replaced the pot before he turned it on. "The joke spread. Pretty soon everybody was giving me lunch boxes. I still get them. I'd be buried in them, except that I use them as prizes in Sunday school."

She was entranced. "Prizes?"

"Every year we have a lunch contest on the last Sunday in June. All the children bring the strangest lunch they can think of.

117

But it has to be something they'll eat. Six winners get their choice of lunch boxes, at least the ones I have on display. Pac-Man's off limits."

Elisa laughed. "This is a church school?"

He lounged against the counter as the coffee began to brew. "Actually, I tell them the lunch box story, pretty much the way I told it to you. Then I tell them how much sweeter it is for me to have these lunch boxes now, that waiting for them made them that much more special. The kids get the message. Sometimes you can't have everything you want the minute you want it, so you have to wait. And when you do?" He shrugged. "It means more."

She wondered if, when the kids became teenagers, Sam's story made them pause in the race to explore their sexuality. If so, it was certainly a novel approach to sex education.

"I use a different box every day," he finished. "In case one of the kids happens to be around." He allowed himself a grin. "Actually, I'm lying. I use them because they're fun. And Mom would not approve of me having anything I don't use."

She liked his memories. She liked his parents and his sister and brother. She was increasingly sure she liked Sam. She was

118

just as sure that she needed to keep her distance. He would be an easy man to confide in.

"Cream? Sugar?" he asked.

"Nothing. The darker the better."

"I've never quite acquired the taste."

"That's probably because what passes for coffee in this country is the cheapest beans badly roasted and stored too long."

"You're lucky. I thought about serving you instant."

She watched as he reached for mugs and poured milk from the refrigerator in his. Then he added coffee and took the mugs into the family room.

The walls here, as in the other rooms, were covered. But here the artwork was clearly that of children, fastened on the walls with plastic pushpins. She suspected the Sunday school children again, or perhaps nieces and nephews. This was a man, like Diego, who loved kids.

Sam set the coffee on the low table in front of a comfortable-looking ultrasuede sofa. "I've told you about me. Why don't you tell me a little about you?"

She joined him and lifted her mug for a sip while she settled on a story. "My father was a teacher. In fact, he taught English, but there was illness and bad luck." She shrugged. "I set off to find my own way in the world to relieve my parents of their burdens."

"Wednesday night you mentioned El Paso?"

She was surprised that with everything else that had been going on, Sam had caught, much less remembered, that. She had nearly forgotten it herself. She would need to be careful. "I have covered a lot of ground."

"I gather you're not married?"

She paused to consider what else to say. She decided not to elaborate. "No."

He went on. "We give two weeks paid vacation, hopefully to be taken when the schedule's not too busy. You would have enough time to fly home and be with your family."

She sipped her coffee and nodded.

"I'm offering you the job," he said.

She set her mug on the table, relieved. "Thank you." She started to say he wouldn't be sorry, but she knew that might well be a lie. When she left without a word, he would feel betrayed.

"There's one condition," he said.

When a woman was poor and clearly in need of a job, there usually was. At least this time she doubted she would be asked to sleep with her boss. "If I can meet your condition," she said carefully, "I will."

"Good. Because I want to throw a car into the bargain."

This was so different from anything she'd expected that she didn't know what to say.

He filled the silence. "I have two cars. The SUV I drove this morning, and a Honda Civic with about 80,000 miles. I didn't want to buy the SUV, but the roads around here can be pretty grim. Last winter I got stuck twice trying to visit shut-ins. And one Sunday I had to walk to church for services because the snow was so deep. I don't need two cars, but I'm sentimentally attached to the Honda, and I couldn't make myself get rid of it. So I want you to use it while you're working at Community Church. Consider it a bonus, because we're not paying as much as we should."

"I don't see how I can accept that. It's too generous."

"Elisa, you can't do the sexton's job without a car, even if you make a super-human effort. This makes it feasible, and it also relieves me of the guilt of owning two vehicles."

When he needed it, he had the most disarming grin. Judging by the warmth and goodwill in his eyes, she could almost believe she would be doing him a favor. She considered a moment, but the possibilities were too tempting. This was a huge gift, much more than he could possibly know.

"Yes, all right," she said at last. "But I have a condition, too. I'll clean *La Casa* thoroughly for you each week. That will be *my* job, not yours. The car will be payment."

"You'll have time?"

"In the time it would take me to walk back and forth to the church, I could clean it from roof to cellar."

"Excellent." He picked up his mug and swung it in toast. "Then it's all set."

Elisa clanked mugs, then peeked at her watch. "I'm sure you're tired. If you're going to drive me back —"

"Don't worry about that. I'll give you the keys to the Civic now, and you can take possession. It's nothing fancy, but it will get you anywhere you need to go."

She needed to go many places. She was thrilled.

She got to her feet, and he followed. The dogs, who were now taking up most of the floor between the family room and kitchen, wagged their tails but didn't rise. She stepped carefully around them and followed Sam — who had taken a better route — to the door, dropping off her mug in the kitchen first.

The car was parked at the side of the house. It was a white hatchback, and it looked to be in good condition for all the miles it had traveled. Sam opened the door and fished under the seat. He got out and held up a keychain with matching keys, and handed it to her. "Most of my neighbors leave their keys in the ignition. You have a license?"

"Yes. Sometimes I drive Adoncia's car. Will I need insurance?"

"I called my agent. We discussed it. I'll call her tomorrow and tell her to be sure everything's in place. You probably shouldn't go far tonight, just in case."

"You're very kind." She couldn't help the next words. "And trusting. I'm really just a stranger to you."

"I'm a good judge of character."

She didn't know what to say. He wasn't as good as he thought.

"Is there a place at your house for another car?" he asked.

"On the side, yes. Diego always parks there. But I won't be living with Adoncia much longer. Diego wants to move in, and he can't as long as I'm there. So I'm looking for something else." She held up the keys. "Now I can look a little farther away."

"How soon do you want to move?"

"Yesterday?"

"Helen Henry needs somebody to stay with her. She's had a young couple with a baby living in her house, but they're moving to Phoenix for several months. Zeke is going to school, and Cissy and Reese are going, too."

Elisa had only needed minutes to see that Helen Henry was not a woman to be railroaded. "Helen wants somebody to move in?"

"Well, so far she's said no to every plan, but Tessa and her mother are convinced somebody needs to be there in case of emergency. So there's a stalemate. I'll warn you. Helen might say no to *you,* as well, but it's worth a try. I'm sure your room would be rent free."

Elisa had not been able to save more than a few hundred dollars. Now she saw the possibilities. Two jobs, a car and a house she didn't have to pay for. She would have money to make discreet inquiries by telephone, to follow new leads if any came her way.

"You're interested?" Sam asked.

"Yes, if she wants me. Adoncia needs the bedroom for her children."

"Then I'll check. We can go out there tomorrow afternoon if you have the time? It's my day off, and I can pick you up."

"Right now I have nothing but time, Sam."

"I sense that."

The conversation had gone from impersonal to personal in the space of seconds. They weren't touching. Indeed she thought that if one of them had brushed the other accidentally, they would have jumped apart. But Sam's gaze was concerned, and very intimate.

"You've only told me the barest bones about your life," he said. "And I suspect you didn't want to say that much. I'm not going to press you, Elisa. But if you ever need to talk, I'll be here waiting."

She couldn't tell him that talk might bring her world crashing around her ears, or that talk might leave him with a moral dilemma even a man of God would find troubling.

"You're very kind," she murmured. "But you've already done too much for me."

They could not seem to look away from

each other. Seconds passed. She was the one who managed it first. She gazed down at the key in her hand. "Thank you."

"Drive safely." He was gone before she unlocked the car door.

Chapter Six

At first glance Helen Henry's farmhouse seemed to bask contentedly in the sleepy late summer sun. But that peaceful snapshot was only a ruse.

"She don't normally take to strangers," Cissy Claiborne told Elisa after Elisa scooped Cissy's baby daughter into her arms and settled her on one hip.

Chubby Teresa Nancy Helen Claiborne was just one year old, with a full head of pale cotton-candy hair. In the space of moments, Elisa had already learned this rosy-cheeked cherub went by two nicknames, Reese on good days, Hellion on not-so-good. With the encroaching move and changes to her schedule, these days she was answering to Hellion.

The baby had toddled down Helen Henry's walkway directly to Elisa and lifted her arms, the way Fernando always did. She smelled like baby shampoo and powder, and immediately nestled in Elisa's arms as if being there was part of her daily routine. Elisa felt a surge of maternal affection.

She saw from Cissy's expression that there was no rivalry here, that, in fact, Cissy was grateful someone else was holding the little girl for a change. "I'm not sure why, but I seem to attract babies."

"Babies know who to trust," Sam said.

"Maybe they just know how much I like them."

"She fussed all day from the minute she got up. This is the first time she's taken a break." Cissy held out her hand. "Cissy Claiborne, Reese's mama."

"Elisa Martinez, Reese's nanny — as long as she'll let me hold her."

"You ever try to pack up just about everything you own with a baby in your arms?" Cissy was young, younger than Elisa had been prepared for, but she said the words with good humor. She had a pretty face, pale golden hair and peach-toned skin, topped off with a friendly smile.

"I can only imagine," Elisa said. "I'm sure she knows something is changing."

"She'll like it in Phoenix. Zeke says our

apartment has a baby playground just down the street. And just as soon as it cools off a little there, we can go for walks."

Elisa had met Sam in the church parking lot so they could drive together. On the trip over, she had learned that Zeke was studying the construction and repair of guitars and other stringed instruments, with the ultimate goal of opening his own shop one day. She could hear all the questions in the young mother's voice. Surely a move this far away was going to be stressful for everybody, not just the baby.

"You're worried about Helen, aren't you?" Sam asked.

Cissy lowered her voice. "Well, you know, Ms. Henry shouldn't really be alone. She thinks she's taking care of us and all, but truth is, Reverend Sam, she needs some looking after. I do the cooking most of the time and keep up with the housework, but most of all I keep her company. She just plain gets lonely."

"I'm going to try to talk her into letting Elisa stay here while you're away. Nancy and Tessa are all for it. Elisa's working at the church now." He turned to Elisa. "Nancy is Helen's daughter, Tessa's mother."

"That's great," Cissy told Elisa. "Reverend Sam's the kind of boss everybody wants."

"Don't tell her that. I won't get a lick of work out of her," Sam said.

Cissy sobered quickly. "I don't want to hurt your feelings, but I don't think Ms. Henry's going to agree. Doesn't matter how nice you are, she's just a stubborn woman. Nancy's brought half a dozen ladies by in the last two months, and Ms. Henry's sent every one of them back out the door faster than a jackrabbit."

"Well, we'll give it a try." Sam put his hand on Elisa's back to urge her toward the front door. For a moment she was all too aware how long it had been since a man had touched her. She and Sam had not said one personal word to each other since he'd ushered her into his car fifteen minutes ago, but she had been only too aware of *him.*

Cissy led them inside. No one was downstairs, but judging from the sound of voices, the second floor was occupied.

"She'll cry when I leave to get Ms. Henry," Cissy warned.

"I'll come and find you if it gets too bad," Elisa promised.

Cissy took off as if she couldn't get away fast enough.

"She's a good mother," Sam said in a low voice. "Conscientious, thoughtful, patient. But this is a lot for a young woman her age to handle. I hope she finds friends in Phoenix to make her feel at home. Reese isn't much for conversation yet."

Elisa murmured endearments to the little girl in Spanish. Reese cooed right back. "See?" Elisa said. "No one's spoken to her in the right language. She just told me she prefers enchiladas to mashed peas."

She smiled at Sam when he laughed. His eyes were warm, and he reached out to fluff Reese's hair.

"What do you think?" he asked. "Could you live here comfortably?"

She'd only had a chance to glance around, but she nodded. "It's a lovely house, filled with character."

"At one time it was filled with trash. That's one of the things you'll have to watch out for if you move in. Helen has a fondness for collecting. It took Nancy and Tessa a whole summer to get the house in shape."

"They did a good job." The living room where they stood was tastefully decorated in an uncluttered country style. She had not lived anywhere so inviting in many years.

A woman with short blond hair appeared on the stairs. "Sam?"

"Come down and meet Elisa."

She came down the steps at a fast clip. She was dressed casually, but Elisa recognized good quality clothing. She was moving through middle age, but she was a woman who clearly took care of herself.

"Nancy Whitlock," she said, thrusting out her hand in greeting. "Helen's daughter." They exchanged the requisite remarks before Nancy turned to Sam and spoke in low tones.

"I'm sorry we weren't in church yesterday, but you can see what we're up against here. I hope you explained to Elisa that Mama probably isn't going to go for this?"

"I did."

"I'm sorry," Nancy told Elisa. "They invented 'stubborn old coot' to describe my mother."

Sam defended Helen. "She just wants a say in her life. I think she might consider Elisa. She practically ordered me to hire her at the church."

"Good thing you did, then, or you'd never hear the end of it."

Elisa brought them back to the real point. "I like your mother, but if she doesn't want me here, I don't want to be here."

"That's a good start. As long as she thinks you're listening to her, she'll be a lot more cooperative."

A noise on the stairs announced Helen's arrival. She was not spry, but she managed the steps with little difficulty. "Nobody told me we had company."

"I was just coming to get you," Nancy said. "Did you finish packing the baby's things?"

"I did, but I can't say I'm happy about it."

"They'll be back."

"Well, at least it'll be quiet here for a change." Helen nodded at Elisa, then at Sam. "You two here for a reason?"

"Do I need one? Couldn't you use a good minister every now and then?"

"If we had one in the vicinity."

Nancy poked her mother in the arm. "I can hear the devil stoking up his bonfires, Mama. For heaven's sake!"

"She doesn't like a thing I say," Helen told Elisa.

"Maybe not, but I think she likes you."

Helen's lips twitched. "Nancy'll go back to Richmond soon enough, I guess. We can get along until then if we have to."

"Helen, I wanted you to know I hired Elisa the way you told me to," Sam said.

"What are you all standing around for? Sit down and I'll get coffee. There's a pot warming in the kitchen." Helen gestured to Reese, still contented on Elisa's hip. "You're spoiling her."

"I hope so."

The corners of Helen's mouth twitched again.

Once she'd gone, Nancy's shoulders slumped. "Well, she likes you," she whispered. "I can't tell you how much better we'd all feel if you were here. Sam says you work at Shadyside, too?"

Elisa nodded.

"Mostly Mama just needs company and somebody to bar the door if she tries to start a recycling center in the living room."

Helen returned with a tray of mugs, and a pot of coffee with cream and sugar, which she set on the table. "Nobody's sitting down!"

Taking a seat, Elisa tried to pull Reese up on her lap. The baby decided she'd had enough togetherness and wriggled free, sliding off the sofa and starting toward the stairs. Helen reached her before Elisa could even stand.

"Oh, no you don't," she said, scooping

the baby into her arms. "Cissy!"

Cissy appeared at the head. "Well, I got a break. It was nice, too. Unusual."

"Oh, stop complaining. We can keep her down here, but you'll need to bring the baby gate down."

"No thanks, I'll just bring her up with me. Tessa says she'll hold her while I finish packing my clothes." By the time the speech was finished, Cissy had arrived to whisk the baby away.

Helen made herself at home in a flowered armchair. "So you just came to tell me you got smart and hired Elisa? Or maybe you have another idea in that holy head of yours?"

"We won't ask you to spell holy." Sam poured coffee for Elisa and passed it to her. He held out the pot toward Nancy, who shook her head, as did Helen.

Without fanfare, he moved on to the reason for their visit. "Elisa is looking for a place to live. It's that simple, Helen. Her roommate's getting married and needs Elisa's room. You know how little rental housing there is in the area."

"I know all about your plan. You people think I'm deaf and don't know what all this whispering on the phone's been about?"

One look at Helen's expression and Elisa

dismissed the possibility that she would be moving here. She could see that the family had made too much out of hiring a companion and completely antagonized the old woman in the process. Helen had no choice now but to assert her independence and refuse Sam's request.

Elisa stood before Helen could deliver the bad news. Setting her mug on the table, she wandered over to a quilt rack in the corner. "I'm sure you don't want a stranger in your house. I don't want to trouble you about this. I'll find another place, but I'm glad I had a chance to visit. Is this one of your quilts?"

Helen was silent a moment, as if she had to reorient herself before she answered. "Just something to take off the chill. I never got cold in the summer before Nancy went and put in an air conditioner."

The quilt was red and yellow, with bright splashes of blue in some of the symmetrical blocks. Elisa discovered several more quilts underneath.

"Oh, they're all beautiful. Such fine workmanship."

"I'll show you more." Nancy got up.

"You don't have to bother the girl none." Helen sounded flustered. "It was a simple compliment, not a request for one of your quilt shows."

"Elisa, would you like to see a few more quilts?" Nancy asked.

"I really would."

Nancy opened a wooden trunk beside a comfortable armchair. "I keep some of my favorites down here. If Mama had her way, she'd pile them in a corner upstairs, where nobody could look at them."

"I sure didn't teach you enough about vanity, did I?" Helen demanded.

"There's vanity," Sam said, "and then there's good old-fashioned self-respect."

Nancy pulled out a quilt and held it in front of her. "This is a new one. Mama calls it 'Oklahoma Made a Monkey Out of Me.' "

Elisa stepped closer to admire the quilt. Helen had used a number of fabrics, mostly greens and browns, like the colors in a forest.

"This is a Monkey Wrench pattern," Nancy explained. "And this is the Road to Oklahoma block. See the unique way she combined them? And if you look carefully, you'll see monkeys in lots of the prints."

Elisa smiled, delighted. "I do. Look at that."

"It's just a silly quilt," Helen said.

137

"Nothing to fuss over. Reese likes monkeys, that's all."

Nancy pulled out several others, each completely different from the last. Obviously Helen enjoyed variety.

Elisa touched the last one Nancy took out and felt as if she had come home.

"This one is . . ." For a moment English failed her. She thought in English as often and fluently as she thought in Spanish, but sometimes the right word was in the wrong tongue. "You did this by hand? All by hand? And the colors? This is a rainbow."

"So you like quilts?"

"I know very little about them." As always, she paused, then decided to go ahead. "In the place where I grew up, there were weavers who made beautiful cloth in every color. This reminds me of that." She fingered the quilt. Tiny vertical strips in bright colors met horizontal strips in a variety of lengths and widths. "This quilt would keep anybody warm, wouldn't it? Like sunbeams."

"I just tried something new, one of those art quilts, only I didn't see any reason not to make it big enough to use. I take my art on the bed, and that's the only way I want it."

"Utility and beauty. That's what the

weavers believe. And each piece is part of who they are and where they come from." She turned. "The way your quilts are."

"Nancy told you to say all this, didn't she?"

Nancy sputtered. "I didn't tell Elisa to say a blessed thing."

Elisa laughed. "I've been in trouble a time or two for *not* doing what I'm told, but never the reverse." She glanced at her watch. "We're keeping you too long."

"Did you ever learn to weave?" Helen asked.

"It's like so many things. I thought the chance would be there forever, and now I'm here and the chance is gone."

"You could quilt."

"I have never sewed much," Elisa said doubtfully. "I don't have a machine."

"I have three. You'll be living right here. You can have your choice, and I'll teach you."

Surprised, Elisa heard the offer and everything that came with it. She had a home if she wanted one. She also had a responsibility to this woman if she accepted the offer. This would not be as simple as she had hoped. If she packed and left in the middle of the night, Helen would be alone. And Helen would not take in another companion.

Yet what could she do? She was certain that if she refused, Helen would not offer this invitation to anyone else. And living here would solve Adoncia's problem, as well as Elisa's own.

"I would like to try," she said carefully.

"Just so everybody in the room knows it," Helen said. "I like Miss Martinez, and that's the *only* reason she has been invited to stay here."

"Mama, there's not a person in this room dumb enough to think you'd do anything just because we wanted you to," Nancy said. "You can count on that."

Elisa was surprised at the way the remainder of the afternoon developed. Instead of going home, she and Sam stayed at Helen's house to help. Assuming that his fiancée was still in town, she had expected Sam to make their visit short so he could spend the rest of his day off with her, but he had explained — too casually, she thought — that Christine had driven to Washington on Saturday to spend some time with old friends before she returned to Georgia.

Sam's personal life was none of her business, but she wondered about his engagement. She knew from the little she had picked up that Sam and Christine rarely saw each other. If Sam were her fiancé, she would not be inclined to spend so much time with other people.

As the others packed, Elisa was pressed into service as Reese's nanny, while Sam helped Zeke Claiborne pack the old minivan he had bought for the trip. Zeke was a young man still growing into a lanky physique, but Elisa could see how seriously he took his responsibilities.

Manual labor agreed with Sam. He seemed to relish physical activity, running up and down the stairs with boundless energy. For someone who spent so much of his life in spiritual and intellectual pursuits, he had the body of an athlete. Ten minutes into multiple trips outside, he had changed from khakis and a sport shirt into shorts and a T-shirt he kept in a gym bag in his car. He had muscular calves and thighs, and arms strong enough to have lifted George Jenkins off the ground Wednesday night and held him there until he sobered up.

Tessa came downstairs and showed Elisa where to put the baby, who had finally fallen asleep in her arms. Tessa had managed a brief hello earlier, but there hadn't been time for more.

"Gram tells me you're moving in?" she said when Reese was safely tucked into a port-a-crib in the back of the house.

"You approve?"

"You'll be great for her. We're all so relieved."

"I'll enjoy living here."

"How would you like a tour? Outside, I mean. It's a little chaotic to show you much about the house, but I need to stretch my legs. Mom and Cissy will keep an eye on Reese, but I can guarantee she'll sleep at least an hour."

Evening was on its way, but the temperature was in the high eighties, at least, and Elisa needed to stretch. She followed Tessa outside, taking a quick breath when the wall of heat and humidity hit her on the third step of the porch. "Your family has lived here a long time?"

"For generations. There were Stoneburners and Lichliters all over the area until World War II. Gram lost nearly everybody to the fighting or the aftermath or the economy. Her husband was killed at Pearl Harbor. He was a distant cousin of the Claibornes, so he had roots here, too. Gram raised my mother alone."

Elisa was never surprised at the sadness people could recount. "It must have been hard to keep the farm."

"That's why she's so stubborn, and why she doesn't waste time on tact. She never had time for anything but plain speaking and doing what she knew was right. Whether it was or not."

Elisa laughed softly. "We'll get along. Most of my life I've been surrounded by people who were sure they were right."

"Were they? Right?"

Elisa sobered. "Too often for their own good."

Tessa remained silent, as if inviting Elisa to share. But she had already shared more than she was comfortable with. She changed the conversation's direction. "All this land belongs to Helen?"

"Yes. She leases chunks to local farmers, some for corn, some for cattle." Tessa pointed out boundaries in the distance and the locations of fields. "There are more farms to the west and south of us, and about fifty acres of woods and fields over toward the river that someone's bound to build on someday. Let's go this way and I'll show you the pond. Last summer we were afraid it would dry up, but all the rain this year has filled it again."

They passed a fenced-in area with something that looked a little like a gypsy's wagon. It was surrounded by chickens pecking in the grass, chickens of different colors and sizes.

"The chickens are Gram's weakness," Tessa said. "And that's a portable chicken coop in the center. When they've pecked up every weed and bug inside the fence, we hitch it up to the tractor and move it to another spot, stake out the fence again and let them have at it."

"Ingenious."

"Gram never kept a pet. But you'll find she comes out here and talks to the chickens two or three times a day, then makes sure all the barn cats are fed. You won't have to do a thing for any of them. And you'll have all the eggs you can possibly eat. I don't seem to be able to get enough of them now that I'm pregnant."

Elisa had been looking for an opening and jumped right in. "How are you feeling? Have you had any more dizziness?"

"No, and I wanted to thank you again for all your help the other day."

"I did very little."

"I called my doctor and made an appointment for tomorrow. But he said exactly what you did. Since I don't have any other symptoms, it doesn't sound like

144

there's much to worry about. And my husband's getting a ride up here tonight to drive me home, so I won't have to sit behind the steering wheel for any length of time."

"Good. You'll feel better when you know for certain. There are enough things to worry about, yes?"

They had reached a pond, perhaps half an acre in size. Reeds grew at the edges, and Canada geese patrolled the opposite shore under giant weeping willows.

"Oh, isn't this lovely?" Elisa was entranced. "I can see where I'll be spending time every day."

"I lived with Gram last summer, and I came out to the pond whenever I needed time to think. I also picked a million blackberries. There's a creek in that direction with blackberries and wine berries all along the edges." She pointed. "But it's late in the season. You won't find too many now. You can wade, though. Just watch out for snakes."

"Sam said you and your mother were here to fix up the house?"

"We carried out tons of Gram's 'collectibles.' Like newspapers and rags and bottles. She's pretty good these days, but you'll need to watch her."

"I've been warned."

"It was a good summer. We're closer. We met Cissy for the first time and got to know her, too."

"She's a lovely girl. Young to have a baby, at least in this country."

"Not in yours?"

"We have many young women marrying and giving birth well before they should. Our maternal health statistics are not good."

"I'm on the other end of the spectrum."

"For a first baby, yes."

"This isn't my first."

From Tessa's tone, Elisa realized there was more to that simple statement than Tessa was saying. "I'm sorry. I'm not sure why I assumed that. You have other children?"

Tessa didn't answer right away. Elisa was sure now that she had walked into something without knowing it.

"I had a daughter," Tessa said at last. "Kayley. She would have been nine this year. She was killed by a drunk driver."

Elisa didn't know what to say. She just put a hand on Tessa's shoulder.

Tessa seemed to welcome her touch. "I was sure I'd never want another child."

"But you decided to take a chance."

"I have to thank Reese. When Cissy brought her home from the hospital, I looked into that tiny face, and Reese stared right back at me. It's a long story how I got there, but I realized I was ready to try again, and I needed to do it soon. I was lucky. I got pregnant two months later."

Elisa squeezed Tessa's shoulder before she dropped her hand. "I know it must have taken courage."

"For the most part I'm doing okay. I think most of us are blissfully ignorant about what can happen when we decide to have a child. On some level we understand risk. We just never think those things will happen to us. But since I know they can and do, I'm too aware of every little thing."

"Like the dizziness? That wasn't a little thing. It was something I —" Elisa changed direction. "Something I'm sure your doctor wanted you to report. I'll bet he told you that when you called. Yes?"

"He did."

"Of course, it won't be the same for you as it might be for a young woman with no experience. But maybe you also realize how . . ." Elisa paused to think of the right expression. "How random the universe is. Maybe you will appreciate what you have even more, because you understand it can

147

be taken away. Through no fault of your own."

"You're speaking from experience."

"I understand the way life can change in an instant."

Tessa waited again, as if she were encouraging Elisa to say more. When she didn't, Tessa went on. "Thank you for listening to me. I'm looking forward to getting to know you better."

Elisa liked Tessa. By the same token, she was afraid she might have found a friend with more insight than Elisa could afford.

They heard footsteps, and Sam approached from the direction they had taken. "Helen said I'd find you here."

He had changed back into long pants and a sport shirt, and looked like a man with a mission. Elisa was contrite. "I'm sorry, do you need to leave?"

"I didn't, but I do now. One of our parishioners was taken to the hospital in Winchester. He's not expected to make it through the night. I need to get over there. I can take you back to the church if we leave right now."

"I'll take her back." Tessa thought better of that. "No, Mom will take her. She won't mind a bit, and that will keep me out from behind the wheel."

"That would be a big help," Sam said. "Shall I wait while you ask?"

"No. If Mom can't, Zeke or Cissy will. You go on. Elisa's one of the gang now. We'll take care of her."

Sam turned to Elisa. "I hate to abandon you this way."

For a moment she thought there was more to his statement than simple good manners. His gaze was warm. She felt her cheeks warm in response.

"You go," she said. "I'll be at the church at eight tomorrow morning to start my training."

"Goodbye, then." He glanced at Tessa. "Thanks again."

They watched him disappear down the path.

"Sam's wonderful at what he does, although not everyone thinks so," Tessa said when he was gone. "He's definitely controversial."

"He has many problems in the church?" Elisa thought of George and Leon Jenkins, and wondered what was behind the controversy.

"He has more supporters than enemies. As long as the balance remains that way, he'll remain as minister. But I wonder sometimes if he's really happy here. It's a small country church, and he's a man with obvious talents. Plus he goes home every night to an empty house, and I think he's a man with a lot of love to give."

Elisa wondered why Tessa had chosen to confide that.

She knew better than to ask.

Chapter Seven

Sam's parents had hoped he would become a doctor. He often thought of that when he walked through a hospital doorway. No one knew how he had to steel himself to cross the threshold. He hated nearly everything inside. The institutional feel, the smell, the unrelenting clatter, the reminders of his own mortality. He wanted to lay hands on every patient and send them home. He hated suffering and disease, but his was not a healing ministry. He could only comfort with his belief that God was a constant presence. He was always moved when that turned out to be enough.

Dinnertime was near when he arrived at the hospital in Winchester where Newt Rafferty had been taken to die. Newt, a widower, was a former Community Church deacon who had resigned from the board eight months ago when his health took a turn for the worse. Claiming the grandchildren would keep him young, he had moved to Winchester to spend his final months with his oldest daughter and her family. But every time Sam made the trip north to visit, he had seen that Newt was failing.

The call to Newt's bedside wasn't a surprise, but Sam was sorry it had come so swiftly. He had prayed that Newt would have more years. Like so many of his prayers, this one hadn't been answered the way he hoped.

He found his way to the appropriate floor and through the rabbit warren of corridors to Newt's room. Several people stood outside. He recognized Newt's daughter Gloria and her husband, and greeted them before he shook hands with some of Newt's more distant relatives. Newt's youngest daughter and only son were inside with their father.

Gloria, whose thin face was streaked with tears, looked shaken but resolute. "Last week he refused further treatment. He says he's ready to die."

Sam took her hand. "How do you feel about this?"

"He knows what he wants. It would be

different if the doctors could really help him. But he's in pain, and anything else they can do will just prolong it. It's only . . . it's hard to let him go."

"Newt's always had good judgment. I think he must have passed that on to you."

Gloria reached for a tissue in her pocket. She was a striking brunette, but the past months had added worry lines where none had been before. "I know letting him go is the right thing, but it's good to hear it from an impartial observer."

"I'm not impartial. I count him among my friends."

"He feels the same way. I'm so glad you could get here. The hospital chaplain prayed with him, but I know Daddy wanted to see you one more time."

"He wants to be buried in the church cemetery. Did he tell you?"

She wiped her eyes. "We'll do the funeral there."

The door opened, and Newt's other children came into the hallway. Both were obviously exhausted.

Newt's son looked much as his father probably had at the same age, tall and scholarly. He shook Sam's hand. "He's resting, but you go in and wait until he opens his eyes. He asked if you were here."

"What does the doctor say?"

"That we should say our goodbyes while we can."

"Has everyone had a chance to see him?"

"A few old friends are on their way."

"Then I'll wait inside." Sam gave Newt's youngest daughter a quick hug. Of all his children, she looked the most upset.

Inside, Sam saw that Newt's bed was one of two, but the other was empty. He hoped it remained that way until Newt was gone. He was relieved to see there were no machines regulating the last hours of his friend's life. Newt had an IV in his right arm and nothing more. He was not thrashing or moaning. Sam thought he was probably deeply sedated.

He perched on the chair at Newt's bedside and took his hand. Then he prayed silently that Newt's death would be easy and his family comforted by the knowledge he was a good man who had led a good life.

Ten minutes passed before Newt opened his eyes. At first he seemed confused, but after Sam spoke to him a while, he focused.

"Sam?"

"I'm here. I've been praying for you."

"You're putting in a good word . . . or two?"

Sam managed a little laugh. "Not much need for it, but every little bit helps."

"I had . . . a good run."

"So you did. A very good one. Fine man, fine family, upstanding member of the church and community. I guess your work is finished."

"You'll check on my kids? Give them a call down the road . . . a piece?"

"I'll tell them you insisted."

"I'm not dying right yet. Not quite."

"You've got it planned?"

"I . . ." Newt was silent for a little while, and Sam thought he might have drifted off again, but when he tried to release Newt's hand, the old man opened his eyes.

"Jenkins . . . causing trouble."

Sam couldn't have been more surprised if Newt had just come back with eyewitness reports of heavenly hosts. "George? Why are you thinking about him?"

"Called last week. Calling all over." Newt licked his lips. "Wants you fired. Trying his darnedest."

"This is not something you should be worried about now."

"You'll watch out?"

"I promise." Sam was deeply touched

that in the last hours of his life, Newt was concerned for him. "It's a good church with good people, Newt. You helped make it that way. That doesn't mean there's not an occasional snake in the grass, but I promise I'll be careful where I step. Maybe I can sit down with George and have a real dialogue."

"I didn't know you believed . . . in miracles."

Sam squeezed Newt's hand. "What can I do for you, friend?"

"Will you say a prayer while I'm awake? I want to hear this one."

On the way back to Adoncia's house, Elisa took several detours. Having a car again was a heady experience. She hadn't been able to fully explore the area where she lived and worked, but now that the opportunity had presented itself, she took full advantage. Like one of the many sightseers who came through on their way to and from Skyline Drive, she turned down unfamiliar roads, examining farms and the occasional family business that lay off the beaten path. Kennels and country veterinarians, eggs and handicrafts for sale, vineyards and nurseries.

The vineyards and nurseries interested

her most. She knew men from Ella Lane often did day work in the surrounding area. They lined up early in the morning at certain locations, where they were chosen for assignments based on previous work they'd done, the breadth of their shoulders or simply their place in line. Sometimes they were paid under the table; sometimes checks were cut. Some employers paid fairly; some took advantage of the slow economy. Although the system was flawed and sometimes illegal, men who would not work otherwise were in no position to complain.

Near Woodstock, on a scenic side road, she slowed at the sign for Jenkins Landscaping. Diego had mentioned this as one of the places men often went to be hired by the hour. Now she realized the business belonged to George Jenkins, the man she had poured into the front seat of a pickup with this same logo so his son could take him home.

Diego himself had often worked here until he found a steadier job waterproofing basements. In the winter, Jenkins Landscaping employees plowed and removed snow and took down or pruned trees; in the summer, they mowed lawns and planted trees and shrubs. The amount of temporary help Jenkins needed each day depended on the weather and the demand for his services.

Since it was Sunday, no one was working or waiting outside, although several small dump trucks piled high with mulch waited in the driveway. She wondered how badly Jenkins' head had ached Thursday morning, and if Leon had been forced to bear the brunt of his father's bad temper.

She stopped once at a service station just outside Woodstock and parked beside a telephone booth she had used before. No one was nearby, exactly the condition she'd hoped for. She inserted the coins she'd gathered for the phone call and dialed a familiar number. When a woman answered, she spoke without preamble.

"It's Elisa."

She waited, swallowed disappointment, nodded as if the woman at the other end could see her. "Okay. I'll talk to you again." She hung up and stood a while staring across the street at a cow in a field who seemed to feel the phone booth needed to be watched.

She hoped only the cow found it so promising.

By the time she got to Adoncia's, she was ready to rest, although with Fernando and Maria at home, that was probably not an option. She had not seen Adoncia since leaving with Sam yesterday. The family had gone on their outing with Diego and returned late, and they were already gone when Elisa, who tried to stay out of their way as they prepared for the day, got out of bed.

Now, as expected, when she walked through the door, she was tackled by both children.

"They are spinning like pinwheels," Adoncia said. "We just got home. Nana Garcia fed them nothing but sugar all day."

Elisa stooped and hugged them both. "Did you have a good day at work?" she asked her friend.

"If hacking chickens in pieces can be good work." Adoncia, who looked exhausted, motioned toward the bathroom. "Will you watch them while I shower?"

"Of course." Adoncia always took a shower when she got home to scrub away the smell of the poultry factory. The job was tiring and dangerous. The fast-moving line, sharp instruments and repetitive motion meant that many careers in poultry processing were short-lived.

Elisa played with the children until her friend came out of the bathroom looking a bit more refreshed. Adoncia fell to the sofa and towel-dried her hair. Fernando crawled up on her lap and laid his head against her chest.

"You had fun with Diego yesterday?" Elisa asked.

"We ate at a restaurant, went to a movie. The children were very good. Now, did you get the job? Is that why the minister was here yesterday? *¡Qué cuero de hombre!*"

Elisa smiled at the description. Sam *was* remarkably easy to look at, and of course Adoncia had not failed to notice. "I'll start training in the morning."

"But you work at Shadyside tonight, don't you? When will you sleep?"

"I won't. But most of the time that won't be a problem. Once I'm trained, I'll have Mondays and Tuesdays off at the church, so my Monday night shift at the home won't compete. And I'll just have to sleep Friday afternoon after I've done whatever is needed at the church."

"You think you can sleep here, with the children screaming?"

The lead-in was too good to waste. "Donchita, I've found a new place to live, with a woman in the church who needs a companion. She needs *me;* you need my room." She held back her friend's interruption with her hands. "It's perfect. And now I have a car to drive, part of my pay for the job at the church."

"You don't have to leave. You know you don't."

"It's time I did. Diego wants to move in. You want to marry him." She watched Adoncia's expression change. "Don't you?"

"No, I decided today. He can move in, yes. That I want. But until we can agree about children, I won't marry him. We'll live in sin." She said the last without concern.

"And you'll practice birth control?"

Adoncia grimaced. "No pills. I won't take them."

Elisa knew that Adoncia's chances of getting Diego to use a condom were about the same as getting him to run for president. "You know, not marrying him isn't going to keep his sperm from having their own little party."

"There are other ways."

Elisa wondered how much reliable information Adoncia knew. This was the friend, after all, who had once rubbed Fernando with an egg to protect him from the *mal de ojo,* or evil eye, of a neighbor. Adoncia was extremely bright, but she covered her bases.

"I won't have another baby so soon after Nando," Adoncia said, almost as if she were practicing what she would say to Diego.

Elisa tried to sound casual. "My sister protects herself the way the church suggests. She has only the two children she wanted."

"Do you know what she does?"

"Her husband wouldn't approve, although he's happy enough to have only two children to provide for. So she finds an excuse each month not to make love when she's fertile."

"And her husband agrees?"

"It's always a very good excuse."

Adoncia laughed. "And how does she know when to be careful?"

"Her periods are regular." Elisa paused. "Are yours?"

"Like the sun and the moon."

"Good. Here's what she told me." Elisa gave a short explanation of cycles, temperature and ovulation prediction kits. "And once you've calculated when you are most likely to be fertile, you don't have sex five days before and five days afterward."

"Ten days? Ten whole days?"

"If you want to be very careful and not take chances."

"Diego will know."

"I think my sister's husband knows, as well. But he doesn't mind." Unfortunately, Elisa was afraid that Diego was going to mind very much, even if he and Adoncia weren't yet married.

Adoncia sounded worried. "It will take work."

"It would be less work to use another more reliable method."

"No," Adoncia said firmly.

Elisa knew that without Diego's cooperation, this plan was flawed, at best. But she respected Adoncia's views. This was her body, her religion, her right.

"Diego will be a guest in my house," Adoncia said. "If I tell him we don't make love, then we don't. If he questions me, I will send him to sleep on the sofa."

Elisa knew how much Diego loved her friend, and how badly he wanted children. She hoped Adoncia could keep him at arm's length when needed.

She made supper, and afterward Adoncia cleaned the kitchen. The children fell asleep early, and Elisa managed to take an evening nap before it was time to dress for her drive to the nursing home.

163

When Adoncia's thirteen-year-old minivan had been available, Elisa had also driven, since her friend was not in need of her car at that late hour. But more often the minivan rested on blocks on the side of the trailer, with some part removed by Diego for repair, and Elisa had been on her own and on foot.

The late shift began at eleven, and the roads were always eerily silent. She had never relished this walk in the darkness, although it could be accomplished in fifteen minutes. The area was still rural enough that wildlife abounded. She had seen raccoons and foxes, and once a family of white-tailed deer crossed her path, never once glancing at the odd two-legged creature trudging to work. Unfortunately, she had never shaken the unlikely notion there might be bears watching, as well. Or men with evil intentions.

Tonight she parked in the employees' section of the lot, and enjoyed every moment of locking up and pocketing her own keys. She reminded herself not to get used to this luxury, that the car was a loan that could be taken back at any time. If nothing else, the past three years had taught her to appreciate what she had, but not to hang on to it tightly.

Inside she punched the time clock and put her purse in her locker. On her way to the central nurses' desk she greeted staff, admiring one aide's new haircut and accepting a cup of coffee from another who was just leaving the break room. At the desk she greeted the nurse on duty and chatted a few minutes before tackling the day log. She caught up on her unit, scanning notes from all shifts since her last and initialing the notes to show she had read them.

On her own unit, she and Kathy, the aide she was replacing, did a crossover, making sure Elisa knew everything she needed to about what had gone on before, who to watch out for and special problems she might encounter. Kathy, middle-aged and exhausted, already had her keys out. She was looking forward to a glass of wine and the several hours of reality shows she had videotaped.

"Did anyone have visitors?" Elisa asked. Visitors were never an issue on *her* shift, but sometimes the previous shift experienced problems settling residents after family left for the night.

"Mrs. Lovett's daughter came, but Mrs. L. was glad to see her go, and so was I. There were a couple of others, but no problems afterward."

Elisa didn't look up from the small spiral notebook where she kept her own notes. "How about Martha Wisner? I saw she had visitors day before yesterday. People from her church?"

"Nobody today. I don't think she has any family. At least no one she's close to. But the church people come regularly."

"I'm working at her church now, too," Elisa said. "They showed me a quilt they're making for her. Maybe they already gave it to her?"

"The one with the leaves? It's really something. The ladies signed their names on the back. It's a good way to help her stay in touch with her memories. If you get the chance and she's up, you could ask her about it."

"I'll do that." Elisa finished her notes, then said goodbye to Kathy, who couldn't get out quickly enough. The aide liked her job, but by shift's end she was always ready to head home.

Kathy had done rounds as her shift came to a close, but as she always did, Elisa went from room to room checking on the residents and making sure they were asleep, or at least contented. The unit was a transitional one. None of the residents here suffered from serious dementia, but none fit into the assisted living wing, either. They needed a secure unit and regular supervision. Some were returning from hospital stays and needed daily nursing care. Sadly, some were headed toward the Alzheimer's unit, where the care was more specialized and controlled. For now, though, they were able to live with less care and fewer restrictions.

One resident was awake and insisted on a shower. Elisa helped her in and out, and laid out a fresh nightgown. Another couldn't find a book. Elisa found it and helped her get comfortable in bed, making a mental note to come back in a little while to put the book away and turn out the light.

She was not surprised to find so many residents awake. "Sundowning" was a common enough occurrence here and nearly universal on the Alzheimer's unit. The internal clock of many of the residents was turned around, and they preferred to sleep during the day and be active at night. Although the staff tried hard to readjust the residents' sense of time, they were often not successful.

Halfway down the hall, she peeked into Martha Wisner's room, but the old woman was fast asleep and everything was in order. She passed on.

Hours later, when she returned to do Martha's vitals, she found her sitting up, staring out the window into the darkness.

Martha was a short woman, with a thick head of permed white hair, and a round face with smooth pink cheeks and furrowed brow. She was dressed in a long cotton gown, which fell straight from her shoulders and outlined neither breasts nor hips.

"Martha? You're up awfully early," Elisa told her. "It's not even five a.m."

"Is it time for dinner?"

Elisa had sometimes awakened from a nap unsure where she had fallen asleep or what time of day it was. She imagined this was the way many of the residents on this unit felt, only for them, a little light through a windowpane, a glance at the clock, didn't solve the mystery. She could relate to the confusion and empathize.

"It's not quite time for breakfast," Elisa told her. "The sun will be up very soon though. It's early morning."

"Didn't I just have lunch?"

"No. You had dinner about twelve hours ago. That's why you're hungry."

"I want to eat now."

Although it was best to keep the residents on schedule for meals, Elisa was also allowed to bend the rules. She was sure Martha would not go back to sleep.

"I'll bring you cereal. Then you can eat a hot breakfast with the others later." There was a small dining area where the residents could eat their meals together if they chose. Some enjoyed the company.

"And juice?"

"And juice. I'll be right back."

Elisa returned a few minutes later with a tray. She wondered if Martha would remember asking for it and was pleased to find that she did. She settled the old woman in a chair and set the tray on a table in front of her.

"Let me check your vitals first," she told her. She used the wrist meter that measured temperature, blood pressure, pulse and respiration, and recorded the data. Then she took the cover off the tray.

"Orange juice. Good. And I like this cereal." Martha looked pleased.

Elisa watched her pour milk from the small carton and mix it into her Special K. "How do you feel? Did you sleep well?"

"Are you new?"

"No. But I'm not here as often as some of the others. I'm Elisa Martinez."

Martha paused, as if searching her memory. Then she shook her head. "I haven't met you before."

Martha's lack of recognition wasn't a good sign. She and Martha had spoken many times. "Well, I'll be working at the Shenandoah Community Church when I'm not working here. I've just been hired to be the new sexton. You remember the church?"

Martha frowned. For a moment Elisa was afraid she had forgotten that, too; then Martha nodded her head. "Of course, and do you think I can't remember my own name?"

Elisa smiled. "People there care very much about you."

"They gave me something." Martha added new furrows to her brow. "Just lately." The furrows smoothed. "A quilt. In the dresser over there. Will you get it for me?"

Elisa found the quilt folded neatly in the bottom drawer. She shook it out and took it back to Martha. "It's lovely. Look at the colors." She turned it over. "And look, here are the names of the women who made it for you." She read them out loud, coming to Helen Henry at the end. "Helen Henry. I'm going to be living with her for a while. Her quilts are beautiful."

"I never cared for doing hand work. My mother despaired of me. But I could cook. How I loved to cook."

Elisa tucked the quilt over Martha's lap. "This will keep you warm."

Martha looked up at her. "Maybe we did meet before. Or maybe you just look like somebody. . . ."

Elisa touched her hair. "You eat your breakfast, Miss Wisner. I'll be back in a little while to get the tray. Can I get you anything else?"

"People here are nice." Martha went back to eating.

Elisa was glad the woman was happy.

Chapter Eight

Sam waited until the day after Newt Rafferty's funeral for his visit to George Jenkins. More than a week had passed since he stood by Newt's bedside with the Rafferty family and watched his friend pass peacefully away. The funeral had been attended by more than a hundred people, and more than a dozen of them participated in the service.

Unless he turned his life around, George's funeral would be a different occasion entirely.

The late August sun was high overhead when Sam pulled into the parking lot of Jenkins Landscaping. Enough time had passed since the fiesta that Sam hoped George would be well into contrition. He wasn't expecting it, though.

At his best, George was a gadfly who saw

the world's myriad faults and made sure they were fixed. George had orchestrated a capital fund drive to replace the church roof. George made sure the trees and shrubs were pruned and fertilized, and the grass cut properly.

Unfortunately, at his *worst* George was a bully who wanted complete control over the way problems were solved. No one on the board of deacons had been able to convince him that the cheaper brand of shingles he'd insisted on was inferior. A year into Sam's ministry, the roof began to leak again. And even though the grounds were tidy and attractive now, Sam was still concerned George was exploiting the men who did the work.

So Sam didn't expect today's visit to go well. In fact, in comparison, that morning's session with the church finance committee to trim next year's budget had been pure pleasure.

He parked just a few feet from Jenkins' office, a small prefab building across the lot from a sizeable greenhouse. A modest beige brick home with a narrow front porch stood back from both, on the side of a low hill. Sam didn't have to knock on doors to find George. He was standing to one side at the front of a group of men, and before Sam even turned off the engine, he could hear him shouting.

"You don't like what I'm paying, you go work for somebody else. You think there aren't a million more just like you who'll do the work cheaper? You think you've got real skills you can sell? Go be a doctor or a lawyer if you want more money!"

Sam got out of his car, but only after struggling with himself. Trying to talk to George was the right choice. But the other possibility, going behind his back to neutralize him — much the same as George was doing — was far more appealing.

George turned his head to see Sam approaching. For the briefest moment he looked embarrassed, like a boy caught bullying the new kid; then the moment ended and his scowl returned. He waved the men away, making it clear he was finished with them. They had started off toward the greenhouse before he stalked over to Sam.

"These people! You think we'd put out a red carpet from here to Mexico, the way they act. Doesn't matter what I give them, what I do, it's not enough. I tell them they start getting paid the minute they start working, but no, that's not good enough. They want to be paid for the hour they stood around waiting to see if I was going to hire them this morning. They can go back to Tijuana for all I care."

Sam took time for a deep breath before he thrust out his hand. "Good morning, George."

George's hesitation was noticeable, but grudgingly he accepted Sam's hand for the briefest of shakes. "I know you and your kind, too. You think I'm not being fair, don't you?"

"I just got here. I wasn't privy to your conversation with those men."

"I know what you think. Treat every one of them like they're good hard workers, even if they aren't. Oh, some are, I'll give you that. I've had a few men I could trust to do exactly what I was paying them to. But most of 'em?" He made a derisive sound deep in his throat. "They'd lie in the sun and drink tequila all day if they had their way."

Sam tried to speak gently, as if he could remember at that moment why he had chosen ministry as his life's work. "For that matter, I'd lie in the sun all day if I could, George. So would you. But that doesn't mean any of us will actually do it. You and I know we have responsibilities, and these men are no different. That's why they're here looking for work at minimal pay instead of hawking drugs in the *barrio*."

"Hell, these people aren't anything like you or me, and that's what you don't get. That's why all this do-gooder stuff you're forcing down our throats is just a big waste of time. These people don't belong here. Not here at my place, not here at the church, not here in this country. And now I'm forced to hire a Spanish-speaking foreman just to stay on top of them. You know what that's going to cost me?"

About half what it should, but Sam knew better than to say so.

"I ought to send them all packing," George said.

Sam attempted to reason. "Just out of curiosity, if these men weren't here, who would do your work? I don't see any born-and-bred Shenandoah boys lined up at your gate. How many of Leon's friends applied for jobs working outside in the hot summer sun?"

"That's not what you came about, is it?"

"I'm afraid it's an example. It's clear you and I don't see eye to eye on a number of things, and even clearer that you'd like to see me disappear so you can find a minister who's more your style."

"That about sums it up. You sure came

with three strikes against you, didn't you? I don't know how many more the board thought they needed not to hire you."

Sam ignored George's speech. "The problem is, there may not be any ministers you'd find agreeable. We ministers are supposed to challenge you. We all need to be challenged or we'll never change. If the next minister didn't challenge you, he wouldn't be earning his pay, and we know how you'd feel about that."

George shoved his hands in the pockets of baggy pants. "You think I need changing? I'm raising a son by myself. You don't have kids. You probably never worked a full day at a real job. You don't know what it's like to run a business or do the things I do."

There was no point in explaining that a church was like a business, and that nothing was more real — or exhausting — than the mission each good minister or rabbi, priest or mullah, embarked on: to open hearts and minds to the love of God.

"I've got a story about this," Sam said instead.

George sniffed. "I don't have time for your stories."

"Humor me." Sam heard the edge creeping into his own voice.

For a moment he thought George would leave him standing there, but the other man shrugged. "Make it short."

"Your situation here is what reminded me," Sam began. "Only the man in my story owned a vineyard, not a landscaping business. One morning this man needed some extra laborers, so he went to the market where they congregated and hired the number he thought he'd need. Then, later in the day when he went back to the market, he saw a few more men who needed work and thought, 'Maybe I'll just hire them, too, and get things finished quicker.'"

"Are *you* finished yet?"

"Given the chance, I'll be finished in a minute."

George narrowed already narrow eyes.

Sam continued, trying to tamp down his anger. "So the vineyard owner hired the extra men. Fortunately, he was a man who could change his mind, and as the day progressed, he hired more and more workers as he saw there was more to be done."

"What in the hell are you getting at?" George demanded.

"Let me cut to the chase. When the workday was finished, there were a number of men waiting to be paid. But when the

178

foreman paid them, the men discovered every one had gotten the same amount of money, no matter when they started."

"Then either the foreman or the owner of your vineyard was a fool."

"Maybe not," Sam said. "You see, right at the beginning the owner told the first men what he would pay them, so that's what he paid. It was *his* decision to pay the other men just as much. In fact he said, 'So the last shall be first, and the first last.' "

"You're speaking in a bunch of damned riddles."

"You'll find that particular *riddle* in the book of Matthew. It's one of the parables of Jesus. He didn't want His words to be easy. We're supposed to think hard about their meaning before we apply them to our lives. I think the point is that God is merciful and His grace is given through mercy, not through a calculation of the hours we've put into doing the right thing or working hard. Likewise — and no less important — it's our job to be as merciful in our dealings as God is in His."

"You think this means something to me?"

"I think it could, if you let it. There's nothing to be gained by working as hard as

179

you do, George, unless you're doing it with a merciful heart. And there's nothing to be gained by putting ourselves above anybody else. The last shall be first and the first last. We're all God's children, and He doesn't care if we start life with a vineyard or as the laborer pruning the grapes. The reward's the same."

"You think I should lie down and roll over, let these men — let *you,* of all people — walk over me?"

Whatever patience Sam had snapped. "I think you need to take a deep breath and ask yourself any number of questions, starting with whether you could better serve the Lord by being kinder and more understanding."

George tried to interrupt, but Sam cut him off with an angry swipe of his hand. "You have a job to do here. You can encourage these men, help them find a place in the community and your company, and pay them fairly. You can practice mercy at every turn. We're all better for making the attempt, even when we don't feel like it."

"Get off my property."

Nothing would have pleased him more, but Sam didn't move. He took a moment to calm himself, to ask what he wanted to accomplish before he spoke again. And in those quiet seconds, he realized where he had failed.

"No matter how badly I tell it, it's a good story. We're all tempted to feel superior to other people. Maybe I've been guilty of that myself. I came here to understand you better, and I haven't asked you how you're feeling, or what's going on with you to make you so angry at everybody and everything. I've just been preaching at you, because you make me angry, too."

George glared at him. "I don't have a thing to tell you. You're less than nothing to me."

"I would like to be your minister."

George snorted. "I have work to do. You know the way out my driveway. Don't find the way back once you're gone." He turned and strode away. In a moment the office door slammed behind him.

Sam had been a minister long enough to know his own boiling point and realize that prejudice stoked the flames. He wondered if George had set out to anger him. And what had he himself accomplished? Sam had quoted Jesus, given a little sermon. On the surface, how could anyone object?

Unfortunately, Sam knew better. He had effectively used the New Testament as ammunition to gun George down. Everything he had said was true, but he had nothing to be proud of here.

"Reverend Sam?"

He hadn't realized he was staring at the stump of what had once been a mighty tree. He looked up to see Leon approaching from the direction of the house. Sam started up the path to meet him. "Hey, Leon."

The boy looked wary, but he nodded. "I didn't know you were coming today."

"I had business with your dad. How are things going?"

Leon shrugged. "Just getting ready for the school year, that's all."

"Are you going out for football this year?"

"Nah. I'm not much for sports. Except basketball."

"Good luck when the time comes." Sam waited to see what Leon wanted.

"I —" Leon cleared his throat. "I, well, I've been wanting to say that, like, I'm sorry. You know."

"Do I?" Sam tried to smile. "Know?"

"About the sign and all."

For the first time that morning, Sam was glad to be a minister. "I appreciate you telling me. Those aren't easy words."

"I guess I was showing off."

"Luckily no harm was done."

"I feel bad. I didn't mean to scare Miss Martinez."

"She strikes me as a woman who doesn't scare easily. Did you tell her you were sorry?"

"Uh-huh."

"You've done what you needed to, then."

"I'm sorry, well, about my dad, too. He shouldn't have taken a swing at you that night."

"He wasn't in control of himself," Sam said. "And he didn't take a swing today when I probably needed one."

"Huh?"

"It's not your problem. For the record, you can't make your dad behave. He doesn't act the way he does because of you, or because of anything you've done." He hoped that made sense to the boy.

"Well, I just wanted you to know." Leon, who didn't look too sure what to do next, turned to go back to the house.

Sam put his hand on the boy's shoulder. "We'll be looking for volunteers to work with the kids at *La Casa.* Having you there would be great. I think you'd have a lot to offer."

"My dad would kill me."

Sam hadn't thought that far ahead, but

183

he realized Leon was right. George would be furious. The lines were clearly drawn now, George on one side and Sam on the other. *La Casa Amarilla* was squarely in the middle.

"I'm sorry. You'd be an asset. But I'll still see you at church?"

"If my dad lets me come."

Sam was fairly certain his visit this afternoon would make that less likely. He watched the boy trudge up the hill.

"You had six calls this morning, and one of them was Miss Fletcher." Gracie Barnhardt, who had been the church secretary since Martha Wisner's retirement, handed Sam a fistful of pink memos, signed and dated, with "comments" in careful script at the bottom. "Sounds mad," one read. "Lonely," another theorized.

Gracie, whose frail body hid an iron constitution, was always right on top of church politics. Luckily for Sam, Gracie shared her opinions with him, and him alone.

Sam glanced at the message from Christine. "I'll be gone a few days. Call you when I get back to town." His gaze flicked to Gracie's comment: "Sounded rushed."

With the school year right around the

corner, Sam guessed Christine was taking the Labor Day weekend to relax before work began in earnest. She had probably accepted one of the many invitations she received and gone down to the Keys for some late summer sun, or up to the Hamptons for a "country weekend." A Hamptons country weekend would be more her style than the one she had experienced in Toms Brook, and they would see each other late next month when he visited her in Atlanta.

"Nothing I can't deal with," he said, looking back up at Gracie, who was pinning errant strands of snow-white hair into a tight knot on top of her head. "Anything else going on?"

"Marvin's leaving at the end of the day. We're having cake and punch, and I've already bought his going-away gift. I got him one of those alarm clocks with the big numbers so he won't have any excuse to be late on his next job."

"You didn't."

"Well, I wanted to."

Marvin was happiest playing banjo with Zeke Claiborne's bluegrass band, or hanging out at one of the truck stops on I-81, playing the phone card sweepstakes machine. Sam wished his new employers well and hoped they found a way to make him work harder.

"How's Elisa doing?" Sam asked.

"You want the truth?"

"When have you ever told me anything but? In grisly detail?"

"The church hasn't been this clean in years. She's supposed to be helping Marvin, you understand, and he's supposed to be showing her what to do. But mostly he sits around and watches her do the work. It's a good thing today's his last day or I'd have fired him myself."

"I'd better watch out. I could be next."

"Well, not by me. But there's a deacon or two who would like to pack your bags."

After Sam's morning at Jenkins Landscaping, he was all too aware of that.

"Elisa said you were going to show her what to do at *La Casa* sometime this afternoon," Gracie continued. "She's coming by in a few minutes." She held up her hands. "I'm just reporting."

In his office, Sam returned the most important calls and tried Christine, but she was already gone. He got her answering machine and left a brief message telling her to have a good time.

There were two women in his thoughts these days, and he was all too aware of both. Unfortunately, Christine occupied the smallest space. They spoke a couple of times a week — or rather, she spoke. She wasn't interested in his struggles or his work here, but she was certain that stories of people he had known in Atlanta or plans her father had suggested for their future would interest him greatly. The distance between them, with all its subtleties and implications, was her biggest blind spot.

The other woman was Elisa. Sam hadn't spent any time alone with his new sexton since the day he had taken her to meet Helen Henry. He greeted her when he saw her at work and knew from a conversation in passing that she had moved into Helen's house. Helen had told him that Elisa arrived with little more than a backpack and a shopping bag, and settled into her room in a matter of minutes. Helen had covered the bed with the "art" quilt with which Elisa had been so taken.

"Looks to me like nobody's been good to that woman in a long time," Helen had said. "Something as picayune as a pretty quilt and she gets all dewy-eyed."

Sam hadn't avoided Elisa. He had simply not sought her out or put himself into situations where he might find her by herself. Same thing exactly.

His attraction to her was physical, yes. Elisa was one of the most appealing women he had ever known. He had not taken a vow of celibacy at his ordination, nor promised to wear blinders.

Had it *only* been physical, he was certain he could have moved beyond it. But in addition, he knew an emotional bond was forming. He admired Elisa. She was courageous and hardworking. Despite her confrontation with Leon Jenkins, she had showed compassion for the boy that same night, and for his father, as well. She was intelligent, insightful . . .

And he was in trouble.

Once a future with Christine had seemed assured. Then their relationship had been tested, was still being tested. Now he wondered at what point a man told a woman he was grateful for the support and love she had given him, but, sadly, no longer needed either.

When did he know if it was true?

The intercom buzzed, and Gracie told him Elisa was waiting. He met her in the reception area. She was wearing black pants and a white shirt, which seemed almost to be a uniform of sorts. He didn't recall seeing her in anything else. Today her hair was in a neat braid starting high on her head and ending in a shining fall below a simple gold clip. She wore tiny gold earrings and not one smudge of makeup.

She turned, and he felt the punch in the gut that was becoming his standard reaction. He liked everything about her. The graceful curve of her neck, the sheen of her hair, the slight tilt of her huge dark eyes, the hesitation before she spoke, the musical cadence of her words.

Somehow he managed a friendly, but not too friendly, smile. "Thanks for stopping by."

"No problem. Is this a good time? I can come by tomorrow. I'm nearly finished for the day."

He remembered that she had worked a shift at the nursing home last night, and probably wanted to go home and take a nap if she could. He was just as glad he had a good reason not to drag out this encounter.

"It shouldn't take long." He told Gracie he would be back to proof the newsletter she was typing; then he ushered Elisa out of the office.

August was nearly over, and the walk across the grounds was pleasantly warm. Several days without rain had reduced the humidity, although the clouds gathering overhead warned that might change, and soon. His roses were preparing for new blooms in a few weeks, when the weather cooled.

"Do you feel ready to take over?" Sam asked. "Has Marvin showed you everything?"

"I'm all ready. It's fairly straightforward, except for setups, and I think I know where everything is and how things should be arranged. If you notice any problems, just let me know."

"And the schedule isn't too exhausting? You worked last night, didn't you?"

"I'm fine."

"Things are going well at Helen's?"

"We enjoy each other." She glanced at him. "How are the dogs?"

"They need a good run. I've been too busy."

"You should bring them to Helen's for a run through the hills. I'm sure she wouldn't mind, as long as they leave her chickens alone."

"They'd be scared to death of chickens." He searched for something else to say. He was rarely at a loss for words, but right now he felt tongue-tied and shallow. None of the things he wanted to say could be put into words. He wanted to know more about her, to feel what she felt, see what she saw. And he knew that the deeper their conversations went, the harder they would be to control.

They arrived at the house, and he followed her up the steps. As he had promised, it only took a few minutes to go through the house and discuss what needed to be done. Elisa's suggestions were good. He promised that the children and the volunteers would take a few minutes at the end of each day to clean up their projects so that all she would have to do was basic cleaning. She promised to stop over once during the week and once on weekends for a thorough scrubbing.

"It's just a little over a week before we start," he said, outside once more on the front porch.

"You're looking forward to it?"

He glanced at her, and for the first time he realized how tired she appeared. Before he knew what he was doing, he'd motioned her into one of the rocking chairs a volunteer had donated. "Sit a minute before we go back. Marvin can wait for you."

She protested but finally took the chair, closing her eyes a moment. "That feels good. I'm filling in a shift at the home again tonight. A last-minute emergency. I won't be doing that very often."

"Two nights in a row without sleep?"

"I'll have time for a good nap if I leave soon."

"You can sleep at the drop of a hat?"

"I can sleep standing up if I don't have another choice."

He had not wanted to be alone with her. Now that he was, he had to admit he didn't want this to end. He sat on the top step and leaned against a pillar, watching her rock slowly back and forth.

"I don't think I'm the only one who needs to regather forces," she said.

"What do you mean?"

"Your mind is somewhere else. You don't look happy today."

He wasn't pleased she had seen right through him. He had tried to convince himself they were not yet at a point where they were this close.

"I'm fine," he lied.

"We have a saying in my country. The deepest waters make the least noise."

"I went to see George Jenkins this morning. It didn't go well."

"You thought it might?"

"I'm forever hopeful."

"And forever disappointed when people

don't behave as they should, yes?"

"How do you know that?"

"I think you take too much on yourself. This is Mr. Jenkins' problem. You can only offer him the chance to make amends. You can't force him."

"It sounds like you've had experience."

"It's been some time since I believed my own good will had much effect on the bad will of others."

He wanted to know more but sensed she wouldn't tell him. "I believe in second chances. I'm here because of them."

"At Community Church?"

He wondered why he had admitted that. He was opening a door that could easily have stayed closed, a peek into his life she hadn't asked for.

"It's a long story," he said, "and you're exhausted. You need to go home and get some rest before tonight."

"I'm resting now. Tell me what you meant."

He wanted to. He wanted to tell her more, perhaps to warn her away. He caught movement from the corner of one eye and turned to watch two crows challenge each other on the dead limb of the nearest oak. They dove at each other twice and missed. Then, satisfied, as if each thought he was the winner, they flew off to celebrate in separate directions. He hoped his problem with George would be solved that easily.

"I was the associate minister of a large church in Atlanta," he said. "A very influential church. I was chosen for the position right out of seminary. The senior minister wanted to handpick his successor and groom him to take over when he retired. I had all the qualifications they wanted."

He didn't go into specifics. Scholarships he had won, articles he had published, the sermon series on forgiveness that had won him a round of preaching engagements in major churches before he even graduated. He had been the star student in a top-notch seminary. And none of that had gone unnoticed.

"The Savior's Church is fairly conservative," he went on. "But the congregation was intelligent and well-educated. I believed I could change them. Their budget was huge, and I saw potential for social service ministries all over the city, for outreach programs, for ministries to youth and college students. I thought I could make a difference."

"Did you?"

He was surprised he could tell this story

now with so little pain. He felt as if he were describing someone else's life. Without rancor. Without blame. Without self-pity.

"I think I did. I was forced to pull back any number of times, to moderate my sermons, to ask for less from parishioners, to expect less in general. But a lot was going well. I met Christine. She's the headmistress of the school that's connected to the church. Her father and others were sure I had a career in politics. I began to believe I could change the world."

He gave a wry smile, because even to his own ears he sounded very young. "Then one day I tried to."

"What happened? Or is this too personal?"

"Do you know anything about the School of the Americas?"

She looked surprised. She had been making herself more comfortable, shifting in her seat, but she froze. "Why do you ask?"

"It's a big part of the reason I'm here."

"I . . . Yes, I've heard of it. It's a program to train military leaders from Latin America."

"The school is housed at Fort Benning, Georgia. Officially it's called something else now, although it's still known as the

School of Assassins by the people who oppose it. There have been a few changes,
some lip service to human rights and the
finer points of democracy, but not nearly
enough for most of us. The list of gradu-
ates is a hall of infamy. These men formed
death squads in El Salvador, assassinated
Archbishop Romero, and raped and murdered nuns. They killed thousands in
Guatemala. It's a matter of public record
that the school taught torture techniques,
kidnapping, extortion. The Pentagon was
forced to declassify those documents.
Some people think the school is still a
huge force for destabilization in Latin
America. Religious leaders of all denomi-
nations want it closed down. I was one of
them."

"Was?"

"Am." He couldn't — didn't want to —
deny it. "Am," he repeated.

"And you lost your job because you
don't believe a training ground for military
dictatorships is a good thing?"

"There's a difference of opinion about
this, of course. Many good people believe
the school is necessary. I happen to think
they're wrong, but I understand their take
on things. I didn't lose my job at The Savior's Church because we disagreed. I lost it

because I was arrested at the annual protest at the Fort Benning gates. I stepped over a line I shouldn't have stepped over, and I was convicted for it."

She was staring at him. He wasn't sure what she was thinking. He understood that, for many people, wilfully flouting the law, no matter the cause, was unacceptable. No matter that Gandhi had brought England to its knees and India its freedom by nonviolent resistance. No matter that Martin Luther King and his compatriots had made civil rights a national priority by facing dogs and fire hoses without fighting back.

He tried to explain but not to apologize. "I did it in the heat of the moment, and I came back from my sentencing to find I no longer had a job. My decision was not popular."

"You went to prison?"

"We expected the first-time offenders, people who had not been arrested before, to get probation, although of course we knew that wasn't a sure thing. That's what I expected. I didn't expect . . ." He shrugged. "The judge decided otherwise. Dozens of us were sentenced together. Priests, nuns, farmers, teachers. I was in a minimum security facility in Pennsylvania for six months. Club Fed, they call it. Unless you've been there."

Usually when he talked about his time in prison his throat closed and his hands began to sweat, and he was glad they didn't now. He still had attacks of claustrophobia in the middle of the night, slept with the hall light burning, opened doors and windows whenever he could, avoided crowded restaurants and long lines at sales counters.

"You said you wanted to change the world, that you believed change was your mission at The Savior's Church."

"I was young and full of myself."

"In the end, what did you learn? That trying to change the world will only get you in trouble?"

He thought for a moment. "No, I learned that nothing is about *me*. It's about God and God's plan. Unfortunately, I didn't take much time to consult the Almighty. I went to Fort Benning because it seemed like a good idea, but I didn't put much thought behind it or make sure that was my path. I saw an injustice and waded right in. I didn't think for long, and I didn't pray. Ever since, I've spent a lot of time wondering if I did what I did for the right reasons. Was that my calling? Or was

I acting on impulse, showing how courageous I was by putting my future on the
line?"

"And you lost everything."

He was sorry those words hadn't been
uttered as a question. "If I gave that im-
pression, I didn't mean to. I'm still not
sure what I lost, Elisa. I certainly lost my
job. Maybe I lost the only chance I'll ever
have to make a difference on a wider scale.
I don't know. For a while I lost my self-respect, because I acted impulsively and
didn't think about consequences. I nearly
lost Christine. I did lose my freedom. The
School of the Americas continues to
flourish."

"Then you're sorry you went that day. I
can see why you would be."

On this, at least, he was sure of himself.
"No, I'm *not* sorry I marched that day,
even if my reasons might not have been
clearly thought out. And although it was
inadvisable, even melodramatic, to step
across that line onto the base without
praying hard enough, I'm not sorry I did
that, either. My life changed in an instant,
but I'm not sure it wasn't supposed to."

"You're not sorry you're here? That now
you're in a small church in the country?"

That was less clear. He tried to explain.

"I've probably told the story badly. But the truth is, I still believe deep in my heart that what I did that day was right, even though prison was a nightmare. Will those months change anything? I don't know. Do I wish I was still in Atlanta, preaching to thousands on Sunday-morning television?" He shrugged once more. "I'm not sure of a lot of things now. I haven't stopped wanting to make a difference with my life, but is that ego talking, or is it the still small voice inside me?"

When she didn't speak, he was sorry. He didn't expect anyone else to understand what drove him or even his ambivalence about the consequences. But he had expected something of Elisa, some hint of understanding, perhaps. He didn't need it to validate what he had done or the struggles he still faced, but he would have liked it just the same.

"I don't expect *anyone* else to see this from my perspective," he said. "Very few people I'm close to do."

"What you did . . ." Her voice was charged with emotion. "It was *right,* Sam. *Everything* you did, whether you were absolutely clear about it or not. You spoke for people who have no voice. And your words and your actions will ring in ways and in places you will never know. How could your God want less of you?"

She got to her feet. He was so surprised, he didn't know what to say. He sensed that if he asked her what she meant, she wouldn't tell him. She started down the steps, but just below him, she turned. She touched his shoulder. A brief, gentle touch. Her eyes were stormy with emotion.

"Don't let anyone tell you that you made a mistake," she whispered.

She was gone before he realized that he was still sitting on the steps staring at her slight figure retreating in the distance.

Chapter Nine

Shenandoah Community Church
Wednesday Quilting Bee
and Social Gathering
— September 3rd

The meeting was called to order ten minutes late in the quilters' beehive. Punctuality is a virtue and we are fallen women. Although it is not within my realm of duty to report the culprits, I can say that when the gavel fell, Cathy Adams and Anna Mayhew were still conferring in the corner.

We dispensed with committee reports when it became clear that no one, not one committee chair, had anything to report. The day I forget to transcribe these minutes will be the day I order my casket. However, it is not my right to question the workings of other women's minds.

We agreed, under pressure and protest, to drop "Wednesday" from our title in the future. Need I report here which impatient quilter was responsible?

Show and Tell was far more popular. We have taken it upon ourselves to make wall hangings and lap quilts for La Casa Amarilla, *which will soon be filled with children each school day afternoon. Of course, in keeping with the theme, each quilt must have yellow in its pattern. Helen Henry is piecing bumblebees for the kitchen walls. Peony Greenway is appliqueing a lap quilt of baby ducklings. Kate Brogan is piecing a small table runner with gold and green sunflowers. Cathy Adams, Anna Mayhew and I have combined talents to produce a Virginia Reel quilt of bold primary prints on a bright yellow background.*

Show and Tell took the entire morning. Had we not debated the placement of every scrap of fabric on every quilt, perhaps it might have gone more quickly. Those who could still chew after flapping their jaws all morning remained to enjoy bag lunches.

Sincerely,
Dovey K. Lanning, recording secretary

Adoncia was having a party. Or at least that was how it looked when Elisa drove up and parked beside the mobile home on the first Wednesday in September. She had stayed late at church last night cleaning and setting up for meetings, including the quilters' weekly bee, so there was no reason to hurry in this morning.

Her biggest mission today would be a thorough cleaning for *La Casa.* Tutoring was scheduled to begin next week, and volunteers would arrive over the weekend to set up and make sure all the supplies were in order. Elisa wanted to be sure that everything was ready.

Adoncia and several friends from the park were sitting at the sagging picnic table under the lone tree that graced her lot. Fernando and Maria were splashing in a plastic wading pool. The women were drinking coffee and dunking *biscochitos,* the anise-flavored cookies that were

Adoncia's specialty. Salsa music spiced the air from a portable radio.

Everyone enthusiastically greeted Elisa in Spanish and made room for her at the table. Despite Elisa's protests, Adoncia went inside for another mug and returned with a pot of fresh coffee.

"We came to congratulate Adoncia," Inez told Elisa. She was Adoncia's age and newly married. Elisa was glad to see she had been included, since the young woman was pretty enough to have worried the other women in the park at first.

"Congratulate?" Elisa glanced at her friend. "For what?"

"Diego gave me a ring." Adoncia held out her left hand and wiggled her fingers.

Elisa duly admired the small diamond, which must have cost Diego a large part of a month's salary. "Are you setting a date?"

Adoncia gave a mysterious smile. "Not until we have, how do they say it here, a meeting of the minds?"

Elisa was sure she knew what that meeting would be about.

Patia, who was also young but worried no one due to a wide girth and protruding teeth, took another cookie and passed the platter. "I'd like to have a meeting of the minds with my Manuel. He says when I have babies I don't need to see a doctor, that childbirth is natural, and when I have pains, he will take me to stay with his aunt. She has delivered babies before." She rubbed her belly. "My sister says he is crazy."

Elisa had met Manuel and found him both rational and concerned. This attitude surprised her, but she suspected it had more to do with a lack of insurance than with superstition or custom.

"When the time comes," she told Patia, "we'll find you a doctor right here who will help for whatever you can afford. There are too many problems an aunt might not know how to fix. A doctor is better, or a good midwife."

"I had a midwife," Adoncia said. "For Maria. She was as good as a doctor."

"But she was a trained midwife, and there was a hospital nearby, right?" Elisa said.

"You know so much about these things," Inez said. "You knew what to do when I had cramps. No one else could tell me."

"What did you tell her?" Adoncia asked. "Me, I take aspirin and complain as loud as I can."

"Inez is allergic to aspirin," Elisa said.

"I turn red, like a berry," Inez said.

"I told her to try oregano tea," Elisa said. "Boiling water, oregano. Let it steep and strain it. It helps some women."

"It helped me," Inez said. "The doctor had nothing to try except patience."

"How do you know so much?" Patia asked. "You were the one who told my sister to eat yogurt when she itched down there all the time." She pointed under the table.

"She itched on her feet?" Adoncia said.

"No! In places above her feet."

Adoncia was grinning. "Her knees?"

"Adoncia," Elisa chided. "She had a yeast infection. From too many antibiotics for a sore throat. You can stop pretending you don't know."

Everyone laughed.

"Yogurt?" Adoncia said.

"And cream from the drugstore. The yogurt helps keep it from coming back."

"How do you know so much?" Patia repeated.

Elisa noted the interest on all their faces. "My sister is a midwife. I used to help with her patients. She taught me a lot. I wanted to be a nurse, but my life went in a different direction." That part, at least, was true.

"I wanted to be a movie star," Patia said.

She waited a moment as everyone struggled silently for a response. "You think I'm not joking?" she demanded.

Everyone laughed, and the subject changed to recipes and Brad Pitt as more *biscochitos* and hot coffee made the rounds.

After the other women had gone home, Elisa helped Adoncia clear the table. Inside, she washed the dishes, while Adoncia dressed the children. When they were happily settled in front of the television, she came into the kitchen to put the newly dried cups and saucers in the cupboard.

"You have many sisters, many *convenient* sisters," Adoncia said. "And your life changes each time you tell the story. I don't think you have a bad memory, Elisa. I think you have bad memories."

Elisa was surprised. She and Adoncia had never talked in depth about her past. Adoncia had seemed to understand it was off-limits.

"Part of being here," Adoncia continued, "in this country, is putting the past behind us, yes? I have done this. I have buried my Fernando. I no longer cry for my family in Mexico. But I have secrets, too, and stories I would rather not share. Once Fernando came after me with a knife when he had been drinking too much. He wanted to kill me. I have never told anyone about that night, but I have a scar right here to remind me." She pulled down the neck of her blouse and showed a jagged scar across her breast. Clearly it had never been stitched, and it had not healed perfectly. "I told Diego I fell when I was a little girl."

Elisa put her arm around Adoncia's waist in comfort. "I'm sorry. I'm glad Fernando's not here to threaten you anymore."

"Diego would never hurt me. This is part of why I love him so much."

Adoncia slipped her arm around Elisa's waist and squeezed, and for a moment the two women just stood together, glad for each other's friendship.

Adoncia pulled away at last. "I love *you,* too, Elisa. And I will never hurt you. Someday, if you want to tell me the truth about yourself, if you need to tell somebody, I will be here waiting."

Through the years, the house that was known as *La Casa Amarilla* had undergone many renovations. Elisa could only guess what had been added and what was part of the original dwelling.

It was hard to imagine a family living in

a fraction of this building, as the original settlers must have. Of course, she had been in mountain villages with homes that were smaller than the living room here, homes with large families that still made room for strangers in need.

But this was different. There had been no village here, only a lone house separated from its neighbors by distances it might have taken a day or more to cover on horseback. No grandmothers or cousins lived nearby to discipline a child who was misbehaving. No uncles or brothers lived in the next house to help with harvests or a winter supply of firewood.

As she vacuumed and dusted, mopped floors and scrubbed bathrooms, she wondered what those settlers would think of the house and community now.

Once the children arrived the house would be dirtier, but today she finished everything except the kitchen in an hour. Once there, she scrubbed the double sinks, removed everything from the counters and sponged them clean, wiped the stove and checked inside to be certain the oven didn't need cleaning, too. She scoured the refrigerator, threw out the old ice in the freezer and put fresh water in the trays.

Almost everything went smoothly. The

old-fashioned walk-in pantry was the only trouble spot, overlooked by the volunteers or assigned to someone who hadn't wanted to do the work. The shelves were thick with dust, and old mousetraps — luckily empty — remained ready and willing in the corner.

She began by throwing away the traps and a few food items that hadn't been removed when Martha Wisner left the house. Then she hauled a chair into the narrow space and climbed up to begin dusting, closing the door into the kitchen so the dust wouldn't undo her good work. One bare bulb lit the area and shed just enough light to let her see what she was up against. She removed the top layer of dirt from the highest shelves, then climbed down and proceeded to the lower shelves, shaking her rag often into the plastic garbage bag she'd brought with her.

With the first layer removed, she went back into the kitchen and filled a bucket with water and detergent, and brought it back into the pantry. She set the bucket on a lower shelf, soaked a new rag in it, and began to wipe down the shelves, stopping often to soak and wring it out again, until the water was too dirty to be helpful. Two more trips to the kitchen for fresh water and she finished the top round of shelves.

Disaster struck on the second level. Leaning forward to reach a corner where two shelves connected, she lost her balance. As she fell forward, she threw out both hands to grab a shelf, hoping to break the impact. The chair tilted, and as she fell against the shelf with all her weight, it came loose and flipped over, toward the wall behind it. She went with it, her hand slamming against the wall.

The accident was over in seconds. She was grateful to find that only her arm was scratched and her ankle throbbed slightly, because she had landed so hard on it. The other shelves had remained in place, and the disaster that had flashed through her mind, every shelf following the one she had dislodged, had not occurred.

"¡Carajo! ¡Me lleva quién me trajo!"

The expletives were mild enough, but she felt better. She tested her ankle and decided it would be fine. The scratch wasn't even bleeding. Then she looked at the wall.

A section was missing, as if it had never been there.

For the briefest moment she wondered how one small woman could have knocked out an entire section of wallboard. Then she realized that wasn't what had happened at all.

She removed the shelf that had flipped, then another and another. And in a few minutes, her suspicions were confirmed.

She wondered if Sam was available to see what she had discovered.

Sam was just about to start on his lunch when Elisa stepped into his doorway. "Do you have a few minutes?"

For a moment he was afraid she had come to resign. She'd been doing the sexton's job for a week now without Marvin, and he was worried she might find it too difficult. One glance at her expression set his mind at ease. Elisa looked unruffled. If there was news, it wasn't bad.

He got to his feet. "Have you had lunch?"

"I thought I'd eat when I got back to Helen's."

"I brought enough for two. I'll share. What do you want to show me?"

"It's over at *La Casa*."

"We can eat on the porch. It's a good afternoon for a picnic." He lowered his voice conspiratorially. "But we can't let the quilters catch us. They'll find out I don't work every single minute."

She laughed. "You're sure you have enough lunch?"

"Plenty." He held up a Rambo lunch box. "It's packed full."

"How old is that one?"

"Mid-eighties. It was the last metal lunch box, a real collector's item. Kids started using them as weapons; there were lawsuits, so the manufacturers went to plastic. A great choice for a minister, don't you think?"

"Very macho. I don't remember seeing any pink lunch boxes at your house."

"Cabbage Patch and Barbie haven't found their way into my collection."

"That could be fixed."

"The whole thing is humiliating enough, thanks."

He shoved the lunch box under his arm and joined her for the walk to *La Casa*, feeling better than he had all morning.

Since the day he had told her of his fall from grace, they had begun spending more time together. Coffee breaks, planning meetings, obscure errands on the grounds together. One afternoon he had taken her to see a patch of lady-slipper orchids at the edge of the property and asked her to put up a sign so the plants wouldn't be disturbed. Another day he had taken her out to the compost pile to show her where coffee grounds and tea bags should be taken each week. Nothing too intimate by any stretch of the imagination, but he knew the episodes for what they were: a chance to be close to her.

"So are you going to give me a hint?" he asked as they neared the old house. "Since you don't look distressed, I'm assuming you didn't find rats or bats or asbestos?"

"I thought I'd found termites, but it's something entirely different."

His curiosity was piqued, but he was in no hurry to get to the house. He liked walking in the sunshine with her, the current of attraction crackling between them. At home alone he would be thinking of something else and a picture of Elisa would suddenly form in his mind. No matter how hard he tried to ignore his own reaction, willpower was no match for desire.

He had progressed in his thinking, or perhaps it was the opposite. Either way, he had decided that ignoring Elisa was counterproductive. The less he saw of her, the more he thought of her. Perhaps if a simple friendship flourished, everything else would die a natural death.

"It's early yet, but if you look closely you can see some of the leaves are starting to change," he said. "Autumn in the valley is beautiful. The tourists will start to descend when the colors change in earnest. Attendance picks up at church, because everybody comes back home to visit."

"I'm looking forward to seeing them."

"What was fall like in Mexico?"

"Hotter. But we looked forward to cooler weather, so it was always appreciated."

"Do you miss home?"

"Yes and no."

He wondered if it was possible to be more vague. "How are Adoncia and her children?"

"She's wearing an engagement ring." Elisa glanced at him, as if to read his expression. "Diego wants to be married right away, but Adoncia's not sure. He wants a family, but she wants to wait until her two are a little older before she has another."

"I can understand that."

"Not every man is so thoughtful. Diego is hungry for family."

"I can understand that, too."

"Because you want children?"

The question was as personal as any she had asked him. He saw from her expression she was sorry.

"I absolutely want kids," he said. "I love kids." Christine claimed to want them, too, although he wondered. Even though she worked with children, it was their parents who interested Chrissy most.

"How about you?" he countered. "Do you want children?"

"I did. Once. But it's not a problem I need to think about now."

"There's no man on the horizon?"

"Not as far as the eye can see."

They reached the house. He paused on the porch. "Lunch first? Or the big revelation?"

"How hungry are you?"

"I'm always hungry."

"The big revelation will keep. It's definitely not going anywhere."

They perched on the top step, and Elisa set about unscrewing the tops of two water bottles Sam had taken from the refrigerator before leaving. Sam opened the lunch box and spread out his bounty. Two sandwiches, apples, a banana, cake and several candy bars.

Elisa leaned over and examined the food. She was close enough that he could smell lemons and a whiff of pine, most likely from cleaning products she had used that morning, but crisp and pleasant nonetheless.

"Sam, you eat this stuff?"

"What's wrong with it?"

Her braid fell over one shoulder and glistened against her cheek as she pried open the first sandwich. "Ummm . . . What is this?"

He took the sandwich from her hand and separated the slices of bread, since he couldn't remember. "Leftover chicken, a fried egg, ketchup and some extra hash browns I didn't have time to eat for breakfast. Oh, and a slice of American cheese." He looked up. "Don't tell me that doesn't sound good. You have no idea how much I yearned for a lunch like this when I was eating prison food."

She looked faintly ill. "And the other's the same?"

"I pride myself on diversity." He lifted the top slice of bread on the second sandwich. "Broccoli, hummus, blue cheese — I love the stuff — and some ham the book discussion group gave me from yesterday's luncheon. The cake was last week's contribution, but it's not very stale."

"This contest you told me about, the strange lunch contest? Are you practicing?"

"I have fruit, I have cake, I have candy." He shrugged. "Strange?"

"The apples have worm holes. The banana was perfect last month. The candy?

I've never seen such tiny candy bars."

"They're left over from Halloween. I only had a couple of trick or treaters last year. I've been working on the bags ever since."

"Is there anything you don't eat?"

"No."

"Is there anything you don't eat with anything else? Say, no lima beans on a grilled cheese sandwich?"

"I'm surprised your food preferences are so narrow."

"I'm surprised you're alive and well and able to put one foot in front of the other."

They were smiling at each other, and for a long moment neither spoke. There were too many of these moments, he knew, just as he knew he was powerless to put an end to them.

"What will you eat?" he asked at last.

"I'll take my chances with the worms."

"They're perfectly good apples, I promise."

They worked on his lunch in companionable silence. She spoke when both apples had disappeared with no further complaint. "What do you know about the origins of this house, Sam? That first day you told me it's pre-Civil War. Do you know anything more?"

"A Miller family settled the land. They arrived from Pennsylvania, I think. A lot of the valley settlers did. Many were of German origin, but some of them were Mennonites, or what they called Dunkards back then and we call the Church of the Brethren now. Those are peace churches, and the members refuse to fight. You can imagine that makes for tension when the country's at war."

"So they didn't fight in the Civil War? That was fought right here, wasn't it?"

"They say this part of the valley never had a lot of slaves, but there were people on both sides of the slavery issue, fighting for opposing armies when war broke out. Brother against brother, neighbor against neighbor. Some people who were against slavery in principle still fought for the South. The capital of the Confederacy was just down the road in Richmond, after all."

"So the Millers might have been right in the middle of things."

"Probably were. I don't know much more than that. I do know they held on to the land until the beginning of the twentieth century. At some point it was passed down through a female Miller — I can't remember her married name — and eventually sold and divided. But apparently it was still called the Miller Place when the church bought this parcel at auction. The whole area had fallen on hard times by then. The Depression took a toll. There's a rumor a lot of farmers sold the local white lightning to get themselves through the toughest times. Who could blame them?"

He balled up his trash and crammed it back in the Rambo lunch box. "So, what's my surprise?"

"Well, I think the Millers might have had a secret life. Or at least somebody who lived here did."

He followed her inside and into the kitchen. She pulled the chain on the pantry light, and he saw that some of the shelves had been removed. Then he saw the hole.

"After you," she said, stepping out of the pantry to let him inside.

"What's this?"

"I think a storage area of some kind. I was cleaning, and I fell. I tried to catch myself, and I hit the wall back there — or at least what I thought was a wall. It turned out to be a door."

He stepped up closer and peered into complete darkness. "You're okay? You weren't hurt?"

"Just a scratch and wounded pride. Don't go any farther, Sam."

"I'm assuming there's no light in here?"

"No, but I found a flashlight in the emergency kit in the hallway. Here." She handed him a high beam flashlight.

Sam aimed the light into the darkness and saw a room, or, more accurately, a cave. There were steps down, four of them — which was obviously the reason Elisa hadn't wanted him to go farther — and the room seemed to be carved out of the hillside behind it. As many times as he had been in this house, there had never been an indication this room existed. It was about six by eight feet, perhaps six feet high, with a dirt floor and stone walls lined with empty cobwebbed shelves.

He stepped back into the kitchen. "That's a surprise."

"I thought you'd say that."

"If it's a root cellar, it's the only one I've ever seen that was hidden away. Generally Grandmother's canned peaches don't warrant a secret room. Besides, there's a root cellar with an outside entrance beyond this one."

Elisa turned off the pantry light. "Maybe the Millers used this room to hide supplies during the war. Wasn't looting a problem when troops came through? Maybe this is where they put their valuables."

"Or maybe it's more recent. Maybe some resident really did traffic in corn liquor during the Depression, and that's where he stored it."

"Maybe it's both."

He wondered how they might find out. Elisa beat him to the most logical answer. "Do you think Martha Wisner might know?"

"How much does she remember about anything?" he asked.

"Her long-term memory is relatively unimpaired. Her short-term?" She shrugged.

"So it's possible if she ever knew about the room she might remember now?"

"It's possible. I work tomorrow tonight. I could ask her."

"Why not? Unless it upsets her."

"Are you going to tell people?"

That was a harder question. Something told him that wouldn't be a good idea, at least not yet. *La Casa* was about to open its doors for the first time, and he didn't want sightseers trooping through to see the hidden room. Until they could discover more about its purpose, he thought it might be wise to keep this discovery secret.

He told her as much, and she nodded in agreement. "I'll put things back the way they were. But it's a very clever arrangement of shelves. The door is positioned be-tween vertical studs and horizontal shelves. There's no question someone wanted that room to be invisible."

He was intrigued by the mystery. But he also realized he was even more intrigued that he and Elisa shared this secret. Now there was another excuse for conversation, for spending time in each other's company.

He had hoped that being together more often would put his attraction to her in perspective. Now he realized there were no easy answers. He was in way over his head already.

Chapter
Ten

Elisa had been too busy her entire life to spend significant time flirting or even thinking about men. Some had interested her, of course, and some had gotten past her defenses. There had been one man, perhaps the most unlikely of all, who had settled into her life and heart. Gabrio Santos had been twenty years her senior. She thanked God every day that she had not let his age sway her. She would never look back on the years of their marriage with anything like regret. Their love had not been romantic, but it had been no less powerful or profound.

Now, faced with something else entirely, an attraction that touched not only her heart but her senses, she was at a loss to know what to do. She was afraid she was falling in love with Sam Kinkade, and a more dangerous and inappropriate emotion could not be imagined.

Risking her heart was impossible. There was no room in her life for anyone else, no hope that anyone could be trusted to understand who she was and what drove her. Not Sam, *particularly* not Sam, whose ideals had already cost him too much, who still suffered the effects of his months in prison. Sam whose desire for air, light, color and space finally made sense to her.

Sam, who could not be trusted to abandon her when he learned the truth.

Even if he weren't already in love with another woman, there was no hope she and Sam could surmount the obstacles in their lives. Unfortunately, despite all this, the moments they spent together were fast becoming the moments that made everything else worthwhile, the work, the lies and secrets, the endless, fruitless search that had brought her to Toms Brook.

The night after their lunch together at *La Casa*, Elisa's sleep had suffered. Now it was the next evening and she was at the nursing home, where she was paying the price. So far she had checked the day logs, done the crossover and checked the residents in nearly every room. But she was moving in slow motion. She prayed there would not be a crisis tonight requiring quick thinking and laser-sharp reflexes.

Having saved Martha Wisner's room for last, she fortified herself with the dregs of a large coffee from the break room and started down the hall. Both Sam and the secret room were taking up too much of her thoughts. She hoped that she would at least be able to put questions about the room to rest tonight.

The moon was a waning crescent, and so far the night had been quiet. She was thankful the moon wasn't full, since invariably that meant more problems. Once she had assumed that was superstition, but experience had taught her better.

Martha's door was cracked, and she pushed it open, peeking inside to see whether the old woman was sleeping. The day shift had noted that Martha had slept most of the afternoon, missing lunch despite every effort to keep her awake and active. Just as Elisa suspected, Martha was up and standing at the window, gazing out at the parking lot. She turned when she heard Elisa approach.

"Why are the lights on out there?"

"It's late at night. Past midnight. The lights are on for security."

"It doesn't feel like midnight."

Elisa was relieved Martha wasn't going to argue about the time. Some residents did, convinced they were correct despite all visual signals to the contrary. Some, of course, weren't coherent enough to argue, but they were combative.

"You slept a lot of the afternoon," Elisa told her. "You're turned around today. If you can sleep a bit more now, maybe tomorrow you can stay awake in the afternoon."

Martha frowned, as if working to make sense of that. Then she sighed. "I can't sleep now. I feel rested. And hungry. Is there something I can eat?"

"I'll get you something. Would you like some ice cream? Or a sandwich?"

"Both." Martha smiled like a little girl hoping to wheedle a week's allowance. "Chocolate?"

"I have to check your chart and the fridge, but I think that's an option."

"Oh, good."

Elisa returned a few minutes later with a tray. She liked making the residents happy if she could. Their pleasures were fleeting, particularly those in the worst health or facing worsening dementia. Martha had seated herself in an armchair and was waiting patiently. Elisa set the tray on the table beside her.

"Turkey sandwich," she said. "I brought mayonnaise and tomato in case you'd like to add them. And chocolate ice cream, just like you ordered."

"I remember eating dinner." Martha looked up. "I think."

"Broiled fish, a green salad, scalloped potatoes and corn bread."

Martha clapped her hands. "I do remember." She lowered her voice to a conspiratorial whisper. "The fish wasn't very good."

Elisa laughed. "It's not what the kitchen does best."

"You've eaten it?"

"I'm afraid there's a plate in the break room fridge with my name on it."

"Oh, that's too bad." Martha sounded sincerely sympathetic. "But the potatoes are excellent."

"I have to go, but I'll be back for the tray. If you need anything in the meantime, you can use the call button."

"I'm going to be busy with my sandwich."

Elisa left to answer the calls of several residents, none of whom had serious problems. By the time she returned, Martha was finishing the last bites of her ice cream. Elisa got a warm washcloth so Martha could wipe her hands and face; then she removed the tray to the stand beside the door. "How was it?"

"Perfect. Were you here before?"

Elisa's heart sank. "I brought it to you."

Martha frowned; then her face brightened. "Oh, yes, you're the one who has to eat the fish." She leaned forward and searched Elisa's face for a long moment. "I know you! You're Sharon, aren't you? I don't know why I didn't recognize you before."

For a moment Elisa didn't know what to say. She took Martha's cloth, and went to the sink to rinse it and hang it to dry. "No, I'm Elisa."

"Sharon is such a pretty name. Your mother named you for the Rose of Sharon in the Bible, but you were never a proper biblical heroine, were you, dear?"

Elisa lowered herself to the chair across from Martha's own. "I think you have me mixed up with someone else."

"Your father thought he could spank the sassiness out of you. I tried to stop him, you know. I used to hide you in my room when you were small if I thought he was in a bad mood. For a minister, he wasn't always a very good person. I suppose I can

230

say that, since he was my brother."

Elisa couldn't help herself. She was fascinated. "Wasn't he? A good person?"

"I'm sure that's why he was asked to leave the church. I don't think he had a really successful ministry anywhere. He had a terrible temper. Your mother put up with it, but she shouldn't have. She should have taken you and run away, but she was weak."

Elisa waited, but nothing else was forthcoming. "Was this when you were living in the Community Church parsonage, Miss Wisner?" she prompted.

"Oh, just call me Aunt Martha, dear, the way you did when you were little."

"You were living in the parsonage?"

"Yes, before your father was sent away. I stayed afterward, you know. I didn't want to go with him, although, of course, I worried about you. But now you're back. It all turned out so well, didn't it?"

Elisa didn't want to spoil what Martha saw as a triumph by reminding her once again that she was not Sharon. "I was at the parsonage today, cleaning."

"Were you? That's funny. How does it look to you after all these years?"

Elisa plugged on. "It's been repainted and fixed up. It looks lovely. But I found something very strange in the pantry."

Martha had been staring at the window and the security lights in the parking lot. Now she turned her gaze to Elisa. "Did you?"

Elisa was sure Martha knew exactly what she was talking about. She seemed particularly alert now, and a smile tugged at her lips. "There's a door behind the shelves that leads to a hidden room," Elisa said. "I showed it to the minister, too. He was as surprised as I was."

Martha leaned forward. "I remember the room. Did you think I might not?"

"I wasn't sure."

"I know I can't remember some things, but I remember that as clearly as my own name." She sat back.

"Do you know why it's there? Was it added while you lived there?"

"Oh, no! It's been there practically as long as the house. It started out as a fruit cellar, you know, but it was much more than that in its time."

"There's a real fruit cellar just to one side of it, with an outside entrance."

"Yes, I know." Martha smiled. "It was added later, to help disguise the secret room."

"What else can you tell me?" Elisa asked.

"This sounds like quite a story."

"I suppose it's all right to tell *you.* Your father didn't even know. I was the only one who did. You see, when we moved into the parsonage, the wife of the former minister took me aside and told me. She showed me some papers and said I could be trusted with the story. The ministers had always kept it a secret. They didn't want people treating the parsonage as a museum. I don't think she liked your mother and father. I'm sorry."

"Then you're the only one who knows?"

"Oh, I was supposed to tell somebody before I moved away, I guess. I just, well, I just had other things to think about."

Elisa didn't know what to say, so she just smiled. It was enough to prompt Martha.

"Now I can tell *you.* Then it will be your secret to pass on someday."

Elisa wasn't sure that there was a real secret, or if there was, whether Martha would remember it from one sentence to the next, but she hoped for the best.

Someone buzzed her and frustrated, she gestured to the hall beyond. "Let me do a few things while you think about the story. Then I'll be back and you can tell me."

"Oh, do come back, dear. My memory isn't getting any better." Martha smiled to show she was teasing.

"You're doing just fine tonight. And I'll be back as soon as I can."

"It's a long story. I might not be able to tell all of it before I fall asleep."

Elisa wondered if this was Martha's way of assuring herself she would have some company on other nights, too. Elisa felt a wave of fondness for the old woman. "Whatever you can tell me. But let me guess. Does this have to do with bootleg whiskey?"

Martha chuckled.

"So it does?"

"No, dear. It has to do with a woman named Dorie Beaumont. You come back, and I'll tell you what I can tonight. I promise you won't find it boring."

Chapter
Eleven

May 18, 1853

My dearest Amasa,
How far away you are, and how unlikely you will receive this letter before the events I recount are long past. Such it always will be, now that you have gone home to Lynchburg to assist your father. I picture you every day at his forge, although I have never seen you thus. In my loneliness, imagination is my worst enemy, for sometimes I also picture myself beside you, bringing water to ease your thirst or wipe your brow. I know this cannot be, that there is no room for me there. But still, the thought will not fly away.

I hope your father improves, though I fear the worst. Daily I pray that he will be delivered from his illness, but I also pray that if death is his deliverance, you will find a way to return to me. I would live in the poorest mountain cabin with you, dear Amasa, even though I know you will never allow it. I would share the humble room over your father's shop, as well, although I know that this, too, can never be.

I study my Holy Bible each night, looking for a sign for our future. Last night, in James, I found this verse: "God is opposed to the proud but gives grace to the humble." You are a humble man, yet I wonder if it is not pride that stands in the way of taking me as your bride? I have never asked for more than you can give. Yet too well I understand your desire to care for and protect me as well as Jeremiah does in our family home. Nightly I struggle for patience and the acceptance of God's will.

I do find solace here. Jeremiah needs me, I know. The man you remember, a man overflowing with wit, piety and affection, has not yet returned to us. He is silent still. Days pass and the only words I hear my brother utter are prayers before meals. His tone is mocking, as if he is daring our Lord to strike him dead, even *as he prays outwardly for grace. At night from my room above the stairs I hear him pacing. Sleep is a rare thing indeed for either of us.*

Rachel has been dead nearly a year, and the children two weeks longer. I visit their graves and lay fresh flowers on them when I can. Jeremiah never goes to the cemetery, and I have seen him turn his head to avoid gazing in that di-rection. The fever that took his family still steals the breath from my chest when I think how suddenly they were gone and Jeremiah was left behind. Would that I only knew how to help my brother feel joy again.

But I promised you news, and there is news. We are no longer alone here. You must not tell anyone of this, Amasa, but, of course, I know you will not. So I will confess to you what has transpired.

This evening a storm swept through the valley like few I have seen before. Our sunny day was followed by a sudden rain and hailstones larger than a fist. I had just put supper on the table, but we quickly abandoned it. Jeremiah went out to the barn to be certain all was well with Betty Gray, his plow horse, and her new foal. Lightning shattered the sky and struck the chestnut tree behind the spring house. The sound was something I never hope to hear again.

I was frightened. I can tell you this because you have seen me when lightning flashes and know I am not the bravest of souls. I was terrified for Jeremiah, and I am ashamed to say I was afraid for myself, as well. I ran to the porch to peer into the storm to search for him, hoping he was safe. By then the skies were dark, and the ground looked as it does after the first snow of winter. As I watched, the hail began to melt under the relentless pounding of the rain.

I had left a quilt on the porch to air, and as I bundled it into my arms to bring it inside, I thought I saw movement near the house. I peered over the railing, wondering if Jeremiah had not gone to the barn after all. There was nothing to be seen until lightning split the sky once more. Only then did I spy a figure on the ground some feet to the side of our porch. A woman lay there, completely still, water washing around her as it ran off our roof. She lay as if on an island, as the rain made twin creeks around her.

I confess I screamed. No one could hear me, of course. The storm was still raging, and as rain battered the ground, thunder roared at regular intervals. I was afraid to go out in it, but even more afraid to leave her to the storm's mercy. Inside, I pulled my shawl from its peg, covered my head and ran to help.

By now I know you are wondering why I am taking so long to tell this story. I fear it is because I do not know how. I do not know what to tell and what to leave out. All of it seems immense to me, you see. The woman, the rain, my own fright. The storm was powerful, but what transpired was more so.

When I reached the woman, I knew immediately what I had found. She is darker-skinned than I, Amasa, with soft rippling hair, like that of the enslaved people I have seen on my few trips to Winchester or to the neighboring farms that imprison them. I could see little but this, but I knew what it meant. This was not a neighbor who had lost her way but a woman escaping bondage.

I tried to revive her, but with no success. I tried to lift her in my arms, but again, I could not. The storm had not abated. I feared for both of us. We were fodder for lightning bolts. Perhaps this is what made me strong? I managed to squeeze my arms between hers and lift her high enough to drag her toward the porch.

Jeremiah found us at the bottom of the steps. He knows how storms frighten me, and he had returned as quickly as he could. (As you can see, he is not completely lost to his own sorrow.) He took one look and lifted her in his arms, then carried her up the steps and into the house.

She is tucked safely into my bed tonight, and I sit beside it writing to you by candlelight. She has wakened only once. I told her she was safe and we would not betray her. That seemed to satisfy her. I asked her name, and she whispered, "Dorie. Dorie Beaumont." Then she fell asleep again.

I close now as my candle flickers and dies. I will write again when there is more to tell. Pray for us, my beloved.

Yours alone,
Sarah Miller

Chapter
Twelve

For once Elisa didn't have to jump up the moment she awoke. Monday and Tuesday were the sexton's days off, and she was ready for a break. The church year had begun in earnest, and children were now coming to *La Casa* for tutoring and enrichment programs, so there was more work to do. She planned to take it easy until it was time for her regular biweekly shift at Shadyside.

In no hurry, she lay in bed and thought about Dorie Beaumont and wondered about the rest of her story. On her past two shifts she had not seen Martha Wisner. Unfortunately, the old woman had contracted pneumonia after what had seemed like a minor cold and spent several days in intensive care at the hospital before being released to a unit at the home that had round-the-clock nursing care.

Elisa had visited during her breaks, but each time Martha had been sleeping soundly. Luckily she was improving and would return to her old room soon, but probably not in time for Elisa's shift that night. Elisa was sorry both for the woman's ill health and because she had not been able to finish Dorie's story. Martha had so enjoyed telling the portion she had recounted before growing sleepy.

Elisa hadn't told Sam what she had learned. She told herself there was more to come, and there was no point in recounting bits and pieces. But truthfully, she was afraid to tell him. If the house had real historic value, it would come under scrutiny from historians and journalists. She did not want to give interviews about how she had found the hidden room. She wanted to fade into the background, and she did not want to tell Sam why.

Once she swung her feet over the side of the bed, she heard noises downstairs, not the usual noises of Helen making coffee or frying bacon, but conversation. She showered quickly and changed into clean clothes before she descended the stairs. She expected to find one of the Wednesday morning quilters swapping fabric with

Helen or using the swaybacked Ping-Pong table in Helen's basement to lay out a quilt for basting. As far as Elisa could tell, basting was the sole reason Helen had asked Zeke's father to load the table — a discard from someone's yard sale — in his pickup to haul it here. Elisa hadn't had the heart to enforce the "no trash" rule. Besides, the Ping-Pong table was getting plenty of use.

On the first floor she found a family reunion. Nancy had arrived with her husband Billy, a distinguished-looking gray-haired man with a warm smile, and Tessa, who was wearing a loose green sundress. Tessa's husband Mack arrived just as Elisa was greeting the Whitlocks, and a gray-and-white sheepdog, eyes hidden under long bangs, bounded in behind him and went straight to Elisa to be petted. Four pets into it she knew this dog, too, was a friend.

"A person can hardly breathe around here today," Helen grumbled. "I take a wrong step and there'll be somebody or something underfoot."

"You love every minute of it," Nancy said, unperturbed. "Besides, most of us are heading out in a minute, and we're taking Biscuit with us."

"You just got here," Helen said, in a transparent about-face. "What's your hurry?"

"We're going to clean out the bluebird boxes one last time and winterize them," Mack told her.

Elisa liked Tessa's husband, although she'd only spoken to him briefly. Like Sam, he was a man who was rarely still. He had curly dark hair and a tan that proved his hours of practicing law were balanced by time in the sunshine. She liked the way he looked at his wife, too.

"I'm staying here," Tessa told Helen. "They're walking farther than I have the energy to go. And besides, I need help on the baby quilt. Will you have time?"

Helen looked as if she was thinking that over, but Elisa could tell she was absolutely delighted.

"I have errands to run this morning," Elisa said.

"No, you don't," Helen said. "You're just trying to be polite, and you don't need to be. Am I polite?"

Elisa laughed. "I will be polite and not answer that. If I'm not polite, I might find my clothes in the middle of Fitch Crossing Road."

"Please stay," Tessa said. "She won't

criticize my quilting so loudly if there's someone else in the house."

"Like that would stop her," Nancy said.

"You stay and I'll teach you to quilt today, too," Helen said, glaring at her daughter, but addressing the words to Elisa. "You said you wanted to learn. Today's the day."

"I don't have fabric or thread," Elisa said.

"You've lived here a couple of weeks already, girl. You're trying to tell me you haven't noticed I have plenty of both?"

Elisa knew her fate was sealed. "Maybe Tessa and I can protect each other."

"Don't you wish," Nancy said with a smile. "I'd stay, too, only I probably like hiking more than I like sewing."

"And you like shopping about a million times more than either," Helen said. "And getting your hair fixed and your nails done."

Nancy kissed her on the cheek. "Bye, Mama. You have just the nicest possible morning. We'll be back when we can't think of any other reasons to stay away."

Helen's struggle not to smile was unsuccessful. "Oh, go on and get out of here. All of you."

There was a flurry of goodbyes, and a minute later the three women were alone.

"So what kind of problem are you having?" Helen asked Tessa.

"None. I just needed an excuse to stay here. If Mack thought I really wanted to walk the bluebird trail, he would slow down and make me rest every ten minutes." She made a face. "And it's still hot enough that he'd be right."

"Let's see that quilt."

"Only if you promise not to criticize."

"Have you ever known me not to criticize?"

Elisa joined in. "Let's see, Tessa. I'll throw my body between you if I have to."

Tessa reached into a green canvas bag and brought out a rainbow hued patchwork top. "I sewed the last row last night. I think I'm ready to put it together and quilt it."

Elisa was enchanted. The top was made of small rectangles of many different fabrics sewn into rows. Because of the way Tessa had placed the rectangles, diagonal bands of color waltzed across the top. "Oh, this is just beautiful," she said. "And so bright. A baby will love this."

"Do you think so?"

"I think it's perfect."

Helen took the top from her granddaughter's hands and examined it. "Well, I see a few places where the corners don't quite meet, but I have to say, this is better than I expected. You seem to have the knack. Not that one quilt is much proof of anything."

Tessa smiled. "Do you think so?"

"I said so, didn't I?"

"What do you think, should I sew a border? Or leave it the way it is and start quilting? Here's some border fabric I bought, just in case."

Elisa listened to them discuss the merits of both ideas. Obviously the two generations were on their way to a meeting of the minds, and quilting was going to be a new bond between them.

The two women settled on a border using a solid lavender fabric to tone down the busyness of the prints. Helen suggested a width, and Tessa started upstairs to the sewing room to use Helen's cutting table.

"Now, your turn," Helen told Elisa. "No baby in sight, so let's talk about what you'd like to start with."

Elisa hadn't thought that far ahead. Now she realized how futile a large project would be. She owned nothing that wouldn't fit into a medium-sized backpack and almost nothing to which she had any attachment. "Something to hang on the wall?"

"Do you see quilts hanging on my walls?"

"I . . . how do you say it here . . . I travel lightly?"

"Travel light. I forget sometimes you're not from here. You talk like you are most of the time. Your English is better than mine."

"Sometimes the idioms trip me up."

"A sofa quilt, then. Something to keep you warm while you read or watch television. And we'll use a lightweight batting so it can be folded into a small bundle. What use is a wall hanging? Does the wall need to stay warm?"

Despite herself, Elisa liked the idea of a small but sensible quilt.

"First, though, we need to see if you can sew a straight seam. Can you?"

"I took sewing in school. But that was a long time ago."

"You get yourself some breakfast, then you come up and see my machines. You can use one of the extras."

One bowl of cereal later, Elisa was given the sewing machine tour. Helen's reluctant pride and joy was a state-of-the-art machine made with Swiss precision.

"Nancy and Billy gave me this for Christmas," Helen said. "Even though I told them it was a waste of money, because I don't want all these fancy stitches."

"You're using them, aren't you?" Tessa asked. She was bending over the cutting table that stood by the windows looking down over the chicken yard and the pond. "I've seen evidence."

"Well, somebody spends all that money, I guess I have to use them whether I want to or not," Helen said with a sniff. "But my mama'd be turning over in her grave if she saw the stuff that machine can do. What's next? I push a button and it picks out the fabric, cuts it and sews it together while I go get my toenails polished?"

"If that happens, we'll have to buy one for Mom so she can quilt, too," Tessa said.

Helen's eyes danced as she turned back to Elisa. "You'll want to start with something simpler."

Elisa agreed. She was afraid Helen's new machine would require a crash course in twenty-first century computer technology before she could even turn it on. She glanced at the two machines set up against the wall, as Helen told her about them, but her eyes shifted to the end of the room.

"Mrs. Henry," she said, when Helen

took a breath. "What's that one?" She pointed.

"That's my mama's machine, made by New Home back in the early 1900s. Every quilt she made, she made on that machine. Never wanted anything different. Never needed anything better. She used that and kept her family warm."

Elisa wandered over to the machine and ran her fingers over it. The lettering said "Ruby," although it had faded through the years. There were ornate gold scrollwork designs on the machine and the metal bed. The cabinet looked like cherry. Obviously Helen dusted it regularly, and Elisa bet the machine was oiled and cared for regularly, too. "Do you ever use it?"

"I'm too busy trying to figure out how to use the eight hundred and something stitches mine come with." She watched Elisa trail her fingers over the machine. "You ever use a treadle?"

"I had a few lessons once." She paused, proofed her words, then added, "A woman without electricity showed me how to use one. She made clothes and anything else she could to help provide for her family. She taught me a little. Her husband also wove cloth on a treadle loom. I like that rhythm, the back and forth, back and forth . . ."

"Why don't you use this one, then? My mama — her name was Delilah — she would have liked nothing better than for someone to use the machine."

Elisa was sorry she'd made such a point of it. "It's an heirloom. What if something went wrong?"

"You think something's going to go wrong now? When nothing did all those years? Besides, it's better if it gets used, better for the machine and maybe better for my conscience. I've had it looked after through the years. I don't like to have a thing in my house not being used."

"Nor does she like to throw things away," Tessa said, from the other side of the room.

"You know, Miss Tessa, you want help with that quilt of yours, you just better plan on being a little nicer."

Helen left, then returned a few moments later with thread and some fabric scraps. She showed Elisa how to thread the machine, then gave a quick demonstration.

"Place both feet on the treadle. I was taught to put the right one a little ahead of the left, but you have to find out what works for you. You start it by turning the wheel with your hand." She turned the wheel and began to rock her feet. The machine made a soft, steady clanking noise.

"There are a lot of little tricks Mama taught me. If you stop with the treadle flipped toward you, when you start back up, most of the time the wheel goes the way you want it to. Takes some getting used to, all of it. You play with it a while with no thread, and see if you want to go to all this trouble. I got a White and a Pfaff powered by good old electricity, if you change your mind."

Elisa was enchanted with the rhythmic click and clack of the treadle. "I'll try this a while and see if I can get the hang of it."

Helen lifted her big-boned body off the chair and moved to one side so Elisa could sit. "Only other person I ever knew with the good sense to hold on to one of these old machines was Martha Wisner. She had her mother's old Singer. Used it to make doll clothes and such for the church bazaar, but never did no work by hand on them. Somebody else had to do that and finish them."

Elisa remembered that Martha had said she was no needlewoman. "What happened to it?"

"I suspect Dovey Lanning took it when they moved Martha, along with a few other things Martha couldn't take along. They were good friends, those two. Been hard on Dovey, seeing Martha slipping the way she is."

"Were you close to Martha?"

"Me? I stopped going to church much for years. Just got back into it when the Bee started up again. I knew Martha a long time, of course, but just to say a word to now and then."

Elisa had hoped Helen might know something about the hidden room, but obviously that wasn't the case. She wondered what Dovey knew and decided to ask if the chance arose.

Helen went to help Tessa with her borders, and Elisa practiced turning the wheel and rocking the treadle. The lessons she'd had seemed like a thousand years ago, and at first the needle moved up and down in fits and starts. After a while, though, she began to relax, and as she moved her feet and hand, she established a regular tempo. Eventually she tried stopping and starting after a few stitches. She pretended to turn the imaginary fabric, starting up again, stopping.

Helen came back and watched. "Looks like you're more or less getting the hang of things. Thread it up the way I showed you, and see what you can do."

Half an hour later, Elisa had managed to sew several seams without breaking her thread. She was tired but pleased. This was unlike anything else in her life. During the time she'd practiced using the treadle, she hadn't thought of anything. Her mind had floated.

Helen and Tessa were ready to go back downstairs. "You coming?" Helen asked.

"I'll just practice a little longer."

"When you're done, you look through that fabric and see if anything looks promising." Helen pointed to a shelf against the wall. "I got lots I don't have any plans for yet. It's all stacked there. You look through it and take anything you want. Then bring it down and we'll talk about a pattern."

"Something simple."

"Too simple and you'll be bored silly."

Elisa practiced until her shoulders began to ache. She cleaned up the scraps of fabric, then wandered over to the shelves where Helen's extra fabric was stored. The accumulation was extraordinary. She had folded the pieces neatly and sorted most of them by color. A few shelves seemed to be sorted by types. One held fabrics that looked to be hand-dyed. Another held children's prints of assorted colors and patterns, puppies and kites and frogs. But it was the bottom shelf that caught Elisa's eye. She squatted on the floor and pulled out pieces of handwoven fabric in primary colors.

Helen found her there a little while later, surrounded by small piles of fabric in a circle around her. "Tessa's making an early lunch. She's setting the table for three."

Elisa looked up. "Thank you."

"What'd you find?"

"These are so beautiful." She held up pieces of the fabric. "They're from Guatemala, aren't they?" It was a rhetorical question.

"I guess so. Peony Greenway, from the Bee, went there on a tour and bought a whole lot of pieces. She used some in a quilt and gave me the scraps when she was cleaning out her sewing room. Peony's one of those people who just can't stand a mess. She has more than three colors on the shelf, it makes her nervous." Helen shook her head in wonder.

"You can't really mean you don't have plans for these."

"No large pieces there. Just scraps of this and that. I don't need it, but I just couldn't throw it out. The colors are too pretty." She read the expression on Elisa's face. "You want this? You'd be doing me a big favor to use it up. There aren't enough years left for me to use everything I have already, and that's not something I got any plans for."

"You're sure?"

"We'll have to find a pattern that lends itself to scraps, but that won't be hard. You can combine this with that, and before you know, you've got a quilt. There's plenty of fabric here."

Elisa gathered up the scraps, folded those that needed it again, and set them in piles on the bottom shelf. She already felt like the scraps were old friends, and she was sorry to relegate them to disuse, even temporarily.

Downstairs, Helen told Tessa what fabrics she'd chosen, and Tessa offered to help look through quilt magazines after lunch to find a pattern she liked. Helen had promised to make a cake for a church bake sale, and after they'd eaten tuna sandwiches, she exiled them to the living room, where the most recent quilting magazines and her large collection of books were neatly displayed.

They sat on each end of the sofa, and piled books and magazines in between. "I want something graphic and bold," Elisa said. "Something geometric."

"Gotcha," Tessa said. "Nothing fussy. You want the fabrics to speak for themselves."

That was exactly right. They began thumbing through patterns. Elisa liked a lot of what she saw, but nothing was quite right for the wide collection of fabrics. The segments needed to be small, but large enough to show off the patterns.

Tessa showed her a few, and one — a traditional flying geese block set in vertical rows — interested her, but not enough for the work involved. They sat in companionable silence going through books, commenting on what they saw from time to time like old friends.

"I'm surprised the hikers aren't back yet," Tessa said, finishing one book and picking up a stack of magazines to leaf through next.

"How far were they going?"

"Almost to the river. But I guess it takes time to clean and winterize the houses. Dad wants to give any bird that needs one a warm place on the coldest days. Then early next spring they'll remove the insulation and get the boxes ready again."

"That sounds like a lot of work."

"Have you seen bluebirds? They're worth saving. I'll take you bird-watching one day after the baby's born. I took my daughter as soon as she was old enough to prop up in a backpack."

Elisa wondered if she would be in Toms Brook that long. The thought of leaving saddened her. Despite her best instincts, she was making friends.

And then there was Sam.

"Mack's not much of a bird-watcher, but he likes hiking," Tessa said.

"He does lots of it?"

"No, he doesn't have nearly as much time as he'd like. His law practice would take up every minute if he let it."

Elisa knew Tessa was a high-school English teacher on maternity leave for the school year and that Mack was a lawyer, but she didn't know any details. "What kind of law?" she asked.

"When it comes down to it, Mack just defends people who need him. Sometimes criminal law, sometimes civil rights, sometimes just lawsuits nobody else wants to bother with because the potential rewards are few. He tilts at windmills."

"Don Quixote. I know the story."

"Actually, Mack's a lot more successful and perceptive than poor Quixote ever was. But sometimes he goes blindly into cases, absolutely sure he's right even if he knows he won't win. He takes on some very big enemies."

Elisa stopped turning pages. "This doesn't worry you?"

"Sometimes. I know it takes a toll on him."

"But what I mean is, don't you fear for his safety?"

Tessa looked up from her book. "No, he works with the poor and the disenfranchised, not the Mafia. To my knowledge, no one's ever wanted to fit him with concrete shoes."

"He speaks out for the poor, and this doesn't threaten anyone?"

Tessa read her expression accurately. "In this country — and we're not perfect, I know — but most of the time we're safe when we express an opinion, even an unpopular one. Things aren't as easygoing as they were before the attacks on the World Trade Center, but Mack sees his job as speaking for greater freedom. And that's still legal."

"Where I come from, speaking out has often been more dangerous than cancer or heart disease. What your Mack does is important."

Tessa was silent a moment; then she nodded. "I don't always remember that, I admit. But of course you're right. I'm proud of him."

Elisa thought of Sam again, another man who thought about what was right and not about results. Sam and Mack had more in common than energy and warm smiles.

"What do you think of this pattern?" Tessa held out a magazine to Elisa. "It's bold and geometric. Small pieces, but I think bright colors and sharp contrasts would be very effective."

Elisa took the magazine and examined the photograph of a quilt. "Endless Chain." The blocks were hexagonal, with spokes radiating from a circle in the middle. The spokes connected, so that the design seemed to have no beginning and no end.

"Yes," she said. "It's like the fabrics are holding hands."

"To keep out intruders?"

"No, in solidarity. To keep out those who would try to destroy them."

Tessa touched her hand. "I've learned a lot from Gram. Quilts mean so many different things to different people. But in the end, the quilts we make are always about something in our hearts."

Monday was Sam's only real day off. He

was careful to keep it that way, refusing any church obligations except emergencies. He was on call six days a week, and time away made him a better minister. But by evening he wished he had a meeting, a worship service, something to lead. He had been restless all day, and the usual Monday chores and errands had not kept him from thinking.

Christine had called early that morning before leaving for The Savior's Academy, and they'd had a pleasant enough conversation. They had discussed his upcoming visit. She had told him about problems she was having with a teacher and about the new testing guidelines that were going to create extra work for her staff. He told her about the opening of *La Casa* and the eight children who were coming regularly to be tutored. For once she asked all the right questions, even promised to send books to help the children with their English. But he'd felt, as he often did, that Christine viewed his work here as a hobby to pursue while he decided what he really wanted to do with his life. He did not miss her after he hung up.

Sam knew Christine was part of the reason he had been restless. And if he was absolutely honest with himself, he knew the other part was knowing he would not see Elisa today or tomorrow. The break was good. It gave him time for stern, silent lectures about priorities and proprieties. But he missed her, and acknowledging it made him even more uneasy about his situation.

By the time the sun started to set he realized the house was closing in on him, and he had to get out. Shad and Shack were ready for serious exercise, and as the sun disappeared and the air cooled, he realized a run was exactly what he needed, too.

The dogs followed him into the bedroom and managed to make a dance out of changing into running shorts and shoes as he leapt and twisted to avoid them. He promised Bed he would take her for a walk when he and the big dogs returned, and gave her a dog biscuit to compensate for short legs.

Then, Shad and Shack at his side, leashes in his pocket, he started along a path behind his house.

He had developed a jogging route that kept the dogs off the road, and now the three of them wove through lanes and across open meadows and fields until they were nearly at the church, where he wanted to retrieve a book. He snapped the leashes in place, and he and the dogs jogged along the shoulder. There were no cars tonight, but he'd learned the hard way that country people ignored speed limits on "their" roads and took them at Indie 500 velocity. A few months ago Shad had nearly been hit by a van flying around a curve, and Sam was always careful now to keep both dogs tethered when traffic might be an issue.

He was almost at the church before he simultaneously saw and heard two pickups screeching out of the lot. A radio blared hip-hop from one. Tires squealed, and he heard shouts from the occupants, who sounded like teenagers.

He was immediately suspicious. Most of the time the church was deserted on Monday nights, a fact any locals who paid attention knew. He hoped the parking lot hadn't become a Monday haven for drug and alcohol use. This was a school night, and he wondered if the parents of these kids had any idea where they were.

He checked the new sign immediately to see if it had finally succumbed to vandalism, and he was glad to see it was unharmed. Trash was strewn in the parking lot, fast-food wrappers and, as he'd feared, beer cans. He cleaned up as he walked, but he started to get worried when the trash didn't stop at the edge of the lot. He followed the trail around the side of the building with the dogs scampering ahead of him, noses to the ground.

The trash ended eventually, but the dogs kept moving toward *La Casa.* He considered pulling them back. He felt certain the kids would have parked closer if vandalizing the old house had been on their minds, but checking would help him sleep better that night. He let the dogs off their leashes and followed in their wake.

The skies had darkened, and he was only yards away from the house before he realized that the teenagers *had* been here. Perhaps they had parked here first, or perhaps they had wandered the grounds until they came upon the house. Whichever it was, the cheery yellow paint of *La Casa Amarilla* was now marred by shiny black graffiti.

"Go home, wetbacks," he read out loud. His hands clenched. "Spics get out."

He was so furious, he was glad the boys had left when they did. He wasn't sure what he would have done to them if he had found this first.

The dogs were up on the porch now, and he heard a yip from one of them. He jogged up the steps and found Shad standing amidst broken glass. He used the toe and side of his jogging shoe to clear a path for the dog and coaxed him away. He determined that Shad's front paw was cut, but the cut didn't look deep. The window looking out on the porch was broken, though, and in the last of the day's fading light, Sam could see that the inside of the pretty little house had been vandalized, too. Furniture and shelves had been over-turned. Every single poster had been ripped off the walls and thrown into a heap. He saw the wall quilt that had deco-rated the stairwell lying in a wad.

He stooped and pulled out his cell phone, and, with his arm around his trem-bling dog, he dialed the sheriff's office.

Chapter Thirteen

On Tuesday, Elisa pulled into the space beside Adoncia's trailer and turned off the engine. Last night's shift at the nursing home
had been uneventful, although once again
she had not been able to see Martha. She
had gotten home at a little past seven this
morning and gone straight to bed, waking
up about ten. She planned to go to bed
early tonight to catch up for the week.

On waking, she had showered and
dressed, then gone to find Helen. Instead,
she had found a note on the table and bad
news. She called the church immediately.

Now, as she got out of the car at
Adoncia's, Maria ran outside to greet her.
Elisa swung the little girl to her hip, lis-
tening as she chattered in a mixture of
Spanish and English about her morning.

Inside, she swung Fernando to the other

hip and listened as he babbled in no language she'd ever heard. When the children were satisfied they'd had her devoted attention, they both scrambled down and went back to "Sesame Street" on television.

"Hey, Elisa," Adoncia said from the kitchen. *"¿Que pasa?"*

Elisa slung her purse on the table and took a chair. "Donchita, *La Casa Amarilla* was vandalized last night. Graffiti sprayed on the outside walls and the inside half destroyed."

Adoncia was sautéing onions and garlic at the stove, her hips swaying as she stirred. "Who would do such a thing?"

"I guess Sam saw a couple of old pickups filled with teenage boys. Too bad he didn't catch them in the act. He called around this morning to see if he could find volunteers to help him get the outside cleaned and painted. Mrs. Henry went to help. She left me a note."

Adoncia turned off the burner. "Not everyone is glad the church helps our children?"

"I'm angry he didn't call *me.* I'm the sexton."

"Isn't Tuesday a day off?"

"Sam knows how strongly I would feel about this."

"Perhaps he also knows how hard you work and how tired you are."

Helen had not scribbled many of the details. Elisa had discovered most of her information from the call to Gracie Barnhardt.

"He wants the front looking as normal as possible when the children arrive on the bus. It's too late to get the school to change plans and take them home. Red tape."

"They put tape on the house?"

"No, I mean the authorities at the school have to follow a plan once it's put on paper. They can't adjust it so quickly."

Adoncia nodded. "So the children have to go to the church."

"Yes, but once they're off the bus, Sam and the volunteers are going to take them to the Sunday School wing, then home after tutoring."

"This is very thoughtful, no? They are trying to protect our babies."

"Here's the truth," Elisa went on. "The only people who are around during the day to help are older or infirm, or at home with small children. Helen is in her eighties. Everyone else is off at work. What can they do? Can they repaint the entire front of a house in a few hours?"

"Probably no."

"I'd like to see if we can round up some of our friends, and maybe some of the men who aren't working today. *La Casa* is for our children, isn't it? Shouldn't we be doing anything we can?"

Adoncia thought for a moment. "I will take Nando and Maria to Nana Garcia. She will watch them for me. She lives to watch my children."

"We need to do this quickly. I'll see who I can round up."

"The Ortegas have guests. Two young men who just came here and are looking for work. Maybe they would help."

"Are they family?"

"I don't think so. I'm not sure why they came here, but they can be trusted. Patia and Manuel are letting them stay until they can find a better place and a job."

Elisa's heart sped a little. She told herself not to hope. "I'll go there while you dress. Patia will help me enlist the others. We can drop the children at your mother-in-law's on our way to the church."

Outside, she hurried between mobile homes until she came to the one belonging to Patia Ortega. She rapped on the door, then stepped back to wait. Her breath caught when a young man in his early twenties answered the door. He was medium height, with light brown skin and black hair falling over his ears. But a closer look proved he was a stranger. He was not Ramon.

He was not her brother.

"I . . ." She took a deep breath and let it go slowly. "Patia? Is she here?"

Patia came to the door in jeans and a huge T-shirt that spilled halfway to her knees. "Elisa. Come in."

Elisa refused and told the other woman why she had come. "Can you help?" she finished.

"These people at the church, will they really want us there? They want to help our children, but our children aren't taking their jobs. . . ."

"They'll be happy for any help we can give them." As she said the words Elisa wondered how true they were. "If they aren't glad to see us," she added, "then perhaps we should not trust them with our children."

Patia's homely face was a mirror of Elisa's own conflicting emotions. "I'll get ready. Maybe Paco will come if I explain we need a strong man."

"Was that Paco who answered the door? He's here with a friend?"

"No, his friend is staying with family in

Harrisonburg. Paco plans to join him next week unless he finds a job nearby."

"I'm going to see who else I can find to help. Thank you, Patia."

Elisa had known it was unlikely either of Patia's guests would be the young man for whom she had been searching for three long years. She told herself there was still hope her brother would show up in Toms Brook one day soon. Ramon was a survivor. *She* was a survivor. They would find each other again.

She still had to blink back tears.

Sam was managing, somehow, to be both encouraged and discouraged simultaneously. He was encouraged that the quilters had shown up, along with a deacon, who was home from work recovering from bronchitis, and four young mothers with six children in tow. The mothers were taking turns babysitting and scraping paint off the house; the deacon was inside clearing away what he could with his limited strength; and the younger quilters were slapping a second coat of primer on the sections of the exterior that were dry enough to paint.

Last night Sam had trained a hose on the front of the house for the half hour it had taken the sheriff's deputy to arrive. The latex spray paint had still been wet, and he had washed away some of it, turning racial slurs into shapeless gray blobs. Sadly, the words had still been legible if anyone looked closely enough, and even the first coat of primer had not been helpful enough to erase them completely. He hoped a second coat would do the trick. If white splotches were all the children saw, he would be grateful.

He turned when he heard Helen Henry's voice.

"We called everybody we could think of. The place will be humming after five."

"We can use everybody we get. There's enough damage inside to keep them busy until midnight."

"They pulled all our quilts off the walls and poured paint from the supply closet on them. Who would go out of their way to be that hateful? Used to be a little mischief around here, just for fun, but most of the time parents rode herd on their kids."

"I'm particularly sorry about the quilts." And he was. So many hours had gone into them, and their bright colors and warmth had made the children feel at home.

Helen sniffed. "Gracie said to tell you the sheriff called. He got a lead on one of those pickups. Somebody seen it burning rubber down the road about the time you got here last night. She might have recognized the driver. Sheriff says he'll come by later if he has any news."

Sam wondered if Leon Jenkins had been involved in the vandalism. He doubted it, considering the boy's sincere and unsolicited apology, although Leon might know who the boys were. One way or the other, Sam doubted Leon would tell the sheriff much.

"It's nigh lunchtime," Helen said. "We collected money from everybody. Dovey and me, we'll make a trip to the store and slap together something simple when we get back. I can't clean or paint worth a hoot, but I can still make a sandwich."

Sam thanked her, and a few minutes later Dovey's car pulled away. The parking spot was claimed immediately by a silver Lexus sedan. An unfamiliar woman got out. She was tall and reed-slender, with curly brown hair that fell to her shoulders. As she came toward him, he noted a freckled face disguised at least partly by a light tan, wide-spaced hazel eyes and a generous mouth. He wasn't quite sure how she had done it, but somehow, in beautifully cut jeans and a sage green shirt, she projected modesty and urban sophistication at the same time.

"Reverend Kinkade?"

He faced her. "I'm Sam Kinkade." He held out his hand.

"Kendra Taylor. We had an appointment at eleven."

He remembered now. She had called to find out more about the church, and he had invited her to come to his office and talk. She lived in Washington, he thought, or one of its suburbs, but she and her husband owned land nearby.

"I'm sorry I wasn't in the office," he apologized. "We had an emergency, and to be honest, everything else slipped my mind."

"Your secretary told me what happened."

He hated to leave the workers, but this woman had come a long distance to meet with him. Fortunately, she waved her hand when he suggested they go back to his office.

"Not on your life," she said. "I'm going to help. We can talk another time."

"That's very thoughtful."

"Tell me why the boys did this," she said. "I write features for the *Washington Post*, and this kind of behavior intrigues me."

"It's an isolated incident. I don't want

this blown up into a story for the paper."

"Is it? An isolated incident? Or is it a part of a wider backlash against immigrants in the area? There's evidence Latino gangs are forming in the Valley, and I'm sure some people are worried. Is this a reaction?"

Sam wasn't certain, and he told her so. Kendra seemed to accept this. "I'll probably do some digging, but whatever I find has nothing to do with helping here today. I'll do that as a friend."

"We can always use friends." He called Anna Mayhew, who was one of the painters, to meet Kendra. Anna suggested that Kendra work inside, cleaning and sorting, and Kendra graciously agreed.

He was about to start tossing bags of trash into the back of his SUV when he heard another car. He looked up and saw his own Honda, packed with women, parking on the side of the lane leading to *La Casa.* Elisa got out, and like circus clowns, five more women wriggled out, all stretching and breathing deeply once they emerged.

"Elisa?" He walked over to greet her. "What are you doing here?"

"So, you don't even let me know, Sam?" Her dark eyes flashed. "You think this should be kept a secret?"

"I think you should have Tuesdays off, the way we agreed." He was so glad to see her that he couldn't look contrite or simply pastoral. He was afraid his eyes said everything. "But I'm glad you're here."

Some of the fire went out of her. "Next time, you trust me enough to let *me* decide whether I want to help. ¿*Entiendes?*"

"If I say yes, what have I agreed to?"

"You need some Spanish lessons."

For just a moment he envisioned Elisa teaching him. The vision didn't include a classroom.

She stepped back. "These are my friends. You've met Adoncia. This is Patia, and Inez." She put names to the next two faces. "They are here to help clean the mess those boys made. There is another car coming with some men, as well."

Sam shook hands with all the women. He tried to convey how pleased he was to have them there. The other car pulled up, and Elisa introduced him to two more women and two men. He said a prayer of thanksgiving for the men, since until that point his had been the only strong back in the place.

He greeted everyone with enthusiasm, but he saw the way their gazes went to the hateful words, still legible on the front of the house.

"I'm sorry," he said simply. "But cans of spray paint don't express the real feelings of a community, just the thoughts of some ignorant boys who had nothing better to do on a Monday night."

"You think we don't hear these things or see them in other places?" Adoncia asked. "If it were just these boys, the world would be a better place than it is."

"Everyone is welcome in this church, and all of you are very much appreciated today. I'm glad you're here."

Adoncia nodded. "We are glad you want to help our children. Today we'll help you." She motioned for the others to follow her. Elisa stayed behind as the painters came to greet the new arrivals and put them to work.

"I guess I was trying to protect you," he told her, before she could say anything more. "I didn't want you to see what the boys sprayed on the house."

"It's been a long time since anyone wanted to protect me." Her gaze softened. "But you understand that this is part of daily life, particularly for those whose English isn't good? We're wanted for our strong backs and willingness to work, but not for any other reason."

"Has that been your experience?"

Her smile was thin enough to be a veneer. "Only when I let it be. I've spoken English since I was a child. To look at me, I could be Italian or Greek or even Mideastern. Of course, Mideastern would make me even less popular these days. Prejudice in this country is like chapters in a book. Chapter One: Hating the Africans and Indians. Chapter Two: Don't Forget the Irish. Chapter Three: Polish jokes." She shrugged. "Hispanics? Latinos? Whatever you call us? Maybe we're Chapter Fifteen or Sixteen on the East Coast, but we're the preface in the West."

"If you know about Polish jokes, you've been well acquainted with this culture for some time."

She seemed to step back without moving a muscle. "What shall I do, Sam? Would you like me to clean inside?"

"Helen's gone to buy food. When she gets back, I bet she'd like to have help putting lunch together."

"Adoncia's a wonderful cook. Maybe that's where she'd be best, too."

He could not let this opportunity pass. He felt he'd been on the verge of discovery. "You've spoken English since childhood?

That doesn't surprise me. And you've had a good education, haven't you? Someday, will you tell me what you're doing here?"

"*La verdad a medias es mentira verdadera.*"

"The Spanish lessons have begun?"

"Half a truth is a whole lie." Her expression was troubled. "I would prefer not to lie to you, Sam."

He suspected she was telling him a lot, without telling him anything. She started to turn away, but he put his hand on her arm. "Have you lied to me already?"

She didn't answer directly. "I have always tried to tell you as much of the truth as I can. Make of that what you will."

He dropped his hand, although he didn't want to. "I can be trusted. You don't have any reason to be afraid of me."

"I have reasons to be afraid of everyone."

She left to intercept Adoncia for a trip to the church kitchen. Sam wondered if he would ever know who she really was.

"Ah, you think you know what it's like to be poor," Adoncia told Helen, "but I bet you never made soup from the same chicken four times."

"Four times? We were so poor when I

was a girl, on Thanksgiving day we split one miserable little hen among my family and my aunt's besides, and still made soup from the bones and feet and sucked the toes." Helen's eyes sparkled. "Then we buried the feathers in our garden for fertilizer!"

"Ha! You had a garden? We were so poor we just had pots on a windowsill. We had to grow everything we ate in four little pots. For a family of twelve."

"You could afford pots? We used rusted tin cans from the landfill."

Adoncia giggled. "You had a landfill? We had no trash to put in such a thing. Who could afford trash?"

Adoncia and Helen had been trading absurd stories from the moment they'd set eyes on each other. Rarely had Elisa seen two people take to each other so quickly. She wondered how long it would be before Helen had Adoncia and maybe the other women at the park making quilts.

"Okay, you two," Elisa said. "It's a tie. You were both poor. And each of you is as good a liar as the other."

"Oh, don't spoil our fun," Helen said. She was sitting at a wide metal table in the middle of the kitchen, slapping sandwiches together from cold cuts and bread she and

Dovey had bought at the store. Adoncia was at the industrial-sized stove, finishing a slapdash chili using ingredients she'd dug out of the church freezer and cupboards. Adoncia could make a meal out of anything.

"I think Helen and I should go to this landfill of hers and see what we can find together," Adoncia said. "We could probably furnish a house or two."

"Both of you need to be carefully watched." Elisa poured the tea she'd brewed into glasses filled with ice, then set them on a tray. She had already set up tables in the social hall for the workers.

"Adoncia, I'll need your telephone number," Helen said with a loudly audible sniff. "So we can talk when she's not around to snoop."

Elisa laughed. "I'll tell everybody lunch is ready."

"Oh, good, some time alone," Adoncia told Helen.

Still smiling, Elisa left the church for *La Casa*, wondering what she would find.

Sam was standing in front with hands dug into the pockets of his jeans, admiring the progress. She halted beside him and gave a low whistle. "The words are gone."

"It took a lot more primer than we'd expected, but it'll be ready for yellow paint as soon as that dries."

"You're going ahead?" The original plan had been to simply block out the words so the children wouldn't see them.

"Everybody wants to. We can finish painting after lunch. And they've made so much progress inside, we might even be able to use the house today, although there'll be no computers for a while, not until we get new monitors, at the very least." The boys had smashed every screen, but she knew Sam was hopeful the computers themselves weren't damaged.

"Wouldn't that be great if the kids could come here today?"

He glanced at her. "How do we keep everybody from sitting with their own little group at lunch?"

"We trust them."

"I like the sound of that. I usually trust people to do the right thing."

She suspected he wasn't simply talking about the work crew.

At lunch, just as they'd hoped, the workers sat wherever there was an empty space. Paco, Patia's boarder, whose English was minimal, ended up between Dovey and Gracie Barnhardt and gave impromptu Spanish lessons, using items on the table for vocabulary. If there had been any lingering reservations, they melted completely when several women who hadn't been able to assist that morning arrived with dozens of homemade chocolate chip cookies and giant jugs of freshly squeezed lemonade to finish the meal.

Elisa landed across the table from Sam. The conversation turned to the teenagers in the pickups and hopes the sheriff would apprehend them.

Sam caught her gaze. "The sheriff might need to talk to you, in case he thinks these are the same boys who were with Leon that day. You might be able to help me describe them."

Elisa's last bite of sandwich felt dry in her throat. She didn't quite look at him. "I doubt I can tell him anything. It's been weeks, and I wasn't paying attention to anyone but Leon."

Sam waited until she looked right at him. "They'd only want to know about the boys," he said, softly enough that only she would hear.

"I don't remember a thing."

He didn't look away when he nodded. She was the first to break eye contact. She was sure he had realized that she did not want to talk to the police, whether she remembered details or not. And if he was that astute, he would be growing even more curious about her.

Elisa knew she had already put her future here in jeopardy. Sam had slipped past her defenses too many times. She silently vowed to be more careful.

— By two, the first coat of yellow paint had been spread to cover the multiple coats of primer. Everything that could not be repaired had been hauled away, and Kendra and several of the mothers had driven to the nearest discount store to purchase posters to replace the ones that had been destroyed until more vocabulary posters could be ordered. They returned with several chairs for the kitchen table and another rag rug to replace the one that had been urinated on before the boys left the house.

It was a contest in Sam's mind which act of destruction had most violated the spirit of love and cooperation they had set out to build here.

Sam had not had an opportunity to have more than a moment or two alone with Kendra Taylor or to thank her for her hard work. He found her as she was gathering her things to return to Washington.

"I promise this isn't a typical day at Community Church," he told her.

"Not typical, perhaps, but a good example of people of good will doing whatever they can to change the world."

"Despite setbacks."

"I may well write that story I mentioned, but I'll be sure to make what happened here today as important as what happened yesterday."

"I can't ask for more." He held out his hand. "You'll come back for that talk?"

They shook. "We — my husband and I — own land not far away. I have fantasies of building a house here, Isaac doesn't. I guess I just wanted to check out the community."

"Ammunition to convince your husband?"

"Or to dissuade me. It goes a little deeper than that, but we can talk another time."

"Feel free to come back, Kendra. You'll always be welcome, and so will your husband."

"Isaac is not a churchgoer."

"Then come alone."

"I may be calling for your take on what happened here."

"I'll be available."

One by one the volunteers said goodbye. He watched Elisa leave with her carload of friends from the park, followed by the others who had come separately. He had thanked each of them personally, and he hoped they knew how genuine his appreciation was. He'd had an idea, too, when saying goodbye to Patia and Paco. If the young man checked out and was willing, Sam thought he might be able to persuade the deacons to allow Paco to stay upstairs at *La Casa* for extra security. There was a room that wasn't in use that could be fixed up quickly in exchange for patrolling the grounds in the evening and keeping his eyes and ears open. And Paco could use the kitchen and bath downstairs. Of course, they would have to teach him some rudimentary English in case he had to call the police.

The tutors began to arrive, although some had come earlier to clean and merely needed to stay on. Soon after, the school bus arrived and eight children got off, walking shyly up the drive to their newly painted yellow house. Sam was proud and sad simultaneously, and he hoped that they would not be upset that the computers wouldn't be available today.

Three little girls, holding hands, came to

greet him. Two boys of seven and eight had run full tilt for the porch, waving as they passed. An older boy of twelve and two older girls walked slowly past, pretending not to notice him. But just when it was almost too late, each one shot him a smile before climbing the steps to be greeted by the tutors. Together everyone had decided the tutors would explain only the basics. Some boys with nothing better to do had damaged some things, but in a few days the house would look almost the same.

Once the children settled in, Sam planned to bring popcorn and cider for their snack, to go with chocolate chip cookies saved for them by the morning's volunteers. An extra treat seemed in order.

The front door had closed and the children were safely inside under the care of the tutors when another young man came trudging down the drive. Surprised, Sam waited for Leon Jenkins to reach him.

"How did you get here?" Sam asked.

"School's out. Somebody dropped me off."

Sam was casting around for the right way to begin his interrogation when Leon jammed his hands under his arms. "I, well, I just wanted you to know, like, I didn't have anything to do with this. I guess you probably thought I did, right?"

Sam searched the boy's face. Leon looked sorry, but not as if he felt personally responsible.

"I considered it," Sam said honestly, "but I decided it didn't fit. I believed your apology the other day. Nobody dragged it out of you. And I think you're too strong to go along with something this vicious."

"I tried to destroy the sign out front."

"People change if they're given the motivation. I think you learned what you needed to from that experience."

Leon met his eyes. "The thing is, Reverend Sam, I'm pretty sure I know who did this. But I can't tell you."

"Why not?"

"Because somebody else told *me,* and, well, I promised I wouldn't say anything. She's afraid she'll get in trouble. One of the guys is her cousin."

It took Sam a moment to put all that together. "So you're caught? If you tell, you betray a friend. If you don't, you betray your church."

"I, well, uh-huh. That's about it."

"I saw one of the pickups, and somebody down the road got a better look when it passed her house. It's only a matter of time. The sheriff will figure it out."

The boy looked relieved.

"Is there anything you can tell me?" Sam asked. "Without betraying any promises?"

"I could tell you the names of the guys who were with me, when, you know, I tried to knock down the sign that day. You could figure that out just by looking at the yearbook. I guess I could make it easier."

"And that would help?"

Leon was careful not to give too much away. He shrugged. Sam knew that was as good as a yes.

"That afternoon when I, well, you know?" the boy went on. "I was trying to impress some people. Now look what happened."

"Son, you're talking to the master of 'act, don't think.' I can't tell you how many times I've followed an impulse and regretted it later." Sam thought about Elisa, but he knew that explanation was too simple. His feelings about his sexton had grown well beyond impulse into something deeper and harder to control.

"It doesn't get easier when you get older?" Leon asked.

"Some things just get more difficult, but hopefully by then you have the strength to do what's right." Sam put his arm around

Leon's shoulders and pulled him toward the church. "Come on and help me pop some corn and pour some cider. Then I'll take you home."

"If you do, you'd better just drop me off at the gate."

"One morning next week I'm going to have another talk with your father and tell him what a good job he's doing with you."

"I don't think he listens much to anybody these days."

Sam knew when silence was better than false reassurances. He just clapped the boy on the back, then they started toward the church together.

Chapter Fourteen

Atlanta's Hartsfield-Jackson airport was as busy as Sam had expected it to be. He had claimed his suitcase by the time Christine made it through the crowd at baggage claim to slip her arms around his waist and rise on tiptoe for a quick kiss.

"The traffic gets worse every single day," she drawled. "If I didn't love you so much, I would have turned around and gone home for iced tea and a dip in the pool."

He hugged her back and felt the welcome softness of her body against his. Fall had not worked its cooler magic today, and Christine was dressed for summer weather in white Capri pants and a coral-colored T-shirt that left just enough of a gap above her waist to tantalize any man with a libido.

"I'm glad you made it." He released her.

"Can I buy you lunch to make up for the traffic?"

"Mother and Daddy are expecting us." Christine made a face, although in no way did it detract from her flamboyant beauty. "Mother's gone all out. She's on a nouveau southern kick, so expect something like chicken gizzards in pesto cream sauce, or pecan and pine nut pie."

"Can we tell them we were in a wreck?"

"Don't say that too loudly. We have a long drive home."

They wound their way to the hourly lot where Christine had parked, and in minutes they were heading north.

Christine drove a silver Audi TT convertible, sporty, classic and perfectly suited to her. She wasn't precisely a menace behind the wheel, but she definitely took no prisoners. Where he was more apt to give his fellow drivers the benefit of the doubt, Christine saw every gap in the adjacent lanes as a challenge.

"You look good, Sam." She looked over her shoulder and squeezed between two semis to make a little extra headway. "Do you realize it's been more than a month since I've seen you?"

He did realize it. Even more, he realized he hadn't thought about her often enough during those weeks. "I'm glad we could work this out."

"Torey is just thrilled you're going to take part in the service tonight. She could hardly say enough good things about you."

He had returned to Atlanta not only to see his fiancée and spend some much-needed time with her, but to do the opening prayer and benediction at the wedding of one of Christine's oldest friends at The Savior's Church. Torey Scoppito had insisted that Sam share honors with Savior's senior pastor, Nigel Fairlington. Sam guessed that between the Fletchers and Scoppitos, enough pressure had been applied that Nigel hadn't been courageous — or foolish — enough to refuse.

Sam knew he should not have come, and he definitely should not have agreed to help with the ceremony. Once again he had put Nigel in an awkward position, and Nigel was not a man who turned the other cheek. In addition to possible career repercussions, Sam would simply have preferred never to darken Savior's door again.

"I'm surprised you had time to pick me up," he said. "No pre-wedding festivities?"

"I'm out of most of them. I'll go over to the church about four to dress and help, but Torey's got a bevy of Scoppito aunts and cousins in addition to her mom and sister, so she already has more women than she needs."

He listened as Christine described Torey's gown, the frou frou dresses originally chosen for the bridesmaids by Torey's mother, and the Vera Wang replacements Christine had tactfully engineered. He watched the familiar scenery race by and felt nostalgia scratching at his defenses.

Christine's account of the trials and tribulations of the Scoppito-Malvern wedding took them nearly to Roswell. The Fletchers lived in North Fulton County, known locally as Atlanta's Golden Corridor. The town was picturesque, wealthy and, for the most part, white. After Hiram's term as governor, the Fletchers had razed the smaller home they'd owned here to build one more suitable for Georgia royalty.

He liked Hiram and Nola Fletcher. There was nothing not to like except, perhaps, a certain casual disregard for people who weren't exactly like them. But he was never comfortable in Christine's family home. Mentally he compared it to the tiny aluminum-sided colonial he had shared with his own parents and siblings.

Throughout his childhood, he and Mark had huddled together in an attic room, steaming in the summer, freezing in the winter. Rachel had been forced to cut through the family's only bathroom to reach her closet-sized bedroom. Now Rachel claimed that waiting endlessly to enter or leave her room while people showered or used the toilet had scarred her for life.

He was definitely not ashamed of his roots or his upbringing. But the contrast with Christine's pointed out the problems between them. She believed Sam was upwardly mobile, desirous of all the benefits and blessings she had been born to. She saw her own background as a gift to bestow on him. All too often Sam saw it as a barrier, an outward symbol of their differing values.

Christine turned on to the road running above the scenic Chattahoochee River, and, after several twists and turns, she slowed. The Fletchers' Georgian home came into view. The house was not quite a mansion, and the eight live-oak-shaded, horse-dotted acres surrounded by white paddock fencing were not quite an estate. But the property bordered on both. The house was cherry brick and just one room deep, angling back toward an awe-inspiring bluestone verandah overlooking the river. A wisteria-draped pergola framed the view and offered shade. The verandah and house could easily contain a crowd of hundreds, and Christine had planned to have their wedding reception here.

In the days when there had been a wedding on the horizon.

Christine slowed to turn into the magnolia-lined drive. "Mother will be serving lunch on the verandah since it's so warm. You know her, she doesn't want to give up a minute of that view."

"I can't blame her. I love it, too."

"Do you?"

"Who wouldn't?"

"Because I was thinking we might get married here."

He let that settle a moment. Then he kept his tone light. "Married? That's a word I don't hear very often in reference to us."

"We're engaged, Sam. Or aren't we?"

He wondered. Exactly what did "engaged" mean except a ring on Christine's finger and occasional chaste forays into each other's lives?

"I assume you don't want to get married at Savior's?" she continued. "I'm willing to forget that, even if they do employ me. If we have the wedding here, no one will think twice about it. They'll simply think I want to take advantage of the setting. And if we have bad weather, we could still do the ceremony indoors. I could come down the staircase."

The staircase in question was a masterpiece, spiral and stone. The Fletchers had purchased it prior to the demolition of a plantation house in southern Georgia and built the house around it. Sam could well imagine Christine slowly walking down the stairs to the requisite oohs and ahs.

"It's a wonderful place for a wedding." He realized how noncommittal that sounded, but he wasn't sure what Christine wanted. She was the one who had backed away from their original wedding date.

"Then you'd agree to it?"

He tried to imagine marrying Christine *here* instead of imagining himself marrying her at all. "I know it's the bride's prerogative to choose a place, but I'm the minister of a church in Virginia. I'm just trying to predict how my congregation would feel if I got married anywhere else."

She pulled into a parking area surrounded on three sides by dogwoods and rows of azaleas so that the cars couldn't be seen from the house. Water droplets clung to leaves, doubtless from a hidden sprinkler system, and they glistened in the morning sunlight.

Christine turned off the engine and faced him. "You don't really expect me to invite my friends and my parents' friends to a wedding at Community Church, do you?"

"Because it's so far away? Or because they'll see how far the mighty has fallen?"

Anger sparkled in her eyes. "That's unfair."

"I don't think so."

She stared at him a moment. "Okay. If we're being honest, I'm hoping you won't even be in Virginia."

"What, you're hoping Nigel will embrace me tonight and beg me to come back as his successor?"

"No! You burned that bridge and blew up the riverbanks while you were at it, didn't you? But there are other churches where the history isn't so painful. Important churches in cities I'd be willing to live in."

He knew it wasn't fair to ask Christine to live just anywhere. The day when the minister's partner simply gave up his or her own career and life and meekly followed a spouse to the next assignment was on the wane. But there was more here than Christine's dislike of rural Virginia. And both of them knew it.

"Mother's going to wonder what we're doing," Christine said at last. "We need to talk this through, but not now, and certainly not here, like this."

"I'm not sure talking will change the basics. I'm not sure I can be who you want me to be."

"I think there's a lot you're not sure of. Don't you think it's a little late for who-do-I-want-to-be-when-I-grow-up and a little early for a midlife crisis?" She sounded matter-of-fact. Christine was not one for self-pity. She had rarely seen a loss she couldn't change to a gain.

His temper flared. "It's also a little late for using bribery to get what you want, Chrissy."

"Bribery?"

"Your hand in marriage if I do what you want and go where you want me to. I got six months for one act of civil disobedience, but you've punished me ever since."

"How fair is that? Everything changed. What was I supposed to do?"

"Not *everything* changed. I'm still the

man I was when I was standing in Savior's pulpit."

"Well, apparently there was a lot of you that wasn't visible. That robe covered more than a nice, solid masculine body. I thought you were logical and rational, that you wanted the things I did and were willing to make some compromises."

"Then you weren't listening to my sermons."

Immediately he wished he hadn't spoken. He had hurt her. Badly enough that he had pierced the brash facade to reveal a woman who saw her life changing and, for once, was powerless to stop it.

He covered her hand with his in apology. "I'm sorry, you're right. This isn't the time or place."

"Maybe it's past time."

"Maybe so, but for the last three years, neither of us wanted to hear what the other had to say."

Christine opened her door. "Sam, let's enjoy the weekend. We need to have fun together and remember how good things can be. Then we can finish this."

As emergency measures went, that wasn't a bad one. He nodded. But were they simply delaying the inevitable?

And how much had his attraction to

Elisa Martinez factored in his responses today? Because throughout the entire conversation, Elisa had hovered in the background, and he despised himself for that.

The Reverend Nigel Fairlington, hale and hearty, silver-haired and silver-tongued, was more welcoming than Sam had expected. He made sure their reunion was witnessed by sympathetic members, of course, and not by those who had signed the petition that had helped remove Sam as Savior's associate pastor. But even this carefully orchestrated sleight of hand had not dimmed Sam's pleasure at the lack of confrontation. In a brief private moment Nigel had thanked him for agreeing to help preside, admitting that appeasing the Scoppitos, who were the church's largest givers, had taken precedence over any lingering resentments about Sam's exit.

"You were young and idealistic," Nigel said magnanimously. "We should have been more understanding."

Sam knew there was no point in telling his former boss that under the same circumstances, he would probably do the same thing again, despite the consequences.

The wedding went off without a hitch,

due largely to the team of wedding coordinators who oversaw everything from the number of pint-sized attendants who helped carry Torey's train to the vanilla-hued candles on the altar that precisely matched Torey's gown. The maids, in warm autumn colors, were a harvest cornucopia. Christine, in a mellow pumpkin hue, nearly outshone the bride.

Sam was greeted warmly and enthusiastically introduced to those in attendance who didn't know him. When photos were finished he drove with Christine to the reception. Torey's parents, like Christine's, lived in North Fulton County, but in a country club community of luxury homes. He remembered from pastoral visits and social events that the Scoppito house had more bathrooms than an airport and cathedral ceilings that rivaled the Vatican's.

The country club itself was modeled after a mountain lodge. Built of cedar and stone, and set in stands of all the desirable Georgia trees, it overlooked the eighteenth green of a Jack Nicklaus signature golf course. Sam had played here numerous times, even though his golf game was enthusiastically mediocre.

"Butlers" were passing trays of gourmet hors d'oeuvres by the time Christine tossed her keys to the valet. The bar was in full flourish, and one wine spritzer later, Sam stood at the huge windows overlooking the golf course and sipped, while Christine went to find her parents.

"We miss you terribly, Sam. I don't think I'd feel my daughter was properly married if you hadn't come today."

He turned to smile at Rose Scoppito. She was a charming woman, dark-haired, brown-eyed, not one ounce overweight, due to a rigid schedule of aerobic exercise and weight training. He suspected she'd visited her plastic surgeon since last he'd seen her. He thought Rose herself would probably have preferred to age naturally, but her husband's position as the CEO of a biotech corporation made that difficult. Rose's contributions to his success were her beauty and skills as a hostess. And just in case, she wasn't giving the charismatic and handsome Anthony Scoppito any excuse for a roving eye or a new trophy wife.

He grasped her outstretched hand. "I appreciated the invitation. Torey and John are well suited."

"She's marrying for love, not for money, that's obvious. I hope she'll be happy on a professor's salary. They certainly won't accept any money from us."

Sam tried to imagine Christine refusing money from her parents if she married him. It was another obstacle they would have to overcome.

Rose wilted a little, or at least some of the discipline left her spine. "Do you miss us as much as we miss you? I find Savior's Church to be deadly dull these days. I never knew what you were going to say in the pulpit, but I can predict every word Nigel pontificates." She held up her hand before he could speak. "I'm sorry. That's rude of me, I know. Talking about one of our ministers behind his back is what brought us to this."

"I miss you, and Anthony, and a host of other people. But the church and everything that goes with it?" He tried to find the answer in his own heart and failed. One thing was clear, though. "I like where I am. I like what I'm doing. I'm happy there."

"It's not just a few years of exile? Siberia for rebellious clergy?"

He laughed. "It feels more like an opportunity."

"Just remember, any time you're in Atlanta, you're expected to come and visit." She gripped both his hands and kissed his cheek before she moved on.

Christine arrived with both her parents in tow. Sam had caught up with their lives at lunch, and by now was well versed in Nola's fund-raisers for the local women's shelter and Hiram's plans to build a guest-house on the lower edge of their property so when Sam and Christine married, they would have privacy when they visited.

Unlike Rose, Nola was a woman who fought aging purely on general principles. Christine resembled her a little, having inherited her mother's red hair, height and love of fashion. But Nola's beauty was more fragile and not at all due to force of personality. She was a tentative woman who knew what to say in every circumstance, but only because she had studied the possibilities with heartbreaking indecision.

Christine didn't resemble her father outwardly but was much like him in other ways. Hiram was a short man, built like a punching bag and able to take as much abuse. He'd lost most of his hair but none of his bulldog persistence. On his deathbed, he would be planning some new project and probably wouldn't notice the Grim Reaper waiting to claim him.

"I bet you haven't been to a reception this fancy since you left Atlanta." Hiram took several shrimp from the butler without acknowledging the young man. "Christine says you don't get into D.C. very often."

"I'm in a couple of clergy groups in the area, but that's about as often as I make the trip."

Nola selected smoked salmon on a cucumber round and gave the butler a tentative nod to dismiss him. "I've always liked the capital. I never wanted to live right in the city, you understand. But there are some lovely suburbs."

"We have a friend here tonight from D.C.," Hiram said. "I knew him when I was in Congress, and we've stayed friendly enough, even if his politics are a bit too far left of center to suit me. I'll see if I can find him and introduce you. Might be a good contact."

Sam immediately sensed something new in the air. Expressions didn't indicate it, nor did body language. It was the studied nonchalance that gave it away.

Hiram left, with Nola in tow. Christine leaned closer. "My feet are killing me!"

He understood why. The shoes she was wearing had spindle-thin heels at least four inches high. "Take off the shoes."

"I can't do that. But we could find some

place private and you could massage them. For starters."

The invitation was just for show, and he knew it. "By the time we found a place that private, dinner would be over."

"Are you having a good time?"

He wondered. He'd expected to feel out of place here, the star pitcher who goes home to his former team only to discover that his skills are either rusty or just plain deficient. Instead, even if he didn't feel like the hometown hero, he felt comfortable, if somewhat detached. He had not yearned for old times, nor had he struggled over the few clear snubs he'd received.

And he had spent a surprising amount of time wondering how things were going back in Virginia.

"Sam?"

He realized he hadn't answered Christine's question. "It's been good," he said. And it had been. Good to see that he was happy with his life — at least most of it.

She looked as if she wanted to say more, but the senior Fletchers returned with an older man in an expensive gray suit that exactly matched his hair, and Hiram introduced him. "Sam, this is Pete Deaver. Pete used to be a lobbyist up on Capitol Hill, but now he works behind the scenes on his own time and dollar."

Sam shook hands and approved of Pete's firm grip. The man looked vaguely familiar, as if Sam had seen him recently in a different context. "What kind of things interest you, Pete?" Sam asked, trying to remember where.

"I work for a couple of different organizations." He named one that Sam was familiar with, an environmental group whose stands were often too oriented toward big business to please Sam. Still, he admired everyone who put time and energy into what they considered good causes.

Christine excused herself to see if Torey needed anything. Hiram took Nola's arm and they drifted away. Sam was left alone with Pete.

"I've heard you preach," Pete said, getting right down to business.

Sam realized this was where he'd seen Pete. In the second row at Community Church. "Yes, I remember. What, three weeks ago?"

"Four. You talked about casting the first stone."

"I hope I talked about *not* casting it. That's what I intended."

Pete had an unremarkable face, but his smile transformed it into something more interesting. His gaze had been shrewd and assessing, but the smile softened calculation into simple interest.

"I've known Hiram for years," Pete said. "He's quite a salesman."

Sam was afraid he knew what Hiram had been trying to sell. Or, more accurately, whom. "And knowing Hiram brought you to the Shenandoah Community Church?"

"I'm on the search committee for my church, Capital Chapel, in northwest D.C. We're not far from Dupont Circle, not far from Georgetown. We date back nearly to the Revolutionary War, and we've numbered three presidents among our parishioners. Hiram mentioned you, and I was intrigued."

Sam had heard of the church. The congregation was not as large as Savior's, and while once the theology had been challenging, almost radical, its days as a beacon for the community had ended. Nowadays it was still influential, but it was a comfortable church to attend, the right place for a man like Pete, who believed that drilling for oil in Alaska could be accomplished with few important changes in that fragile, irreplaceable ecology.

"I've seen your building," Sam said. "Impressive? Good size congregation?"

"What we lack in size we make up for in prestige. Our members are wealthy and important."

"I'm sure."

"And we're looking at you as a candidate to lead us."

Sam didn't know what to say. This was unexpected, but it certainly explained a lot. His earlier conversation with Christine about their wedding. Hiram's guesthouse. Even Nigel's surprising lack of animosity. Sam was no longer in disgrace. He had managed to attract interest in his skills, considerable interest from a church he did not have to be ashamed of. He was out of the liturgical doghouse. He was upwardly mobile once again.

Sam realized he had left Pete standing there without a word. "What kind of minister are you looking for?"

"One who doesn't bore us to death."

Sam nodded to encourage more information.

"We're well-educated, and we're not interested in a Bible thumper. We expect intellectually stimulating sermons on relevant topics. I don't mean you can't preach from the Bible, of course, but give us credit for a little common sense. I thought you did that in the sermon I heard. I was impressed."

Sam smiled a little. "I'm glad you found it meaningful. But there's a lot more to ministry than those minutes each week in the pulpit. What's your vision for your church?"

Pete was clearly warming up to this task. "We don't want to be lectured to. We had that with our last pastor, and he got the boot. We want to be gently led."

"You don't want controversy." It wasn't a question.

"We have people of many different political and philosophical persuasions in our midst. We don't want anyone to feel alienated. We want to think, we don't want to . . ." He was at a momentary loss for words.

"Feel? You don't want to come out of the service on a Sunday feeling stirred up?"

"That's right." Pete was too smart not to know that Sam was supplying more than the right words. "You have a problem with that, Reverend?"

"Sam. And it's probably too soon in this relationship to have a problem with anything. I'm gathering information."

Pete nodded, as if Sam had passed the first test. "The last minister had some very strong ideas about what we should be doing in the community. We're too diverse to —"

Sam felt a ping of interest. "Diverse? Racially? Economically?"

Pete grimaced. "No."

"I'm guessing you're sorry about that?"

"Personally, yes. But not everyone will be. We don't do much outreach. We do tend to keep to ourselves. And about the only thing we agree on is that we don't want anyone telling us what we should do about it."

Sam decided to cut to the chase. "You know my background?"

"Yes, I do. I've talked to the pastor here about you. He says you're a rising star who got knocked off course. I'll tell you right now, we would not be any more tolerant than these people were of a minister who doesn't put his commitment to us right out in front."

"In other words, if I felt led by God to act in a way you disagreed with, I would not be welcome."

"It's never that clear-cut, is it?"

Sam shrugged.

"We're looking for youth, intelligence, drive, charisma. You have them all."

Sam was gratified to hear that, but not as

gratified as once he might have been. On some level he was afraid the words were an indictment, particularly the last two. "What's the next step?"

"I'll bring our committee to visit your church some time in the next two months. A surprise visit, most likely. Then we'll figure out where to go from there. But right now you're the best candidate by far. You have everything —"

"Except an unfortunate tendency to do what I think is right."

"Are you less impulsive than you were three years ago?"

Sam thought this was the question of the hour. What was impulse and what was God's voice? He was not foolish or brash enough to believe he always knew the difference.

"I'm less impulsive," he admitted. "That is not the same as calculating."

"We want a man with real values. We just don't want one who forces them down our throat." Pete stuck out his hand, and Sam shook it again. Then Pete disappeared into the crowd.

The wedding reception had ended, and the elder Fletchers had gone to bed. Christine and Sam were lounging together on the sofa in the upstairs sitting room. The pickled pine walls with elaborate trim and crown molding were showcases for many of the oil paintings of the nineteenth-century South that Nola collected. Resurrection fern and Spanish moss hung from mighty live oaks; rivers wound lazily through cane fields; horses stretched and preened on bluegrass fields. The southern theme was repeated all around him. Camellias on the floral print sofa, wisteria on the delicate china tea service on a side table. None of it cloying or overdone.

"This is a good life, isn't it, Sam?" Christine's words were only slightly slurred. The party had gone on into the wee hours, and the champagne had flowed freely. Wisely, Christine had let Sam drive home.

"It's a good life," he agreed. Her head was in his lap, and he stroked her hair back from her forehead, although he couldn't keep up with the curls that sprang back as soon as he released them.

Despite a remarkably clear view of her cleavage, he was amazed to discover all he really wanted now was to go down the hall to bed. And not with Christine. He'd gotten up before the sun, and it was now well past midnight. The day had been emotionally exhausting, too.

"How did your talk go with Pete Deaver?" She sat up and shook back her hair. Obviously she wanted to see his face as she questioned him.

"You know what he wanted, don't you?"

"Isn't it exciting?"

He supposed it should have been. But he knew better than to confess the whole truth, that he was troubled, not excited, by this opportunity.

When he didn't answer right away, she frowned. "Don't tell me you told him no."

"I didn't tell him anything. I listened."

"Well, that's something." She cuddled up to him, but turned so she could still see him clearly. "Sam, this is a wonderful new chance for you. Don't you see? Washington's an exciting city. I loved it when Daddy was in Congress. I always wished we could really live there, have all those monuments right in my backyard. Maybe it's not Atlanta, but it's nearly as good."

"I like Washington."

"It would be a great fit for you."

"And for you?"

She tilted her head. Her eyes searched his. "Yes. Is that a crime? I could be happy there. Don't I deserve that?"

"I want you to be happy." He took a

deep breath. "Chrissy, it's possible you can't be happy with me." She started to speak, and he put his finger against her lips. "Hear me out. It's time, don't you think?"

She frowned, but she remained silent.

"If Pete Deaver knows what he's talking about, Capital Chapel is looking for a minister who will make the congregation feel good about themselves. They don't want somebody who'll challenge them. They don't want somebody who'll ask more from them than they're willing to give. They're complacent and happy to be so. He as much as told me I have to promise I won't go off half-cocked the way I did here. No protests. No civil disobedience. No sermons that make anyone uncomfortable. Certainly no prison sentences. I can be intellectual, but not emotional. I can't thump the Bible too loudly, particularly, I'm guessing, those parts of it they'd rather pretend aren't there. I'm making an educated guess here, but I suspect my sermon on rich men and the eye of a needle won't go over big."

"I can't believe you've already decided against it without seeing the church or talking to anybody else!"

"I haven't decided against it. I just don't

want you to think this is a shoo-in, even if they want me." He considered his next words, but knew he had to go on. "I will never be part of a church that insists on making decisions for me. It's my job, my struggle, to be a moral human being and to go where I'm led."

"Oh, stop it! This is the real world. You can't have everything you want. You have to make some compromises, you have to play the game a little. Didn't you learn anything when they threw you in jail? What good did that do?"

"It changed my life. It changed *me.* And more and more, I think it was supposed to."

She sat up straight, no longer touching him. "I've just about had it, you know that? I can't wait forever. I *won't* wait forever! We should be married. By now we should be thinking about having kids!"

"Then marry me. Make the commitment once and for all. Share my life with no strings attached. Make choices *with* me, not *for* me. I know you don't want to live out in the country. When it's time to leave Community Church, I'll look for a place where you'll be happier. We'll look together, but don't tell me you won't marry me unless I do exactly what you want."

"You're being selfish. You're trying to control me. You don't give a damn what I need or want."

"I can't be somebody I'm not just to please you."

"Neither can I."

They stared at each other. Sam halfway expected her to slide his diamond off her finger. But she sat very still, as if she was afraid if she moved, she might move out of his life forever.

The silence continued until he thought he couldn't stand it any longer. Then she shook her hair back over her shoulders. "I won't be coming to Toms Brook next weekend, the way I said I might."

He gave a slight nod.

"I've been invited to go foxhunting in Middleburg, and I think I'm going to accept," she continued.

"Do you want me to drive up and see you?" Middleburg, a picturesque village in Virginia's lush horse country, wasn't that far from Toms Brook.

"No. A man has invited me. I doubt he'd appreciate you showing up on his doorstep."

He heard the revelation — and the challenge. "He knows you're engaged?"

"He's not one to care too much."

He kept his voice low. "Are you having an affair?"

"No." She paused. "Not yet, anyway."

"I see."

"Probably not. I'm staying with his sister. I could get you an invitation for the weekend, if I thought you had either the time or inclination. But there's no point in simply showing up to visit for a few hours."

"Take it or leave it?"

"Something like that. I'm tired of playing second fiddle to your church and your conscience, Sam. I'm tired of waiting for you to see the light and realize what you gave up."

He was all too aware that he was not angry with her. Hurt, perhaps, and his pride was wounded. But he was not angry. For one moment he had wanted her to say there was another man she was serious about, that they were sleeping together and she no longer wanted Sam in her life.

He was ashamed and dismayed that he had hoped for the easy way out, and apprehensive about what would happen next. But most of all, he was relieved that once and for all the tension between them, the very real possibility they would never marry, was out in the open.

"Nothing I've done was to hurt you. Not

three years ago and not tonight." He covered her hand, but she slid hers away and stood.

"Well, I *have* been hurt. But I guess I know what you say is true."

"Are we going to leave it this way?"

She shrugged. "For now."

He wondered if she was clinging to the hope he would fall in love with Capital Chapel and take the position there. In Christine's mind, if that happened, every problem between them would be resolved. Sadly, Sam knew better.

"Sleep well," he said.

She nodded and left him to stare at landscapes of a gracious, romanticized life that was not so different from Christine's hopes for her own future.

*C*hapter
Fifteen

Elisa had never had a serious hobby. As a child she enjoyed jigsaw puzzles, so her mother set up a table on the wide porch where the family liked to congregate, and a puzzle had always been in process. As an adolescent she listened to music, buying tapes, then CDs, with her allowance. But neither activity ever bordered on obsession.

Piecing the endless chain quilt was a different story.

Perhaps her interest had developed so quickly because piecing the quilt reminded her of fitting a puzzle together. As she worked, she was warmed by memories of her mother's laughter and her father's pretend indignation when he couldn't find the right piece. The quilt was much like a jigsaw, only it was Elisa's job to cut the fabric and be certain it was exact so the block was a precise hexagon. She had already learned what could happen if she was careless.

Or perhaps her interest had bloomed because the rhythmic clinking of the treadle was like the steady beat of the music she once had loved, repetitive and soothing. As she sewed, she was lulled into oblivion, her thoughts drifting back to the happy days before her parents were killed, before she became a mother to the brother who was so much younger than she.

Perhaps it was the familiar splashes of color, the texture of handwoven fabric against her fingertips, the pursuit of beauty when her life had been so devoid of it.

And perhaps it was the image the quilt created in her mind of links so strong they could never be broken, of a solidarity and strength she dreamed of for her people.

"You were a million miles away."

Startled, Elisa looked up to find Helen standing beside her.

"Oh, I'm sorry. I guess I was."

"No matter. I understand. I get that way sometimes. Quilting's what took me away from all my troubles. Guess that's why I done so much of it in my time."

"It's addictive."

"Let me see what you got so far."

Helen had already seen and discarded the first half dozen of Elisa's blocks, showing her where she had gone wrong and what she needed to make her work more accurate. Elisa gathered up her rapidly mounting pile and handed them over, standing to stretch as Helen pawed through them.

"You've gotten better."

Elisa knew this was high praise indeed. "You think so?"

"I wouldn't be all that ashamed to say I made a few of these myself."

High praise.

"They look a little silly with a hole in the middle, don't they?" The block formed a hexagon of twelve wedges of alternately light and dark fabrics that did not meet in the middle. When Elisa had finished the number she needed, the next step, according to Helen, was to sit down with a circle of fabric and applique it in place in the middle, like the hub of a wheel.

"You got enough there for your first applique lesson."

Elisa had already manufactured a pile of excuses to go with her blocks. She plucked out the best. "I've never been much for hand sewing. My mother had to let out the hems on my dresses because she said my stitches were too big."

"You think I'm going to do this for you, come time to start putting the quilt together?"

"You mean you won't?"

"Don't get smart with me, missy. You come on down and we'll do the first part of it today. You bring the fabric you plan to use for the centers. And don't dawdle."

Elisa had errands she planned to do later, so she took a few moments to comb her hair and slip on shoes. It was past time for a new pair, and she made a note to visit Wal-Mart, since she had just picked up her check at the nursing home. She would need something sturdy and comfortable, hopefully something she could adapt with a cheap pair of overshoes when winter snows began.

Downstairs, Helen had spread the collection of blocks on the kitchen table. Beside the blocks she'd made a pile of towels and set her iron on top of them. "Got a trick I learned from one of those television quilt shows. Never saw a single show on quilts 'til Nancy made me get that satellite. Learned to quilt just fine without them, too."

"Nevertheless, we're about to take advantage of Nancy's satellite today."

"Might as well, since she's paying for it anyway, whether I use it or not."

Elisa pulled up a chair beside her. "I could sit all day at the treadle."

"You'll like this well enough, I guess. The needle goes in and out, in and out. It's got a rhythm to it, like the machine."

"The nuns used to slap our fingers if our stitches weren't even."

"Nobody's going to be slapping anybody in my kitchen."

"I'm not getting out of this, am I?"

"Not on your life."

In the next half hour Helen showed her how to trace and cut circles from, of all things, freezer paper. Then how to cut slightly larger circles from the fabric, which she ironed to the shiny side of the paper, and finally how to baste the edges of the fabric to the wrong side of the paper so that when she was finished she had a neat circle to applique to her block.

"Now, here comes the part you got to pay attention to," Helen told her. "You did good with the basting."

"I'm warning you, that's how all my stitches look."

"Not by the end of this lesson they won't."

And they didn't. By the time Helen had

grown tired of playing quilt teacher, Elisa had begun to get the hang of hiding her applique stitch so the fabric circle just seemed to have attached itself with no earthly help.

She sat back and stared at the completed block after she snipped her basting stitches and peeled the freezer paper away. "Well, who would think I could do this?"

"Me, for one. All you needed was a little confidence and nobody hitting you for your mistakes."

"You wanted to a time or two."

"Well, so? I didn't lay a finger on you." Helen got up and placed her hands against the small of her back as she stretched. "You'll be a quilter yet."

Elisa felt as if someone had just handed her a rainbow. "Thank you. That's nice to hear."

"I want you to start coming to the Wednesday Quilting Bee."

"Oh, I couldn't. I've got work to do at the church every morning."

"I'm not going to listen to no. You've got nothing that won't keep 'til later in the day. And if somebody needs you right that second, they'll know where to find you."

Elisa rose, too. "But I'm a beginner."

"So? You're already better than some of

the women. And now you've got handwork you can do. Iron up a pile of those circles and bring them along."

Elisa looked down at all the blocks she had already made. "I'll have to iron a big pile."

"What happened to that small quilt you were fixing to make? You think I didn't notice just about everything you own fits in a backpack? Looks to me like you won't be able to leave the house now. This quilt you're making won't fit, that's for sure."

"I might have to leave it for Cissy and Zeke," Elisa said, struggling to keep her tone playful.

"You know, there are a lot of rooms in this house. Won't be no call for you to leave just because they're coming home in February. You'll be welcome to stay. I'm counting on it."

Elisa leaned over and kissed her cheek. "Thank you for that. And for giving me this gift of quilting."

"No call to get mushy." But Helen's eyes sparkled.

"I have to do some things in town. Do you need anything while I'm there?"

"No, you run on." Helen started toward the refrigerator, then turned. "Oh, I forgot to tell you. Some man, Mexican by the look of him, came by looking for you."

For a moment Elisa couldn't speak. Then she found her voice. "Did he leave his name?"

"He did." Helen paused. "Durned if I can remember it though. Give me a minute."

Elisa couldn't wait. "Young? Old?"

"Anybody under eighty looks young to me." Helen frowned. "Not real tall. Stocky. Hair sticking up all over like a porcupine's quills."

Elisa felt such a sharp stab of disappointment she was afraid to breathe. "Diego? Diego Moreno?"

"That's him."

She struggled not to let her feelings show. "He's Adoncia's fiancé. I wonder what he wanted."

"You tell Adoncia I want her to come and visit me and bring those children she talked so much about. They'll want to see my chickens."

"I'll tell her. I'll stop by on my way back home."

"Well, don't tell her this part, but I'm working on quilts for her and her kids. I hope she waits a while on that wedding of hers to give me time."

Elisa gave Helen's resisting body a hug.

Elisa had intended to stop by Adoncia's anyway. The last time she'd seen her friend, Adoncia had been in a dark mood, complaining of everything but the real reason for her bad temper. Diego was pressuring her to set a wedding date, and she was no longer sure how to avoid marriage without telling him the truth, that no matter what, she was not going to start a family right away.

Elisa arrived at Ella Lane carrying gifts. Bubbles and a fancy bubble wand for Maria, a plastic dump truck for Fernando, new red-and-white dish towels for Adoncia. She'd also brought her completed quilt block to show her friend. Adoncia had expressed curiosity about Elisa's new project.

Adoncia was sitting on her little porch on a folding chair when Elisa pulled up. Fernando and Maria, in fleece sweatshirts and long pants, were chasing each other around the trailer.

"My timing is good," Elisa said, waving the gifts as the children ran by. They squealed in delight, as much to see her — she hoped — as for the gifts. Fernando took his truck to a nearby sandpile, and

Maria followed to see if she could make bubbles land in his hair.

"You saved me," Adoncia said. "They would have made two, maybe three, more trips around the house, then what would we have done?"

Elisa gave her the towels. "Your old ones are falling apart."

"They're pretty. I won't want to get them wet."

Elisa perched on the edge of the porch and looked up at her friend. "How are things?"

Adoncia shrugged. Elisa knew that didn't bode well.

"Diego came to see me, but I wasn't home," Elisa said as an opener.

"He came? To your house?"

Elisa nodded.

"Well, he has stopped coming to mine."

"Stopped coming here?"

"He is angry at me, and at you."

Elisa settled back, afraid this was going to be a longer visit than she'd hoped. "Exactly what happened?"

"A man who cannot go to bed with his woman whenever he wants to begins to . . ." She turned up her hands. "What is the word?"

Elisa was sorry this was an English day. "Complain?"

Adoncia shook her head.

"Shout?"

"No! Begins to . . . *sospechar!*"

"Suspect?"

"Yes! Begins to suspect that something is wrong. Diego thought perhaps there was another man. So I told him the truth. *¿Qué otra me queda?* I told him that I will not have another baby, even when we marry. Not until I am sure I can be a good mother. *No entiende.* And he does not understand why we must not make love for more than a week each time."

"Well, surely he understands how it works, just not why you want it that way."

"He is furious."

"And you?"

"I am furious at him. This is my body, my life. And these two —" she gestured to Nando and Maria who were giggling in the sand pile "— *mis niños,* need a mother who is not so tired she cannot cook and clean for them or hear their prayers without falling asleep."

"You don't have to convince me."

"No, but I have to convince him."

"I'm not sure you can."

Adoncia's eyes filled, and angrily she wiped away a tear. "Then he can stay away. *Encontraré a otro novio!*"

Elisa was sorry for both her friends. She loved Adoncia and liked Diego. He was a good man, not usually a controlling one. But this was an issue that meant the world to him. Until the moment Adoncia had given him a child of his own, Diego would feel he had only borrowed a family. Not because he didn't love Maria or Fernando. But because he needed proof he was a father in every way.

"You say Diego is angry at me?" Elisa asked.

"I told him that you explained how I could keep from getting pregnant."

Elisa was sorry it had come to this, but she didn't blame Adoncia. And Diego was an intelligent man. Surely he understood, at least on some level, that Elisa was only helping her friend.

"What if I talk to him?" she asked. "What if I explain that you love him but you need time without a baby in the house. If it comes from me, maybe he'll begin to see it's just temporary, until you feel ready."

"He won't listen." Adoncia's eyes sparkled with tears. "*Es terco como una mula.* He won't budge. He is not thinking like a man with intelligence."

"No, he is thinking like a man in love."

Adoncia sniffed.

They talked of other things. Adoncia's shifts at work had changed, and she had been moved to a better, less dangerous job. Fernando had added several new words to his growing vocabulary, half in Spanish, half in English, which proved to Adoncia that her efforts to use both were working. Inez had found work at a salon in Strasburg and was studying to apply acrylic nails. Paco, who was now living at *La Casa*, had found a day job picking apples.

Elisa showed her friend the finished endless chain block, and Adoncia made all the proper noises of appreciation. She was calmer by the time Elisa left, had even laughed and applauded when Patia's dog, long-eared, short-tailed, ambled over to snap playfully at Maria's bubbles. But Elisa was still worried.

Obviously Diego was worried, too, because he was waiting in his truck in front of Helen's house when Elisa got home.

She pulled up behind him and got out to meet him. He was leaning against the driver's door, but he straightened when she approached.

"Diego? What's going on?"

"You can ask me that?"

Her heart sank. He sounded angry, and

while she was not afraid of him, she did not like angry men. She reminded herself that she was standing on a Virginia country road, that the sun was shining and Helen was in the house just beyond her.

"I won't pretend, then," she said carefully. "I've just seen Adoncia, and she told me you're fighting."

He pushed away from the truck, but he didn't move closer. "You think what goes on between us is your business? You think you have the right to keep her from having my baby?"

She just looked at him, waiting for him to calm down and be reasonable. The issue was emotional, and she wished she hadn't been caught in the middle. But she didn't regret helping Adoncia. She'd had a responsibility to do so.

She watched him struggle with himself, and finally he fell back against the door. "Why do you care what we do?"

"This is between you and Adoncia. I didn't advise her not to get pregnant. I just told her what to do when it was clear that was what she wanted. But for what it's worth, I agree with her. Pregnancy is hard on a woman's body, and she's tired. She works hard, she takes care of the children, she just wants some breathing space. She'll be a better mother to another baby when she's had time to recover." She paused. "Is that too much to ask? That you wait until she's ready?"

"How do you know all this? You don't have a husband. You don't have children of your own. No man looks at you, because you won't look back. You think I don't know you don't like *men?* A woman like you giving Adoncia advice!"

She tried to ignore the attempt to hurt her. "Before I came here, I saw a lot of women with too many children. They were tired and old before their time."

"The church —"

"The church says she can use the rhythm method of birth control. No priest is going to tell her she can't. It will buy her time between babies, even if it's not perfect. That's all she's asking for."

His eyes narrowed. "This is my life and my family. You stay away from us!"

She narrowed her eyes. "I like you, and I know you like me, no matter what you say. But don't try to control me, and stop trying to control Adoncia, or this isn't going to turn out well. She adores you. You're good for each other. Please, just be a little more patient."

"Don't tell her what to do." He pushed

away from the truck again. "Maybe I can't make you stay away, but I can make you sorry if you don't."

For a moment she wasn't sure she had heard him right. "That's a threat, Diego? You're making a threat? Because that's what it sounds like."

He looked surprised at his own words, as if they had come from someone else. Then he glared at her, as if to show he had meant every word.

"You're upset right now because you miss her," Elisa said.

"I'm going to marry Adoncia."

"Please, give this a little thought. You can have everything you want if you're just a little patient. Doesn't what Adoncia needs matter?"

This time he didn't reply. He got in his pickup, slammed the door and drove away.

Chapter Sixteen

*Shenandoah Community Church
Quilting Bee and Social Gathering
— September 24th*

*The meeting was called to order at
9:10 in the quilters' beehive. We would
have started on time except that Helen
went storming off to find her favorite
chair, which somebody had borrowed
for a committee meeting. Helen claims
that in the future she's going to chain it
to the floor.*

*Because we have no fight left, we will
henceforth drop "social gathering" from
our title.*

*The top we are quilting for the
Christmas bazaar is progressing nicely,*

although some members (whose names will not go down in history by my hand) have been warned their stitches are too long. The red and green design will make a pleasing raffle item if nobody notices that the backing (donated by Anna Mayhew) is not the correct shade of green. Peony Greenway pointed out that some healthy percentage of the male species are color blind, and we should concentrate on selling them tickets.

Kate Brogan's babysitter moved away (Kate promises the move had nothing to do with a certain wildflower bouquet and a patch of poison ivy) and Kate brought her children as guests once again. Helen announced she is teaching Elisa Martinez, our new church sexton, to quilt, and Cathy suggested that Helen bring Elisa to our next bee. Helen promised she will, even if she has to drag her in by her ponytail.

The meeting was adjourned and a potluck of salads was served. Rory and Bridget were given picnic lunches in the play yard. The children were not the only ones present who saw this as a special treat.

Sincerely,
Dovey K. Lanning, recording secretary

Helen got to her feet, a task she wasn't finding any easier as the days progressed. "I have a guest with me today. Elisa Martinez is joining us, and I didn't have to drag her anywhere. So next week when you read your minutes, Dovey, I don't want to hear different."

The little group applauded, and Helen was gratified to see that Elisa's welcome was genuine. She hadn't expected anything else, but she'd given up thinking she understood people a long time ago.

"I may get called away," Elisa told them, "but I'll stay as long as I can."

"She was over here at seven cleaning and setting up," Helen said. "And the church never looked so good."

"That's a fact," Peony Greenway said. "If anybody comes to get you, you slip under the quilt frame and we'll say you just left."

"It's good to be with you."

Helen thought, as she always did, that Elisa's rare smiles were warm enough to light up the room.

Elisa didn't smile often enough. Helen wanted to know why, although of course she would never ask. Elisa's life was her own business, and her past, well, that was over with, wasn't it? But it was clear to Helen that she had suffered. There were nightmares. Helen knew that. Sometimes she heard Elisa tossing and turning at night, speaking in Spanish. A couple of times she'd heard cries, but before she could decide what to do, the house had grown quiet again. Either Elisa had awakened or the nightmare had ended.

Giving her a place to live, well, that was a good thing, she supposed. But Helen wished she could do more.

"Have you done any hand quilting?" Peony asked Elisa.

"I'm a complete beginner."

"She's learning to piece, and she's not so bad at it," Helen put in.

"What blocks are you working on?" Anna asked.

Elisa pulled several that she'd completed out of a cloth bag Helen had given her to put her quilting supplies in.

"That's not an easy pattern," Anna said, frowning. "Helen, you let her start with this?"

340

Helen defended herself. "My mama always said you should learn to do something just the way you were going to be doing it for life. Start on something you don't care a thing about, and you'll never finish and never learn what you need."

"That sounds like good advice," Kate said. "My mother taught me to knit potholders. Do you know many eight-year-old girls who need a potholder?"

"Do you knit today?" Helen asked.

"Not a thing."

"See?"

"Well, whatever you're doing is working," Anna conceded. "These look very professional."

"And she's using my mama's old treadle." Helen felt like that just about made her point, all by itself. "Not everybody here can use one, I'd say."

"I couldn't," Kate said. "Besides, can you imagine a treadle in my house? Something powered by human energy? At least with my machine I can hide the electric cord so Rory can't sew Bridget's fingers together."

There was silence as everyone imagined that possibility.

"These are made from the Guatemalan fabric scraps I gave you, aren't they?"

Peony asked Helen. "And what a perfect use for them. Are you from Guatemala, Elisa?"

For a moment Helen thought Elisa looked blank, as if digging out an answer was impossible. Then she shook her head. "No, Mexico."

"Oh, I've been to Mexico a lot," Cathy Adams said. "My husband has family living in Mexico City. I bet you get home-sick."

"More than I can say," she said.

Helen knew Elisa well enough to feel the current of emotion in her friend's voice. Helen felt an alien desire to reach over and put her arm around Elisa's shoulders, to hug her as she might reluctantly hug Tessa, if she thought she really needed it. But she knew better. Whatever haunted Elisa Martinez, the young woman did not want to share the story nor the feelings behind it.

"Let me show you how we're quilting this top," Helen said instead. She figured the gift of a new topic of conversation was the only one she could readily give.

"Thank you," Elisa said. And her gratitude showed.

An hour later Elisa was surprised at how easily she had been accepted by the quilters. Most of the jobs she'd had since coming to the United States had demanded a clear separation between staff and the people they served. That was less true at the nursing home and one of the reasons she enjoyed her work there. Staff was looked up to by most of the residents, who yearned for friendship along with competent care. And the residents were in no position or frame of mind to ferret out information about the nursing staff. She was safe *and* accepted. It was ideal.

She had not expected the same of this job. She had assumed she would be a shadow working behind the scenes. Perhaps she would have been, if she hadn't been invited to share Helen's home, or if she hadn't volunteered with her friends on the day after *La Casa* had been vandalized. But whatever had turned this particular tide, she was touched, but also worried that she had been included as one of this group so readily.

Keeping her distance and moving on had kept her safe in the years since Gabrio's death. Now that thought saddened her, even though she would have to move soon enough if Ramon didn't arrive. She had stayed too long, raised too many questions.

Made too many friends.

"You just about got the hang of rocking your needle. I'll give you that," Helen said, peering over her shoulder. "But the size of those stitches is a disgrace."

"Helen!" Dovey shook her finger in Helen's direction. "That's no way to teach her to quilt."

"No, it's okay. She's right." Elisa laughed at the mess she'd made. At least her uneven, wandering stitches would pull out easily enough. "Besides, when Helen tells me I'm doing something right, I know she's not being nice."

"If she tells you you're doing something right, we'll serve champagne," Dovey said with a sniff.

Elisa pushed back from the quilt frame. "I need a break. My fingers have been pricked a million times. I'm surprised I haven't bled to death."

"You'll toughen up," Helen said. "You'll be practicing at home. I'll see to it."

The door to the beehive opened, and Sam appeared. "May I come in?"

Elisa realized her heart was suddenly lurching erratically. She had only seen Sam from a distance since his return from Georgia. She'd spent a disturbing and inordinate amount of time during his absence wondering if he would come back only to say he was leaving for good to take a church closer to Christine.

"Come on in, Reverend Kinkade," Peony Greenway said. "Come see what we're doing for the bazaar."

Sam was dressed in neatly pressed khakis, a light blue dress shirt and a dark blue jacket. His hair had been recently cut. A deeper tan made his eyes seem even bluer, as if he'd spent time beside a pool or on the golf course. His smile embraced everyone as he came into the room, but it faltered when he saw Elisa at the quilt frame.

"I see you've got a new member," he said, looking away immediately. "It's about time Elisa took a break from work."

"Her heart's in the right place," Dovey said tactfully. "And she shows promise."

Sam entered the room, and Elisa saw he had a woman with him. She recognized the curly brown hair and slender figure immediately.

"Do you remember Kendra Taylor?" he asked the group. "She was with us the day we cleaned up the mess at *La Casa*."

Most of the quilters had helped that day, and everyone greeted Kendra.

"Kendra was interested when I told her about you, so she's here to see what you're doing," Sam told them.

Elisa noticed every move he made, and with them the fact that he had very consciously not looked at her again. For a moment she wondered if he had begun to put pieces of her particular puzzle together and was wrestling with what he had discovered about her. Then she reminded herself it was always good to be careful and dangerous to be paranoid.

"Are you a quilter?" Helen asked.

"I collect old quilts," Kendra said. "I like the history and the stories that come with them."

"Come set a spell with us then and see history in action."

Kendra looked pleased to be asked. Sam admired the quilt, exchanged a few words with the group, then left. Kendra settled in between Dovey and Peony. "I'll just watch. What pattern is this? A pinwheel of some sort, right?"

"Clay's Choice," Helen said. "Don't know why it's called that, that's for sure. Who was this Clay, anyway?"

"I like the fabrics." Kendra leaned over, her hair falling across her shoulders. "This one in particular. Christmas mice. Not even a mouse, right?"

"We'll raffle it off unless nobody buys a ticket. Then we'll give it to the homeless."

"Oh, you'll sell tickets. It's wonderful." Kendra sat up, and her gaze caught Elisa's. "Don't you think so?"

"I think it was more wonderful before I put my needle to it."

"I can't sew a straight seam."

"I wouldn't say that too loudly around here. Some people will take it as a challenge, and before you know it you'll be pricking your finger right along with the rest of us."

The conversation swirled around for a while, but soon Kendra brought it back to Elisa. "How are things at *La Casa* now? There's been no more trouble?"

"Not so far," Elisa said.

"We have a young man from El Salvador staying there at nights," Cathy told Kendra. "He keeps an eye on the place. And the police claim they'll make an arrest eventually."

"Were you surprised there was so much animosity about the program?" Kendra asked.

"It was senseless vandalism," Peony said. "And worse than anything, it was aimed at children. What kind of people destroy a classroom simply because they don't like the nationality of the people using it?"

"The kind who have not been taught

better," Dovey said.

Elisa couldn't let that go. "Violence is not only a matter of teaching, but a matter of courage. It is so easy to hurt others if you are afraid you are in danger yourself. This can be counted on and used by leaders of any age."

"You've seen this kind of thing before?" Kendra asked.

Elisa sensed that Kendra rarely asked questions just to pass the time. She was a journalist, after all. Next to a government official of any kind, journalists were to be feared most.

"I was speaking generally," Elisa said. And far too much.

"I think you might have some interesting things to say about what happened."

When Elisa didn't respond, Kendra took her cue and didn't push any harder. The conversation changed, and soon the quilters got up, one by one, to get the lunches they'd brought and help themselves to coffee. Kendra thanked the group but refused their offer to share the bounty, claiming she had another commitment.

Elisa felt relieved when Kendra left. She was about to leave, as well, when she realized that Dovey was standing by herself at the coffeepot. Elisa joined her, not wanting to miss this opportunity to speak to her alone.

"Martha Wisner is feeling much better," Elisa said, after she and Dovey had chatted for a few moments about the quilt in progress. "Helen tells me you are good friends?"

"Yes, and I'm glad to hear she's out of the woods. I did call several days ago and went to visit yesterday."

"She enjoys visitors when she's feeling well."

"The pneumonia was a nasty bout."

"Yes, I didn't see her for weeks. She needed more nursing care than we could give her on our unit."

"Well, I know you're taking good care of her now that she's back."

Elisa tried to feel her way. "When we have a few minutes together, Martha talks about her house. She knows I'm working for the church. She doesn't know about *La Casa*, or doesn't remember. But she likes to talk about the history of the house."

"Yes, she lived there for many years."

Elisa had hoped for more, although she wasn't sure what, exactly. She didn't want to tell Dovey what little she knew about Sarah and Jeremiah Miller and the slave named Dorie Beaumont. But if Dovey did have information, Elisa was hoping she might share.

"She knows quite a bit about the origins of the house," Elisa said. "Did she tell you those stories?"

"I can't say she did." Dovey looked puzzled. "If she knew the history, you would think she'd have written it up for the church archives. To my knowledge, we have very little there."

Elisa knew a dead end when she hit one. "Well, if I learn anything interesting, I'll be sure to let somebody know." It wasn't true, but as lies went, it was not a large one.

"We're glad you're here, Elisa," Dovey said. "You are a welcome addition."

Elisa wondered how welcome she would be if anyone knew the truth about her.

Sam was glad that Mondays and Tuesdays were Elisa's days off. Not seeing her when he returned from Atlanta had given him time to think about Christine and the changes in their relationship. He had tried to put Elisa out of his mind so he could focus on the future. He didn't want to end his engagement because he was deeply attracted to another woman. He had no relationship with Elisa now and didn't want to explore one until he was certain he and

Christine had no hope of a happy marriage. He took his commitment to her seriously.

He wondered, though, if they had ever really been in love. Had he let attraction sway him, let the good life beckon him into an engagement that wasn't right for either of them? He didn't know, but he did know that just coming upon Elisa sitting with the other quilters had almost stopped him in his path. He had wanted nothing more than to find some excuse, any excuse, to ask how she was and what she had done while he was away.

When he returned from the beehive, Gracie handed him two messages. "Tilly Bratweiser wants another meeting of the youth advisory committee this afternoon. She wants to hold it in the teen lounge, probably to prove what terrible shape it's in so she can insist it be remodeled to her liking. I'll bet Elisa hasn't cleaned it yet. She usually does it midweek. It takes longer than the other rooms."

The teenagers had appropriated one of the larger rooms in the old Sunday school wing and furnished it with scraps of carpeting and cast-off sofas. It was a dust magnet, not to mention a haven for mice, whose interest was prompted by forgotten snacks and errant crumbs embedded between cushions. More than once the youth advisory committee had threatened to evict the teens. Elisa scrubbed and vacuumed the room as if it were a personal crusade. Clearly she had a fondness for adolescents, despite the behavior of some of the local teens.

Sam scanned the note and imagined sending Gracie, whose arthritic knee had kept her at home half of last week, in search of Elisa. There was no one besides himself to do it, no matter how much he had hoped to keep his distance from her. "I'll ask her to get to it right after lunch," he promised.

"The other one's happier news. A wedding in the offing."

Sam scanned that one, too, and saw that a couple he had met with had decided to tie the knot in a simple pre-Christmas wedding. No matter what transpired with Capital Chapel, he was sure he would still be at Community Church to perform the ceremony.

"Gracie, will you call them back and ask them to come in sometime next week to make the arrangements? And tell them I'm delighted."

"You'll find Elisa?"

"I'll go find Elisa."

"Done, then." Gracie picked up the telephone.

By the time he returned, Elisa had left the beehive. She hadn't stayed for lunch, and no one was sure where she'd gone. Back to work was all they knew.

Sam finally tracked her down in the social hall. She was spreading wax on the red oak planks, her hair pinned on top of her head, the sleeves of her shirt rolled up to her elbows. Under the circumstances, he wondered how she could look so lovely.

"Elisa?"

She didn't turn at first. He thought her mind must be somewhere else. He moved closer. "Elisa?"

Startled, she turned. "Oh, Sam." She took a deep breath. "I was a million miles away."

He wondered exactly where she had been, but he didn't ask. Not only wouldn't she tell him, it was not a conversation he ought to start.

He looked down at the floor. "Will this take a while?"

"About an hour. I have to buff it before it dries completely."

In as few words as possible, he explained why he was there.

"No problem. I'll just switch doing the lounge today with something else. I'll start as soon as I finish here and make sure it's spic-and-span."

"Good. I appreciate it."

"Did your trip go well?"

"It went fine."

"Your roses are blooming, and the garden's beautiful. It would be perfect for a fall wedding right now, wouldn't it?"

"There's one scheduled next week. Hopefully it won't rain."

"I gather you don't have any control over the weather?"

"I didn't take that class in seminary."

She smiled. He wanted to look away. Her smiles flipped switches inside him that badly needed to stay in the off position.

"I wanted to ask you about Kendra Taylor," she said. "She seems, well, interested in what happened at *La Casa*, and I know she's a reporter for the *Washington Post*."

"She writes features."

She pressed her lips together, as if trying to figure out what to say next. "She . . . is she planning a story? Do you know?"

"I think she's just a woman who keeps her eyes open for anything her readers might find interesting."

"Then you don't think that's why she came again today?"

"We had a counseling appointment." His voice softened. "She wasn't here for a story." There was nothing else he could say without breaking a confidence. And there wasn't much to say yet, anyway. Kendra was feeling her way, waiting, he thought, until she felt completely comfortable before she bared her soul. At the moment, all he knew was that she was not happy with her life, and she wasn't sure what to do about it.

Elisa relaxed so visibly that he could see it happen. He wanted to ask her why it mattered, but she wouldn't tell him. Besides, he didn't want to sound as if he planned to be involved in her life.

He turned to go, but he felt her hand on his arm. Her fingertips barely touched his jacket, but he felt the touch in unrelated places and unrelated ways.

"Have I done something to upset you?" she asked. "Or are you just very busy catching up?"

His first response was to tell her she was imagining his withdrawal. But he wasn't good at lying, nor did he want to be. How much of the truth could he tell her? He had never confessed his feelings, so how could he tell her he was fighting them?

He faced her, and her hand drifted to her side. "I'm going through some personal stuff. I guess I'm just trying to figure out my life. I seem to need space from you to do it."

She searched his eyes. He was afraid that everything he *hadn't* said was there for her to read. "Don't make me part of any equation," she said at last.

He knew he needed to nod and leave, or even to pretend he didn't understand. He couldn't make himself do either.

"Because you don't want to be?" He heard the uncertainty, the catch, in his own voice. He heard himself uttering words he should never say. "Or because you can't be?"

"Please don't ask."

"This is a conversation we shouldn't be having."

"I'm sorry. I just . . ." She shrugged.

He knew what she had wanted to say. *I just miss you.*

He understood only too well.

This time he managed a nod. Right before he left.

Elisa's next shift at the nursing home seemed to pass in slow motion. Throughout the long night she had done all that was required, but in her head she had constantly replayed Sam's words and her own response.

She knew now that she was not the only one who felt the attraction sizzling between them. And she knew all too well how doomed any relationship was.

Martha had been asleep the first time Elisa went into her room that night. She had slept soundly through Elisa's Monday shift, and they had not had an opportunity to talk. Elisa wondered if the hospital stay, then the stay on the nursing care wing, had helped Martha stop confusing day with night. If this was so, she would have to come visit the old woman some afternoon to see if she wanted to tell the rest of her story.

On her second visit to the room, however, Martha was wide awake, sitting up in bed, paging through a magazine. Elisa wondered if it was one that Dovey had brought on her visit yesterday.

"Miss Wisner?"

Martha looked up. She squinted in Elisa's direction, then she smiled. "Sharon."

Elisa had not expected this mistake a second time. She tried to smile. "No, I'm

Elisa Martinez, your night nurse."

"It is night, isn't it? I just couldn't sleep. I think I slept too much before." She waved her hand weakly, as if she couldn't remember when.

"I'm so glad to see you again. We missed you."

"I was in the hospital, then . . . somewhere else."

"That's exactly right. After the hospital they moved you to a different wing right here, so you could have more care. But now that you're feeling so much better, you're back home."

"This isn't my home."

Elisa was sorry she had used that word. "I know it doesn't feel like it sometimes."

"My home is behind Community Church. Do you know it?" She laughed. "Of course you do. What am I saying? You lived there as a little girl."

"That must have been Sharon. I'm Elisa."

Martha was frowning. "Didn't I . . . ? Didn't I tell you . . . you know?"

Elisa moved across the room to sit beside her bed. "You told me about Sarah and Jeremiah Miller, and the night they found Dorie Beaumont in the rain."

"I did!" Martha's eyes glowed. "I remember. And I remember why. You found the room."

"Yes, I did."

"But I didn't tell you more?"

"No, it was time for you to go back to sleep."

"I'm not sleeping now."

Elisa smoothed a wrinkle in Martha's covers. "You certainly aren't. I have a little time, unless someone calls me. Would you like to tell me the rest of it?"

"Oh, my dear, there's too much to tell all at once."

Elisa wondered if this was true, or if Martha just wanted to drag it out to help pass the time. "Whatever you want to tell me," she said.

"Oh, good." She was silent a moment. "Did I tell you how sick she was?"

Elisa settled in for the story. "No, you didn't."

"Very sick, you know. It's a wonder she survived."

Chapter Seventeen

May 25, 1853

My dearest Amasa,
So much has transpired since last I wrote
that I am uncertain where to begin. First,
I pray this letter finds you and your father
well. I have not received a letter in many
weeks, but, I know, as often happens, I
will receive several upon Jeremiah's next
trip into town.

I no longer feel free to make that
journey with my brother. The reason will
be clear after I tell all that has happened.

I am sure you remember the story that
had just begun to unfold. That night I sat
beside the bed of our frail visitor, wiping
her brow as fever shook her. Her illness
was not unlike the one that took Jere-
miah's family, and I was frightened that I

would not be able to affect its course. I was helpless as Rachel and my beloved niece and nephew succumbed to its evils. Only Jeremiah was helped by my ministrations, and I think he holds my aid against me, for I truly believe he wishes he could have perished with his family.

Dorie Beaumont is very thin, so slight that I feared the worst for her. But by morning she was taking sips of water, and while the fever did not break, it abated. Hope returned to my heart.

Near dawn, Jeremiah came into the sickroom to see if a new grave would be required. After helping to settle her in my bed, he had told me he would notify no one if she died, but bury her on the hillside with our Miller kin, where she would be free forever from enslavement or the taint of it.

Jeremiah stared at Dorie's face, a lovely face even though it is gaunt and sad, and asked the question I knew he would. Why had this woman survived, when his plump, healthy Rachel had not? He does not want to talk of God's will, even though the words never fly far from his thoughts.

By noon Dorie's eyes had opened several times, never for long, never with *comprehension. But by the time it was necessary for me to leave her and set food on the table (certainly not the large meal Jeremiah is accustomed to) she seemed to be sleeping deeply and comfortably.*

I made haste to serve Jeremiah and flew back to the sickroom with my own meager dinner on a plate. When I arrived, Dorie was sitting on the edge of the bed, the quilt I had rescued from the porch and with which I had covered her gripped in her hands.

"This is not the quilt," she said, although I cannot properly convey the way she said the words. With little strength, certainly. Her voice was halting and difficult to understand. Not because she doesn't speak well. (She does.) But because she was still so very ill.

I bade her lie down, but she would not.

I approached to smooth her pillow and she cowered as if I meant to strike her.

I stood back and assured her I meant no harm. "But this is not the quilt," she repeated.

"Do you want another?" I asked, in hopes that this simple kindness might calm her. I have many quilts, as you know, Amasa. My mother's final years

were spent stitching them when she could no longer find strength for much else. "I will bring another," I promised our poor guest. "Only you must lie still and rest so that you will grow strong again."

"The quilt." She lifted her hands, the fabric gripped tightly within them. "The quilt. The centers are not black."

The pattern of that quilt, Amasa, is that of squares surrounding squares. If it has a name, I know it not, being less a seamstress than most women. Each square surrounds one of Turkey red, a red that appears often in my mother's quilts, since this color of poppies and sunsets was her favorite.

Seeking to understand, I pointed at a red square cocooned by strips of brown and dark blue sprigged calico. "This is not black?" I asked.

"Black. For safety. Black like a starless sky," she said.

I pondered this, and at last I understood. "You were searching for such a quilt? You were searching for a house with such a quilt hung out to air?"

"Black," she said softly. "Like night, when it is safest to travel."

I understood then what she was trying to tell me, or perhaps to tell herself. In the darkness, in the storm, she had come across our home and seen Mother's quilt draped on the bench across our porch. She believed she had found the house she sought, a house where she had been told she might be safely sheltered.

A house with a quilt of many black squares.

"You have found the wrong quilt but the right house," I promised her. "We will tell no one of your presence. We will help you."

"Are there others here like me?" she begged to know. "Have there been others?"

I was so ashamed, my dearest, to tell her there were none, nor ever had there been. We believe not in slavery, Jeremiah nor I. Our church, the same church in which you worshiped, believes it is a sin to hold any man or woman in bondage. Yet we have done nothing to assist our African sisters and brothers. Silently we decry the practice that has brought them to our shores, but Jeremiah and I offer no assistance nor speak out publicly. Some say that war will come of this one day, and perhaps it shall. But I think that had Dorie not arrived on our doorstep, we would not have been tested until war was upon us.

"You are the first," I told her. "The first of many to come." As I said this, I knew it must be true, and that Jeremiah and I must make it so.

I did not know that Jeremiah stood behind me until he spoke. "Promise nothing," he admonished me, "except that this woman shall find no harm here. The rest is not our business."

Jeremiah's heart has been hardened. This you know. But to hear it spoken so clearly, to hear how sadly transformed he is since the death of his family, frightened me.

"I will speak only the truth," I told him. "If others come, and they will if we speak of our commitment in the right places, then we will take them in. Or I will not remain."

Jeremiah did not answer. He strode to the bedside and helped Dorie back under the quilt that had frightened her so. "The future matters not," he told her. "It matters only that you must rest and recover until you are ready to travel again."

She was soothed by his words as she had not been by mine. She lay back against the pillows and closed her eyes.

"You must sleep," he told me. "I will stay with her and make certain she takes no turn for the worse."

I asked him then the question I had not yet been inspired to voice. "And what will come of her if the slave patrol is searching? Will you give her over to them so that we will be safe from their punishment and that of the law?"

"We will hide her," he said, never once looking at me. His gaze was far away, somewhere no one else will ever go.

I had pondered this through the long night and found no answer. "There is no place they will not look," I told my brother.

"They cannot look at that which they cannot see," he said.

A week has passed since Jeremiah uttered those odd words, Amasa. And in those seven days my stern, broken-hearted brother has wrought such changes that sometimes I am uncertain, upon waking and going downstairs, that this is my childhood home.

In the week since Dorie held the quilt in her trembling hands, she has eaten and slept, but rarely spoken. As each day passes, however, she grows more confident that we want only for her to recover her strength so she can continue her journey to freedom.

She still is not well. As of yet I do not know if it was the enslavement or the journey out of it which has laid her so low. I am thin, but she is thinner. Her wrists are as narrow as reeds, her face is skin tightly stretched over bones like a sparrow's. Her hair, which is only a little darker than my own, is lusterless. She coughs, and I fear she will never draw in another breath. But each day, I believe, she improves a bit.

Pray, Amasa, that the transformation of our home will be completed soon, and that until it is, no one will discover her presence. For if they searched for her now, I fear they would find her. If only she will grow stronger as her safety is secured here, so that soon she will be strong enough to hide without fear.

I will write again, and soon. I know, even though you are far away, that you are as sad and concerned as I am for Dorie's fate.

With all my heart,
Sarah Miller

Chapter
Eighteen

Three weeks later, Elisa was addicted. She'd seen people addicted to the needle, but not to a quilting needle, a size 10 "between," to be exact. Helen had been as good as her threat, and whenever Elisa had a few minutes to spare, Helen had insisted she perch on a chair at her own quilt frame and practice her stitches.

Hand quilting was as mesmerizing as the click and whir of the antique treadle. Elisa had quickly found she could lose herself in the rivers of thread. Helen, who had recognized the symptoms, stretched a simple rail fence top of red, white and blue on her mother's frame, which was nothing more than boards and clamps on sawhorse legs, and turned it over to Elisa for practice. Her stitches were straighter now and much more even, but they were still too large.

The quilt, meant for summer picnics and not for judging at the County Fair, stood up to Elisa's practice sessions and seemed to preen under the spotlight.

Now, in the beehive at Community Church, Elisa was trying to pass on her new obsession.

"You think I'd really like this quilting stuff?" Adoncia narrowed her eyes at the nearly completed Christmas quilt still stretched across the Quilting Bee frame. "It doesn't look easy."

Elisa had invited her friend to visit *La Casa* that afternoon to teach the children how to follow the steps in a recipe. She planned to teach them how to make Mexican hot chocolate, and had even brought authentic chocolate tablets and her precious *molinillo,* the carved wooden stick that she balanced between her palms and spun back and forth to whip the finished product.

"Helen would like you to come." Elisa traced a line of stitching with her fingertip. The quilt was nearly finished. "Everyone would enjoy having you here, and Maria and Fernando would have playmates."

"Maybe . . ." Adoncia winked at her friend, then lifted the edge of the quilt where her children were hiding. "Oh, you're still here? I thought you had gone away forever."

Maria giggled. Fernando scooted out on his bottom and held up his arms, his trademark grin firmly in place. Maria followed, carefully pulling down the edges of the quilt, as if protecting her hiding place.

"Diego won't like me coming here," Adoncia said. "He does not trust this place."

To some degree Diego and Adoncia had patched up their relationship. Elisa knew Diego's experiences in this country had been mixed, and he wanted to protect his future wife from the same prejudices he had faced. But Diego's desire to remain separate from the larger community and Adoncia's desire to find a place in it was just another conflict. Adoncia had told her the atmosphere at the little trailer was still thick with tension on this subject and on the subject of babies.

"I don't want to come between you." Elisa reached down to reclip a barrette in Maria's fine black hair. "Diego is already angry at me."

"He is angry at me for asking you what I should do. And I worry, because trying to please him makes me forget sometimes what days I must be careful to stop a baby." Adoncia lifted her son into her arms. "If I give in to Diego on this, I will be giving in for the rest of our lives together. Diego and I must learn to compromise or not marry."

Elisa had hoped for the right moment to present her friend with a gift, and now it had arrived. "I bought something for you that will make it easier to be careful."

"What, sleeping pills for Diego?"

Elisa opened her purse and pulled out a bag. "It's very simple. Open it and see."

Adoncia opened the bag, took out a box and removed what looked like a beaded necklace. "Jewelry? It won't fit over my head."

"They're called CycleBeads. They help you chart when you're fertile and when you aren't. See this little ring? On the first day of your period you slip it over this red bead. Then every day after, you move the ring one more bead. When the beads are brown, like these, it is safe to have sex with Diego."

"There are not so many brown beads."

"There are many days that are safe, and fewer that are unsafe. The white beads are for days when you must not sleep with him." Elisa explained briefly how to tell from the beads if Adoncia's cycle was the right length to make the rhythm method safe.

"It's just a way to make certain your timing is correct," she finished. "The church would approve."

"Diego will not." Adoncia clasped the beads against her chest. "But this is for me to decide. Thank you. I will keep them where he does not question me every time I touch them."

"He's a good man. I think he just needs time to think about this."

"He is a good man, but he is angry at you, as you say." Adoncia put the beads back into the box and put it in her handbag. "He will make trouble for you if he finds out you gave these to me."

Elisa remembered Diego's threat in front of Helen's house.

"What could he do?" The question didn't sound as offhand as she hoped it might.

Adoncia lowered her voice. "He says your green card does not look right, that maybe someone should be told."

Elisa was at a loss for words.

"I told him that if I believed he would do such a thing, I would make him leave. I don't believe he would do this. If he did, I would not stay with him. But I wanted you to know he is angry enough to say it."

Elisa believed Diego was a better man than that. She also suspected his own documents might not stand up under close scrutiny. Even if she was wrong, he wouldn't want to interact with the INS. Not unless he was so furious he was beyond intelligent thought.

"Maybe I won't come around for a while," she said.

"He has a new job. He's not home during the day. You are always welcome, but most welcome then."

"Job?"

"He is the foreman at Jenkins Landscaping. It's not a happy place to work, but the money is good. He is saving to buy a real house for us."

Diego and George Jenkins working as a team was something Elisa couldn't picture. For all his faults, Diego had a good heart. She had few reasons to believe the same could be said of his employer.

Elisa checked the clock over the door. She knew better than to prolong the discussion. Adoncia had to make her own decisions, and Elisa had interfered too much as it was. "Time to get to *La Casa*. I'm so glad you agreed to help today. Some of the children speak almost no English, and you can prod them a little."

"They are not like you, huh? They do not grow up speaking English with their parents?"

At moments like these, there was nothing Elisa could say.

"I am right," Adoncia said as they exited into the play yard and started across the grounds. It was not a question.

"What does it matter?"

"To me? Not at all. To you? So many things you don't talk about, Elisa. Are you afraid I will tell somebody?"

"I'm happy with things the way they are. I don't want to dwell on the past."

"Dwell? No. But mention sometimes?" Adoncia turned up her hands, not an easy feat with Fernando in her arms.

"You're a good friend to care."

"You need somebody else to care, not just me. You need a man. Men look at you, but you don't look back. This is part of the past you won't talk about?"

"First I have to find a man I want to look at."

"I think you found one, but you turn away."

Elisa knew Adoncia was talking about Sam, even though the subject of Community Church's minister had until now been off-limits. "You have a good imagination, Donchita, but there's no man."

The air was crisp, and fermenting apples from the abandoned orchard bordering church property scented the air. Nature's spectacular autumn pageant had nearly ended, and only the hardiest leaves still clung to the trees. Adoncia lowered Fernando to the ground, and he and Maria chased each other through the decomposing piles that lined the road leading up to the little yellow house.

Wisely Adoncia said nothing more, but thoughts of Sam were now firmly planted in Elisa's mind. For three weeks they had avoided each other as often as possible. Most of the time Gracie gave her instructions and passed along messages. Sam was polite but distant. She was the same.

But she missed him. She had filled her time and erased what longing she could with quilting and with *La Casa*. Somehow, without really planning to, she had become a regular volunteer at the after-school program, spending most afternoons helping any way she could.

By the time they got there, the children had already arrived, and several were sitting on the steps, including a sixth-grade boy named Miguel who was new to the program. Elisa had tried to talk to him several times, but he didn't respond to questions in English or Spanish. One of the volunteers who had elementary Spanish skills had expressed real concern about Miguel's adjustment and gone to visit his parents. The family seemed close-knit and supportive. The mother was worried, too. Her older sons had stayed behind in Mexico, and Miguel missed them desperately.

Elisa introduced Adoncia and her children to Miguel and the others. Miguel managed the briefest of nods but didn't reply when Adoncia tried to draw him out. The other children were more receptive and followed Adoncia inside to begin the cooking lesson.

Elisa dropped to the step beside Miguel. She remembered her brother at this age and the way that everything had seemed larger than life, one minute as bright as the north star, the next as dark as a cloudy night.

She spoke in Spanish. "Don't you want to join the others, Miguel? I'll work with you on the computer if you like."

He shook his head. Once.

"I think I know how you're feeling," she said softly, so no one would overhear. "I had to leave my home, too, and I haven't seen my brother since I did. I miss Ramon and all my friends."

He glanced at her, as if trying to figure out whether to move away or answer.

She pressed this slight advantage. "I can't talk about this to many people. It's hard to understand unless your own experience is the same."

She could almost see him processing her words and trying to decide if answering was worth the energy. In the end, though, he only shrugged. One brief shrug.

She was working on her next move when an aging green sedan came down the lane a little too fast and stopped, brakes screeching, just yards from the porch.

Leon got out on the passenger's side and opened the back door, pulling out a couple of boxes, one which was oversized and nearly flat, before he closed the door and rapped on the roof. The driver, a teenager who didn't look old enough to sit behind the wheel, backed into a parking space, turned and drove off.

"Hey, Leon." Elisa stood up to help the boy carry the boxes up to the porch. "What do you have here?"

Leon's cheeks reddened, but he smiled shyly. For the first time Elisa got a picture of the future Leon Jenkins and thought he was going to be quite appealing.

"I . . . well, I thought, you know, that I owed this place something."

"Did you?" She smiled at him, and the color in his cheeks deepened.

"I, well, those guys might not have come here, if I hadn't . . . you know."

"You can't take responsibility for the things other people decide to do. But I think it's great you want to do something for *La Casa*." She glanced down at Miguel as she spoke and saw something like interest sparkling in his eyes. "What did you bring us?"

By now Leon's cheeks were nearly burgundy. "I, well, I noticed there's not much to do outside. You know. So I got this basketball hoop. We can put it back there."

He pointed in the direction of the ramshackle frame garage behind the house, which these days held only garden tools. The asphalt driveway circled the house and ended there, and the paved area to one side of the door was flat and perfect for basketball games. Elisa wondered why nobody else had thought of this.

"You know, you're a genius. That's exactly what we need. The days are still too beautiful to spend inside."

He looked so relieved, she had to suppress a smile. "I can put it up for you, if you want," he volunteered. "I just need a ladder. I brought tools and stuff for the backboard."

"I'm almost sure there's a stepladder in the garage." She glanced down at Miguel again. Leon had opened the box to reveal the hoop and a wide composite backboard to mount it on, and Miguel was definitely interested.

"But you'll need help," she said. She fired off a rapid entreaty in Spanish to the boy sitting on the steps. At first it looked as if he would refuse or ignore her again. Then he got to his feet.

"This is Miguel," she told Leon. "I don't think he speaks much English, but he would be happy to help you. And he could use a friend."

Leon frowned, and she thought he was trying to decide if he was able to cope with the language difficulties and the need to reach out to a sixth grader. But he spoke after only the briefest of hesitations. "Hi, I'm Leon." He looked up at her. "How do you say that in Spanish?"

"Hola. Me llamo Leon."

Leon wrapped his tongue around the words and did a credible imitation. Then he motioned for Miguel to join him around back. Miguel trailed the older boy, but even following at a distance was a breakthrough.

Inside, she alerted the tutors about Miguel and the hoop; then she joined the cooks, making sure Fernando stayed away from the stove and the older children stayed close enough to see the day's lesson. Adoncia was clearly enjoying herself. Elisa thought her friend would make a good teacher. She had spoken to her about going to college, but Adoncia had too much to deal with at the moment to think about that.

She gave the boys half an hour to install the hoop before she went to check on them. She had just glanced down at Fernando, who was perched on her left hip sucking his thumb sleepily, when she stumbled against someone bounding through the front door.

Strong hands steadied her, and she looked up to find Sam.

"I'm sorry," he said. "I didn't see you."

Sam often checked on the children's progress in the late afternoon. They never wanted to put away their finished homework until Sam could inspect it. Elisa usually avoided him during those times by leaving before he arrived. But today her timing was off.

He was dressed in elegantly faded jeans, a navy turtleneck and a subtly patterned tweed sports coat. One lock of dark hair fell over his forehead, and his eyes were bluer than the October sky. She noticed that he had not yet dropped his hands. They were warm and heavy on her shoulders. "Did you see what's happening around back?"

He moved away then, his hands falling to his sides. "No. What's going on?"

"Come see."

He hesitated. Had anyone else asked this of him, he would have gone without comment.

She moved past him, letting him decide for himself whether walking to the backyard constituted an overload of intimacy. She felt a flash of anger that their friendship, which had been so important to her, had been forced to end this way. Neither of them had asked for the attraction that leapt between them, yet even now, after weeks apart, her body felt warm and liquid, as if the very tissue that held it together was melting away. Female desire had once seemed an academic subject worthy of study, a combination of biological imperative and an instinctive preference for traits to pass on to offspring. Sprinkle in estrogen, testosterone and pheromones, and yearning for a certain man was the result.

It was anything but academic now.

She felt, rather than heard, him follow her. She sped up so they wouldn't have an opportunity to speak again without the boys present. She wasn't sure which would be worse, speaking, or finding that he had no intention of doing so.

Leon and Miguel had made great progress, and Elisa was pleased to see the installation was a joint venture. The composite backboard was already installed, and Miguel was up on the ladder tightening what looked like the final screw on the hoop as Leon held it steady. "Look at you," she said. "It's up already."

"Can we play once he's done?" Leon turned his head but continued to hold tightly to the ladder. "I promised Miguel."

Elisa couldn't imagine any activity more enriching than that one. Miguel, mourning his brothers, needed boy time more than he needed anything else.

"I say yes," she said quickly before Sam could comment. "But only if I can play, too."

"Hey, wait a minute." Sam came to stand beside her. "Two per team."

"What about the baby?" Leon looked doubtful.

Elisa realized if she carried Fernando back inside now, he would wail inconsolably. And there was no spot outside safe enough for him to play without close supervision.

"I'll take him."

Elisa saw that some of the older girls had followed them. Damita, who had spoken, held out her arms. "Maybe you'd rather play?" Elisa asked.

Damita, long hair flying, shook her head. "I have a baby brother. I'll take care of him."

Elisa knew a deal when she heard one. She set the little boy in Damita's sturdy arms, and when she saw Fernando looked perfectly at home, she turned. "Reverend Sam and I against you boys. Prepare to lose."

Leon slung his arm around Miguel's broad shoulders. "We'll beat them, won't we?"

The quirk of Miguel's lips was barely wide enough to qualify as a smile, but it looked like the sun coming out to Elisa.

Leon retrieved a brand-new basketball

from the second box. Elisa imagined he had spent much of his pocket money on this equipment, which looked brand-new, and she was proud of him. He tossed the ball to Miguel. The boy tried a few tentative bounces, then he took off for the hoop. He made a basket in one shot.

"Wow!" Leon clapped his hands. "Good going!" The ball bounced in Elisa's direction, and he stopped clapping in time to intercept it after she tried to pass it to Sam. He dribbled toward the net, but Elisa was in front of him in a flash, raising her arms to make the shot more difficult.

Leon dodged right, then swung left, but she was ready for him. She had taught Ramon that very maneuver, and for one bittersweet moment she pretended this was Ramon in front of her.

Leon whirled 180 degrees, dribbled a few feet, feinted left, feinted right, turned again and shot despite her attempts to block him. But the shot missed, and Sam was right there to catch it. Miguel charged him, and Sam fumbled. In a split second Miguel had the ball and made another successful basket.

Sam looked properly chagrined, although Elisa was sure both the fumble and the sheepish expression were Oscar-winning performances. She provided an encore, retrieving the ball and narrowly missing the next shot. Miguel caught it as it bounced off the backboard.

Miguel shot another basket, and as before, she grabbed the ball as it fell through the net. This time she dodged Leon's attempts to block her. As the two boys bore down on her, she flashed them each a grin, dribbled a few feet, turned her back to the hoop and lofted the ball high over her shoulder.

She knew from their startled expressions when the ball went through.

"How did you do that?" Leon stopped and stared at her. "You weren't even looking!"

"I knew where it was. I saw it in my mind's eye."

"That's crazy!"

Miguel, who was less concerned about what she had done and more concerned about what *he* could do, grabbed the ball as Sam neared him, dancing back and forth until he had a credible opening. Then he tossed the ball over Sam's head. It bounced on the rim and fell back. Elisa scooted around Leon to grab it, but mid-dribble he knocked it out of her hand, clearly determined now that she would get no favors because of age or sex. He made a basket.

More children came to watch, and cheering sections formed. They weren't keeping score, although Elisa noted that Sam made certain the boys had an equal number of baskets. When he allowed himself the pleasure, his game was fluid and expert. But clearly Sam had the most fun watching the kids.

They had been playing for about twenty minutes when Fernando clamored to get down. Damita tried to cajole him, but several kicks later she put him on the ground, unaware how quick he could be. From the far side of the court Elisa watched the little drama unfold. Damita set the toddler on the ground, keeping a hand on his shoulder to detain him, but Fernando, who was absolutely clear about what he wanted, dodged her hand and ran on to the court.

Leon and Sam were vying for the ball near the edge when Fernando arrived. Before either of them could stop, they plowed into the little boy, and the three of them went down in a tangle of arms and legs.

Sam managed to protect Fernando by lifting him so his head didn't hit the pavement. But there was no way to keep him from scraping his shins on the asphalt.

"You okay?" Sam asked Leon as he stood and swung Fernando into his arms.

"Yeah, what about him?"

Elisa arrived to inspect her small friend. His screams had already turned to whimpers. Fernando liked nothing as well as an audience. Sam held him out for her examination. "Scrapes," she said after a cursory perusal. "Maybe a bruise tomorrow."

"We have a first aid kit in the upstairs bathroom," he said. "His mother will want to clean him up."

Elisa took Fernando and cuddled him against her chest, murmuring softly to him in Spanish until he quieted. "Adoncia will want me to do it. Is the kit in the cabinet?"

"I'll show you." Sam turned to the boys. "Looks to me like there are a couple more basketball players here." He motioned to the biggest girls. Leon looked disgusted, but he nodded.

Elisa assured Damita she hadn't done anything wrong and that Fernando would be fine. Then she and Sam started toward the house.

"Where did you learn to play like that?" he said, when they were out of earshot.

"I was the captain of my basketball team."

"You're pretty short to be anybody's captain."

She knew he was teasing. "We have few giants in my country."

"You practiced. A lot."

"I have a brother."

"And he taught you to play?"

"Why do men always think another man must have done the teaching?"

"You're right. You taught him?"

"He is much younger. He came into the world with a football — what you call a soccer ball — in one hand and a basketball in the other."

"That must have been hard on your mother."

"She was so grateful to have him, he could have come with a whole basketball team. She waited a long time for another child."

"Where is he now?"

This was the central question of her life. Was her brother alive, making his way toward Virginia? Was he in Mexico, trying to cross the border? Or . . . She would not even allow herself to think of the other possibilities. Until someone presented her with proof her brother was dead, she would not let herself consider it.

"He is seeing the world while he is still

young." She fervently prayed it was true.

"You miss him."

"More than I can say."

"You seem so alone."

She glanced at him from under her eye-lashes. "We each make our way in the world. Those who have someone to share the journey with are luckier than they know."

They reached the porch steps, and Sam opened the door for her. Fernando had nearly fallen asleep, and although Elisa hated to wake him, she knew the scrapes needed to be cleaned and treated. She took him into the kitchen, where Adoncia fussed over him without looking at his injuries. Elisa assured her they were minor and would heal quickly; then she took him upstairs.

Sam followed. She hadn't really expected his help. She could have found the first aid kit without him, but she was grateful. He removed a plastic tackle box from the cabinet under the sink and set it on the counter. "Want to do it in here?"

"Yes, I'll need running water." She took a clean washcloth from a basket over the toilet and handed it to Sam. "Will you wet this?"

The bathroom was tiny, and he had

closed the door to keep curious children at bay, although he opened the window over the tub immediately, as if he needed the fresh air for reassurance. In the confined space, she was more aware of him than ever. As she swayed to comfort Fernando, her hips brushed Sam's. She crooned softly in Spanish, trying not to notice the solid feel of Sam's hip against hers.

When the washcloth was ready, she perched the little boy on the edge of the counter, one arm around him to be sure he didn't slip off. "Will you keep him steady while I wash my hands?" she asked Sam.

Sam leaned over and put an arm around Fernando, too. For a moment they were linked by their connection to the little boy. Their faces were only inches apart. He smelled faintly of lime, and she could see twin depressions at the bridge of his nose, probably from reading or sunglasses. Then, suddenly aware that she had lingered too long, Elisa let him take Fernando's weight and she slipped away. She lathered her hands with liquid soap and rinsed twice. Then she took the washcloth.

"I can take over from here," she said.

"I'll stay and keep him company."

She was aware of his eyes on her and the

warmth of his body beside her as she sponged Fernando's leg. The toddler was too interested to protest. She concentrated on examining the scrapes — two areas — carefully and swung him close to the faucet. "I'm going to take off your shoes, Nando," she crooned. "Then your leg will take a bath in the sink."

He giggled.

"Is he always this accommodating?" Sam asked.

"He's a wonderful little boy." She put her forehead against Fernando's. "Aren't you, *querido?*"

Fernando put his arms around her neck and kissed her.

"He's a *lucky* little boy," Sam said.

Her heart took off again, and she couldn't look at him. Her fingers fumbled with the Velcro fasteners of Fernando's sneakers, but she managed to get them off quickly enough. She put his socks — so tiny they gave her a pang — inside his shoes and whirled him around so she could run water over his leg.

He didn't like this part as well. He whimpered a little, but Sam began to make faces at him, and in a moment Fernando, trying to imitate them, forgot to worry.

"Adoncia won't thank you for that. He'll

be making faces at everybody." Elisa made certain there was no debris clinging to Fernando's skin. When she was satisfied all the dirt had been washed away, she lathered the cloth with soap and gently cleaned his leg. Sam's faces got wilder, and Fernando only protested twice.

"Okay, Nando," she said at last. "We're all finished here. Let me dry it, then we'll put some cream on it and you can have a Band-Aid."

"You should have children," Sam said.

She looked up at him. "So should you."

"Why aren't you married, Elisa?"

Her chest felt tight. They were only inches apart. It would have taken no effort at all to lean against him. "I was." Her voice sounded like it was coming from far away. "My husband died."

"I'm sorry." He cocked his head. "There were no children?"

"My husband didn't want them." So much had happened, so many years had passed, and still the truth of that saddened her. "He did not want to bring children into this mess we have made of our world. But he helped me raise my brother."

"*You* raised your brother?"

Again she knew she had said too much. "With my husband's help."

"Where were your parents?"

"Dead."

He lowered his voice. "The day I hired you, you told me that you left home when you were young because your parents had too much to handle."

There were so many lies, and it was so easy to be caught up in them. "They died after I left. I went back, took my brother, and married my husband."

She glanced at him. He did not look convinced.

"You must be close to your brother if you raised him yourself. Will he come to visit?"

She hoped for nothing so much as that. "God willing."

"You'll introduce me?"

She took her time selecting a Band-Aid with Fernando's help, taking the cap off the antibiotic ointment, drying Fernando's leg. Then she looked up again.

"I don't know what to say to you anymore, Sam. Do you want me to include you in my life? The rules have changed?"

His expression was unreadable. "I thought we were still friends."

"I don't think so." She dabbed the ointment on Fernando's leg, then covered the worst scrape with the favored Band-Aid.

"I didn't ask you to shut me out entirely."

She lifted Fernando off the counter and cuddled him against her. She was aware that the little boy was now a barrier between them, no longer a bridge. Only then did she meet Sam's gaze. "It's the only way."

He didn't deny it. When she opened the door, he let her go without another word.

Chapter
Nineteen

Elisa liked fall mornings in the countryside. She could lie in bed without opening her eyes and pretend she was in one of the mountain villages that she and Gabrio had visited. There, just as they did here, roosters announced the sunrise, and the dew-saturated air swept in through open windows and cracks in the walls.

If it was market day in the mountains, the family would be up before dawn readying produce or handicrafts for the journey. The air would be scented with coffee, smoke from the cooking fire and, too often, the acrid odor of inconsistent sanitation and poverty. But no matter how poor people were — and many of them had been all too desperate — they had shared what little they had, grateful for what she and Gabrio could offer in return, grateful that someone they could trust had come to listen.

Elisa knew at exactly what point in her reminiscences to force her eyelids open. As dawn slowly lit the room she would stare at the ceiling above her bed and resolutely follow the spiderweb crackling of the paint, compelling herself to seal her memories back in the box she envisioned deep inside her — a box far too close to her heart.

On November first she knew better than to allow herself even those few moments of remembrance. Some dates were so powerful that the memories became a plague, a feverish infestation of images she couldn't bear. On this morning she slipped out from under the covers immediately upon waking and made the bed, folding and draping the extra quilts neatly across the footboard.

The sun was not yet up. Normally she would have been careful not to wake Helen, who wasn't a sound sleeper, but Helen was in Richmond, spending the weekend with Nancy and Billy, and Elisa was alone in the house. This was not good for her state of mind. With people around her, she could exist in the present. Without them, it was too easy to let her mind drift. She scooped up clean clothes and took them to the bathroom, where she showered quickly, changed and left through the back door.

The sun was just lighting the horizon when she trooped out to the barn to feed the bevy of fat unnamed cats Helen swore she didn't love. The morning was already warmer than she'd expected, promising a glorious Indian summer day. She removed the sweater she'd been sure she would need and flung it over her shoulders; then she continued on to the chicken yard to scatter feed and check for eggs. Finding none, she fastened the chicken wire fence, made sure the house was locked and left for church.

Nothing special was on the schedule today, and there were no unusual meetings to prepare for. A community group that normally rented the social hall on first Saturdays had postponed until December, since they had celebrated Halloween last night with a party at the American Legion Hall. Unless something unexpected had occurred, her work would be minimal. Then she would have the rest of a long day to get through alone. There were no children to tutor, and although she could spend the afternoon at the treadle or the quilt frame, neither held much appeal. It was too easy to think while she did both, too easy to relive her husband's death. Too easy to wonder if she would ever see Ramon again.

As she'd expected, the lot was empty. She parked close to the entrance, then with a plastic garbage bag in hand, she made a sweep of the pavement, gathering candy wrappers that looked as if they had blown in from a ghost or goblin's trick-or-treat bag. Behind the church, she walked through the tiny graveyard, then the rose garden, picking up gum wrappers, a paper cup and several straws, but clearly no one had set out to damage church property last night. Three boys who had vandalized *La Casa* had finally been arrested and charged. Sam was hoping they would be sentenced to make restitution and perform community service.

She bundled what little trash she'd recovered and tossed it in the bin at the back. She entered through the side of the church, flipping light switches until she gathered her things from the sexton's closet in the upstairs hallway. She donned a canvas apron with wide pockets to keep her clothes clean, and trundled the mop and bucket into the social hall.

The wall clock reminded her it was not

yet eight. She hadn't eaten or made coffee at Helen's, and by the time she'd mopped the floor and set up tables for tomorrow's fellowship hours, she realized she'd made an error. In her hurry to exchange the empty house for an empty church, she had overestimated her own reserve of energy and, worse, her emotional resources.

She rested against a table and rubbed her eyes with the back of her hand; then she stared at the wall across the room, as she had stared at the ceiling that morning, and sought composure. She was still staring, trying to pull herself together, when she heard a noise in the hallway. She jerked her head up to see Sam in the doorway.

"You startled me!" Heart pounding, she straightened, pushing away from the table.

"What are you doing here so early?" he asked.

He was dressed in fleece sweatpants and a long-sleeved T-shirt with an American flag and words she couldn't read from this distance. She thought he had shaved, but his hair was rumpled, and when Shadrach and Meshach wandered through the doorway, she realized he had probably jogged here.

"I could ask you the same thing," she said.

"I couldn't sleep." He shrugged.

"Me either."

"It makes for a long day. You look like you've had one already."

She bent, extended a hand and clicked her tongue, and the dogs bounded over to greet her. She was glad to have two hands, one for each bobbing furry head. To their credit, neither of them jumped up on her, although she imagined that had more to do with exhaustion than good manners.

Sam followed the dogs. "I hear Helen's out of town."

"The house is too quiet and very empty."

"You look tired."

She looked up from the petting session and silently read his shirt. *Dissent is Patriotic.* "Another sermon?"

"There's never enough time in the pulpit. And you're trying to change the subject."

She tried for a wry smile. "I was just thinking I should run out for some fast food. I didn't eat before I left the house."

"You should know better."

"Did *you* eat?"

"I had a choice between saltines and

canned beets. I passed."

She knew he sometimes worked on his sermon on Saturday, but she had never expected to find him here so early. "Were you planning to stay? I could bring something back for you, if you like."

"No, I was planning to finish my run."

She looked down. Both Shad and Shack were panting. "The dogs look finished to me."

"It's early for them, too."

She glanced up at the clock again to dismiss him. "Well, enjoy the rest of your day."

"Fast food isn't good for you."

She thought she'd ended the conversation. "I'll take that under advisement."

"Fat. Salt. Sugar." He frowned.

"Sam, since when has nutrition concerned you?"

"Let me take you to breakfast."

For a moment she wasn't certain she understood. "Breakfast?"

"You know, that meal most people eat first thing when they wake up? I guess we could wait for lunch, but I don't think you'd make it that long."

"Oh, no, I —"

He rested his fingertips on her forearm. "Yes, you could."

She knew better than to go. Her feelings must have showed in her face. "It's just breakfast," he said. "We'll go somewhere and sit across from each other at a table." He hesitated, as if he was trying to figure out how to word the next part. "It's not going to hurt anybody. You don't look happy. Let me do something. At least let me feed you."

"I couldn't. You have the dogs. It will be so late by the time you run home —"

"We'll drop them on the way, if you don't mind them in your car."

She didn't bother to remind him it was his car. "You don't think it might create problems? If we're seen together that way?"

"There's no reason for anyone to gossip."

She didn't want to bring up the wisdom of spending time in each other's company. Calling attention to what had been merely wisps of conversation was a risk. She could make too much of this and by her very words create a situation where there was none. They had set no ground rules, made no declarations or refusals. He had implied he was attracted to her and that this was a problem for an engaged man. She had used even fewer words to tell him there was no hope of a relationship anyway. They had been careful, controlled, evasive. Anyone listening might have missed the inferences. But she had not.

And neither had he.

She had considered long enough and by doing so drawn too much attention to this. "All right. I have all day to finish my cleaning."

"Correct me if I'm wrong, but it won't take all day. Right this minute I'd be comfortable eating off any surface in the building."

"Maybe an hour," she admitted.

"Then you have plenty of time for coffee, bacon and eggs. And the place I'd like to take you has the best sweet rolls in Virginia."

"Fat, salt and sugar, remember?"

"You've never had better." He whistled for the dogs and disappeared back through the doorway in the direction of his study.

She squeezed the last drops of water from her mop, then wheeled the bucket back to the sexton's closet, emptied the contents in the sink, cleaned it out, then went next door to the ladies' room to wash up.

Sam was waiting by his office when she arrived. "I made a reservation."

She was charmed but skeptical. The countryside had its pluses, but superior restaurants were not one of them. At the most she had expected a step up from the fast food she'd offered or one of the truck stops out on the interstate. Of the restaurants that were available, she imagined few served breakfast.

In the parking lot, she tried to hand him the car keys, embarrassed to be driving him in his own car. But he refused. "I'll direct you from my house."

Out on Old Miller Road, she glanced at him. "You're being mysterious."

"I'm basking in the glow of my creativity."

She put her foot on the brake. "Tell me we're not going to *your* house for breakfast and you're not cooking."

"You're implying there's something wrong with the way I eat."

"You *are* going to cook."

"No, remember? I need to go shopping. So, no. We'll just drop off the dogs."

Her foot moved back to the accelerator. They reached his house, and after the dogs were safely inside and he had changed into a sweatshirt that matched his pants, he returned to the car. "Just continue on Old Miller another mile."

She was willing but skeptical. "Is this a back way somewhere?"

"Turn right at the next crossroads, then make your first right and your fifth left."

"Heading toward the river?"

"You're going to have a ringside seat."

Despite herself, she was getting into the spirit. If she didn't feel cheerful, at least she was no longer in danger of bursting into tears. She gave herself over to driving, following his instructions with a little prompting each time. Otherwise they didn't speak.

At the fifth left she was forced to slow down when the paved road ended suddenly. "A picnic?"

"Do you see a basket?"

"What could possibly be out this far?"

"Slow down."

"I'll come to a dead halt."

"We're about to turn."

She slowed to a crawl, and he pointed left. She stopped when she saw a sign that read: Daughter of the Stars, and beneath it, A Bed and Breakfast Inn.

"Gayle Fortman owns and runs it," Sam said. "She's the president of our board of deacons. The river's just beyond."

"Does she know we're having breakfast with her guests?"

"Now that the leaves are almost gone, she says her guests have dwindled. When I called from my study, she said she'd be glad to have us this morning." He touched her arm when he saw she was still hesitant. "I've been here before. She's been asking me to come again. She wants to do this."

Reluctantly, Elisa turned into the drive. The inn was old and rambling. The brick red paint, white trim and black shutters gave it a colonial feel. Porches jutted from every side. Gold chrysanthemums and purple pansies outlined flower beds and filled pots on the front porch. Wicker and wood furniture nestled under hanging ferns in comfortable groupings.

"The house has been here a long time," Sam said. "Gayle and her husband found it when people could still afford property in the area. I gather the renovation took years. He left in the middle of it. She finished with loans and elbow grease."

Elisa could imagine the work involved in running a place like this one and keeping it profitable. "She lives here alone now?"

"She has three teenaged boys. Good kids."

"Friends of Leon's?"

"I don't know, but we ought to encourage that."

Despite her best instincts, she was pleased at the "we" in that sentence.

She parked, and with typical good manners he got out and came around to open her door, but she was already out, too. "I still feel strange, Sam. Is this where Christine stays when she visits?"

"No. Chrissy wants to be away from church members."

She wondered if that had caused him any embarrassment with Gayle.

"And it doesn't matter," he went on. "I told Gayle I found you working too hard, too early. And I did."

She wished she hadn't mentioned Christine. By doing so, *she* was the one who was making more of this than he had intended.

They walked up the path to the porch, and Sam let them in, rapping his knuckles on the door as he opened it. "Anybody home?"

The entry hall extended at least twenty-five feet to swinging doors. There was a desk to the right, with an open book for guests to sign, and pottery containers with brochures advertising Luray Caverns and the Blue Ridge Parkway. Guide books for the area were neatly overlapped in a vertical row, and an apothecary jar was filled with colorful jelly beans.

The floor was pine, with a runner the same red as the siding extending to the doors. Behind the table was a seating area with plush jewel-tone love seats and windows overlooking the porch. In front of them and off to the right was a wide staircase leading to a sunlit landing before it made a full turn to continue to the next floor. The staircase was pine, as well. The entire effect was of space and warmth. Elisa was enchanted.

The doors at the end of the hall swung open, and a woman with short blond hair and a smile came through. She was drying her hands on a dishtowel, and she slung it over one arm and extended her hand before she reached Elisa. "I'm Gayle. I don't think we've met, although I've seen you hard at work."

Elisa shook. "It's kind of you to have us."

"Actually, it's something of a conspiracy. I keep trying to feed Sam, but he's always too busy. Do you know what he eats?"

"I'm afraid so."

"I decided it's too pretty outside to let you eat indoors, so I set a table on our patio for you. I hope that's okay. It may be the last morning of the season that's warm enough."

"Your other guests are already out?" Sam asked.

"No, sometimes everyone eats together, but people are coming and going this morning. So you'll have a table to yourself." She read Elisa's expression correctly. "Please don't worry. I've told Sam, I make extras of everything. My kids will eat what the guests don't. With teenage boys, I don't worry about wasting food; I worry about having enough. So I make tons."

"This is a treat," Elisa said.

"Take it from me. When you take care of other people all the time, you need somebody to wait on you for a change. Both you and Sam work too hard." She turned to Sam. "Don't you?"

"Abolish death, sin and basic obstinacy, and I'll take it as easy as the next man."

"Your obstinacy or the congregation's?"

"Take your pick."

"Go that way." She pointed to the room beside the hallway, a larger version of the nook behind the desk, furnished with comfortable chairs, sofas, country antiques and glass-fronted bookcases. "Through the dining room and out the back door. The patio's just below the back porch. You've been there, Sam."

"We'll find our way."

"I'll bring you coffee and juice. Make yourselves comfortable."

Elisa admired the rooms as they walked through, particularly the antique star quilts Gayle had used on several walls. She could hear noise from the kitchen, but all doors leading to it were closed. Outside again on the back porch, she got her first glimpse of the river. "Look at that."

"It's wonderful, isn't it? Gayle could sell this place and retire on the profits, but she loves it too much. Somebody would tear down the inn and build a village of mini-mansions. She wants as many people as possible to enjoy this part of the river."

He took the steps down, and she followed. The fieldstone patio was level, but the land from that point was terraced. They were many feet above the river. The banks on both sides were thick with trees, but there were enough breaks for them to easily view the water sparkling in the sunshine.

They seated themselves at a round table that was already set for two. Elisa was enchanted with the view. "Why did she name the inn Daughter of the Stars?"

"You don't know the legend?"

"I guess not."

"Some people think that's what the word

Shenandoah means. Of course, there are detractors, who are probably right, who say the name comes from other sources. But the legend is better."

Gayle arrived with a tray. She placed two glasses of grapefruit juice served over crushed ice and rimmed with sugar on the table, along with a pot of coffee with a pitcher of cream.

They thanked her, and she promised to return in a few minutes with food.

Elisa sipped her juice and felt better almost immediately. "Tell me the story."

"It's an Indian legend. First the Great Spirit made the world. And did a fine job of it, too. Afterward the morning stars, arrayed in robes of fire, wanted to celebrate this beauty together, so they found the loveliest place in the world, a shining silver lake rimmed with blue-green mountains, and they sang a song of joy. They were so pleased, they promised to meet there every thousand years to do it again."

He stopped. "You're smiling."

"I'm imagining plugging that date into an appointment book. Singing songs of joy. Same day, next millennium."

He smiled, too. For a moment he just looked at her.

"What?" she asked.

"That's the first real smile I've seen from you all morning. I feel better."

She looked down at the table, picking off an imaginary crumb. "Go on with your story."

"They met again and again, but one day, while they were singing, a huge boulder broke loose from a mountain rimming the lake, and all the water poured out in a rush to the sea."

"You didn't tell me this was going to be a sad story."

"It's not. Because a thousand years later, when the stars looked for another place to reunite, they came upon a beautiful green valley with a silver river running through it and knew this would be a perfect place to sing. Finally one of them realized these were the same mountains where they had cast their robes of fire, and the silver river ran along what had once been the bed of their lake. They were so pleased, they plucked the jewels out of their crowns and threw them in the river. And that's why the Shenandoah sparkles the way it does, and why it's called The Daughter of the Stars."

"And Gayle named the inn after the legend."

"It's beautiful, don't you think?"

It *was* beautiful, but the timing for

hearing it was wrong. The timing for being here was wrong, too. She had realized both those things when Sam started to speak, when he commented on her smile, when the cool autumn breeze sent wisps of hair dancing around her face. At first she had felt better, before the sudden inexplicable overload of beauty, of sentiment, of the company of a man she cared too much about, crashed around her. Now she felt worse, and she steeled herself against the flood of sadness.

"Yes, it's beautiful, but the story's every bit as likely as Adam and Eve and the Garden of Eden." Her voice sounded tight, her words stilted.

"Legend's never about words and phrases, it's about deeper meaning. A scientific explanation of the Big Bang has very little poetry and wouldn't be recounted around a campfire for one generation, much less millennia."

"I was always the debunker of myth."

"You come from a culture with rich, colorful traditions *based* on legend and myth. Wouldn't you say they provide meaning for a lot of people, whether they're strictly true or not?"

She toyed with her fork. "I don't think I'm up to theological discussion this morning."

"One of those traditions is the Day of the Dead," Sam said. "Which is today, as a matter of fact."

She rested her head in her hands, elbows perfectly splayed over gleaming white pottery. "I know what day it is."

"Is that why you're feeling sad? Why you came in to work so early?"

"I'm fine. Maybe a little tired."

"Maybe a little sad?"

She straightened and looked up to see Gayle approaching with another tray. She managed all the right responses, exclaiming over Virginia country ham, cheesy garden omelets with the tail end of the season's peppers and tomatoes, the cinnamon pecan rolls that Sam had rhapsodized about in the church social hall. Gayle excused herself to take care of a couple who were checking out, and they were alone again.

He dove right into his food, and for a moment she thought he might forget his questions, but a few mouthfuls later, he looked up. "That's what's bothering you, isn't it?"

Denial drew more attention than a simple yes. She nodded.

"Tell me how you celebrated in Mexico."

"You probably know all about it."

"Humor me. I'm sure the traditions are different in different parts of the country."

He wanted her to talk. She thought it was one part counseling, one part curiosity, one part concern. Then there was that elusive fourth part, neither affection nor attraction, exactly, but some volatile mixture of both that they could not discuss.

"It's a day to honor and remember the dead," she said. "A day to bring them back to life, if only in our hearts."

"And from what little you've said, too many people you've loved have died." When she didn't answer, he held out the basket of cinnamon rolls. "This will make you feel better."

She took one. "Cinnamon roll therapy?"

"More like somebody who cares about you wishing he could do something to help."

His kindness brought tears to her eyes. She blinked them away. "Thank you."

"Did you go to the cemeteries? Have processions or parades?"

She bit into the roll. It was every bit as good as he had promised. "There are flowers and candles, sweets. Skulls of spun sugar. The cemeteries are decorated. There's music."

"What's your favorite memory of the day?"

That was so easy, she spoke before she had time to censor herself. "There was a village some distance from . . ." Good sense intruded. "The place I grew up. They had a special way to celebrate and honor the dead. Once, when I was a little girl, my family drove there to be part of it, because my father's family had come from a place not far away." She stopped, aware that she was about to say more than she should.

"What did you do?"

She wanted to describe that day to him. For so long there had been no one to talk to.

"I like to hear about your life," he said.

She weighed the dangers of recounting one small story, but in the end her desire to do so outweighed caution.

"We got up very early, well before dawn. There were only three of us. My mother, father and me. My brother was not yet born. It seemed to me we drove for hours. The roads were not good, and I remember being unhappy I could not be with my friends. My mother had set up an altar in our home with photos of family who were gone, candles and offerings of food. My parents were not Catholic, but this one time of the year they acted like everyone else. I wanted to go to the same cemeteries as my friends, but my father said that it was more important to be with my family. And we had cousins buried in this village, people I had never seen or known."

She paused to eat a little, and Sam didn't hurry her.

"We arrived at last," she said, when she was feeling a little less hungry. "There were so many people in the streets, all dressed in their finest clothing. There were vendors selling food, and I asked for corn. I remember my mother bought me some. It's not like the corn we eat here, larger, not as sweet, but with lime and salt it was delicious.

"There was a procession to the cemetery, and we walked with everybody else. When we got there, I saw the kites." She looked up. Sam had stopped eating and was simply watching her. "Your food will get cold," she said.

"Kites?"

"The most extraordinary kites you could imagine. *Barriletes*. Some so large they couldn't be held by one man. The people made them of bamboo and wire, cloth or colored paper. Some had taken all year to make, and each was unique. They could not fly the largest, of course, but all that morning and into the afternoon, they flew those they could. From a child's perspective, the kites reached all the way to the heavens."

"It must have been a spectacle. But why kites?"

"Some say the dead know the color of their family's kites and slide down the string to be with them. Others tie messages to the tails, to tell departed family members what has happened that year and whether they are well. Most of all they ask for favors and blessings, because their loved ones are nearer to God than they are."

Sam sat back. "Did you fly a kite?"

"A little one my father bought for us there." She finished the food on her plate.

"It's a moving ritual," Sam said. "A way to face and release a little grief."

"There is a lot of grief in this world to release."

"And if you were home, you might be able to put some of your own grief in perspective today."

She had certainly been indiscreet enough in the past that it was no surprise Sam had drawn conclusions. "Loss is part of living."

"Not the best part."

She managed a smile. "No."

"Thank you for sharing the story."

She wanted to tell him she felt better, that talking about her family had put her losses in perspective. But, of course, it wasn't true. Still, she was glad he had cared enough to pull the story out of her, even though caring complicated their relationship and both of them knew it.

"We left to go home that afternoon," she said. "But years later I learned that the kites are burned at the end of the festival. The dead must be released to go back where they came from. Only for that one day are they allowed to be with us."

He put his hand over hers. "But you always carry them in your heart."

"And that is why my heart is so heavy."

"You can't let go?"

She looked up, straight into his eyes. "If I let go, who will be left to remember?"

Chapter
Twenty

By afternoon Sam had a mission in mind, and for once Bed got to join the other dogs. Sam packed all three mutts in his SUV, although he had to lift Bed into the back when her short legs and heroic leaps wouldn't do the trick. In the driver's seat, he turned and admonished them.

"You will be on your best behavior. You won't take off after squirrels or rabbits. If you see a bear, you'll run in the other direction. If you don't see a bear, you won't complain. And no matter what else you do, you won't do anything that will frighten Elisa. Got it?"

Two wagging tails were visible. Sam was sure that somewhere out of sight Bed's stumpy tail was stirring the air, too.

He covered the miles between the parsonage and Helen's house at a moderate clip. His brain was a battlefield, but he had already declared a winner. Perhaps leaving well enough alone today was the most rational strategy. Certainly waiting until he and Christine resolved their future was the most mature strategy. But seeking out Elisa again was the most human strategy, and the one he had chosen.

Last night Christine had called from the country club to wish him a happy Halloween and to tell him that instead of a traditional Thanksgiving dinner, the Fletchers had decided to host a catered gathering for fifty of their closest friends. She expected Sam to come, of course, and when he suggested instead that she drive to Pennsylvania with him to spend the holiday with his family, she refused outright. By the end of the conversation they had settled on a quiet weekend in Toms Brook after they both completed their separate holiday plans.

Sadly, Sam realized he had only suggested this alternative because he and Christine could no longer delay the conversation that was hovering at the edges of their lives.

Sam was relieved when he saw his little Honda parked in Helen's drive, since he hadn't consulted Elisa, and he hadn't warned her he was on his way. He parked behind it and told the dogs he would be back. Then he removed the large plastic bag from the passenger seat and put it on the roof of the car so the dogs couldn't damage the contents while he was gone.

He knocked, then stood back and waited. He didn't have to wait long. Elisa, in blue jeans and a dark red blouse tied under her breasts, answered the door. Her shining black hair streamed down her back and over one shoulder. He had never seen it when it wasn't braided or clipped.

All nobility fled, and he faced the real reason, or at least the biggest one, that he had come to see her this afternoon. He could no longer make himself stay away.

"Sam." She made two syllables out of it. "Did you leave something in your car this morning?"

"No, but there's something on my SUV you need to see." He remembered this feeling from adolescence. Suddenly he didn't know what to say or where to put his hands. And he was steeling himself, all the while, for rejection.

"I was just in the middle of . . ." She hesitated, then she smiled a little. "Nothing."

He relaxed an inch, took a breath and forced his way back to maturity. "I'm glad

I'm not pulling you away from something you can't leave."

"I was trying to read."

"What?"

"A textbook on geriatric medicine."

"It's a beautiful day outside. Did you notice?"

"I borrowed the book from the home. I . . . I thought it might help me understand some of the medical terms better."

"Can you put it down for a while?"

"I could put it down forever."

"Come see what I brought." He turned, trusting her to come.

She followed him down the steps almost to his car. "The dogs? You want me to see the dogs?"

"You've had that pleasure once today. No, something else." He glanced sideways, and once again felt her beauty in places that were, under the circumstances, best ignored.

"Breakfast, and now this," she said.

He thought of Gayle Fortman's last words that morning. He'd stopped to thank her one more time after Elisa had gone outside to retrieve the car.

Gayle had watched as Elisa disappeared down the steps. "A lot of people who emigrate to this country were lawyers or architects or brain surgeons before they came, and now they're cleaning churches or asking if we want fries with our burgers. Elisa was one of them, wasn't she?"

He hadn't been able to answer. But every time he was with Elisa, he hoped he got a little closer to unlocking her secrets.

"Breakfast was a good idea," he said now.

She stopped a few feet from the car and waited. One of the dogs — Shad, most likely — signaled his impatience with a pathetic howl. Sam removed the bag and snapped it open wider with the flick of his wrist. Then he pulled out a huge rainbow-colored kite, still in its original package.

He held it out to her. "It's a perfect day. Sunny. Just enough breeze. Helen's acres waiting to be trampled by willing feet."

"Oh, Sam . . ."

He touched her shoulder, then withdrew his hand. "Don't say no."

She put her hands palm to palm and rested her fingertips against her lips. "Where did you get it?"

"Rachel gave it to me for my birthday. When we were kids I used to tell her to go fly a kite whenever she was bothering me. My childhood comes back to haunt me frequently. At least this time it wasn't a lunch box."

Her voice was husky. "I like your sister, and I haven't even met her."

Sam knew Rachel would like Elisa, too, as would Mark and his parents. They would find Elisa approachable and warm.

"I hope it's a good one. I grew up in a kite-eating coal patch. The overhead wires were so low, the birds were afraid to sit on them because the alley cats might reach up and grab them. The town saved money by cutting the electric poles so short any kid who grew to be more than six feet was —"

She took the kite out of his hands and looked up at him. "I'd love to fly it with you."

He fell silent. He thought he'd never seen anyone so appealing as she was at that moment, hair streaming over her shoulders, eyes luminous, lips softly parted.

"You're a good man," she said softly.

"We'll tie messages on the tail."

"And the dogs will come with us?"

"If you'll have them."

"We'll just keep them on a leash until we're past the barn and the chicken yard. The ducks at the pond can fend for themselves."

"Do you need anything inside?"

"Go ahead and let them out. I'll go the way I am."

Once the dogs were out of the car, Elisa lavished attention on them; then both of them kept the big dogs in line as they moved past the house and into the open countryside. Bed followed at their heels.

Sam had brought a light jacket, but the sun was hot on his arms and neck through his sweatshirt. He tied it around his waist in case the wind picked up and Elisa needed it.

When it was safe to release them, the dogs scampered ahead, except for Bed, who was still content to be their escort. Cardinals, chickadees and wrens serenaded from low tree branches, and the creek that ran beside the path Elisa had chosen sloshed and bubbled over stones and fallen limbs.

Despite himself, he imagined a life like this one. Simple pleasures appealed to him. His days in Shenandoah County had taught him this, or at least reminded him. But simple pleasures with Elisa seemed anything but. The day already had a resonance, a clarity that was unfamiliar, as if he were seeing it through a lens that sharpened and reduced it to its essence.

She braided her hair, and he was

charmed by the fluid movement of her arms even as he mourned the result. She stooped to commiserate with Bed, who'd fallen behind, and the sight of her with his smallest companion, speaking to the dog as if Bed were human — something he, of course, had never done — filled him with tenderness.

They had hiked for twenty minutes to the top of a hill, and for the first time he realized he could see a branch of the river sparkling in the distance. "This would be a wonderful place to build." He made a slow circle gazing at every view. "Who would need anything but this scenery?"

"Tessa and Mack want to build a house here someday. Can't you imagine it?"

"Things are turning out well for them. I wasn't sure they would."

"I know. She told me they were close to a divorce."

"People who love each other can't always live together."

"Do you counsel people to stay together and preserve their marriage at all costs?"

"Sometimes the costs are too great. But I don't suggest they give up easily, either." He thought of Christine and the promises they had made. Neither of them had taken them lightly.

Her next words surprised him. "Marriage was harder than I'd expected. And better, too. But it's no surprise to me that it doesn't always last. People who choose for love wake up one morning to discover they're married to strangers."

"Is that what happened to you?"

"No. I chose Gabrio precisely because he was the man he was. I looked up to him. I knew I could trust him, that there would be no surprises."

He waited for her to say love had also been part of it, but she didn't.

"I chose him because he would support me," she finished. She seemed to realize how that had sounded. "Emotionally. Not financially. Gabrio was there for me in the dark hours of my life."

"Will you send him a message today?"

She lifted her chin and shaded her eyes with a hand. "Gabrio was an atheist. He would laugh at me for trying to communicate with the dead. He would say it's not scientific."

"Are you an atheist?"

"More often than I'm a believer."

"Does it matter today?"

He watched her consider. "Not at all."

"I'll assemble the kite while you word your messages and decide who gets them. I warn you, though, no one has ever accused me of being handy. This might take a while."

"We have the whole afternoon." She paused. "Or do we?"

"I've cleared my empty schedule just for you. We have a guest preacher tomorrow, and I have no sermon to write."

Her eyes sparkled. "How lucky I am."

He was the lucky one, and he knew it. There was no place he would rather be, and truth be told, no one he would rather be with. And that was now the central problem in his life.

He handed her note cards and strips he'd torn off a sheet that had seen better days. They found a tree to lean against and made separate nests in the fallen leaves at its base. Lounging comfortably, Sam took the kite from the bag and read the directions. Elisa stared into space. Beyond them, the dogs chased each other through the grass or investigated the plethora of new scents.

The kite was simple to assemble. He finished it quickly, then read through the book that had come with it, wondering how in all his years on the earth he had never put a kite in the air.

He turned to gaze at Elisa. She was

writing, and he saw how grave she had become. He sobered, too. Her long braid, fastened with a rubber band from her pocket, fell over the shoulder closer to him. Her profile showed traces of Indian heritage more clearly than a full facial view. Her cheekbones were wide, her nose narrow and short, her eyebrows black winged slashes against sun-kissed skin. He wondered how much of that warm latte color was sun and how much her natural skin tone, and he realized where his thoughts were leading.

She tapped the pen against her cheek. She looked pensive and undecided.

"Hard to know what to say?" he asked.

She didn't answer for a moment. He wasn't sure she was going to. Then she looked at him. "Hard to know who to say it to."

"Hard to choose?"

"I . . ." She looked torn.

"You don't have to tell me."

"There's someone . . . I don't know whether to send him a note, as well."

He saw this was not a simple exercise. As it was with many religious rituals, this was more about facing herself and her fears.

"What will it hurt?" he asked.

"I don't know if Ramon is alive or . . . dead."

Whoever Ramon was, he was important. Sam could see how important in her eyes. The fact that she had shared this fear with him was more evidence. He wondered who this man was and what he meant to her.

He knew better than to actively probe. "Ramon is special to you."

The answer came much more quickly than he had expected.

"My brother."

He turned to his side so he could see her better. "The same brother you told me about?"

"I have only one."

"And you don't know if he's alive?"

She gave one shake of her head.

She had revealed more than she'd wanted. He could see that. He could also see that if he asked her to tell him more, she would shut him out. Elisa had to explain her past a little at a time, and today he was almost certain she had shared as much as she would.

"You could ask the departed to watch over him, Elisa. Wherever he is."

Her expression softened. "I almost think you've flown these kites of remembrance yourself."

"In one way or another, we all have."

She went back to writing. He went back to watching her. She was lost in thought, adding a bit at a time, but finally she sighed and began to fold the bits of paper into squares. "This is enough."

"Then you're ready to fly?"

"The wind has picked up."

He held up the instruction booklet. "I'm officially an expert."

She got to her feet and held out a hand. He pulled himself into a sitting position and took it, careful not to pull her over when he rose. Her hand was not soft against his, but callused and strong.

They tied the messages to the kite's tail with the thin strips of cloth. "The stronger the wind, the more tail it needs," Sam told her.

"That makes sense." She stepped back. "If the wind hadn't picked up, I would have had to choose among loved ones."

He looked around. "Where did the dogs go?"

"There's Bed." She pointed to the other side of the tree, where Bed was happily snoozing.

"I shouldn't have taken my eyes off them."

She held a finger to her lips. He listened

and heard barking in the distance. Before he could stir, she smiled. "Coming toward us."

"You have good ears."

The smile faded. "I have learned to listen."

The dogs, running side by side, burst into the clearing, tongues lolling, tails wagging.

"Didn't we have a talk?" he demanded, pointing a finger at each of them in turn.

"I'm sure they're properly rebuked," Elisa said. "They won't run off again."

"Not until I turn my head. At least they came back."

"They'll always come back. They adore you."

"Is that how it works?"

"They would search the world to find you."

From her tone, he thought they were talking about more than dogs, but he knew better than to ask.

With the dogs at their heels, they took the kite to the wide open area on the hilltop where Mack and Tessa would someday build a home.

"Listen carefully," he lectured. "You hold the spool, and I hold the kite. You'll notice I have my back to the wind."

"This was the reason for the finger in the air?"

"It's a scientific method, millions of years old. They've found skeletons of Cro-Magnon man with one finger in the air."

"I won't ask which finger."

He grinned. "You'll be ashamed of yourself when the kite takes flight."

"I will silently practice my apology as you launch it."

"I'm going to run. When I release the kite, your job is to pull the string hand over hand as it climbs. When it's high enough, you can let more out until you're using the reel."

"No, I think we have this wrong. The expert needs to be on this end. I'll run, you work the string."

"But they're your messages."

"Oh, I'll take over when it's up." Her eyes were shining.

He had a feeling this was a challenge. "No problem. Just watch and see how it's done."

They switched places. She took the kite and held it aloft. Then she began to run, keeping the kite aimed into the wind. He didn't have time to admire her technique. Once she released it, he did everything the booklet had suggested, but when she let

434

go, the kite fluttered to the ground and nestled there on a clump of grass.

"Maybe I need to hold it higher?" she said.

"Try that."

They went through the motions again with the same result.

He was perplexed. He reeled in some of the string, took a firmer hold and nodded. They tried and failed twice more.

He didn't think a kite on the ground was going to be very therapeutic. Elisa joined him as he looked down at it.

"Maybe we do have to shorten the tail," he said.

"No, let me try." She put a hand on his arm and held the other toward him for the reel.

"It's clearly harder than it looks."

"It looks very, very hard when you do it."

"Don't feel badly if it doesn't go up when I let go."

"Oh, I think I'm going to just try this alone."

"You don't want me to run with it?"

She smiled and shook her head. She took the reel, wound it until there was very little line left, then she moved away from him. He watched her turn this way and that, and finally settle on a spot she liked.

Then, as he watched, she held the kite aloft with one hand and began to let the line out with the other. In a moment she released the kite with one toss and it began to climb. She gave it line, then tugged and it rose higher, released more string, tugged hard again, and it continued to climb. In a moment it was well and truly launched.

"I've been had," he said.

"Were the power lines really so low in the town where you grew up?"

"Clearly they weren't in yours."

"On the Day of the Dead we flew kites to communicate with loved ones. But at other times we flew kites in our cemeteries to keep evil spirits away. And more practically because there they would not be caught in trees or wires."

He joined her, smiling at her obvious pleasure. "And how many would you say you've flown?"

"A hundred? Two? I taught Ramon to fly kites. He was very enthusiastic. It was something we did together for many years."

The kite flew higher, a rainbow burst of color against autumn's sapphire sky. He watched it climb, watched her tug and release. When it was high enough, she offered him the reel, but he refused with a shake of his head. "I'd rather watch you."

"Will the departed know I'm here?" she wondered out loud. "Will they think to look in Toms Brook for me?"

"They will now that they've seen your kite."

She was silent, and so was he, watching the kite toss in the rising wind.

The sun was filmed by stratus clouds and moving lower in the sky. In the next minutes he watched more clouds moving in and the sky subtly changing color. The kite continued its flight, dancing, pirouetting, diving, turning. She handled it like a professional.

The dogs took off, then returned. Shad fell to the ground at his feet to scratch an ear. Bed woke up from another nap and sniffed her way down the hill and back. More clouds rolled in, but he was content to stand and watch the kite waltz.

Much later, when the temperature began to drop and the shadows of the trees at the clearing's edge had lengthened, he realized with regret that it was time to start back. He started to speak when he heard her gasp. He glanced up and saw the strip of tail with the messages tied to it, snap free. The wind carried it off immediately. The tail didn't fall to earth as he would have expected. It simply blew away, in the direction of the river. In a moment he lost sight of it.

He wondered how Elisa felt.

She reeled in the kite. He stayed beside her until it was just beyond them. Then he went to catch it and bring it down safely.

He returned and held it as she finished gathering in the remaining string.

She waited until she was finished. Then she looked up. Her eyes glistened. "They have my messages now."

He wanted to put his arms around her. He wanted to tell her he was there for her, in any way she needed or wanted him. But he did not. He touched her hair. Lightly. Briefly. Then his hand fell to his side.

"Yes." It was all he knew to say.

"Thank you, Sam."

He nodded.

"You've made this a good day after all." She looked down at the kite again, then up at him. "Did you mean it when you said your schedule was empty?"

"Yes."

"I'd like to make dinner for you. I'd like to share it with you. But if you're too busy, I —"

He spoke before he had time to think.

He didn't *want* to think. "I would be honored."

"Then give me time to prepare. Come back at eight?"

"You're certain you have the energy?"

"You've given me energy."

They stood facing each other, reluctant to move. Then Sam felt a furry body nudge his leg. He bent, picked up a stick and threw it for Shack, who bounded away in pursuit.

When he turned, Elisa was slipping the kite back into its wrappings. They headed down the hill together.

Chapter Twenty-one

As a child, Elisa had always looked forward to a feast on the Day of All Saints, a meal that the family's devoted cook prepared well in advance. It was the culmination of many hours of celebration, and a wide circle of friends always arrived to share the meal and tell tales of the day.

After the deaths of her parents, Elisa had learned to prepare her own meals. There had no longer been money for cooks or housekeepers, or for the house with the shaded courtyard brightened by brilliant scarlet bougainvillea and a sparkling mosaic tile fountain. She had moved to another city, to a two-room apartment near a park where Ramon could still play outdoors. And she had learned to cook the meals he loved so well.

She was sorry there wasn't time to make

the traditional meal tonight, but she was determined the food would be authentic. She returned from the grocery store and the tiny Latino *mercado* in Woodstock with two bags of groceries.

By seven-thirty the house was fragrant with garlic and onion, and as the main dish simmered, she ran upstairs to change. She had so few clothes it wasn't hard to decide. A trip to the thrift store with Adoncia and Patia had turned up a dark green knit dress that suited both her and her limited budget. Now she slipped it over her head and smoothed the skirt over her hips. She unbraided her hair, and while she was brushing it, she decided to leave it down. Most of her adult life her hair had been short so it could be easily cared for. Tonight she liked the feel of it against her shoulders and back. She thought Sam would like it, too.

While she shopped and cooked, she had warned herself that this day had changed nothing. Sam was still engaged. She was in no position to have a friend, much less a lover. They were adults, capable of controlling themselves and the situation. She had invited him tonight to thank him for his kindness to her.

But the words were hollow. She wasn't

good at fooling herself. She had made the invitation because she wanted to prolong the bittersweet agony of being close to him.

A touch of makeup, a squirt of lotion on her work-roughened hands, and she went downstairs to put several CDs in Helen's stereo system. This was another gift from Nancy, one Helen claimed she didn't see the need for, but somehow a new collection of disks with titles like "The Essential Statler Brothers" and "Classic Crooners" seemed to play themselves at regular intervals. Elisa had splurged on a few of her own to go with them.

She was ready when Sam knocked. He wore khakis and a navy sports coat, with a pale blue shirt and no tie. He carried flowers, white spider mums and red carnations in green tissue paper. He kissed her cheek when he presented them to her, the perfunctory greeting of friends. It still resonated in a body long out of practice coping with desire.

"I bought wine," he said. "I have red and white in the car. Either or both?"

"We're having chicken." She was still looking down at the flowers. She was afraid her cheeks were pink.

"White?"

442

"Let's ignore the experts. I like red better."

"So do I. It's from Chile."

"It sounds perfect."

She left the door ajar and went to find a vase for the flowers. She was placing the newly trimmed stalks in water when Sam came into the kitchen.

"This was recommended. It's a blend of three grapes." He held up the bottle for her perusal.

"Sena. Yes, it's a good one."

"You've had it then?"

She finished arranging the flowers. "I visited the area where it's produced on a holiday." She presented the glass vase to him. "Will you put these on the table?"

"The dining room?"

She nodded.

"Did I tell you how lovely you look in that dress?"

"Thank you."

He took the vase. His absence gave her a moment to chide herself for over-reacting. Just a few words and a quick kiss, and she felt beautiful and desirable. At this rate she was afraid she would dissolve into longing if he accidentally touched her.

She was peeking in the oven when he returned. "Something smells incredible."

"I think you'll like it. Anyone who eats mashed potato and scrambled egg sandwiches can't be too choosy."

"Do you like to cook?"

"I didn't at first. We were spoiled when I was a girl. Our cook was so wonderful, friends of my family dropped by often just at mealtime. We didn't pretend they were there to see us. We knew."

He lounged against the counter, arms folded. "Did she teach you? What's that you're peeling?"

"Don't screw up your face, it might freeze. And they're not rotting bananas. Plantain, a relative. These are just ripe enough to fry. And no, Rosa Maria didn't teach me. She would not have believed that to be proper. But she did let me watch and help if no one was home. So I did learn some of her secrets. But there were many failures when I began cooking on my own."

"Did your husband care?"

"Gabrio?" She laughed. "I don't think I cooked for Gabrio more than half a dozen times. When we married there was a cook in his house, a woman who had been with his family since he was a boy. She did not want me inside her kitchen. She was not as good as Rosa, but it was safest to pretend I loved everything she made."

"It sounds like a very different life."

She imagined he would be shocked at exactly how different.

As the oil heated, she retrieved a can of pureed beans. Back at the stove, she took a second frying pan from a pegboard hook and set it to heat, as well, adding garlic she had already chopped for extra flavor.

"Want me to open that?"

She offered it. "Do you like black beans?"

She pointed to the right drawer, and he searched for the opener. "I grew up with good old pork and beans right out of the can. Something tells me this is a different experience."

"At home I soaked my own, then cooked and mashed them. Ramon always did the mashing."

"These look good," he said.

She was beginning to trust that he would let her lead the way and reveal only what she was comfortable with. "They *are* good. I made them for Helen. She grew up eating dried beans of all kinds from her mother's garden. She didn't complain."

He handed her the opened can. She

scooped the beans into the pan and began mixing them with a wooden spoon. She added plantain to the other pan, and divided her attention between them.

"I like the music," he said.

"I'm glad."

"Who is it?"

She turned down the heat under the beans and turned it up under the plantain. "Ricardo Arjona. He's one of my favorites."

They were both quiet, listening. Arjona's voice was smooth, with just a hint of vibrato lending emotion. This selection had guitar and just a hint of some rhythm instrument Elisa couldn't identify.

Sam turned his back to the counter again and resumed lounging. The kitchen seemed smaller and cozier with him beside her, and she was aware of the short distance between them.

"I'm at a disadvantage," he said. "I'm working on my Spanish, but I've got a long way to go."

"Are you? Working on it?"

"Usted esta bonito."

She smiled a little. "I think you mean to say *estás bonita.* Unless you are trying to tell a man you don't know well that he's pretty?"

"I probably won't have much use for that. *Estás bonita.*"

"*Gracias.*"

"*De nada.*"

"You *are* working on it."

"Right now, if I go to Mexico I can ask directions to the bathroom, order tamales and count to twenty, in case anybody asks."

"I'm sure that will be tops on their list of requests." The beans were beginning to thicken. She gently shook the pan as they parted from the sides, forming the puree into a roll. "How are you learning?"

"I bought tapes. I listen to them in my car. That's about the only chance I get."

She was touched he was making the attempt. "It will help with *La Casa.*"

"It doesn't help right now. I'd like to know what these lyrics mean."

He looked perfectly at home, as if he stood there each night and watched her cook. "Would you really? Maybe not. Arjona's a social critic, more or less the Bob Dylan of Latin America, except his voice is so sensual and powerful. He is not always kind to his neighbor to the north."

"What's he singing about now?"

This was one of her favorites. She tried to put the essence into words. "It's the story of a man and a woman. She is from Cuba; he is from New York. She is a Marxist and he a Republican, but Arjona asks what do Lincoln and Lenin know about love?"

"What do they?" Sam agreed.

"She is a mulatto, he is blond like the sun. The woman and the man don't speak the same language. But love ties them together."

She glanced at him again. His eyes were following every move she made.

She stopped shaking the pan. Her voice was lower and husky. "The Yankee falls in love with the Cuban. He takes her hand and takes her away. They go to Paris to live, where together they can make fun of the rest of us."

His eyes were warm, their deep blue grayed in the incandescent light. "I like it. Love surmounts all barriers."

Their gazes locked. She forgot to stir or shake, until she realized the song had ended. She looked away, focusing on the wall behind the stove. "I thought you might."

"He's easy to listen to."

"Yes." She turned down the heat under the beans, flipped the plantain once more and turned off the heat.

"Love is more powerful than borders or treaties or treatises," he said.

She didn't look at him. "Arjona would agree."

"Would *you?*"

"In my limited experience? Love is the place where the hard work starts. The Cuban and the Yankee will probably have to learn more than French to understand each other."

"You're not a romantic."

"And you are?" The words were meant to be light. They sounded just a bit breathless.

"I think the Cuban and the Yankee are still together in Paris, madly in love. More in love because of their differences. Right now they're having a glass of French wine at a sidewalk café in Montmartre. She never learned to speak English, he can't speak Spanish. But I think they speak French perfectly."

She smiled. She couldn't help herself. When she looked up again she saw he was watching her, waiting for her to tell him that such things were not possible.

"In my country we like to say that everyone is the age of their heart." She splayed her hand over her breasts. "Your heart is young, Sam."

"Because I believe sometimes people find each other despite every obstacle? Don't you believe it, too?"

"I believe in love. But I'm also a realist."

"I think you're a woman who has seen too much sorrow."

They stared at each other again. She read patience and encouragement in his eyes, and the hint of something that was the antithesis, the desire to know her now, without pretense, without delays, without barriers.

For a moment she was tempted to give in, to tell him who she was and what drove her, to lay her past and future at his feet and ask him to share it in any way he could. Then a new song began, the beans began to smoke, and she forced herself to look away.

"We're ready to eat. Will you open the wine while I take the food to the table?"

"If you'll start this CD all over again."

She carried in platters, and he brought wineglasses and followed with ice water. They worked together, as if they had always done so. When the table was filled, he pulled out her chair.

He moved around the table, shortened for the occasion by the removal of two leaves. He poured a little wine in her glass and waited for her to taste it.

"Very nice." She held up her glass for more.

He filled hers and poured one for himself. "The food looks wonderful. Is this a special meal for the holiday?"

She held up the salad plate. "No, in my family the traditional meal was *fiambre*. As a child I looked forward to it all year, but it takes a whole day of preparation, so I couldn't do it for you on short notice. This is just a little taste of it."

"It looks like antipasto."

"A little bit like it, yes." She looked down at the combination of marinated vegetables and meats. "In its real form it's enough by itself to make a whole meal, and the more things that go into it, the better. There's a story Rosa Maria liked to tell. A rich woman fixed a feast for expected guests and told her servant girl how to serve it. The girl had a lover, and he came to visit. She forgot about dinner until suddenly she realized it was time to serve and she wasn't prepared. So she threw everything on one plate, and that became *fiambre*."

He took a selection of the deli meats and vegetables she'd included and passed the plate back to her. "Love created a feast and a tradition. However it came about, that's the way I like to eat."

"Yes, I've noticed. You would be a fan. Your lunches are *fiambre* on Wonder Bread."

He lifted his wine. "Let me make a toast."

She picked up her glass.

"To my hostess, accomplished cook and kite flyer, fixer of scrapes, wise mentor of young men, tender of churches, companion and aide to the old and sick, quilter, and friend."

Her heart lifted at his words. She was pleased he saw so much that was good in her life. Most of the time she felt she was just marking time, that she had stopped living once she began to run.

"And to my guest," she said. "Healer of hearts and souls, nudger and catalyst, guide and patient *amigo*."

They smiled at each other, then lifted their glasses and sipped.

"It's an excellent wine," she said. "Thank you."

"I was lucky to find it."

"May I serve you?"

Sam passed his plate, and she dished up the chicken and rice, plantain and beans. Then she passed a dish of tortillas she had warmed and covered with a damp cloth.

"I don't think I've had a meal this good in years." He closed his eyes and inhaled. "The chicken smells wonderful."

"It's my brother's favorite."

"I can understand why."

They ate with only a minimum of conversation, listening as Ricardo Arjona serenaded them. Near the end of the meal, when the talk had strayed to church activities, she set down her fork, filled and happy. "You've been at the church for more than two years now?"

His expression said they were sharing a joke. "It seems longer sometimes. Particularly when George Jenkins is lecturing me at board meetings."

"How long will you stay? Do they move you automatically after a certain length of time?"

"No, I can stay as long as it's right for everybody." He took one final tortilla to scoop up the rest of the chicken, with its sauce of finely chopped vegetables, olives and capers. "But I've been contacted by a church in D.C. that's interested in having me in their pulpit. They've been to Community twice to hear me. We've had several long conversations."

She felt a sharp stab of disappointment,

although she knew that was foolish. She would surely be gone before he moved on. This was obviously best.

"That's not for public consumption," he added. "Nobody else knows."

She felt her way. "You'll have to give them notice, won't you? So they can find another minister?"

"The decision isn't nearly that far along." He wiped the last bit of tortilla around his plate, but she thought it was more a delaying tactic. "Truth is," he said at last, "it's a very big promotion. It means I'm out of the ecclesiastical doghouse, that I've been forgiven for my wild-eyed radical past and accepted back into the moderate fold."

"But you don't sound pleased."

"Don't I?"

"Why aren't you?"

"Maybe I'm still a wild-eyed radical at heart." He popped the tortilla in his mouth and shrugged.

She pondered that. "I think you're a man who wants to define his ministry, not have it defined for him."

He tilted his head, as if to regard her from a different perspective. "How do you know me so well?"

Because she paid attention to everything

about him, but she could hardly tell him so. She listened when he spoke, asked the right questions, thought about him far too much. None of those things could be said.

"You struggle with who you are, with what you believe. I think you always will. I just don't think you want somebody else making those decisions for you."

"Apparently not. They want me to go to D.C. in March and conduct a service. They'll introduce me to the congregation, and when I leave, they'll decide whether to invite me to become their minister. I've put off my answer every time they ask, citing this problem or that, Thanksgiving, Christmas, the alignment of the planets, a parishioner's hangnail." He smiled a little.

"Why don't you say no?"

His eyes held hers. "Because first I have to end things with Christine."

"Sam . . ." She wanted to turn back the clock to earlier in the conversation, but she wasn't sure when it had gone wrong.

He went on, ignoring her attempt to stop him. "Then I'll know if what I'm feeling about creating a ministry in D.C. is a reaction or the real thing."

She didn't know what to say.

"Our relationship is over," he said, when she remained silent. "I've known it for a long time, and I'm almost sure she has, too. People think she's flighty, that Chrissy's attention span is about as lengthy as a manicure, but it's not true. She stood by me when no one thought she would or should. She never gave up on us. But the us we've both been holding on to hasn't existed in a very long time and won't exist again."

"You don't have to tell me this. I don't know why you think you do."

"I'm sorry."

She reached across the table and rested her hand on his. "No. I'm not asking you to be sorry. I just didn't want you to think that because I asked you here tonight, you owed me anything. Certainly not an explanation."

He covered her hand before she could withdraw it. "For two people who can't talk about this yet, we've already said plenty, Elisa. You know I'm leaving my fiancée and that you have some part in that, even though you've never done a thing to lead me on. I know that you're running from something or someone and you don't want any complications, much less a man who's falling in love with you."

She pulled her hand away. "Maybe tonight was a bad idea."

"I don't think so. Do you? Really?"

"You don't want me in your life, Sam. You don't know how badly you don't need me."

His tone hardened. "When will you trust me enough to tell me?"

She stood and began to clear the table. "It's not trust."

He joined her, piling his silverware on his plate, although she shook her head. "Then what?"

"I have dessert. Mango sorbet. It's very good."

Frustration showed in his eyes, in the tightening corners of his lips, but he didn't push her. "I'll help with the dishes."

"You don't have to. It won't take me long to —"

"I'll dry."

In the kitchen they stood nearly shoulder to shoulder, but there was a space between them now, a carefully controlled space that neither breached.

Until the dishes were nearly done, the counters cleared and the music changed.

"That's not Ricardo Arjona anymore," Sam said.

She kept her voice light, as if nothing had happened. "It hasn't been for a while.

We listened to 'Music From the Coffee Lands.'"

"I guess I wasn't thinking about it."

"Now this is salsa, guaranteed to make you pay attention."

He swung her around the moment she lifted her hands out of the dishwater. "Dance with me."

Her breath caught; then she laughed. "Did we drink too much wine?"

"No. Dance with me."

"Here? In the kitchen?"

"No. Come on." He took her hand, still dripping and soapy, and pulled her through the kitchen into the living room.

"I bet you don't have the least idea how to dance to this music," she chided. She dried her hands on a napkin left on the table. "Have you ever danced it?"

"Can you polka?"

"You're serious?"

"I was hopping and half-stepping around the room at Union Hall to Grand Stan Muziack and the Polkateers by the time I was eight. Rachel and I won a prize the year I was ten, which was the last year I would have been caught dead dancing with my little sister. She claims it never happened."

"This is very different from a polka."

"Show me."

After the silent tension in the kitchen, this was an about-face she wasn't quite ready for. But his enthusiasm was infectious, and she felt herself relaxing again. "Okay, but don't say I didn't warn you."

He held out his arms.

"Are you sure? I could step all over you. Or worse."

"I'm strong and brave."

"Then first you have to get the rhythm. Come stand beside me. I'll pretend I'm leading."

"I'm liberated. I can follow."

"I probably can't. First, pay attention to the beat. Think fast-fast-slow. Move your hips a little, but only a little. Think mambo, if they mambo at your Union Hall. Fast-fast slow. Right foot back, left foot forward, knees slightly bent all the time. It's the same for both of us, only not at the same time." She demonstrated.

He moved to the beat with her, catching on quickly. He didn't lumber or spring. He had a quiet natural rhythm and command of his body that was both restrained and sensual.

She reminded herself that she was a dance instructor. She took his hand and they danced together, still side by side. The song ended, and the next was a little faster and more raucous. They paused, but as the tempo picked up, they fell back into step. Then, as he continued the basics, she moved in front of him, switching the direction of her feet to coordinate with his.

"Very good." She was surprised he wasn't tripping all over himself.

"I'm still counting," he said.

"You don't look like it." She dropped his hand, then held up her arms. "Now try it holding me. Probably just like your polka. My hand on your shoulder, your hand at my waist."

He didn't pull her close, but they slipped into position as if they had always danced together. The intimacy of facing each other as they moved to the sensual rhythm wasn't lost on her. She couldn't ignore it. She could only pretend.

"Move your arm down as you rock forward, up as you step back," she told him. In a few beats he had the hang of that, as well.

The song was half over before she spoke again. "This would get boring, and we can't have that. Salsa is never boring. We'll try a turn."

"Just watch your feet."

"When you go back, you'll raise your left arm, like this. I'll do the rest of it."

"The fun part will be watching you."

She nearly missed a beat. "Ready?"

He lifted his arm as he stepped back, and she took the turn in three steps, ending back where she'd begun exactly when she was supposed to. "See, our repertoire has doubled."

"Let's try it again."

They did, without incident. He was holding her closer now. Not close enough for her to protest, but enough that she could feel the heat of his body. She couldn't remember dancing with a man as tall as Sam, or a man in whose arms she felt this secure. But secure was not the same as comfortable.

"There are many things we can do," she said as another cut began and they picked up the rhythm again. "If we want to move around the floor a little, you do a half turn like this." She demonstrated. "You turn away from me. I follow one beat later, dancing in front of you."

He tried, and she followed. "See?"

He tried again, and again she danced in front of him.

"You can do a lot of different things," she said. "You can —"

The music had stopped. He was holding her tighter now. He gazed down at her. She couldn't make herself move away, and when he kissed her, she was ready.

She slipped her arms around his neck. As he pulled her closer, her body sank into his, no distance, no barriers, no restraint. The feel of his lips and touch of his tongue weren't a surprise. She had known how they would taste, known how he would kiss her and how her body would respond. She was flooded with sensation, as if she had been paralyzed and now each limb throbbed painfully with life. The sensation was excruciating. The sensation was glorious.

He wound her hair in his hand. She thought his fingers were trembling against her back and waist. She could feel herself shaking deep inside, as if this kiss, a mere kiss, was a prelude to something darker and uncontrolled, a blatant sexual response that had lain dormant inside her so long she had almost forgotten its existence.

"Sam . . ."

She wasn't sure which of them pulled away first. He took her hands, as if to keep her from running away. There were no words to express what she was feeling.

"Christine is coming the Saturday of Thanksgiving weekend." His voice was low, deep with feeling. "I'll talk to her then. This isn't something I want to do on the telephone."

"Don't talk to her because of this, not because of tonight."

"Don't even try to tell me you don't feel something."

"It doesn't matter what I feel. You're not listening. I can't have a relationship with you. I may never be able to."

"Tell me what's going on!"

She tugged her hands from his. "I can't do that, either. And if you keep asking, I'll have to leave, Sam. Please don't ask again."

It took him a moment, but as she watched, he understood the scope of her resistance. "You would leave Toms Brook? Because I want to know who you are?"

"I should have left already," she said softly. "I may have to leave anyway. But don't *make* me leave because you think you're falling in love with me."

"Think?"

She was silent. She knew better. And she knew, and thought that he did, as well, that it was not one-sided.

The CD had ended. The room was quiet. He nodded at last. "I'd better go."

"Yes. Please."

"Don't leave because of me, Elisa. I'll back off for good, if that's what you want. I won't ask questions, and I won't make demands."

She wanted to say something. She *had* to say something. She touched his arm. Lightly. "I don't want it to be this way. Can you see that?"

"Probably not. Because it doesn't have to be this way. I won't hurt you."

"But knowing me could hurt you."

"We can face whatever it is together."

"No, because there's no way to face it without being parted forever." She knew she was speaking in riddles, but it didn't matter. Her life was a riddle with no solution.

"I'm not going to understand. I'm not even going to try." He ran his hand through his hair. "It was a wonderful dinner. Thank you."

"I'll walk you to the door."

He let her, as if another argument would have been too much to bear. He said goodbye, and she watched him walk down the steps. Only when the door was locked behind him and the house silent did she begin to weep.

Chapter
Twenty-two

Sam belonged to a small clergy group in Winchester that met on the second Monday morning of every month for coffee and conversation. Although their theologies differed, the men and women in the group had found they had many things in common. Their discussions were enlightening, and he had grown particularly fond of a Catholic priest named Joe Menendez, who served a small country parish.

Father Menendez had come out of retirement to assist the struggling church with the promise that he could still spend more time fishing than hearing confession. The church was small, but his fluent Spanish and warm smile attracted many from the local Latino population on Sunday mornings.

On the second Monday of November,

Sam walked Joe to his car after their monthly get-together. The group had been smaller, and therefore more intimate, than usual. They had gotten off their assigned topic immediately when one of the members, a Presbyterian minister, related a story about a family who was refusing to deal with the approaching death of a grandmother. They had all shared ways they had dealt with similar experiences, and the morning had flown by.

"You didn't say much today," Sam told Joe as they started down the street to the older man's car. "Is that because your church has a sacrament that pretty well announces the time has come?"

"What we used to call Extreme Unction? After Vatican II we started calling that our anointing of the sick, and now it's more of a community healing service."

Joe, still handsome at seventy with a full head of silver hair, searched a pocket for his keys. "But back when it was a deathbed ritual, I was refused permission to administer last rites any number of times because the patient or family refused to acknowledge the end was near. Protestants don't have a market on denial."

Sam thought of all the ways he practiced denial himself, particularly in regard to

Elisa. Since he had kissed her more than a week ago, he had denied himself access to her and even denied himself the right to think about her.

The only thing he could not deny was the fear that now, if he took one misstep, she would disappear forever.

He was still thinking of her when he spoke. "Maybe we don't have a market on denial, but we don't have the colorful pageantry you do, either. I celebrated the Day of the Dead with a friend this month. She flew a kite, something she did once as a child in Mexico, with messages to her departed family. It was therapeutic."

"You mean Guatemala."

It took him a moment to process Joe's words. "I'm sorry?"

Joe stopped beside a green compact sedan. "Guatemala. That's where they fly the kites. Not Mexico. One particular village, Santiago Sacatepéquez, is well known for it. I was there once to see it. People come from all over. Very impressive."

"You never flew kites in Mexico?" Sam knew Joe's father had come to Texas as an undocumented worker and stayed to become an influential citizen. But the Menendcz children, all eight of them, had spent every holiday and vacation with family in Guanajuato, so they would not forget their roots.

Joe unlocked his door. "Not on *Dia de Los Muertos.* Never did it, never saw it done. I'm fairly certain that's peculiar to the Guatemalan highlands, and only a village or two, at that."

"I'm curious. Did you have a special dish you ate that day? Sort of an antipasto?"

"That's Guatemalan, too. Very tasty, as I recall. I can't remember what they called it. In my father's town we feasted on the foods that had been offered on our altar. Any specialty of the house. Only the best was good enough. Molés, tamales, a special bread called *pan de muerto.*" He paused. "You're making me hungry. Do you want to follow me home for some lunch?"

Sam's thoughts were elsewhere. "Thanks, but I'll take a rain check. I've got to get back home to let my dogs out. It looked like a storm was moving in when I left this morning, and I didn't want to leave them outside."

"No dogs, no cats, no wife." Joe grinned. "I think I'll go fishing."

Driving back toward Toms Brook in the SUV, Sam mulled over Joe's words. He was certainly no authority on Latin American culture, but he *was* certain Elisa had told him she was from Mexico. He respected Joe's knowledge of many things, but he wondered if, this once, his friend was mistaken.

By the time he had let the dogs out and rewarded them with treats, he knew he couldn't let this rest. He had intended to spend his day off cleaning out the refrigerator, taking down the screens for the winter and going for a long run. Instead, he made his way to the computer and got on the Internet.

An hour later, he had more questions than answers. But one thing was certain: Joe was correct. The only mention of a ceremony like the one Elisa had described was at Santiago Sacatepéquez in Guatemala. And *fiambre* — he had recalled the name of the dish she had served with a little help from the Web — was a Guatemalan tradition.

He spun in his chair and gazed down at the dogs, who were lying in a circle at his feet, nose to tail. "I have a problem, guys," he said out loud. "I can run Elisa Martinez through my computer and see if she's mentioned anywhere. Or I can forget this and let her tell me why she lied about her background when she's good and ready."

Not one of the dogs looked interested.

He wondered if one of them had jumped up, clearly ready for a long run, would he have turned off the computer? As it was, their message was clear. *We're happy, take your time.* He didn't want to ponder how absurd it was to consult three moth-eaten mutts on issues of trust and morality.

He typed Elisa Martinez into his favorite search engine and waited for results.

The dogs were more than ready for a run by the time Sam was ready to quit. Elisa Martinez was not an uncommon name. By the time the results became too vague or esoteric to pursue, he had searched dozens of Web sites and turned up crime victims, scholars, soccer goalies. He'd seen photos and birth dates that disqualified some women immediately. For others, the facts simply didn't fit. His Elisa was not spending her summer in Prague finishing her dissertation or waiting in Chicago to learn the outcome of a deportation hearing.

For all practical purposes — on the Internet, at least — the Elisa he knew did not exist.

Sam asked himself what he had hoped to accomplish. Had he really believed he would learn who she was and how to help her? Had he hoped to go to her and tell her he understood why she was running and it didn't matter to him? Or had he, in some insidious way, been protecting himself? Had the complications she represented begun to weigh too heavily on him?

He didn't have to think long. Despite what he had discovered, he trusted her completely. He was not looking for reasons to move away from her. He was looking for ways to move closer. He knew, without knowing any details, that Elisa needed help, and that if she didn't find it, they had no hope of a future.

Now he had to find a way to convince her that he could help her, no matter what her problem. Because Elisa was already too large a part of his life for him to back away.

Elisa knew the location of nearly every public telephone in a twenty-mile radius. This evening she used one at a fast-food restaurant near the nursing home. Even though it was late, the restaurant was just noisy enough to keep her from being overheard, but not so noisy that she couldn't hear the voice on the other end.

She waited as the telephone rang in Sacramento and hoped Judy was at home. They had carefully worked out the dates of her calls through a neighbor of Judy's, who had relayed the schedule to Elisa in January. Elisa never phoned on the same day of the week or at the same time. It was unlikely, after all this time, that Judy's line was tapped, but both women knew it was still a good idea to be careful.

Judy picked up on the fifth ring.

"It's Elisa." They had not indulged in polite conversation for years.

"Call me where you called me last January." The line went dead.

Elisa had not expected this. It was either the best or worst of news. Either Judy had something to say at length or she had real reason to believe the line was tapped. Since she had to wait at least ten minutes for Judy to go next door and settle in, she went to the counter and bought a cup of coffee, nursing it at a table near the telephone and worrying about what she might discover when Judy got to her neighbor's house.

An overweight man with mermaid tattoos peeking over a formfitting tank top ambled to the phone and spent the next fifteen minutes snarling at somebody on the other end. Elisa forced herself to read the classified section of the morning paper — all that was left behind by that time of day — and nonchalantly glanced up now and then to see if the man had moved on. Inside she was seething. He left at last, smiling and shuffling off, as if fifteen minutes of abuse had improved his day immeasurably.

It was close enough to closing time that she wondered if she would have time to finish her call now. She folded her paper and went back to the telephone, using the change from her coffee and more she had saved to place the call.

This time the telephone only rang twice.

"Elisa?"

"Yes. What's going on?"

"I'm not sure. But it might be good news."

Elisa had managed, somehow, to maintain her self-control while she waited to use the phone. She had admonished herself not to be hopeful, but now her legs felt weak. She leaned against the wall, propping herself as best she could.

"What?"

"We got a call last week. Somebody asked for you by name! A young man. James took the call, not me. But he knew what to do. James told him to call this number in half an hour so I could talk to him."

"And?" Elisa heard the wobble in that

one word and closed her eyes.

"I'm sorry. He didn't call back."

Elisa waited, hopeful there was more, but Judy was silent.

"That's all?" she asked. "Nothing else?"

"I think James scared him off. If it was Ramon, he might have thought it was a trap of some kind. Maybe if I'd answered instead . . ."

Elisa thought that could be true. Ramon knew Judy, because Judy had been her roommate at Stanford and had come to Antigua to visit the summer before Elisa's parents were killed.

Elisa's mind was spinning. She didn't know what to say.

Judy spoke first. "Listen, James did manage to tell the man the story we'd agreed on."

"Exactly what did he tell him?"

"James said that you and Tom were off on a picnic because you wanted to wade in the brook. Then he told him to call this number so he could talk to me."

"What did he sound like?" But even as she asked the question, Elisa knew how foolish it was. Even if James had described the voice exactly, it had been such a long time since Elisa had heard her brother speak. Ramon's voice would be deeper now. She might not recognize it herself.

"James said he had a deep voice, light accent, a little tentative. He sounded young, maybe early twenties. But the conversation was so short . . ."

"It could have been anybody. It could be somebody who found out you were my college roommate and tracked you, somebody from the government . . ."

"It could have been. Or maybe it *was* Ramon. And now he can put two and two together and figure out where you are."

Elisa wanted to believe that. She was desperate to believe it. "He's had a week to get here and find me. Maybe he didn't understand that 'Tom' and 'brook' go together. Maybe he didn't catch the words."

"It might take several weeks if he's hitchhiking. It might take him longer if he hasn't even crossed the border yet or if he has no cash. Who knows his circumstances?"

"Judy, I'm scared. This scares me more. What if it's not him?"

"Don't leave, whatever you do. Just be careful. I have a feeling about this. It would take Ramon some time to find me. We knew that. And more time to cross the border, years to cross, maybe, until he found someone he could trust to help him.

He couldn't take chances. Look how long it took you. We knew that, too. I'd about given up hope, but I just have a feeling this was really him. I've stayed right next to the phone all week, hoping he'll call back. Call me here on Saturday and we'll touch base again."

"Your neighbor?"

"She doesn't ask questions. And nobody's going to tap *her* phone."

"I'll call. Thanks. Pray for us." Elisa hung up.

She checked her watch, then ordered a final cup of coffee to go. She had a week-old sinus infection, and she had resorted to drowning the last vestiges in as much liquid as she could hold. Because of the infection, she had missed two shifts at the nursing home and cut her hours at the church to the bare bones.

Of course the latter had been as much to avoid Sam as to rest and recover.

Once she was in the car, she took her time driving the short distance to Shadyside, trying not to give in to either excitement or disappointment at Judy's message. This was what she had prayed for, some sign her brother was really alive and attempting to find her. This was why she had come to Toms Brook, because this was a place Ramon might think to look for her. Toms Brook had meaning for them both. This was the reason she had stayed, despite losing too much of her anonymity and falling in love with a man she could never have.

She relived her conversation with Judy. Before this, there had been two hopeful signs her brother was alive. A boy had been seen hanging around the home of old friends of her father's in Manzanillo, a Mexican resort town, only to vanish several days before the friends returned from an extended holiday in Arizona. Then there had been a photograph taken at a funeral in Mexico City for a prestigious colleague of Gabrio's, and a young man on the third row who looked exactly like she thought her brother might look now. She had seen the photograph herself on the Internet. She knew.

The evidence was subjective. Both Manzanillo and Mexico City were places Ramon might well have thought to look for her. But Ramon was dark-haired and dark-eyed, with honey-colored skin like hers. That did not make him unique in Latin America. Hope and imagination went hand in hand. Like her, the people who had given her this information wanted to believe Ramon was still alive. There were additional trustworthy people both in Mexico and the United States who were watching for her brother.

Now she considered alternatives. She could banish hope, accept the fact that she would never see her brother again and plan the rest of her life accordingly. Or she could continue to believe he was alive somewhere, that somehow they would find each other. Perhaps here, perhaps through a network of trusted friends like Judy, who had tried to help from the beginning. Someday Ramon would trust one of those friends long enough to discover her whereabouts.

And this, in the end, was what she had to believe. Because believing her brother was dead was too terrible to bear.

By the time she walked through the nursing home door, she was able to greet her colleagues with a smile. She answered questions about her week and assured everyone she felt well enough to take her shift. She admired the new charcoal sketches rendered by residents that were now displayed in the hallway and reception area. She did the crossover with Kathy, read a week's worth of notes, and listened sympathetically to the sad story of another departing aide who had just been jilted by her boyfriend.

She was glad to have work to do. She lingered longer than usual in every room as she checked on patients, adjusting blinds and bedcovers, straightening night tables, adding ice to bedside water pitchers that really didn't need it. She kept busy so she wouldn't have to relive her conversation with Judy, but it was Martha Wisner who finally took her mind off the telephone call.

Martha was standing by the window when Elisa entered her room. She turned, squinting as if she wasn't wearing her glasses, although she was. "Sharon?"

Elisa had come to expect this, but as always, she was disconcerted. "No, I'm Elisa. How are you, Miss Wisner?"

Martha frowned. "You do look so much like Sharon. Have I called you that before?"

"That's all right. She was someone you were close to once, wasn't she?"

Martha considered. "My niece," she said at last. "But maybe she's gone now. I'm not sure. . . ."

Elisa had found that most patients suffering from dementia preferred to cover up the things they didn't know. She was touched that Martha had shared her uncertainty. "She lives on in your heart," she said. "She would be glad, I'm sure."

"You've been gone."

Elisa was encouraged. "Yes, I was sick." She saw Martha found that troubling and hurried to explain. "Just sick enough to worry about not spreading any unnecessary germs. Nothing serious. And I'm nearly well now."

"Well, that's good. Very good." Martha pursed her lips, as if trying to remember exactly why. "Oh, I know. I wanted to tell you more of my story!"

"I'm so glad you remembered."

"I've been waiting for you." Martha made her way to an armchair in the corner. "Can you sit with me a little while?"

Elisa was glad to. She perched on the edge of the chair across from Martha. "When you're done, I'll get you something to snack on. You should try to go to sleep soon."

"Oh, I will. But I've been waiting every night to see you."

Elisa wasn't certain this was true, but she thought the fact Martha had remembered her and remembered talking to her was a hopeful sign. "I look forward to this time together."

"Exactly the way Sarah looked forward to Amasa's letters. Did I tell you that I know so much of what happened so long ago because of those letters?"

"These letters, Miss Wisner, do you know what happened to them?"

Martha smiled. "Amasa was a lucky man. Sarah loved him very much."

Chapter
Twenty-three

June 1, 1853

My dear Amasa,
Your recent letters were even more wel-
come than the rain that will bring life to
Jeremiah's newly planted cornfields.
Upon his return from town, Jeremiah pre-
sented me with three, a treasure beyond
price. I will not allow myself to savor all at
once and have read only the first.

Now I am almost frightened to open
the others, since the news from
Lynchburg is growing sadder. I pray for
your father in his last days, and for you,
as you do his work at the forge and care
for him. Calvin Stone is a good man, and
the fact that he is not afraid to die affirms
what I know of him, that his heart is pure
and his life was led without shame. How

many can say the same?

I almost smile when I think how little I once had to report. In my letters I told you of birds nesting in my favorite tree, of the black bear with twin cubs who regularly visited our apple orchard, of people from the church who asked to be remembered to you. Now there is so much to tell, I will leave the smaller things for you to imagine. Suffice it to say that the weather has been kind since the storm that brought Dorie to us, and despite our guest and our worries, we have accomplished much.

In my last letter I told you that Dorie seldom spoke. This has changed, and we now know much about her life. Oh, Amasa, it is all so very sad. I will tell it quickly and know you will understand the things I have no wish to put on paper.

Dorie was born in Augusta County to the cook for a wealthy family with land and many enslaved persons to do the work. Her mother was regarded as an asset, and Henry Beaumont, who claimed ownership of her, treated her as well as a person in such circumstances might expect to be treated. Dorie is probably almost twenty years old, and although she does not know her father's name, she does know he was one of many guests in the Beaumont home.

Dorie was brought up as a maid and companion to the Beaumonts' youngest daughter Bertha, and although the law forbade the family to educate her, she was present in the schoolroom where Bertha's tutor, a Maryland woman with abolitionist sympathies, made certain to teach Dorie, as well. In this, Dorie and I have a bond. Both of us were educated above our lot in life. Me by an educated mother, Dorie by the sympathetic and secretive tutor.

The Beaumont family expected Dorie to remain at Bertha's side forever, intending to present her as a gift to their daughter upon her marriage to a local attorney and landowner. Instead, Dorie fell in love with a free man named Silas Green, who hired his services as a carpenter and came to the Beaumont estate to oversee the building of a new barn. When he asked for Dorie's hand in marriage and for the right to buy her from them, the Beaumonts were outraged and ordered him off their property.

Weeks later Silas and Dorie married secretly (as slaves are often forced to) and without clergy. Dorie believed if she promised to remain Bertha's maid, eventually she could persuade the Beaumonts to allow her to marry Silas and purchase her freedom.

As you might guess, Dorie found herself with child, and when Henry Beaumont discovered all that had transpired, he locked her in the smokehouse with no food and little water. When she was finally set free, she learned that Silas had disappeared.

Dorie is certain her husband was murdered. Others who saw a band of men riding toward his cabin on the night Dorie was imprisoned have told her there is no reason to hope. After the men's departure, Silas's cabin was gone, burned to the ground and most probably he with it. As punishment, Dorie was sent to live above the wash house and toil in the yard over the boiling kettle while she waited to give birth.

Dorie's child was born five months later, a girl she named Marie. When Marie was two, she was plucked from Dorie's arms and sold with others from the Beaumont estate to a tobacco plantation in Maryland. So that they no longer were forced to witness her despair, Dorie's services were loaned to a family in Harrisonburg with the promise that if there were good reports of her year there, she would next be sent to Staunton to serve Bertha and her husband.

Instead Dorie bided her time until the new family believed she had grown both docile and obedient. Then, on the darkest night of the month, she ran away.

Oh, Amasa, I have no words for the pain in her eyes when she talks about being separated so cruelly from her daughter. She knows where the little girl was sent, having risked everything before her exile to Harrisonburg to steal into Henry Beaumont's study to find the sale papers. She can read and understand maps. She learned from others how to stay alive on her journey and who might help her. She prepared as best she could, packing food, even forging papers that claimed she had been recently freed (although it is doubtful that any who read such a document would believe it to be true).

Before we found her, Dorie had been on her journey for four weeks, and she was nearly captured twice. Jeremiah is certain there are handbills in every town in the valley describing her and seeking *her return. He has seen one such in our own little burg. For the most part she walked the mountain ridges, staying far from settlements and using the stars as guidance. Several times near the beginning she was moved from one safe place to another by people who were willing to help. She has hidden in caves and in the cellars of vineyards.*

She came to us because she was told that when she reached Mauertown, she must look for certain landmarks that would guide her to safety. My heart is brightened that someone not far away is taking in men and women, even families, who are escaping injustice. In the storm and with illness dragging at her, she was badly lost and mistook our house for theirs because of Mama's quilt. But by God's grace she was not led astray.

Jeremiah has finished her hiding place, and even I, who have lived in this house all my life, would have difficulty discerning it. Dorie knows how to secrete herself there, if need be, and I am adept at swiftly moving shelves into position and jars to cover their width. The room is dank and narrow, but it is freedom's home.

Jeremiah surprises me, Amasa. From

the beginning, he was willing to act to save Dorie, but with a willingness born of conscience alone. He was troubled by her presence and the demands it made of him. He wanted only to live his life in silence and despair.

Now, once again, he is becoming aware that there are people who have suffered more than he. While extending shelter to Dorie, he has extended a new and tender regard for her that swells my heart with pride. Upon hearing Dorie's story for the first time, he resolved to help her find Marie, for he fears that a child so young might change hands many times before she grows to be a useful member of a slave owner's family.

Jeremiah has convinced Dorie to let him make inquiries before she leaves us. I believe he is reluctant to see her go. She has brought new life to our home, and although he would never express it, I think her quiet, feminine ways remind him of Rachel. Dorie's love for her daughter reminds him of his wife, as well. These good memories restore his heart.

I have prayed for something to bring Jeremiah back to us, and Dorie is God's answer.

I will close now. With these words go

my deepest affection.

Always with you,
Sarah Miller

June 4, 1853

Dearest Amasa,
I was about to seal this letter so I could read your next (a childish game I play with myself), when all manner of excitement occurred here. I am sorry to tell you none of it bodes well for us or for Dorie. I will set it on paper now but have no hope that this letter will make its way to town in the coming days, for even if a neighbor stops by, I cannot entrust these pages to anyone. Jeremiah is now afraid to leave even for so long as half a day, a justified fear, I am sorry to say. I will explain.

Last night Dorie and I were sitting on the porch, taking our ease as the sun sank in the sky. I reread my letter to you as Dorie read our Bible. She is fascinated by the story of Moses and the Promised Land. I, too, find the similarities uplifting. Since the Fugitive Slave Law was enacted, the Promised Land for Dorie and other enslaved peoples is Canada. How sad that there is no place in this fertile valley where she can live undisturbed. Tell me, Amasa, of what do we have to be proud if we cannot defend the rights of all people to live without fear?

I was so absorbed in what I had written that the barking of our dogs soon became a familiar noise like that of crickets or bullfrogs by the creek. I will confess I imagined you opening the letter, your hands stroking the paper and your smile blooming slowly. Lost in this reverie, I wasted precious seconds. Dorie herself woke me from it.

"Horses," she said. "More than one. They're coming quick."

I looked up, and in a moment I realized she was right. And what a start this gave me.

Jeremiah was out in the barn, and I knew that even if he heard our visitors, he could not travel the distance from barn to house before their arrival.

With one mind, Dorie and I ran inside to the shelves where our dishes and staples are kept. We moved what we had to, lifted two shelves and pushed open the door. Dorie escaped inside and left me with the task of returning everything to its place with hands that trembled *badly enough I nearly broke a dish.*

We have all grown careless here. What reason is there to suspect this little family of harboring a runaway? Even as Jeremiah fashioned the secret room, I had little thought we might use it. As I returned to the porch, I saw our Bible on one chair and my letter to you (a letter that speaks clearly of our guilt) lying on the next. I closed the Bible and slipped your letter inside, holding it against me as three men drew close to the house. As they slowed their mounts I wondered what other signs of Dorie's presence I had left in the open for all to see. An item of clothing that was clearly not mine? The trundle bed made up as it would be if a guest were here?

Of course I knew the latter might not be apparent to men like these. These are creatures who could never fathom my delight in having Dorie close at night, her soft, even breathing a reassurance that she grows stronger. If they believe Jeremiah and I harbor Dorie or others like her, they believe we exile her to the barn or the chicken coop, not keep her safe in our home and hearts.

A more scurrilous lot of men I have never encountered. The dogs barked and nipped at the heels of their mounts as if they, too, suspected the worst. One man raised a whip to beat Blue, until I told him that if he harmed one dog, I could not be responsible for what the other four might do to him.

In truth, as you know, our dogs are a useless pack, more adept at lying in the sun than guarding us. But the man, who did not know this, lowered his whip.

I called Blue, and all the dogs moved closer to the porch. There they remained, snarling, between me and the men, their round canine eyes suspicious. For once I felt well protected.

I will endeavor to report our conversation, such as it was.

"We're looking for a slave girl," the biggest of the three declared. "Name of Dorie."

I should describe the slave patrol briefly. The spokesman was large enough to do damage to any horse unlucky enough to be saddled by him. He was nearly toothless, but this has not deterred him from eating, for doubtless, he has consumed enough food in his lifetime to feed several others.

The second was not a young man, but wiry and strong, and his watery gaze never stopped darting to shadows and windows, as if he expected Dorie to materialize momentarily. The third was hardly more than a boy, but he had already learned the insolent sneer of the others. Unlike them, he stared only at me, as if to curdle my blood or reduce me to the vapors.

"Why have you come here?" I demanded. "No one has ever suspected us of harboring fugitives."

"You seen her?" he asked, ignoring my question.

"We are law-abiding citizens," said I. (And we are, dear Amasa. God's law, of course, takes precedence always.)

I had been afraid to take my eyes from the men. Luckily I saw a movement beyond their loathsome circle and knew Jeremiah had joined us. I am not a brave soul, and relief flooded me.

"Good evening," my brother said calmly. "What brings you here this night?"

The large man explained again. Jeremiah listened without interest. "There is no one here except those who belong here," he said. "And no reason for you to tarry."

The man was undeterred. "We got

word you might be keeping runaways,"
he said. "We'll just have a look around."

"You've been led astray," Jeremiah
said. And truly, they have been, Amasa,
since their mission strays far from God's
law.

"Don't matter. We're looking," the man
said.

Jeremiah might have protested, I suppose, but it was clear that these men
would do as they intended no matter
what we said to them. My brother took
the wisest course and said nothing more,
simply nodding and gesturing to the out-
buildings. "See for yourself."

They said they would check the house
first. Jeremiah nodded to me, and I
stepped aside. I'll confess my heart
pounded as if it would flee my chest.
Clutching the Bible, I allowed them to
pass, although I think the dogs would not
have let them by if Jeremiah had not
called them to his side.

I followed the men inside, as if to be
certain they did no damage, and Jeremiah accompanied me. How sad it was
to see these men pawing through our
possessions. I believe they find pleasure
in destruction. They touched everything,
pausing often to see if we watched them,

for I believe they were intent on stealing anything they could. Upstairs, the youngest lingered in my room, stroking my clothing, gazing in the silver hand mirror that was my mother's wedding gift from her own mother.

One frightening moment came when he lifted the coverlet on my bed, exposing the side of the trundle. He knelt and looked beneath, but seemed satisfied no one was there. Perhaps he is too limited in intelligence to see that the bed was ready to be slept in. Or perhaps he knows nothing of the need to wash and air bedding when it is not in use? Whatever satisfied him, he left my room reluctantly, and later, as darkness fell, all three men left to continue their journey.

But I make this too easy, because before they rode away they lingered beside the shelves and wall that separated them from our terrified friend. They asked for water and I gave it to them. They asked for food, and I gave them that, as well. They remained there, Amasa, as if to torment us, as if they knew Dorie was only a cough, a sneeze, away from capture.

And then, at last, they disappeared into the night.

Jeremiah told me afterward that he be-

lieves the patrol's arrival was his fault. Alas, our friend and neighbor Hiram Place was also in town that day when Jeremiah saw the handbill with her description. Upon seeing the announcement of Dorie's escape, Jeremiah spoke his feelings out loud. "No person can own another," Jeremiah told him. "How can this woman flee a condition which does not exist? She is free in God's sight, and one day the law will see that she is free, as well."

Mr. Place and his son butcher hogs with us each fall. His wife and daughters come to gather apples from our orchard and bring us sweet cherries each June. He has no slaves, but perhaps that is only because he cannot yet afford them.

Perhaps Mr. Place did not send the patrol to our doorstep. Perhaps they came on their own accord, searching every house along their route. But I will never again look at my neighbor without suspicion. What destruction slavery wreaks, even on those who do not practice it.

Dorie stayed the entire night in her secret room, and in the morning she stayed near to it, in case the patrol returned. But this evening, as we sat inside (no longer confident to sit on the porch) she told us *she must leave immediately. She is afraid she has put us in harm's way, for the penalties for harboring fugitives are steep.*

She is not yet well or strong enough to travel. Jeremiah insisted she must remain a while longer. He has already made inquiries on her behalf in Maryland, through a minister there. He hopes to hear about her daughter's fate in the coming weeks.

Dorie is torn, for she is now our friend and wishes us no trouble. Too, I suspect a rare kinship forming between her and my brother. Where once he spoke to Dorie only through me, now when I come upon them I often find them conversing.

She is both lovely and intelligent, a woman few men could ignore. Jeremiah seems to delight in their conversations. His scowl, which I had thought a permanent part of his face, has smoothed, and his eyes are no longer lifeless but filled with inquiry and even, at times, humor. If he is not the brother I once knew, he is more mature, a man who has survived a great loss and begun to move beyond it.

I am exhausted, my dearest Amasa. This will have to be the end for now, with one last thought. After the slave patrol rode away, I found I was still clutching our Bible against my chest. I opened it carefully to preserve your letter and found I had inserted the pages into Second Corinthians.

As I removed them, my eyes fell on this verse: "Stand fast therefore in the liberty wherewith Christ hath made us free, and be not entangled again with the yoke of bondage."

Your prayers are needed, and you have mine, as always. But I believe with all my heart that God is with us here.

Always yours,
Sarah Miller

Chapter
Twenty-four

La Casa's volunteers tried to make Fridays special, so the children would end one week looking forward to the next. On Friday the twenty-first, with Thanksgiving just around the corner, the children were assembling arrangements of dried flowers, miniature pumpkins and small ceramic figurines of pilgrims and Indians to take home to their families. If some of the tableaus looked as if the Indians were hiding, waiting for the right moment to leap out and attack the interlopers, Sam could hardly — considering history — complain.

It was light jacket weather, and the younger children and older girls were happy working inside. But the older boys, led primarily by Miguel, had gone out to the basketball court, where Leon was informally coaching them. He was a regular volunteer now, an asset to the program. Everyone agreed Miguel had made a significant turnaround, at least partly due to Leon's casual offer of friendship. Miguel was teaching Leon to speak Spanish, and Leon was working on the other boy's English. No miracles. No transformations. Just two boys better off for their relationship.

Sam's visit came at the afternoon's end. Although he and Elisa had never discussed timing, they had made a silent pact. She spent the first hour after the children arrived helping with the program, then left to do other things. Most of the time Sam arrived after she was gone. They saw each other around the church, of course, and chatted informally for a moment or two, but for the most part they were careful to stay out of each other's way. He didn't know what she was frightened of, but *he* was frightened he would send her running. He said a silent prayer of gratitude every day when he saw she was still at the church, hard at work.

After admiring the centerpieces, Sam walked around back to watch the boys play. They had stripped off their jackets and were sweating from the exercise. After a few minutes he stole the ball, shot a few baskets himself, then relinquished it to start back toward his car. He had a dinner meeting to present his plan for either moving to three services next fall or expanding the sanctuary, and he needed to prepare. The two services at Community Church were overcrowded, and he didn't want people to stop attending because there was no room to sit.

He got to his car just as George Jenkins pulled up in a company pickup. Sam watched as the deacon got out and slammed the door behind him. He didn't need his training in counseling to see that Jenkins was angry, a condition that seemed natural to him.

"You look like you're in a hurry, George." Sam casually stationed himself in Jenkins' path, so the older man couldn't make an end run around him. "May I help you with something?"

"Where's my boy?"

"He's out back, playing basketball. He's darned good, by the way. I wouldn't be surprised if he makes the high-school team."

"Just what are you trying to pull?" George made a fist and emphasized the final word by punching the air.

Sam reviewed his week but couldn't imagine exactly what he'd done this time.

"I'm not trying to pull anything, not that I'm aware of. Want to be more specific?"

"You lured my boy over here against my wishes."

"Leon came on his own initiative."

"You set up this place to help those kids, and what's the point, anyway? Nobody cares if they do well in school, because nobody wants them to stay. You're spoon-feeding them, making them think they can call this their home."

Sam struggled to keep his voice low and calm. "What threatens you so much, George? Give it some honest thought, for everybody's sake, especially your son's."

"I can't seem to do anything about this program of yours." George swept his hand to encompass the house and grounds. "But I *can* do something about my son. I won't have him being a party to this. Why is it up to us to help? Tell me that!"

Sam's temper was fraying. Badly. "Do you want me to stand here and review the Golden Rule? It's that simple. Do unto others —"

"Damn it, what I want to review is your contract! You're up for one, you know, and I'm going to make damned sure it's not renewed. We don't need your kind."

Whatever was left of Sam's patience

snapped. "My kind, their kind. What kind do you need? Angry white men who think they have a lock on what's good and right for everybody?"

The moment he'd spoken, Sam knew he had gone too far. Not that he didn't believe what he'd said, but there had been no point in saying it except to discharge frustration and gain the upper hand.

He took a deep breath, but he knew better than to apologize. "Think about this. Why are you turning your anger against the very people who are making you a rich man? What's really pushing your buttons?"

"*You* push my buttons, Reverend. We don't need some ex-con telling us how to live, and if I have my way, you won't be around to push my buttons much longer."

"Then somebody else will come in, somebody else will stand up in that pulpit and speak for what's right, and you'll make it your mission to get rid of him, too. And when does that stop? Do you want to force people to take sides, have endless accusatory meetings? Is that what a church family means to you?"

"I'm going to find my boy, and I'm going to take him home. Then I'm going to start making phone calls. I've had enough of you. I've had enough of *this*."

"In your frame of mind, I don't want you near the children. I'll get Leon for you."

George looked as if he wanted to argue with that, as well. "Don't take all day, or I'll come looking for him."

They were spared the hunt. The basketball players were just coming around the house. Leon immediately caught sight of his father and said something to the others. They trooped inside, and once they were in, Leon walked down the driveway toward his father's truck, donning his jacket.

"Dad." He gave a slight nod. "What are you doing here?"

"What in the hell are *you* doing here? That's the question. I told you to stay away from this place, didn't I?"

Leon shrugged.

"Answer me, boy!"

"You said this place was no good and I sure didn't need to be part of it. But they need me here, and I like helping. What's the problem?"

"You want to work? I've got a million things you can do back at home."

Sam considered trying to intervene. Although he smelled breath mints, not alcohol, he was fairly certain George had been drinking. He was not sure Leon was safe with his father.

Leon settled it by drawing himself up to his full height, which was level with his father's. "I'll come home later, when I'm done here. I can't leave. I promised Miguel I'd help with his homework."

"I don't care if you promised Jesus Christ!"

Leon's eyes were unwavering. "Well, I promised Him, too. I promised I'd try to make things right here, and that's what I'm doing. That's a promise I can't go back on, not even for you."

George clenched his fists. Sam tensed, waiting for George to go after his son, but to the man's credit, he was able to control himself. He stood still for a long moment, as if deciding what to do next; then he shook his head, and his hands relaxed.

He turned to Sam. "This is *your* fault."

Sam wondered if George was right. Knowing George's prejudices, should he have questioned Leon more closely? Or had he been right when he decided it was his job to help Leon make amends? Do unto others? Or honor thy father?

"Maybe I should have checked with you," he told George. "But I think being here's good for Leon. He's a wonderful young man. You and I don't see eye to eye on much, but surely we agree on that? And you've raised him to be the young man he is."

"Get in the truck," George told Leon.

"I'll be home at 5:30. I promise." Leon turned, and without another word, walked back up the drive and up the front steps.

For a moment Sam thought George would follow and physically haul his son to the truck. But with an obvious effort, the man held himself back.

Sam lowered his voice. "Will you please look at how important this is to him? Can you see his commitment's a good thing, even if you don't agree with the cause?"

George's eyes narrowed. "I can see that getting rid of you is more important than I thought. And you'd better believe I'm going to tell everybody who'll listen how you've come between me and my boy. Folks 'round here want to raise their own kids without interference. Nobody's kids are safe now. Start looking for a new church, Reverend."

Sam was exhausted by the time his meeting ended. Resistance to change was normal, and there were some good reasons not to expand Sunday morning services or the sanctuary. By the time they had discussed every option over vegetarian lasagna at Daughter of the Stars, Sam was too tired to know what he thought.

On the way home, he tried to decide if he still had the stamina to take the dogs for a short walk before he went to bed. They'd been cooped up all evening, and he was afraid if they didn't walk off some energy, they might keep him awake all night.

When he unlocked the door, he was surprised when the dogs didn't run to greet him. More surprising was the sensual voice of Norah Jones coming from his stereo and the smell of coffee brewing. He stood with the door open behind him and listened. He didn't have to wait long.

"Sam?" Christine appeared in the family room doorway. She wore a scooped-neck white sweater and matching pants. Her hair tumbled over a series of thin gold chains, and she looked delectable.

He moved forward to greet her. "What on earth are you doing here?"

"Is that any way to say hello? You're glad to see me, aren't you?"

He nodded, although it wasn't strictly true. The visit was a complete surprise, and besides being exhausted, he wasn't prepared. He took her hands in his and leaned over to kiss her cheek. She slipped her arms around his neck, forcing him to release her hands. Her kiss was much more passionate than his had been.

She stepped away at last. "That's more like it." She smiled knowingly. "I thought you'd be glad I dropped by."

"It's a long way to drop. I could probably have changed tonight's meeting if I'd known you were coming."

"Oh, it was very last-minute. A friend was flying his plane to D.C. I went along for the ride, rented a car."

"I didn't see one outside."

"I parked in the back so I wouldn't give away my surprise."

He wondered if the "friend" was the man she'd mentioned on his last trip to Atlanta. "What did you do with my dogs? Call the SPCA?"

"The big ones are in the run out back. They went willingly after I bribed them with something disgusting from your refrigerator. The little one's asleep on your bed. If I have my way, we'll have to move her a little later."

He saw the raised brow, the slight smile, and knew he was being seduced.

If he'd had any doubts his relationship with Christine was over, his lack of reaction was proof enough. He didn't want to go to bed with her; he simply wanted to go to bed. Not just because he was a minister who was trying to practice what he preached, because he was a man who was in love with another woman.

When he didn't speak, she touched his cheek, her fingertips as soft as down. She trailed them to his chin. "Shall I pour you some wine? I took the liberty of opening a bottle I found in your cupboard. One step from rotgut, sweetie, but it serves its purpose."

"I'll pass. I'm so tired I'll fall asleep after the first sip."

She didn't ask why he was tired. He imagined she knew it had to do with the church, and that was a subject that didn't interest her. "Coffee, then," she said. "I made a pot. Sit down and I'll get you some."

Coffee was a good idea. He doubted he could ask Christine to come back tomorrow when he was rested and ready to say the things he needed to. No matter how he felt, they had to put this behind them tonight.

He made his way into the family room and settled on the sofa, aware that if he sat in a chair by himself, the message would be all too clear. She arrived with mugs on a plastic tray and an unopened package of pecan sandies. She settled in beside him, curling her legs under her, and opened the package, offering him first choice.

He took one and set it on the tray, picking up his coffee instead. She filled in the silence as he sipped.

"Mother and Daddy send their greetings."

"How are they?"

"Busy. They're so disappointed you won't be coming for Thanksgiving."

"My family hasn't been together for over a year. I can't miss dinner with them."

"Daddy's had you on his mind."

Sam waited. The lateness of the hour seemed to be working some unusual magic. Christine had a way of sliding slowly into a subject the same way she slid words together with her lovely, liquid drawl. Tonight she was getting straight to the point of coming here.

She picked up her mug and turned it in her hands. "He's been talking to Pete Deaver. Pete tells Daddy that the Capital Chapel's selection committee has asked you to come and preach so they can make a final decision, but you're hedging. I told Daddy that couldn't be true."

He set down his mug. There wasn't

enough coffee in the world to make this easier. "I am hedging."

"Why?"

"Because I can't separate my feelings about the church from my feelings about you. And I thought I needed to be able to do that before I could make a decision."

"You think I'm pushing you? That's the problem?"

He met her eyes. "You *are* pushing me, but that's not it." He reached for her hand, taking and placing her mug on the table beside his. He waited, hoping some easy way of saying this would occur to him, but clearly that was futile.

He squeezed her hand. "Chrissy, we love each other and probably always will, but we fell out of love a while ago. I'm not sure when it happened, but I do know why."

She slipped her hand out of his. "You're speaking for both of us?"

He backed up. "I'll just speak for myself, then. Being honest about our feelings isn't as hard as we've made it, but this is still hard to say. I think it comes down to this. We were never right for each other. I knew it, and I think you knew it, too. But we were so attracted, we ignored it. I loved being with you. You made me laugh. You made me take myself less seriously. And you stuck by me when nobody expected you to."

She didn't speak. For a long moment he waited, but she said nothing.

He tried to clarify. "We're two people who took different forks in the road. I glimpse you every once in a while walking your path, and you glimpse me. We wave, blow kisses." He shrugged. "The paths aren't going to converge again. We both know it."

"You're so sure?"

He gave a short nod.

"Pete Deaver asked my father to vouch for you, to assure him that you'd learned your lesson after prison." Her voice caught. "I made Daddy say yes. I was so sure you'd agree, so pleased. I thought we'd found the perfect compromise."

He refused to accept guilt. "You thought a church like Capital Chapel was what I wanted, too?"

She looked away. "It could have been."

"If I'd cooperated, you mean? At what price?"

"I hoped having me happy at your side would be enough."

"It would have meant a lot. But enough? Knowing that I'd had to move there or you wouldn't marry me? That it was an ultimatum?"

"I thought I could make you want it."

"Even you aren't that powerful."

She didn't speak for a while. He wondered if she was gathering forces for the next round. He wondered what he could say that he hadn't said already.

She was still staring at the wall when she finally spoke. "I thought if I came tonight, I could talk you into that final interview, that you'd see how important it was for both of us. At least at first . . ."

"At first?"

She seemed to struggle, then she looked back at him. "On the plane up here, I realized what I was doing."

He was surprised, and his face must have shown it, because she grimaced.

"I know I always find a way to get what I want, Sam. I learned it at my daddy's knee. If I watched and waited and dove in at just the right time with just the right weapon, I could have anything. That's why he was such a good politician and I was so badly spoiled. And from the moment I met you, I wanted you."

He couldn't disagree or soften her words. "I'm not sure you always realize what you're doing."

"Well, I did this time. I was trying to manipulate you into doing what I needed you to do. And even though I was fighting it, I guess I knew all along that if my plan worked, I'd have to live with the consequences. You would resent moving before you were ready, and you would resent me. Because somehow this is all tied up with your vision of yourself and who you're meant to be."

He tried to be just as honest. "For the record, I've tried not to make a quick judgment about Capital Chapel, but I guess my decision was clear right at the beginning."

"I guess." She said it with only the faintest touch of irony.

"I don't want the church. I need a ministry where I can do what I've been called to do, and I don't care if it's big or small, influential or a dot on the map. I'm happy here right now, but if I found another church that suited me better, would you come with me? To a working-class Chicago neighborhood or a small town in Iowa? Could you come willingly?"

"Then it's about churches and not about us?"

"It's entirely about us. It's about both of us being happy with our lives. And that's not going to happen if we're together, is it?"

She sat back and closed her eyes. He waited, letting her consider everything he'd said. When she opened them, they glistened with unshed tears.

"I know why you've held on to me, to *us,* so long. Do you?" she asked.

He didn't know how to answer. "Why do you think?"

"Because I represented the life you worked so hard to achieve. And no matter what you say, until now, you haven't been sure you wanted to let go of it. I was the dream of a big church, a powerful ministry, maybe a career in government service."

He knew she was right, although not completely. "It was always a lot more than that. I loved you. Don't discount that. I still love you. But it's not a love that can sustain either of us in the years to come. Just the way that other dream doesn't sustain me anymore."

She released a long breath, as if she had been holding it for eons. "Haven't you wondered why I stuck by you when everybody thought I should leave?"

"I guess I'm not really sure."

"I held on because you bring out the best in me. When I'm with you, I'm not as self-centered, as shallow. . . ." She held up a hand to stop him from speaking. "I didn't know I could be anything more than Daddy's little girl until you came along, Sam. I learned that from you. You saw something in me that nobody else bothered to look for. Now I've just got to decide what to do with it."

He was touched and even sadder than he had expected — and he had expected to feel devastated. "Maybe that will be easier if we're not together. You're a good person — you've always been a good person. But you need to find *your* way. Not mine."

"You've mixed loyalty with love for a very long time now. And you've finally seen the difference, haven't you? Because you've fallen in love with somebody else."

He didn't know how Christine knew he was in love with Elisa, except that she had always been more sensitive, more astute, than — as she had said herself — anyone had ever given her credit for. He could not deny it, although the impulse was there. But he owed Christine the truth, if not the details.

"Even if I wasn't, Chrissy, our relationship would have ended. It was time."

She nodded.

"And you? The man you mentioned to me when you were in Atlanta? Was that his plane you flew up on?"

"I don't know if that relationship will go anywhere. I don't even know if I want it to. You were too good for me, but I'm not sure he's good enough. You raised the bar." She forced a laugh. "Not that you're a saint. You're stubborn, and way too sure you're right, and lately you don't smile enough. You need a woman in your life. And I think I'll always be sorry it couldn't be me."

She held out her hand and looked down at the little diamond he had given her. She slipped it off her finger and held it out to him. When he put out his hand, she placed it in his palm and closed his fingers around it.

"I'm going to go now," she said.

"You have a place to stay tonight?"

She gave a half smile, and her voice was husky. "I'll drive over to Middleburg. I could use some time on the road to think." She got to her feet, and so did he.

He walked her to the door, searching for something to say to make this easier. Relief would come later, along with hope for a better and different future for both of them. But right now all he could feel was years of intimacy turning to stone.

She opened the door, then turned to

face him. He put his arms around her and pulled her close. They stood that way for a long moment, her head against his shoulder, her arms around his waist.

Then she turned and left. He waited at the door until her taillights were no longer visible.

Chapter
Twenty-five

Sam's need to sleep vanished with Christine's taillights. He was alone now, with no promise of a relationship with the woman he loved. He was still as far from Elisa as he had ever been.

A lonely howl from the dog run reminded him that he wasn't completely alone. He circled the house to release Shad and Shack, who threw themselves at him as if he had been away for years. He was sorry that love between human beings was so much more complicated than the love of a dog for its master. All he had to do to encourage his dogs' endless devotion was feed them. There were no other expectations. They loved him unconditionally.

Did he love Elisa unconditionally?

The thought was new. His relationship with Christine had failed because there had been too many conditions on both their parts. But what were the conditions Elisa demanded? Secrecy was one. She was not willing to tell him who she was and where she came from. He was fairly certain she had lied to him when she said she was from Mexico. He was also fairly certain she had purposely given him clues that she was lying. Had she wanted him to check her story of kites and *fiambre?* Had she hoped he would find out more so she could tell him the truth?

Or had she merely been pointing out that nothing about her was what it seemed, so he could not hope for the truth, not ever?

The dogs raced around his small backyard, as if making endless circles would cure them of a day of being cooped up. Bed wandered out to see what was up, and Sam realized he had left the front door open. He whistled, and the dogs reluctantly joined him for the walk around front, as if by going inside they were on their way to the "big house" for a life sentence.

They needed to run. He realized *he* needed to run, too. He considered routes and decided he didn't want to confine the dogs, that tonight they needed to be leash free and able to set their own pace. They needed a quiet road with few cars traveling it. They needed Fitch Crossing Road.

Fitch Crossing. Helen's road. *Elisa's* road. At night there was no traffic to speak of, and the road was too rough and narrow to speed. All the dogs had reflectors on their collars. They would be safe.

He was tired of fooling himself. If he saw lights at Helen's house, if he thought anyone was still up, he would stop. He would try to talk to Elisa. He wasn't sure what he would say, but he knew that somehow he had to make her understand that, conditions or not, he wanted her in his life. If she demanded secrecy, he would have to accept that. But he would not accept being shut out entirely. Whatever she was running from, whatever she had done or had been done to her, he would stand by her.

Inside, he decided to stay in the jeans he'd worn to his meeting. He changed into a sweatshirt that was more appropriate for a run, then fished for his keys. The dogs waited beside him while he locked the house, then followed him to the car. He lifted Bed in after the others had made the leap; then he got into the driver's side and started toward Helen's.

He parked off the road about a quarter mile away. Bed was happily asleep, so he cracked a window before he let the big dogs out. The night was chilly, but Bed, who was deeply snuggled into an old fleece blanket, would be warm and content. He locked the car and started down the road.

As he'd expected, there was no traffic. There was also very little light, so he ran in the middle of the road to avoid unseen ruts and ditches under at least a foot of dried leaves along the edges. As they passed their first farm, watchdogs howled a canine overture but did not run out to protect their turf. Sam had hoped the locals penned their dogs close to the house for protection, and so far, he was correct.

He slowed a little as he reached what he thought was the edge of Helen's property. As he drew closer to the house, he found himself questioning a late-night visit. He had acted on impulse, and now he wondered what he'd been thinking. If he was going to talk to Elisa, he needed to do it when he was rested.

As if to affirm this foray back into logic, he saw no lights inside the Henry house and only a dim light shining on the porch. As he neared the turn into the driveway, he also noted that the Honda was not in sight.

He was surprised, since unless she was taking extra shifts to help out for the holiday, it wasn't Elisa's night to work at the nursing home.

He wasn't sure whether to feel disappointed or relieved. Disappointment quickly won out. Apparently logic was a small wedge in a larger whole.

The dogs were panting beside him, but keeping up well. He decided to run to the Claiborne farm and turn around. He could feel the effects of a day that had been too long and too difficult. By the time they got back to the car, he would be ready to sleep it off. And tomorrow he would talk to Elisa.

If he could find her. For the first time he realized it was possible she might be gone for good. Was that the reason the car wasn't there? Was it parked at the church with a note telling him she was leaving Shenandoah County forever? Had he waited too long for this conversation?

He ran to the edge of the Claiborne property and turned back toward his car. As he ran, he reminded himself there were many places Elisa could be. She had friends here. She could be with Adoncia, or off at a movie with one of the other women from the park, or even having a late-night dinner. But the realization that he might have lost her forever underscored what he was only now able to admit to himself. He hardly knew Elisa, didn't know even the most basic facts, yet if he lost her now, he would feel the loss in ways that his farewell to Christine hadn't touched.

By the time he reached his car again, he knew — although it was foolish — that he couldn't go home until he had checked the church parking lot. Out of breath because he had sprinted too fast, he sat behind the steering wheel and gulped oxygen for a moment. He made a futile attempt to convince himself to wait until morning. Then he started the engine, turned around in the nearest driveway and headed back toward the church.

A meeting was just letting out, a rental group of single parents. Tonight they had gathered to watch and discuss the film *Father of the Bride*. People were leaving in small groups, heads together, one couple arm in arm. He wondered if any romances had begun as they discussed letting go of their children. He envied them their problems, as difficult as they were. They had lost at love, but they had children to show for the effort and hope for their futures.

And he was being excessively maudlin.

He swung into the lot and circled slowly to the back, where the staff parked. He was relieved to see that Elisa's space was empty. He made a wide circle to turn around and go home, silently excusing himself for giving in to irrational fear.

Then he saw a familiar white Honda, hidden under the overhanging branches at the lot's edge. He wheeled around and parked in his space. As the dogs watched through the side windows, he went inside and did a quick check of the building. The sexton's closet was locked up tight. And Elisa was nowhere to be found.

Back in the car, he pulled up beside the little hatchback and looked over to be sure Elisa was not inside. When he saw that she wasn't, he parked and got out.

Light from the lampposts set at wide intervals throughout the lot did not reach this far. The car was in deep shadow, and he peered in the side window, nose against the glass, to glimpse the interior, until he realized the car wasn't locked. He opened the door and looked inside. The car was clean and empty. Not a piece of paper, not an empty can or bottle. His gaze drifted to the ignition, but no keys hung there.

He started to close the door; then he leaned down and felt beneath the seat until his fingertips touched metal. In a moment he was gazing at the key ring he had given Elisa the day he had turned the car over to her. There were two keys on it. Both to the car. No house key. No keys to a locker at work. No church keys.

He clenched the keys against his chest and stared out into the night.

He had lost her.

He wasn't sure how long he'd been sitting there when a different scenario occurred to him. He was afraid to hope, but at the very least the misery he felt was best postponed. He got out of the car; then he opened the door to his SUV and invited the dogs to come with him. With the three of them at his heels, he walked across the grass, over a slight rise and through the grove of trees that bordered one side of the gravel drive leading up to *La Casa*. Paco was in Harrisonburg visiting a friend for the rest of the week, and the house should be deserted.

He was nearly there before he saw her. Elisa was sitting on the next-to-the-last step, leaning back against the top one and gazing out at the night. He stopped, something like a prayer rising in his heart.

"Hey." He was surprised at how calm he sounded.

She raised a hand in greeting. "What are you doing here?"

The dogs were overjoyed to see her. They ran up the steps and nudged her playfully. Bed jumped into her lap.

He decided not to pretend the meeting was accidental. "I was looking for you."

"Here?" She put an arm around each dog, but whether from affection or in self-defense he wasn't sure.

"I had this awful feeling you'd left town."

She cocked her head. He moved closer to see her expression.

"Why did you think that?"

"Because you've made it clear you will one day. I went jogging by Helen's, the car was gone. . . ." He shrugged.

"So you came to *La Casa*?"

"At first I thought maybe you'd left the car in the lot for me to find. The keys were under the seat."

"I don't have pockets in these pants."

He joined her on the steps, one dog body away from her. He waited.

"You were checking up on me?" she said.

He wasn't sure what emotion matched those words. Concern? Fear? Anger, perhaps? She was keeping whatever she felt out of her voice.

"For the record, this is the first time I've done anything like this. I'm not keeping track of your movements. I just —"

"You just what?"

"I just need to be with you tonight."

He heard her expel a breath. "You don't."

"Afraid so."

Shack took that moment to explore, leaving a space between them. He could see Elisa's face, although not clearly. "Christine made a surprise visit to see me. We had a long talk. We've ended the engagement."

"And you came just to tell me this?"

"That's a part of it. And I didn't end my relationship with her because of you. So no disclaimers, okay? It was over a long time ago in every way that mattered."

"It can't change anything, Sam."

He leaned against the step and angled his body so he could see her better. "What are you doing here?"

"I knew Paco was gone. I came to check and do some thinking."

"About what?"

"A woman named Dorie Beaumont and a man named Jeremiah Miller. There's a lot I haven't told you."

"That comes as no surprise."

"Not about me. Not really, anyway. I told you I hadn't learned anything interesting from Martha Wisner about the house, but it isn't true. She's had a lot to say."

"Are you so in the habit of keeping secrets that you kept that a secret, too?"

"I wasn't sure what to do. The house probably has some historic importance. I think it was a stop on the Underground Railroad. At least for one slave, and probably more in the years I haven't heard about."

He considered this, not seeing the point at first. Then he realized what she was saying. "You didn't want anyone to know because people would begin poking around. You didn't want them here asking questions about anything."

"Bingo. That's what you say, right?"

"We've been known to."

"Dorie Beaumont was a slave from farther south. I've done some research at the library. There were more slaves in the valley than anyone wants to admit, although not so many in this county as in others. But Dorie escaped after her young daughter was sold to a farm in Maryland. And she ended up here because she believed this was a safe house."

"Go on," he encouraged her after she remained silent a while.

"I don't know much more. Sarah and Jeremiah were brother and sister, and they lived here together. They belonged to a church that spoke out against slavery, and they were opposed to it. They found Dorie and harbored her, nursed her back to health. And while she was here, Jeremiah built the safe room you and I found that day. He was an angry man, distraught over the loss of his wife and children the previous year in some kind of epidemic. But having Dorie living here changed him."

She turned to see him better. "I think they fell in love."

He wasn't sure he wanted to hear the rest of this. Stories like this one never turned out well. Where would the two lovers go where they could both be free? Who would accept them as husband and wife in a time when slaves were thought to be little more than animals?

"Martha hasn't told me the ending," she said, as if she had heard his thoughts. "But it can't be good, can it?"

He shook his head. He was touched, more than he wanted to be.

"All this happened right here in this

house," she continued. "This was deep in the country. The nearest neighbor was far away. The slave patrol came and nearly frightened Sarah to death. But she and Jeremiah stood by Dorie, even though they could have been jailed if she was discovered."

"It's a good story, Elisa. Filled with strong, good people."

"I know how Dorie must have felt." She spoke slowly, carefully, not as if her English wasn't up to the task, but as if she needed to choose each word from many, to be sure it was the best, the safest. "She came here by mistake. She did not ask the Millers for help. I believe she would have crawled into the bushes and died before she asked strangers for anything. How could she trust them?"

"But they helped her. Just because she was a human being."

"Can you see how she must have felt? They gave her shelter. They fed her, nursed her through a serious illness. And even as she realized how much she had to be thankful for, she also knew she was endangering them. These people, who had been good to her for no reason other than that she was alive and in need of them. And as she lay there at night, she knew in her heart that she could bring down such destruction on their heads simply by her presence."

Sam understood Elisa was doing more than just recounting a story from the nineteenth century. "Are we talking about Dorie Beaumont? Or are we talking about Elisa Martinez?"

"Sam, you told me months ago how much you hated prison."

He let that sink in a moment. "And you're afraid that because of that, I need to walk the straight and narrow from now on."

"Of course."

"And you're a detour, of sorts."

She didn't respond.

"Elisa, the detour has something to do with the fact you're not from Mexico at all, but from Guatemala, doesn't it?" He ignored the beginning of what he thought might become a protest. "If this is about something as simple as documents that aren't in order, no one is going to arrest me. Can't you let me help you? Tessa's husband takes cases like this, or knows someone who will. I know he'd help —"

"You don't know anything, Sam."

"I know you gave me clues about your nationality because you *want* me to know more about you. Only you're so con-flicted —"

"Conflicted?" She laughed bitterly. "You have no idea how happy I would be if my life were that easy."

"Tell me something, then. Anything. Trust me with a little more of the truth. Don't make me play guessing games."

She was silent for so long that he thought she was refusing. Finally she spoke. "I *am* from Guatemala."

"You must have a good reason to pretend otherwise."

"My reasons are the best."

"Can you start from the beginning?"

"Just like that?"

"Just like that. Where you were born. The names of your parents. Your favorite subject in school. Then work your way into the reasons you're hiding from something."

"Someday maybe I'll tell you every little detail."

He captured her hand. He could feel her pulse with the tip of his index finger, and he felt it speed up. "Someday is a good word. Just tell me what you can. And it's not a condition. Just tell me because you want me to know."

She watched him with sad eyes until he released her hand and sat back.

"Here are the basics," she said. "My father was a native of Guatemala. My mother was an American named Sharon Wisner."

At first he didn't make the connection, but as the silence stretched, the name sank in. "Wisner?"

"Wisner. Martha Wisner is my great-aunt. She doesn't know it, of course, but she calls me Sharon almost every time she sees me. I must look more like my mother than I thought. Everyone told us there was a resemblance, that the eyes and the shape of my face were the same, but I never —"

"Martha Wisner is your aunt? *La Casa* was your family home? We're sitting where your family once sat?" He had not known what to expect, but he certainly hadn't expected this.

"Once upon a time, until my grandfather was asked to leave the church and find another. Of course, Aunt Martha stayed here."

Sam shook his head in disbelief. "Your grandfather was one of my predecessors."

"A surprise, yes?"

"A big surprise."

"My mother's childhood wasn't happy. Her parents were rigid and humorless, although she never described them that way to me. But from her stories, I could tell. She did say her years here in Toms Brook were the best. When I was growing up she told me stories of this place, of the mountains and the green fields, of the river. She told my brother the stories, too, years later. I've been hoping he would remember."

She fell silent again. He prodded. "Why?"

"Because I'm hoping he will find his way here. After she died, we always said we would come and visit someday to honor our mother."

"You never came to Toms Brook as a child? You never visited Martha?"

"No." She turned her palms up, as if trying to find a way to tell a long story in a few words.

"Did Martha know about you?"

"She probably knew I'd been born. But we were so far away, there was no real relationship. After she graduated from college, my mother joined the Peace Corps. I pieced the story together — my mother was never one to speak harshly of others. She was something of a rebel, and she wanted to see the world. My grandparents had expected her to stay in rural Minnesota, where they could keep a close eye on her. They were so angry with her decision to go abroad, and later to stay there, that they cut off all relations with her. She was assigned to Guatemala, and that's where she met my father. After that, she just never had any good reason to go home again. To my knowledge, my grandparents never called or wrote or asked to see me before they died."

Sam sat back. Elisa's connection to the church, to Toms Brook, to *La Casa*, was entirely unexpected. "You took the job here . . . why? It can't have been a coincidence."

"Because I've hoped Ramon would find me here, that he would come to the church to see where our grandfather was minister. I wanted to be here if he did. And I took the job at the nursing home so I would be near Martha in case he located her there."

He shook his head slowly. "Please, tell me about Ramon. Everything seems to revolve around your brother. Let me help."

"It's all so mixed up, Sam." She looked away. When she spoke, her voice was soft. "I've told you more than I should."

He wanted more. He wanted all of it, and a commitment, as well. He knew, in that heartbeat, that he had already made his own, and that it was not the facts of her life that he needed now, but her trust.

He reached for her hand again and threaded his fingers through it so she couldn't pull away. "Then I won't ask for more. Elisa, I love you." He heard her indrawn breath, but he went on. "Maybe not knowing all your story isn't easy. Maybe it makes no sense that I've fallen in love with a woman whose past is such a mystery. But I did."

"I'm a fool to let you know so much."

"Are you a fool who's in love with me?" He held her hand tighter when she tried to pull it away. "Because if you aren't, I'm going to make you fall in love. I'll find a way. It'll be my life's mission."

"Sam . . ." She began to cry.

He pulled her close, encircling her with his arms. He tried not to notice how soft she was against him or how his own body responded. Her hair smelled like honey warming in the sun, and her cheek slid against his neck like satin.

He knew she was not going to answer him, but he thought he knew the answer anyway. It shone through her tears.

He spoke haltingly, finding the right words slowly, as she had. "I know who you are, even if I don't know all your past. And if there are things in your life that have to remain a secret, then so be it.

But don't leave me."

His arms tightened at that thought, and he heard her draw a breath. "There are worse things than prison. Maybe that's what Jeremiah Miller thought all those years ago. Losing you would be worse. So much worse. When I thought you were gone tonight, all the color went out of my world."

"I can't stay here."

"Don't tell me that." He tilted her face toward his. "Please don't tell me that. Because then I'll have to spend the rest of my life looking for you. And no matter where you go, I promise I'm going to find you. Save me that trouble, okay?"

She was still crying. Silently, with tears trickling slowly down her cheeks.

"Can you promise me one thing?" he asked softly. "Please, don't leave without saying goodbye. Don't make me wonder every morning if you're gone. Don't make me lie awake at night wondering if you're packing. I don't want to find my car abandoned with the keys under the seat and know that this time, it's for good."

"Then you have to do something for me. . . ."

"Anything."

"You have to give me time. And room."

He knew what she really wanted. She

hoped by keeping him at arm's length, their relationship would not deepen, that she would be able, in the end, to leave him, that she would still have the emotional courage she needed.

"Will your problems be fixed with time? And room?"

She didn't answer.

"Is that the only way you'll promise to warn me you're leaving?"

She nodded.

He kissed her gently. Her tears were salty against his lips.

Chapter
Twenty-six

Elisa remained at *La Casa* for a long time after Sam left, thinking about the many terrible ways her life had spun out of control. On the porch where her grandparents had spent summer evenings hoping for a cool breeze, where her own mother had played pick-up sticks and jacks, where Dorie and Sarah had sat until the approach of the slave patrol sent them scurrying inside, she thought about fate and the utter uselessness of railing against it.

She was in love with a man she could never have. If she had wondered what games fate might still have in store for her, now she knew.

When she began to relive the events that had brought her here, she knew it was time to leave.

Once she was in the car, she wished she

had a place to go other than Helen's house. As kind as Helen was, tonight she yearned for something more.

She wondered if a woman ever outgrew the need for her mother. Sharon Wisner had been a woman of intelligence, resolve and wit. She had married a wealthy man in a country of great poverty, but she had never settled for a life of luxury or one of isolation from the real world. She had not hidden behind courtyard walls, ignoring the sea of humanity just outside. And she had insisted that her children view their lot in life as good fortune, not as a divine gift they had fully deserved.

Sharon had taught her son and daughter to laugh and love and keep their eyes wide open. Not a day had passed since her death when Elisa had not mourned that loss, but telling Sam about her parents had brought back the sadness of losing them in full measure. Now she wished Sharon was here beside her, that her mother could tell her what to do.

She had turned on to Fitch Crossing Road before she realized where she needed to go instead. Tonight she had immersed herself in Dorie's story. Now she wanted to know the ending. If Martha was awake, she would be happy to have a visitor; if she wasn't, Elisa had lost nothing but an hour she would have spent staring at her bedroom ceiling.

She took a side road back toward the nursing home, parked and went inside.

The staff members were surprised to see her. She made up a story about leaving something in her locker, then casually mentioned that while she was there, she wanted to check on Martha Wisner. No one seemed to find that strange. Everyone had favorites among the residents. It was to be expected. The aide on duty reported that Martha had been awake an hour ago when she had checked on her.

Elisa peeked into Martha's room. If the old woman was asleep, Elisa would leave. But as she had expected, Martha was up, this time sitting in an armchair, thumbing through a magazine. Elisa rapped on the door, then stepped inside.

"Hello!" Martha gave her a big smile. "You're not wearing your uniform."

Elisa was glad that tonight Martha hadn't called her Sharon. The mistake always tugged sharply at her heart. She wished she could tell Martha who she was. She wasn't sure the old woman would understand or even remember for more than a few minutes, but she thought while they were talking, it would please Martha to know she was family.

Elisa closed the door. "I'm here as a visitor. I thought I'd see how you were doing tonight."

"Oh, I had a good day. We had lemon pie for dessert."

Elisa thought Martha was indeed having a good day if she remembered the pie. "And did you have visitors?" At the Wednesday quilting bee, Dovey had mentioned that she intended to see Martha today.

"I think so. Yes! Dovey came to see me."

"Well, that's wonderful. I hope you got outside. Cold weather's on the way."

"We went for a walk." Martha beamed, clearly as pleased that she could recount this as she was at the news itself.

The room looked subtly different. Elisa had been here so many times that the slightest change was apparent. For a moment she wasn't sure why; then she noted something new on the bookshelf under Martha's lone window. She strolled over and picked up a framed photograph, and her heart leapt in her chest.

"This is new." She was careful to say the words casually.

"Is it?" Martha thought. "Dovey brought

it for me. It used to be mine, and she had it framed, just for me. Do you like it?"

Elisa brought the photograph to her. "Very much. Who are these people?"

"That's me on the right." Martha took the frame and pointed to a lovely young woman with a dark pageboy hairstyle and a shirtwaist dress with a crisp white collar. "That's my brother and his wife there." She pointed to a dour-looking couple who were familiar to Elisa from photographs in her mother's family album. "And that's Sharon on the top step." Sharon was dressed in polka dots and a hairstyle of Shirley Temple ringlets. She looked decidedly uncomfortable. Even so, Elisa saw her own eyes staring back at her.

Martha, clearly perplexed, looked at Elisa. "Aren't you Sharon?"

"No, I'm Elisa."

"I keep getting confused, don't I?"

"Just a little."

"I was pretty, wasn't I?"

"No, you were beautiful."

Martha beamed. "I was going to get married, but Bob was killed in the war. I don't remember if I loved him. I know I never found another man who pleased me."

"Better not to marry, then," Elisa agreed.

"My brother and his wife? They never should have had that poor child. They would have breathed for her, if she had let them. She could never satisfy them. They were always right, and she was always wrong. And they let her know it, too. Luckily, she had spunk. She walked out once she was grown, and they couldn't forgive her for taking her life in her own hands."

Hearing confirmation of the story she had pieced together as a child was jolting. "Do you know where she went?"

Martha pressed her lips together and tried to remember. "No. I don't think I saw her again."

Elisa was surprised Martha had remembered so much. She took the photograph and set it on the shelf once more. "Can I get you anything while I'm here?"

"I'm just fine, dear. It's so nice of you to come by to see me." She lowered her voice. "It's not really visiting hours."

Elisa lowered hers conspiratorially. "They let me get away with it because I'm on staff."

"Did I tell you a story?"

Elisa perched on a chair across from Martha's. "The one about Dorie Beaumont and the Millers? Yes, I'm the one who found the room in your old house."

Martha nodded knowingly. "I thought so."

"I wonder, would you like to tell me the rest of it? When we left off last time, Jeremiah and Dorie seemed to be developing a special relationship. And he was trying to find her daughter. Then the slave patrol came and nearly found her."

"Can you imagine people hunting others down that way?"

"Only . . . too well." The words caught in Elisa's throat.

"I couldn't live in a world like that."

Elisa didn't tell Martha that she did, that there were places too numerous to count where people were still hunted for their political or religious beliefs, the color of their skin, their ethnicity. The peaceful Shenandoah Valley seemed a long way from that reality, and this was one thing Martha did not need to remember.

"Do you feel like telling me the rest of the story tonight?" Elisa asked. "Before you go to sleep?"

"A bedtime story. There's not much more, I'm afraid. But I'll tell you what I know."

Elisa settled back in her chair to listen.

Chapter
Twenty-seven

June 15, 1853

Dear Amasa,
I am sick at heart and reluctant to burden you with my sorrow. I have read all your letters and fear there will be another soon that confirms the dream I had last week, that your father has slipped away at last.

If this be so, I fear not only this news but your decision to find a life in the west now that you are no longer tethered to Lynchburg. I know if you do leave to seek your fortune you intend to send for me one day, and that this is the only way we can hope to have land of our own. But, Amasa dear, I know in my heart if this transpires, I will never see you again. There will be too many miles and too much time passed.

Several nights ago Jeremiah told me yet again that he would welcome you to share this farm as my husband. I know your feeling, too, that there is not enough land to divide between two families and that it is not your right to create such a burden on my brother. Jeremiah says he will not marry again and bring up children on this land, but as you have said before, Jeremiah's grief speaks for him and blocks his vision of a happier future.

Perhaps I am being morose, but when I tell you what has occurred, you will understand why tonight everything seems so bleak.

Yesterday Jeremiah received, at last, a response to his inquiry about Marie. As you know, there are good people everywhere, and some of them have helped us.

The news was not what we hoped it would be. Marie is not at the plantation on the Rhode River where Dorie believed her to have been taken, nor would anyone say what, if anything, happened to the child. We did learn there were floods in that area in early spring and reports of those illnesses that too often come in the wake of flood waters. I fear a motherless child would be the last to be cared for and the first to succumb to such an illness.

Jeremiah waited until evening to tell Dorie his news, afraid if he told her sooner she would disappear without a word. He promised he would continue his search, but Dorie understands the worst. It is likely Marie is lost to her forever, either by death or sale, and the chances Jeremiah will learn her daughter's fate are slim indeed. There are so many slaves on the plantations of that region. Indeed, tobacco is a crop that depends on many hands. What overseer will remember the fate of one small child?

We are blessed in this part of the valley, I believe, that our soil does not happily support tobacco, and that we are not as tempted to force others to labor for our benefit.

Dorie did not weep, but I confess I wept for her. I believe the memory of her daughter's tiny arms around her neck is what has carried her this far. Freedom has little value for her without Marie.

Late that night I was awakened by voices downstairs. I sat up with a start, afraid that the slave patrol had visited late at night in hopes of discovering their prey. They have not left the area, and Dorie has been forced to remain in the house at all times, because someone might be on a neighbor's hillside watching from afar.

Dorie was no longer in her bed. At the head of the stairs I listened, only to realize that the voices I heard were hers and Jeremiah's. My brother was attempting to persuade her to stay, promising he would do everything he could to determine the truth about Marie. Although I could not hear them well, I realized that despite everything that had happened, Dorie was uttering words of comfort. Deep in her own grief, she still found the strength to help my brother.

I know not what transpired next, for I left and returned to my bed. Before I fell asleep, I prayed she would stay, but I had heard enough to know this prayer would not be answered. Dorie knew she could not remain and continue to put us in danger.

She was gone when I awoke just before dawn. I crept down the stairs to find Jeremiah asleep and no sign of our friend. I woke him at once, and we searched the farm and our road in both directions, Jeremiah on horseback and I on foot. But Dorie has vanished.

I believe, as does Jeremiah, that our grieving young mother is slowly making her way to Maryland, to the plantation where her daughter was sent. Last night Dorie told him that she is certain the slaves there will know what happened to Marie.

I believe her own life no longer matters to her, and that if she can only determine Marie's fate, she will gladly give up what little freedom she has found. I cannot bear to think what might happen to her if she is captured by the patrol on that journey, or what fate might await her at the hands of the man who claims to own her. Likely he will imprison her — or worse.

Jeremiah has spoken little today. Once again he is the silent, sorrowful man I had reluctantly come to know. I, too, find little about which I can be hopeful, Amasa.

I have devised a plan to offer Dorie what little assistance I can. Tomorrow I will ask Jeremiah to speak with Hiram Place about the evils of slavery. He should as much as confess we are hiding a slave somewhere on the farm with us. This, of course, will bring the patrol to our doorstep again, but if we are wrong about Hiram, perhaps Jeremiah will find another way to bring the hunters here.

In the days ahead we will tantalize them with Dorie's presence and become openly secretive. I shall draw curtains during the day and scurry around the homestead after dark, as if I have something to hide. I will send pleading glances at Jeremiah when they arrive and tearfully beg them not to search.

I will, in short, do everything I must to convince them Dorie is still about. This will not fool them for long, but perhaps it will give our friend a chance to gain ground.

There is nothing more I can do. As the day has passed I have become resigned to the inevitable. I will never know if Dorie finds her daughter or a home away from bondage. I am resolved, however, that I can help others like her. In the days ahead, once the hunters are gone, I will seek out other sympathizers and tell them to send runaways to me. I will sew black squares on the quilt that Mama left me and hang it on our porch every night. I will laugh in the faces of the slave patrol or preach the gospel of Jesus to them. (I am afraid one will be as helpful to their *souls as the other.)*

Because Jeremiah has been loath to leave us, I have yet to receive a letter from you that addresses all I have told you of this business. In Lynchburg tonight you are doubtless thinking of me as I think of you now. But I feel in my heart that you approve of our actions and grieve at the outcome.

I ask only one thing of you, Amasa. Upon your father's death, please come to me for one last visit. I long so desperately to see you. Come here and let me convince you that whatever the future holds, we must make our plans together. I beg you not to head west without letting me hold you again.

I will close now. You are my heart and my soul. I see your face at night before I close my eyes and on waking each morning. At least I have this much of you.

I wait for the news that I know will be coming shortly, and I pray I can bear it.

Your very own,
Sarah Miller

Chapter
Twenty-eight

The flu arrived with the onset of cold weather. Elisa sailed through unscathed, but despite mandatory flu shots, her colleagues at the nursing home weren't so fortunate. Over the Thanksgiving holidays and into December, she took as many shifts as she could so that the home had adequate coverage.

On the first Friday of the month, she was working the three-to-eleven shift to cover for an aide who had been stricken earlier in the week. The changes in regular personnel had affected the residents, who sensed turmoil behind the scenes. Many of their regular visitors were sick, as well, and their comforting routine had been altered. She lingered in rooms as she collected supper trays and helped with bedtime preparations, soothing fears and assuring those who could voice their worries that the changes were only temporary.

After the last tray was delivered to the kitchen and the last shower supervised, she leaned against a wall in a quiet hallway and closed her eyes.

The extra money was a godsend. Despite exhaustion, the extra work was, as well. She went from the church to the home with few breaks, and she rarely had time to nod hello to Sam. For his part, he was keeping a distance and living up to his part of their bargain, but both of them were acutely aware of the other's presence at the edges of their lives.

She knew the situation was not sustainable. Sam's patience would end. Her vigil in Toms Brook would end, as well. Unlike Dorie, she couldn't disappear without a word, but soon enough she would need to move on. Judy's phone call, the call that had given her such hope, had not borne fruit. Ramon had not appeared on her doorstep.

Her countrymen said, *"El amor todo lo puede."* But unlike romantics everywhere, she did not believe love always found a way. She knew better.

"Elisa?"

She opened her eyes, ashamed she had

been caught by the nurse on duty. Beth Crane was a matronly woman in her fifties, nurturing, professional, relaxed. Everyone liked her, but she was always very much in charge.

"A two-minute break, I swear," Elisa said, managing a tired smile to go with the words.

"You're dead on your feet."

"Not quite."

"Honey, you're working here, working at the church. You can't keep up the pace. We're all worried about you."

Elisa was sorry she'd drawn that much attention. "This is my last shift until my regular shift on Monday. I'll sleep in tomorrow. I'll be fine."

"Why don't you knock off early? It's snowing. Things seem quiet. Jan lives nearby. I'll call her and see if she can come in a little earlier than usual. She'll want to beat the worst of the storm anyway, and you can get home before the roads get really bad."

Elisa started to refuse, but an earlier bedtime was just too tempting. "What will you do until she gets here?"

"I'll be available if anything comes up, and it won't be that long."

Elisa finally realized what Beth had said

about the weather. "Snow?"

"Light now, but the forecast claims more's heading our way. It's too early for a storm. It doesn't bode well for the season, does it?"

Elisa had never driven in snow. The thought of a maiden voyage driving Sam's car clinched it. She didn't want the Civic to end up in a ditch. "I'm going to take you up on this."

"I wasn't going to give you a choice. You skedaddle. And be careful."

Elisa finished her paperwork, punched out and gathered her things, looking in on Martha first, but the old woman was soundly sleeping. Jan arrived as she was putting on her coat to go outside, and Elisa caught her up on what she'd done.

Snow was falling steadily. Just out the door she stopped and, like a small child, turned her face to the heavens, letting the flakes tickle her nose, cheeks and tongue. She had experienced snow in the highest mountain ranges of her own country, and she had seen it in her travels, too, but she had never taken it for granted.

She wished she could share this with Sam. Instinctively she knew he loved the season's first snowfall, as well.

Her love affair with winter's landscape

lasted until the car slid sideways as she exited the parking lot. She remembered what little she knew about driving on ice and steered into the skid. The little car responded well, and she made it out of the lot and onto the road. Considering that Beth had called the snowfall "light," it was piling up remarkably quickly, and there was no evidence a plow had come through. She wondered how long it would be before the county began to clear, and if the plows even ventured as far into the country as Fitch Crossing Road.

She crawled home at a speed one notch above a fast idle. SUVs and pickups passed her at a more daring clip, but even with the hatchback's reliable front wheel drive, she slid off the road in town and narrowly avoided a mailbox closer to Helen's house.

By the time she reached Helen's driveway, she was sure the fault was not her driving. She had passed two cars abandoned at odd angles on the roadside, one with its front wheels in a ditch. The light rain that had fallen earlier in the evening had frozen into a layer of ice under the picturesque snowfall, and the roads were truly treacherous.

As she pulled up to the house, she was so busy avoiding disaster, it took her several moments to realize another car was already parked there, already deeply shrouded. Under the white blanket she recognized the car as Tessa's and wondered what the other woman was doing at her grandmother's house in the midst of a storm.

There was enough snow on the ground by now that she made it to the steps without incident. Slipping and sliding, she grasped the railing to pull herself up, hand over hand. The porch itself had a glaze of ice, and as she skated over it, ineffectually digging in her toes and spreading her arms for balance, she made a mental note to find rock salt to treat the porches and steps. Knowing Helen, she would make her way to the barn and the chicken coop first thing tomorrow to see how the pets-who-weren't had fared. She did not want the older woman to slip and fall.

Inside, Helen and Tessa were sitting in front of the fireplace, where a fire crackled merrily. Nancy had sent a crew to repair and clean the chimney during one of Helen's trips to Richmond. Although predictably Helen had fussed, Elisa suspected tonight she was glad she could use it without burning down her house.

The two women looked up when Elisa walked in. Elisa hadn't seen Tessa in weeks, and in that time the pregnancy had clearly become a force to be reckoned with. Tessa was huge.

"It's awful out there," Elisa said. "The roads are terrible."

"They were just starting to get icy when I drove in." Tessa hauled herself out of an overstuffed chair. "Let me get you hot chocolate. I just made it."

It was too late to wave her back to her seat. Tessa was already on her way to the kitchen.

Elisa glanced at Helen, who held up her hands. "Don't look at me. Is it my fault she takes after the Stoneburners? Not a single one ever did what he was told unless that was what he wanted to do in the first place."

"But what's she doing here on a night like this?"

"Appears she and Nancy've been planning for weeks now to take me Christmas shopping. When she called I told her not to bother, but you can see what good it did me. Nancy's supposed to come in the morning. Fat chance now."

"Tessa's not supposed to be driving any distance."

"Mack drove most of the way. She dropped him in Strasburg for a weekend staff retreat at the old hotel there. She claims her doctor said it was fine to drive short distances, since she hasn't had any more dizzy spells, and fine to visit me, since the baby's not due for six more weeks and not showing signs of coming earlier. Does that sound sensible to you?"

Elisa doubted that the doctor had okayed driving on ice and snow, but the magnitude of this storm had surprised everybody. If Mack had known what was coming, no doubt he would have brought his wife straight to Helen's himself or insisted she remain in Strasburg.

"The important thing is that she's here and safe. And she won't have to go out again until the storm is over."

"I been through a lot of storms in my time. Mark my words, this is gonna be a doozy. But it's too early for the ground to be frozen solid yet. When the snow's done falling, maybe it'll melt fast."

Tessa returned with a mug of hot chocolate. Elisa was reaching for it when the lights flickered, then went out.

"Well, if that don't beat all." Helen was clearly annoyed.

Elisa felt for the chocolate and wrapped her fingers around the mug. In a moment her eyes began to adjust to the firelight.

"Mrs. Henry, you have candles and flash-lights somewhere. I know I've seen them."

"Candles in the kitchen drawer closest to the outside door. I'll light the lantern top of the fireplace. There are flashlights . . ." She paused. "Durn it all to heaven, Nancy probably moved them somewhere. Used to be down in the fruit cellar."

"Now that was a great place to keep them," Tessa said. "If somebody needed light in an emergency, they just had to navigate steep, narrow stairs into a pitch-black room with no windows."

"You take after your mother more than you let on, Tessa," Helen said with a sniff.

Elisa remembered where she'd seen the flashlights and silently blessed Nancy. "There's an emergency kit in the closet under the stairs. I'll get them."

In a few minutes the lantern was lit, candles in hurricane lanterns adorned two side tables, and each woman was armed with a flashlight. The electricity seemed to be out for the count.

"Lights go off out here, sometimes takes 'em days to come back on," Helen said. "Wish I still had the old potbellied stove. That and this fireplace's all we had when I was a girl. My daddy could fill it up and bank it at night, and there were still plenty of coals to start a new fire of a morning."

Not having light was an inconvenience. Not having heat was a real problem, and Elisa wasn't sure if the fireplace was a help or a hindrance. Even though it provided a warm place to gather, she knew it probably sucked more heat from the house than it replaced.

"We got plenty of quilts," Helen said, as if she could hear Elisa's thoughts. "We'll leave the faucets to drip so the pipes don't freeze, then we'll snuggle under as many quilts as we need. I been experimenting with wool bats, so I got a couple of quilts for you girls that can melt an igloo." She got up and stretched, ending with her hands over her head. "I'm going to bed before my sheets get so cold I freeze solid getting into them. I'll turn on the taps and put out a pile of quilts in the hallway. Don't forget to put the screen across when you're done with that fire."

Everyone said good-night. Helen had gone upstairs before Tessa spoke again. "Want some cookies, or crackers and cheese?"

Elisa thought she was probably too tired to chew, but she hated to leave Tessa alone downstairs. "No, but I'd be happy to get you some."

Tessa rested her hands on her sizeable belly and grimaced. "I'm not even sure the chocolate was a good idea. In fact, would you mind if I went up and went to bed? It's been a tiring day, and Gram's right. The bed will only get colder as the night goes on. I'm going to warm mine up right now."

Elisa wasn't sure Tessa was really tired or if she just sensed Elisa's own exhaustion. Either way, she wasn't going to argue. "I'll scatter the coals and put the screen across. You go on up. And be careful. The flashlight beam doesn't extend far."

They chatted another minute, then Tessa lumbered upstairs. Elisa locked up, took care of the fire and followed.

By the time she undressed and finished her turn in the bathroom, she was too tired to worry about heat or lights. Her comfortable bed, now mounded high with quilts, beckoned. Crawling under them, she turned off the flashlight, turned on her side and fell sound asleep.

It was after two in the morning when Sam pulled up in front of the little duplex in Woodstock that his secretary Gracie called home and turned off his engine. Moments like these were the reason for driving a four-wheel-drive gas guzzler, and for once, he was glad to be in this particular vehicle.

"Now you'll be nice and warm tonight," he said.

The two women accompanying him made sounds that ranged from mild to moderate enthusiasm, depending, he supposed, on how tired they were. Dovey Lanning and Peony Greenway had not been happy to be uprooted from their homes to spend the remainder of it with Gracie, but both lived in a section of the county that had lost power early in the evening and knew they would be better off finishing the night in a heated house.

"Let me get you inside one at a time," Sam said. "It looks slippery out there."

"Was a time when Gracie wouldn't have let a single snowflake get ahead of her," Dovey said, "but then, all of us are getting up there in years."

Sam got out and went around the car to help Peony first. As late as it was, he was glad to be doing something constructive. He was spending too many sleepless nights anyway, and his patience was at low ebb.

He helped Peony up the short walkway, and Gracie, in a flannel bathrobe, opened the door before they could knock. "I've got a bed all made up for you," she said.

By the time he made it back to the house with Dovey, Gracie had already shown Peony to her room and helped her settle in.

"Who else you got to move?" Gracie asked Sam, once Dovey was inside, shaking the snow off her boots.

"We've got four SUVs making the rounds, so everybody who might need help will be covered. I'm going to check on Helen Henry next."

"She won't leave her house. I know Helen. She'll say she's lived through a lot worse, and she surely has. And you be careful out on that road. Fitch Crossing never sees a plow."

"I'm going to check anyway." Sam told himself he was making the trip to be sure the elderly woman was safe and warm, but, of course, he was also going to check on Elisa.

"Sam, did you ask Dovey about old Reverend Wisner?" Gracie asked him before he could leave.

Sam shook his head, feeling embarrassed. In a moment of weakness he had asked Gracie to tell him what she remembered about Alfred Wisner, the man who was Elisa's grandfather. He had also spent time on the Internet looking up references to any Wisners in Guatemala, despite only the slightest of possibilities that Elisa's mother had kept her maiden name. He was sorry he had investigated Elisa's past, and at the same time he was sorry he hadn't turned up anything helpful. His hands seemed tied.

"What do you want to know?" Dovey asked. "I remember him pretty well, though I was just a girl."

"Just curious what happened to him after he left here. There aren't any records."

"Well, he went off to Minnesota, as I recall, and became the pastor of another church. Maybe that one agreed with him more, because they kept him a while. But after that church, he never found another. He taught at some community college, I think, until he retired. I believe both he and his wife were fairly young when they passed on."

"Martha must have spoken of him from time to time," Sam said.

"Not much. After he left here, they weren't that close. But she was mad about his little girl. Sharon, I think her name was. Sharon was the one she missed."

"Oh, Martha has a niece?" Sam asked silently for forgiveness.

"From what I remember, she left Minnesota when she was old enough to be on her own. I don't know as Martha had anything much to do with her once she was grown."

Sam waited, hoped, for some tidbit of information that would enlighten him about Elisa and her struggles. But Dovey was clearly finished. Except for a question.

"What's your interest in Reverend Wisner?" Dovey asked.

"I'm just trying to trace a little church history."

"Well, you find out anything interesting, we'll be all ears."

Even as he smiled his agreement, Sam made sure to keep what little he did know to himself.

Chapter
Twenty-nine

Once Elisa woke up and felt cold air against her cheeks. She burrowed farther under the covers. Immediately, it seemed, she was deeply involved in a dream in which Sam and Leon Jenkins were trying to protect Sam's dogs from a flock of predatory birds who swooped down again and again, talons extended, trying to carry the dogs away. As Sam leapt at one, the bird turned into a rainbow-colored kite and began to soar high above the others. She heard a woman call her name, but she couldn't pull her gaze from the kite, which danced above the birds until they, too, turned into kites and danced with it.

"Elisa . . ."

She sat up, startled, and fully awake this time. She fumbled for her flashlight, then her watch, since the bedside clock had stopped at 9:53. Squinting through sleepy eyes she saw it was three in the morning. The quilts had tumbled to her waist, and she shivered as she listened.

For a moment she wondered if the voice calling her name had simply been part of her dream; then she heard it again.

"Elisa . . ."

She threw the quilts to one side and slid out of bed, taking the necessary moment to find the old furry slippers and heavy robe that had come from the church rummage sale. Holding the flashlight in the crook of her arm, she tied the belt as she scuffed her way to Tessa's room.

She knocked softly, then, without waiting for an answer, opened the door and went inside.

"Tessa?"

"Oh . . . I'm glad you . . . oh!"

Elisa knew immediately what was happening. "How long have you been in labor?"

Tessa, a woman who kept her emotions close to her heart, burst into tears.

Elisa sat down on the bed beside her and took her friend's hands. "When you said you weren't sure if you should have had the hot chocolate, were you in labor then?"

Tessa shook her head and swallowed, as

if trying to gain control. "Just queasy. I thought . . . I just thought I'd eaten something that didn't agree with me when I had dinner with Mack."

"How soon afterward did the contractions begin?"

"I woke up with them. There's no clock. I thought it was just a backache or cramps from indigestion."

"Did your water break?"

"A few minutes ago. The bed's soaked." Tessa squeezed Elisa's hand. "I'm not due for another six weeks, Elisa. We have to stop this."

Elisa shook her head. "Not at this point, I'm afraid."

Tessa drew in a large breath. "I have to get to the hospital."

"I'm calling for help. We'll get somebody out here as fast as possible to take you in."

Tessa didn't release her hand. "It's worse than you know. I saw my doctor on Monday. The baby's breech. He thought the chances were excellent it might turn headfirst in time for the delivery. If not, he was going to try a few things to turn it. We had six more weeks!"

Elisa could feel Tessa's panic in the way her friend gripped her hand. At this point, panic was as much a danger as the premature delivery. Tessa needed to be as calm as possible.

Elisa covered Tessa's hand and squeezed in comfort. "Look, maybe this baby is not full term, but of course it will survive. At this late stage it will be small but perfect, maybe even close to five pounds. Once we get you to the hospital, the doctor will probably do a Caesarean. It's the standard of care for a breech delivery. But it's possible the baby has already turned and the delivery will be natural. No matter what, you have to remain calm. That's the best thing you can do for your baby right now."

"You sound like you know."

"I've worked in delivery rooms. Before I came here. I know a calm mother makes all the difference." She got to her feet. "I'm going to call the fire department in Toms Brook."

"What's the fuss?" Helen said from the doorway.

Elisa wasn't sorry she had been awakened. "Tessa's in labor. Stay with her while I call for help."

The two women touched shoulders as they passed. To Helen's credit, she didn't lecture Tessa. She just got a quilt from the foot of the bed and tucked it around Tessa's shoulders, then she sat down on the edge. "Your mama was early. I ever tell you that? Just about six weeks early, too. Scrawny as a chicken leg, but with a howl like nothing you ever heard before or since. I should've known right there and then what I was in for."

Downstairs, Elisa made her way to the kitchen telephone with the aid of her flashlight and picked up the receiver. The line was dead. She jiggled the switchhook several times, but clearly the storm had taken down telephone lines along with the power.

She didn't have a cell phone, an impossible luxury in her situation, but it occurred to her that Tessa might. She went back up the stairs and found Helen still chattering.

She interrupted without apology. "Tessa, do you have a cell phone?"

"In my purse. Over there."

Elisa shone her light on the floor and found the purse in the corner. She rummaged through it, found the phone and snapped it open. She walked out into the hallway and into her room, closing the door behind her.

A few minutes later she set the telephone on Tessa's bedside table, having had too little time to prepare what she was going to say. She wished she could take Helen aside to talk to her, but she knew Tessa wouldn't stand for it. Tessa was a woman who expected honesty and answers.

"It's going to be some time before anybody can get here," she said, coming straight to the point. "The fire trucks are out, and it looks like they'll be out a while. One's a chimney fire for sure. The roads are a mess. There have been accidents."

She sat on the bed and took Tessa's hand again. "I tried Sam. He has an SUV, but he's not home. I left a message for him. He'll come when he can. I know he will. But the roads may be too bad right now for anything except rescue equipment. I'm not sure he'd get through."

"Give me that phone. I'm going to try Ron Claiborne. Maybe he can get her into town." Helen took the phone. Tessa didn't say a word, but she was breathing hard.

"I'm going downstairs to get the lantern and candles." Elisa left as Helen made her call. By the time she returned and set the lantern on a dresser and lit it, Helen was punching buttons with abandon.

"This phone's not working," she said at last.

Elisa took it out of her hand, hoping this was simply the generation gap. "Tell me the number." But after she'd tried it, too, she realized that Helen was right. "Maybe everybody else is using their phones and the company can't handle the volume. Or the weather's causing interference. At least I got through to the fire department. They'll do what they can."

Tessa moaned.

"That could be hours," Helen said.

Tessa leaned forward. "I don't think I can wait hours."

Elisa was searching for any alternative other than the one that was obvious to her. Yet, in the end, it was simple. She had made a promise, taken an oath, and now she had no choice.

She took Tessa's hands again. They were as cold as ice. She chafed them as she spoke. "You have to be calm. You're going to be fine. I can deliver the baby."

"They teach you that at work?" Helen demanded. "How many babies get born in a nursing home?"

"I've had medical training."

"Elisa . . . this is going to take more than first aid," Tessa said. "I've got to get into town. The baby . . ." She gave a low moan and arched, lifting her back off the bed.

They heard a clatter downstairs on the porch, then somebody pounding. Elisa nodded to the doorway, and Helen took off. Elisa helped Tessa turn to her side and began to apply pressure against the small of the other woman's back with the palms of her hands. She prayed that help had really arrived and she would not have to tell the truth after all.

"If that's the emergency crew, you'll be all set. They'll have everything you'll need." Elisa kept her voice low and soothing. "It's going to be all right. Everything's going to work out just fine."

It didn't take long for Helen to return. She was followed by Sam. For a moment Elisa couldn't believe he had come. It was as if she had wished for him, and he had appeared.

"How did you get here so fast?" She tried not to devour him with her eyes. "It's only been minutes since I called."

"I didn't get a call. I've been out, along with some others from church, since the beginning of the storm, making sure our shut-ins were taken care of. I came to check on you and Helen."

"I'm nobody's shut-in," Helen said indignantly.

Elisa was so glad to see him that she couldn't keep it from her expression. "And you can take us into town? The roads are good enough?"

He didn't smile. "No, they aren't. I'm afraid my car's in a ditch about a quarter of a mile down the road. I walked the rest of the way. I'm sorry."

"No matter. We're going to be fine." She turned away from him, concentrating on Tessa again. But she could feel his presence in the room and the unfamiliar comfort of it.

"How often are the contractions coming?" Elisa asked.

"Close. I don't know. Close."

"Helen and Sam, will you excuse us please? I need to talk to Tessa alone."

Helen destroyed that notion. "I'm not going anywhere. You think I'm leaving Tessa now?"

Sam put his hand on Elisa's shoulder, kneading it gently. She could feel the warm welcome weight, the comfort and the question. "It looks like we're going to be a team here. Let's just put everything on the table."

Elisa looked from grandmother to granddaughter and knew they would both have to know the truth. She didn't look at Sam. She couldn't.

"I'm not just a nurse's aide. I'm a physician. An obstetrician, to be exact. I graduated from medical school at the

Universidad de Francisco Marroquin, and I specialized in high-risk pregnancies at the largest hospital in Guatemala City. I've delivered babies in state-of-the-art facilities, in mountain huts, deep in the forest when the mothers were afraid to come into the open. I have delivered every kind of breech birth, with and without anesthesia, and nobody in Virginia is better qualified, because few of your doctors have delivered in those conditions. Are you with me? *¿Entiendes?*"

"Are you making this up?" Tessa looked as pale as her sheets. "Are you just trying to make me feel better? Why haven't you told anyone?"

"It's a long, terrible story."

Elisa saw from the two women's faces that delaying the truth wasn't going to help. "There are people who want to kill me, and if they don't find me first, my government wants to try me for a murder I did not commit. I have been in hiding for three years. And when we are done here, I will have to disappear again. Can you see why I haven't told the truth?"

"How did you get here all the way from Guatemala?" Helen demanded. "If you're wanted for murder?"

"The same way others get here. Forgery,

bribes, payments to human smugglers. My education helped, and so did old friends. And almost nobody in the United States cares what is happening in Guatemala. The story never made your front pages."

Sam's voice was low. He dropped his hand. "Alicia . . . Santos. My God, you're Alicia Santos, aren't you?"

Elisa closed her eyes for a moment. It had been so long since she had heard her real name spoken out loud, although Sam had only gotten it partially correct. She enunciated carefully and slowly. "Alicia Maria Estrada de Santos. Perhaps it is not true that no one in the United States cares what happens in my country. How do you know?"

"Because after my arrest I've read everything I can on human rights violations in Latin America, and your case was in the news. The government claimed you killed your husband. But there were people who said it was part of a political witch hunt."

"It was convenient for some in power to kill and bury Gabrio themselves, before he could bring destruction on them. They tried to kill me, as well, but after I escaped, branding me a murderer was nearly as effective."

Tessa drew a startled breath and

clutched her belly. Helen got to her feet. "Well, we don't have time for this, do we? Just one thing's for sure. You've lived here for months now, and nobody can tell *me* you're a murderer. Can you help my granddaughter deliver this baby?"

"I can." But Elisa didn't move. "Tessa, you have to trust me. We have to work together."

"You're . . . Elisa to me. My friend."

Elisa would have helped anyway. There was no choice. But she was reassured now that, if necessary, they could do this together.

"First I need to do an examination, and I need to scrub up. I'll need a few things. Helen, will you see what you can do about assembling them? And get the fire started again. We'll need warm blankets for the baby."

"The water's hot enough. It's a gas heater. Come to think of it, the dryer's gas, too. I can put some blankets and such in it to warm them."

Elisa hoped neither appliance had an electric starter. She gave Helen a verbal list, then asked her to gather supplies while she went to wash her hands. "Pile some blankets over there for the baby." She pointed to the table top beside the lantern.

"Put the water bottle there to keep them warm."

Then she turned to Sam. "We'll need your help. Stay with Tessa for a few minutes and keep her company while we prepare. Are you willing?"

His eyes were steady in the flickering candlelight. "Why didn't you tell me? Did you worry I would turn you in?"

"You have to turn me in or you can be arrested for harboring a fugitive. Do you want another prison term?"

She left before he could reply. In the bathroom, she clipped her short nails shorter, then scrubbed them three times with a nail brush using antibacterial hand soap from the sink dispenser. She finished scrubbing and made her way back to the bedroom, letting her hands drip dry.

Tessa was breathing deeply, trying to relax, and Sam was gripping her hand. Helen brought in freshly laundered sheets, along with the other supplies Elisa had asked for, and among the three of them they managed to get the sheets under Tessa. Elisa told Tessa how to position herself. The bed had no footboard, a definite plus under these circumstances. Sam stepped outside, and Elisa began her exam.

She could hear Tessa breathing loudly,

but despite fear and pain, she managed not to cry out.

Elisa straightened and rinsed her hands in a basin of water Helen had provided. "The baby is still breech." She knew pretending otherwise or trying to keep the other women in the dark would be foolish. This was a cooperative venture, and everyone needed to understand the details.

She continued before they could question her. "There are three kinds of breech positions, and this is by far the best. The baby is presenting rump first, what we call a frank breech, because the legs are not bent. The feet are near the baby's head. More jackknife than cannonball, if he was competing in an Olympic diving event."

"He?" Helen said.

"Figure of speech. I'm not that good." Elisa managed a smile, knowing that if she appeared relaxed and confident it would help immeasurably. "There's more good news. I've seen frank breech babies delivered without the slightest help. They pop out when Mama pushes, just like babies have done all over the world forever. This isn't your first baby, which is a very good thing. The baby is large enough that I'm not really worried about him. The birth is a little premature, which is a risk factor, but not so premature that I'm concerned. I see no reason why we can't do this."

She looked at Tessa, who was breathing faster and harder. "And it looks like we're going to do this very soon. Are you feeling the urge to push yet? You're completely dilated, Tessa. Either you didn't recognize what was happening, because it feels different, or this is a very swift labor."

"No . . . Not . . ." Tessa's eyes widened. "Lord . . . I don't want to lie down. I need to get up."

"Okay, let's get you up on your hands and knees. Helen, help her, okay? Sam?" This was no time for formality. Tonight "Helen" was easier than "Mrs. Henry," and Sam wouldn't mind being yelled for. He came back into the room, and she gave a brief nod and a short explanation before she turned back to Tessa.

"This will make you feel better if we can do it and get things moving. Squatting for a breech delivery has problems associated with it, and so does standing. So let's try this for a bit. Sam, you get in front of Tessa so she can lean against you. Prop her up like so." Elisa helped them position themselves. Tessa was making noise deep in her throat, and Elisa recognized that sound. Tessa was gathering her strength and focus, preparing herself, as women had done throughout history, to bring her child into the world.

Elisa had missed this moment, the preparation for birth, the anticipation of an important job she could do and do well. She had missed it so intensely that for her own mental health she had been forced to push her real work out of her mind. She had not allowed herself to think what she had lost, but now it flooded back. She had been born for this, and she had been kept from it by fate.

The room was too cold, but no colder than many delivery rooms Elisa had worked in. Helen had blankets in the dryer, and she had filled a hot water bottle with hot water from the sink. The baby would be welcomed into the coziest environment they could produce under the circumstances.

Elisa soothed Tessa, keeping her voice low and even. "Once I delivered breech twins. One came feet first, and the next came out rump first, like your baby. The last time I saw them, they were chasing chickens through the streets of their village. The mother got up after the birth and made coffee for everyone who came to offer their congratulations."

"Don't . . . expect coffee!"

"Do you feel like you want to push now?"

"No!"

"You will, and soon. But we'll do this slowly. I want to warn you. Breech babies come at their own rate, and the worst thing we can do is rush them. So don't be surprised if the actual birth takes longer than it took with your daughter. This is natural and normal. The baby will know what to do, and I will only provide a little help." She hoped this was true. It was the best scenario.

"Sam, are you wearing your watch?"

He sounded calm. "Yes."

"Then you'll time for me. When I tell you."

She continued to talk, telling more stories of successful deliveries to relax everyone. For once Helen was silent, simply providing the physical support her granddaughter needed. Sam said nothing, but Elisa could feel him watching her.

"Ahh . . ." Tessa began to pant. "I need . . . to push. Now. The baby is coming."

Elisa was sure she was right. Had she been reassured that help was on the way, Elisa would have tried to delay the birth by putting Tessa on her side, hoping to slow the contractions. But now she only wanted the birth to progress as naturally as possible. There was nothing to be gained from trying to stave off the inevitable.

Tessa's knees were shaking. She seemed to be sinking. "Are you comfortable that way?" Elisa asked.

Tessa shook her head wildly.

"Okay, we're going to do this sitting up at the bedside. It's a good way to deliver. Helen, we'll have you get behind her on the bed. Right here." Elisa directed her to a spot, then signaled Sam to help her get Tessa in position leaning against her grandmother.

"Sam, can you stand just to the side there? We may need you to help lift and hold her legs. Can you do this?"

He nodded, but he looked the tiniest bit pale. She hoped it was the low light and not a tendency to faint. She was filled with love for him. Even under these demanding circumstances, his response was admirable.

"Okay, we're set now. Tessa, go ahead and push with the next contraction. We'll see what happens."

It took three hearty contractions and an enormous amount of energy on Tessa's part, but at the peak of the third one Elisa saw the baby's rump before it retreated as the contraction waned. "Okay, we're on our way here."

"Sam!"

Sam jumped at Tessa's scream and nearly lost hold of her knee. "What?"

"Cell . . . phone?"

Elisa was about to tell Tessa it was too late to get a ride anywhere anymore when the other woman ordered, "Call Mack. He can listen."

Sam looked to Elisa for permission. There were seconds before the next contraction. She nodded. He pulled it out of his pocket and punched in the number of Mack's cell phone as Tessa spat it at him.

"Is the phone working?" Elisa asked.

"There's a lot of static, but I think it's ringing."

The next contraction began. Elisa was about to tell him to forget it when Sam spoke. "Sam Kinkade here. Your wife's about to have your baby. We're at Helen's, and there's a doctor doing the delivery. This is now on speaker phone." He punched a button, then dropped the phone on the nightstand.

"Mack! Can you hear me?" Tessa shouted.

The phone crackled; then they all heard

a man's voice. "Just get busy."

Tessa took a deep breath and began to push again. This time Elisa saw more of the baby's bottom. "Sam, please note the time," she told him.

After one more contraction and push, the bottom crowned. She was right there, expecting it, and as gently and patiently as she could, she helped the baby's legs unfold. Then she released pressure and waited, providing only the most minimal support. The cord was pulsating and, fortunately, hanging free.

"What are you waiting for?" Helen demanded. "Get that baby out of there."

"Shh . . ." Elisa watched as the baby's legs began to kick and his body twist. And it *was* "his," she saw. Tessa and Mack were having a son. "He's doing what he needs to. He's turning from posterior to anterior. One of the miracles of birth. Go ahead and push with the next contraction, Tessa. He's almost here."

Tessa made an unearthly sound, but she pushed, and an arm slid out as Elisa skillfully turned the baby. Then she gently and surely helped release the second arm. "Just the head now. This may take a few minutes. That's perfectly natural. We need to keep the chin tilted toward his chest, so

I'm going to reach in and help guide. Are you with me, Tessa?"

Tessa made a sound women all over the world echo at the end of delivery. Elisa knew what it meant. "Be patient," she said. "Your son's nearly born. Helen, go get those blankets out of the dryer. Right now. Sam, get behind her and prop her for all you're worth."

"Son?" Mack's question was unmistakable even though the line was crackling loudly.

"Yes, son."

Elisa had hoped this part would be as easy as the rest of it had been, but she could not reach the baby's chin. "I'm going to let him dangle a little. This will help get his head in the right position. Bear with me, Tessa. We're almost there."

"Mack, why the hell aren't you here!" Tessa shouted in the direction of the telephone.

Elisa propped the baby's body against her arm and let him dangle. A professor had once told her the definition of eternity was the time it took a breech baby's head to emerge. More than once in her life, she had remembered his words.

After long moments she searched for the baby's chin again, this time with better results. A thrill passed through her. They were nearly done. The baby was nearly born. "Got it. We're almost there." She lifted the baby's body. A mouth, then his ears and nose appeared. "You're doing great, Tessa. We're almost done. Just the crown . . . and here he is!"

Helen arrived just at that moment. Elisa caught a glimpse of her as she stepped back and rotated the baby so she could see him clearly. He wasn't yet breathing. She strode across the room and laid him on the warm blankets Helen had prepared. She wished for better light, for a stethoscope, for oxygen, for a heated isolette, for a hundred different things to make this easier. A premature baby this well-developed had every chance if the right care was given.

She cleared his nose and mouth with a piece of cloth, then dried him roughly with a warm towel Helen had provided. Just as she was considering resuscitation, he gulped and gave a cry that grew lustier after he'd drawn another breath. She watched his color change to a dusty rose.

"Oh!" Tessa burst into tears.

Elisa did the briefest of exams, monitoring his breathing as she did. He was breathing as if he'd been doing it for years. She wrapped him snugly in three blankets, then brought him to his mother's side, along with the hot water bottle to tuck in beside them. Since he was breathing so well on his own, now they had to worry most about keeping him warm.

Helen and Sam had already helped Tessa lie back, and Elisa placed the baby in his mother's arms.

"I'm guessing he's at least five pounds. I suspect he's not as premature as you thought, maybe only four, or at most five, weeks early. He'll need to be thoroughly checked by a pediatrician as soon as possible, and I can guarantee they'll want to keep him in newborn ICU for a little while, at least, for observation. But he's going to be fine." She raised her voice. "Did you hear that, Mack? Your son is going to be fine."

"Who's speaking?" he shouted through the line.

"Dr. Alicia Santos," she said. She felt Sam's hand on her shoulder. "Of *Hospital General San Juan de Dios* in Guatemala City. Congratulations. Your wife and little boy are real troupers."

Chapter Thirty

When the emergency crew arrived fifty minutes later, Tessa was nursing her son. The fact that the baby knew what to do and seemed interested in doing it so quickly after birth was an excellent sign.

After a quick exam, the paramedics let Tessa continue until they transferred her to a cot and the baby into a portable isolette to carry them down the stairs. Elisa recounted the basics of the birth and the expulsion of the placenta. Then she bent over and kissed Tessa's cheek before the paramedics began their journey.

"You saved us both," Tessa said.

"I doubt it. That baby wasn't waiting for permission. I think you'd have done it without me whether you wanted to or not."

Tessa managed a weak grin. "Not with

such great results. Mack and I won't forget this, not ever."

"Just keep certain details between us? That will be thanks enough."

Tessa nodded. Elisa felt a hand on her back. She straightened and found Sam standing just behind her.

"Tessa was very lucky you were here," he said. "Don't downplay your contribution."

"She *was* lucky," one of the paramedics, an older man with a steel-gray ponytail, agreed. "I've seen these kinds of deliveries end differently. You ought to think about taking some classes and maybe getting certified. You handled yourself like a pro."

Elisa smiled at the irony. "Maybe I will."

"I'm going with them." Helen had left the room to change out of her nightgown and robe just a few minutes before. Now she was back, dressed in wool and corduroy. The cardigan gapped where she'd missed a button.

The ponytailed paramedic started to object, and the old woman narrowed her eyes. "Don't even think about arguing with me or I'll follow on foot and you'll have to explain my frozen body lying in the middle of some road between here and there."

He gave a low whistle. "You're playing hardball."

"Call it whatever you like."

"You'll have to squeeze up front with me."

"Just keep your hands to yourself."

Behind her, Elisa felt laughter rumbling in Sam's chest. She was suddenly exhausted. She leaned against him, and his arms encircled her. He felt so warm, despite the rapidly dropping temperature inside the house, and his strength fortified her.

"Don't plan on staying here the rest of the night if you don't have to," Helen warned before she followed the others out of the room. "It might take days to get electricity, or it might take hours. No telling which."

One of the men called over his shoulder, "You can follow in our tracks to the main road. They were plowing it when we came through."

"Do you want to give it a try?" Sam's breath warmed Elisa's ear and tickled her cheek. "My electricity was on when I left the house. You're not parked very far into the driveway. We might make it out to the main road, then we're home free. If we don't, we can walk back."

As tired as she was, Elisa knew she wouldn't sleep. The birth, the secrets revealed, would keep her awake. She also knew that Sam would not allow her to be alone. She had told the truth, but it wouldn't set her free. She was in more danger now that she had recounted her story, and as his arms tightened around her, she knew he was aware of that. He was not going to let her go without a fight.

"We can probably dig out the car," she said. "The snow shovels are in the mudroom."

"Let's try." He squeezed her tighter before he let her go.

She washed up one more time; then she changed into the warmest clothes she owned, ending with a pair of rubber overshoes from the mudroom closet that looked to be thirty years old.

Sam was already digging when she joined him. Between them, they shoveled a wide enough path to get the Honda out to the road again. Sam threw one of the shovels into the back seat and motioned for her to get in on the passenger side. She handed him the keys, and he started the engine to warm it while he went down to the road and shoveled his way into the wide tracks the paramedics had left behind.

The snow had nearly stopped now, and

except for their footprints and the path they had shoveled, the world was white and breathtakingly beautiful. She drank it in while she waited. Snow crystals adorned the windshield in feathery patterns, completing the fairy-tale illusion. She wondered if she would ever see Helen's house this way — or any way — again. Except for the crunch of Sam's footsteps, the little world that surrounded her was so still, so perfectly at peace, that for a moment it was easy to pretend she was a genuine part of it, that the life she had known in Guatemala was a fiction and this the only reality.

The driver's door opened, and Sam lowered himself to the seat, slamming the door behind him. "Are you ready?"

She wondered what he was really asking. Ready for a short trip? Ready to run? Ready to stand and fight? Ready to believe there was something more for her future than a life of subterfuge and lost dreams?

When she didn't answer, he slung his arm over the back of her seat and carefully maneuvered the little car into reverse.

Sam estimated the trip to the parsonage, which normally took less than ten minutes, took most of an hour. When they weren't crawling, they were stopped. Twice he was forced to get out and shovel sections of the road, then push, while Elisa cautiously applied the accelerator, so they could get enough traction to begin moving again. Even the main road was treacherous. Sam, who had grown up in western Pennsylvania's colder climate, couldn't remember a worse night for driving.

His driveway was piled with snow, and he stopped in front of the house instead, beside a knee-high snowdrift, and turned off the engine at last. "We'll have to wade through to get to the porch."

"I don't care. I can't wait to get inside."

"The lights are still on." He pointed across her. He could see the lamp in the living room lighting their way.

She rubbed her hands together. "The pleasures of city living."

They had talked so little since getting in the car that he paused a moment just to soak up the sound of her voice. "I'll make coffee the minute we get inside. You're heading for a hot shower."

"That would be wonderful."

"I'll see if I can shovel you out and open your door."

Taking short high steps, he plowed his way around the car, but Elisa had managed to shove the door into the drift so she could exit without him. Holding on to each other, they tramped their way up the buried walkway. The dogs were waiting inside to greet them. Their smothering, furry weight against Sam's half-frozen legs was more than welcome.

"Go," he told Elisa. "And take your time. Just save me a little hot water."

She finished more quickly than he'd expected, and came to join him just as the coffee stopped dripping and the toasted bagels were ready for cream cheese. As she entered the kitchen, she was toweling the damp ends of her hair. "Your turn."

He couldn't help but notice the firm outline of her breasts against her wool sweater as she lifted her arms. "I won't be long. Go ahead and start without me."

When he returned in a dry jogging suit and T-shirt, she had set the table for two with blue place mats and folded paper napkins. She'd put out orange marmalade for the bagels, and cream and sugar for the coffee, and added a bowl of freshly washed grapes.

The simple domesticity of it seemed both out of place and extraordinarily welcome. He wished they didn't have life stories to sort, more secrets to uncover, futures to debate. He wished their lives were this simple, reduced to coffee and gentle conversation. He wished all they had to talk about was the birth of Tessa and Mack's baby, and the good things that awaited the MacRaes now, after the sadness of losing their daughter. He wished they could end this night in bed together, making love and holding each other for hours afterward to chase away the cold.

"Feeling warmer?" she asked, and the fantasy ended.

He looked away. "Marginally. Shall I pour the coffee?"

"Please. I warmed the bagels again when I heard you turn off the water. I'll get them."

He poured coffee into two large mugs and brought them to the table. She slid a bagel onto his plate, then one onto her own. In her seat, she lifted her mug and read the logo out loud, idly tracing the words with a fingertip. "Heroes. Sojourner Truth, Helen Keller, Susan B. Anthony, Coretta Scott King." She fell silent. The mug was covered with names.

"Alicia Santos?" He lifted his coffee to his lips and savored the heat of it.

"Gabrio was the hero, never me."

"I want to hear everything."

"I don't even know where to start."

"Then start with Ramon."

"It's all so mixed up, Sam." Elisa tried to smile, but it was simply a movement of her lips; her eyes remained sad. "Eat your bagel."

"I'll need the strength?"

"It's not an easy story."

He picked it up; then he put it down again and picked up his coffee instead. "Go on."

She sighed and cupped her mug just under her chin, as if the steam would infuse the story and make it simpler to tell.

"I told you about the way my parents met. They were so in love. Mamá adopted Guatemala as her own country. Papá's family had come to Antigua two generations before from a nearby village, *San Miguel Dueñas*, and they were still very poor. Some missionaries discovered Papá in one of their classes and realized how smart he was. Through their efforts, he got a scholarship to the university, even though many of the people in his family were still illiterate, or nearly so.

"But even after he got his education and started a successful coffee exporting business, Papá never forgot who he was or where he'd come from. He bought handicrafts, mostly weaving, at good prices no one else would pay, then sold them abroad. He wanted to help all the people, like his family, who had so little and needed so much. And Mamá, after two years in the Peace Corps, wanted the same."

Sam knew enough about politics in her country to realize that sentiments like these had gotten many of her fellow citizens killed in the 1970s and '80s. "I'm afraid to ask where this is leading."

"I was an only child for most of my life. My mother wanted a large family, maybe because her own family was as good as dead to her, and my father's family had dispersed through the years or died. I don't know how many miscarriages or stillbirths she had, but I do know that finally, after yet another, I knew someday it would be *my* job to make certain women like my mother had all the children they wanted, safely and happily."

"Tonight Tessa MacRae is glad you made that decision."

She managed a real smile this time. "Then, when I was fifteen, Ramon was born, and my parents were so happy that everything that had come before seemed worthwhile. Not long afterward I went away to college." She looked up. "Stanford. I finished in three years."

"That explains your excellent English."

"Not entirely. My parents wanted their children to be completely bilingual. We spoke English inside the house, Spanish outside the home. No exceptions. I also know several Mayan dialects, *Kaqchiquel* best of all, some others just well enough to get by. Papá helped found craft cooperatives in half a dozen villages. I went with him every summer to visit and learn."

He reached across the table and touched her hand. "So far it's a happy enough story. You speak of your parents and brother with love."

"No child had better." She cleared her throat and sipped the coffee.

He waited a moment as she composed herself. "What did you do after the years in California? Medical school?"

"Just after I graduated, my parents were killed in a car accident. Although there was no proof it was anything but an accident, some people who knew them and weren't afraid to whisper the truth said my parents had been run off the road. You see, during the worst troubles in my country, Papá had been an outspoken advocate for human rights, and he had been questioned repeatedly by officers in the army. Mamá was a liberal American activist who still had contacts in the U.S. Both of them were dangerous to the people in charge. The only real surprise was that they were not killed sooner. It was not a good time to be outspoken in my country. It was not a good time to be alive."

She said the words matter-of-factly, but Sam heard the bitterness behind them, and what he thought was still shock that the parents she loved had been taken so abruptly and cruelly.

"Ramon was not in the car," she continued. "Or he would have died, as well. That was thirteen years ago. He was only five when they were killed, and suddenly I was no longer a sister but a mother."

"I'm sorry." There was nothing better to say.

She ate a little, more as if she needed the time than the food. Then she picked up the story again.

"Papá's best friend was a doctor named Gabrio Santos. He was a little younger than Papá, twenty years older than me, a generous man with a social conscience who gave much of his time and most of a large inheritance to provide medical treatment in villages where no one else would go. He established several clinics and made quarterly trips up into the mountains. I grew up calling him Tío Gabo."

"And he went from being your uncle to your husband." It was not a question, although Sam was surprised at the large difference in their ages.

"After my parents died, I gave up my plans for medical school in the U.S., of course. The money was no longer there, and I had Ramon to think of. Then Gabrio stepped in and persuaded me to move to Guatemala City, where he had a flourishing medical practice with a specialty in public health. He wanted me to attend medical school at the *Universidad de Francisco Marroquin.* He promised to help find proper schools and care for Ramon. He believed I would make a fine doctor and, by service to our country, honor my parents."

"It sounds like a good plan." Sam hesitated, wondering if he had a right to ask a question. But Elisa answered before he could.

"No, I can see what you're thinking, but Gabrio had no plans except to help me achieve what my parents had hoped I would. The difference in our ages bothered him more than it bothered me. It took a very long time for him to admit he wanted to marry me. By then he had become a real father to Ramon, and that was one of the reasons I loved him."

Sam could see how the relationship had developed, but he couldn't help wondering, had the circumstances been different if Gabrio would have simply remained her father's good friend.

"He was the best doctor I ever knew. Gabrio would take the practices of Mayan people he treated and expand on them, so they knew he respected their culture. So many people had been displaced and had no homes. They wandered in the mountains, afraid to settle, afraid their villages and crops would be burned or, worse, that they, too, would be massacred. Gabrio went to them. He took help to them. He cared in a way too few others did."

Sam clearly heard the love in her voice, as well as the voice inside himself that protested it. But he had no right or reason to be jealous of a dead man. "You were right before. He sounds like a hero."

"A hero, yes, but not a saint. He had faults, and I learned to know them well. He was so driven to help others that he rarely took time for himself. And he never quite overcame the difference in our ages. In some ways he acted more like a father than a lover. On one hand, he wanted me to succeed as a doctor and achieve any potential I had, on the other, he wanted to protect me from the harshest realities of our lives. And in the end, protecting me kept me from having a voice in what happened next."

She pushed her chair back and stood. "You haven't eaten a bite."

"Does it matter?"

She folded her arms at her waist, as if she was still cold. He stood, too. "Let me get you a blanket. You're shivering."

She didn't protest. "But, Sam, you must be exhausted. You need to sleep."

He gave a half smile. "What are the chances? Go in the den and make yourself comfortable. I'll be right there."

He returned with a colorful wool afghan that normally graced the foot of his bed. It was ragged and worn, but it had kept him company through the long nights of adolescence.

Elisa was huddled on the sofa, and he draped the afghan on her lap, tucking it in around her. "My aunt crocheted this out of scraps of yarn when I was ten. I've never been able to make myself get rid of it."

She tugged it higher and buried her arms beneath it. "It's an old friend. You're lucky to have it."

He went back into the kitchen for their coffee, topping it off with more. Then he settled beside her, but not too close. She needed room in every conceivable way. "You don't have anything left from *your* childhood, do you?"

"I hope I have the most important thing."

"Memories?"

"My brother."

"You haven't said enough about him."

"You know about the massacres in my country? You've said as much."

He knew. Guatemala, like other countries in Latin America, had an unfortunate history of experiments with real democracy interspersed with periods of harsh military rule. Under the latter, anyone suspected of left-wing activities was jailed or murdered. Left-wing was interpreted loosely enough to include anyone who advocated human rights, the organization of unions, assistance to the poor.

In the period from the mid-1950s to the mid-1980s, government in Guatemala had been completely dominated by the country's army, and guerilla groups had formed to challenge them. As the rebel forces retreated into the Mayan highlands for cover, the indigenous people, whether they were involved with the guerillas or not, were rooted out by the army, their villages destroyed and thousands murdered.

He condensed the facts. "I know that in Guatemala, the army's policy of murder and mayhem was called the broom, because the army swept through the whole country, clearing away all dissent."

"*La escoba.* Yes. It is surprising, as I said, that, as outspoken as my parents were, they were not killed earlier. But they had friends who protected them. My father had received international acclaim for his cooperatives. It would not have been simple to make him disappear, as so many others did. And he was careful, a man who believed he knew friend from foe and how to play one against the other."

"How does this relate to you, Elisa? Guatemala's come a long way toward democracy since then. There's been a civilian government in place for almost twenty years."

"The year my parents died was a particularly terrible year for my country. Things had seemed better, then we took a turn back to bloodshed and violence. Once more, people who spoke out were murdered, intellectuals known outside Guatemala as well as Mayan villagers. There was a man named Martin Avila Morales who was rising in the political ranks, a close friend of my father's, nearly as close as Gabrio. My father had information about one of those incidents in a village, important information that needed to reach the right people, so he went to Martin and recounted it. He was assured the information would be put to good use."

Sam saw she was shivering and tucked the afghan tighter around her. "Drink some coffee." He handed her the mug and watched her sip. "I gather this Morales was not a man to trust?"

"He is the most dangerous man I have ever known. *Un comodín,* something like what you call a chameleon, a man who changes with his environment, a man who can hide what he is, who is too often invisible to the naked eye. When my parents were killed, Martin attended their funeral and grieved publicly, as if he had lost his best friends. I had no reason to believe he hadn't. Only Gabrio was suspicious, since he knew my father had given the information to Martin, but since he had no proof, he chose not to tell me his fears."

Sam understood now what she had meant when she said Gabrio had protected her. "That was still a long time ago."

"Yes, and perhaps it would have ended there if, a year before he died Gabrio had not begun to hear bits of information from people he treated in his clinics. I'll make the story short. Little by little, piece by piece, Gabrio began to suspect Martin Avila Morales himself had been instrumental in a massacre at a village named Wakk'an where Gabrio had established a clinic. The killings took place in 1985. Martin was an officer in the army at that time, and that fact was well known. But we had always believed he was a voice of reason, a man who had been able to prevent bloodshed."

She set down her coffee and shivered again, but this time Sam knew there was nothing he could do. There was no way to warm her. "Go on," he encouraged.

She reached for his hands, and he gripped them.

"Guatemala began exhuming the sites of massacres eleven years ago. Forensic scientists from all over the world and hundreds of volunteers have come to help. It is necessary, to prove the scope of what happened, and to help the survivors and relatives of the dead move on with their lives. As Gabrio gathered information about Wakk'an and what had happened, he began to organize the exhumation of a mass grave on the square. Of course there was much resistance and many threats made. There always is. Many people want to forget what happened and move forward. And, of course, many of them prefer their own pasts and culpability not be questioned, not be exhumed, as it were, for the world to see."

"And Martin Avila Morales was one of those?"

"Do you know that in 1996 the soldiers who participated in these horrors were given amnesty? It's part of our National Reconciliation Law. For the most part they cannot be prosecuted for what they did, but Martin wanted a career in politics — in fact, he wants to be president one day soon. So even if he could not be tried, it was not in his interests to be identified with what happened in Wakk'an, and it was not in his interest to allow the exhumation to go forward. He came to Gabrio and asked him not to continue, giving excuses why it was not a good idea at the moment, but by then Gabrio had learned the final piece of the puzzle. Martin himself was the officer who had ordered and carried out this massacre, and Gabrio wanted to prove this."

"Did you know?"

"Not then. Gabrio continued to protect me. I think he believed that if I didn't know details, I was safer. He was almost certain at that point, I think, that Martin had been responsible, too, for the death of my parents. But he did not want me to know, to bring back those memories or put me in danger, until he had assembled his case and presented it to someone who would be able to help."

Sam rubbed her hands. "When did you find out?"

"Ramon and I always accompanied Gabrio to the clinics. I worked side by side with him, and we thought it important for Ramon to be with us. He is good at many things, my brother, and I believe he would have followed in Gabrio's footsteps and worked in public health. We could count on him to do things many boys his age would never be able to.

"Several weeks before the exhumation was to begin, Ramon and I were to accompany Gabrio to the mountains to work at one of the clinics. Afterward, when Ramon and I were back at home, Gabrio planned to join the others at the Wakk'an exhumation. But as the time came to leave, Gabrio began to make excuses. He did not want us to come for this reason and that —"

Her voice caught, and she brushed away a tear. "Gabrio and I had been fighting for weeks by then. He was never home, and I missed him. We were arguing constantly, too, about having a child. Ramon was nearly grown, my position at the hospital was well-established, and I wanted a baby. But Gabrio resisted. He cut short every conversation, made excuses to be gone. Now I know he was putting together his case against Martin, that he was assembling evidence, and even that he was afraid to have a child because it would make him more vulnerable.

"But I didn't know these things then, and I was hurt and upset. When he asked me to stay in Guatemala City with Ramon, I balked. I thought he was trying to shut me out of his life even more. Also I knew Gabrio would not take care of himself, that he would work too hard unless I was there to insist. At the last minute I fell ill, and again he tried to make me stay home, but I refused. By then I was frantic. I sensed too much was wrong, and I didn't want him out of my sight."

"Elisa . . ." Sam held her hands against his cheeks.

She shook her head. "I'll finish, then be done with this."

"This is very hard, I know."

"What do you remember reading about Gabrio's murder?"

Sam had searched his memory since the moment at Tessa's bedside when he had realized her identity, but his recall of the facts was sketchy. "Not much. He was murdered on a mountain road. Someone found his body the next day. You were reported to have been with him, but you were gone. . . ." He hesitated too long.

She closed her eyes. "My fingerprints were on the gun."

"Yes. I remember that much."

"We were on our way to the clinic. We were late getting started because I was sick and not moving fast enough, and because Gabrio's car was in the garage for repairs and at the last moment we had to take mine instead. Gabrio was curt and distracted. I was too sick to be polite. We argued as we were leaving the house. I said to him, 'Lately, Gabrio, I think you would be happier dead than married to me.'"

She began to cry. Sam moved closer and took her in his arms. "Elisa, we all say things we don't mean when we're sick and upset."

"Do you know how this one sentence has come back to haunt me? In the car . . .

Gabrio finally realized I had reached a point where I was thinking of leaving him. So . . . as Ramon slept he finally broke down and told me about Martin, about his investigations, about my parents and his belief they had been murdered.

"He was angry at me for forcing his confession. I was angry at him for keeping . . . the truth to himself, but at least I finally knew what it was that had taken him so far from me."

She made a visible effort to pull herself together. "As we drove, rain had begun, and the higher . . . we climbed . . ." She took a deep, shaky breath. "The worse it became. The car kept stalling and getting stuck, until we were afraid to drive farther. Our roads . . . are bad in the best of weather. You have no idea how bad they can be in the rain. Hours later we stopped by the . . . side of the road. We knew we couldn't reach the village that night in the rain, in the dark.

"Everything, the truth . . . the fact he had kept it to himself and treated me like a child, the storm . . . We were exhausted; I was feeling sicker, and Gabrio and I were hardly speaking. Even Ramon, who was awake by then . . . was upset."

He stroked her hair. When she was

calmer, she began again.

"We saw headlights and thought our luck had changed, that we would be safer in a caravan. Gabrio got out, and three men got out of the car behind us. It only took a moment to see we weren't safer at all. They made us get out of the car, held us at bay while they searched it. I thought at first they just intended to rob us, but then they unlocked the glove compartment with our keys and found my gun."

"Yours?"

"The year before I had been attacked by a rabid dog. Gabrio insisted I carry a gun after that. He was not a violent man, simply cautious. We agreed I would keep one locked in the car, just in case, but only in the car. I didn't carry it with me.

"When they took the gun, Gabrio stepped forward." She looked at Sam. "They shot him. The man holding my gun shot him. Then the other man stepped away from us and he turned the gun toward me. . . ."

Sam felt his stomach knot. For a moment he felt physically ill.

"Do you believe in miracles, Sam? I've never asked you this. But either an angel or a devil intervened that night. Because the gun jammed the second time. And when it did, I pushed Ramon into the bushes at the side of the road, and we ran. I knew Gabrio was dead. They shot him through the heart. He had no chance at all, but we did. They came after us, of course. We heard them crashing through the bushes, but it was dark, growing darker, and the storm had started again."

"It's a miracle you survived," he said, tightening his arm around her.

"I very nearly didn't. It became clear quickly that they were going to catch up. I pointed to something that looked like a footpath to our right, and Ramon took off toward it. As soon as he'd gained a few feet, I took off to the left, making noise as I did."

"You were trying to make them follow you?"

"I wanted my brother to have every chance. So I did what I could to lead them away from him. I thought they would catch me quickly. I could hear them behind me. I don't know why they didn't. At some point they made a wrong turn, perhaps, or because of the rain, they could not hear me as well as I'd thought."

"Sound travels differently in the mountains."

"Whatever the reason, I expected to die.

I stumbled into a dense thicket. There were boulders, and I slid between two of them and crouched, waiting for them to find me, praying they would not. Once I thought I heard them pass . . ." She swallowed. "Then I heard gunshots."

He didn't know what to say. He held her tighter.

"Two shots," she said, the words ragged. "I was lost by then, turned around. I don't know what direction they came from, Sam. I don't know why they shot . . . But I never saw Ramon again."

He kissed her hair, and only then did he realize his eyes were wet. "I'm so sorry."

"I stayed in the thicket until the next morning. By then I was so sick I could barely walk, but somehow I found my way back to the road, and I stayed within sight of it, following it as best I could to the village while I stayed hidden. A man was searching for firewood, and he found me. He helped me hide in the woods until nightfall, then he took me to a house on the outskirts, where they took care of me. The man and some others went back to find Gabrio and the car, and to look for Ramon, but there was no sign of any of them. They found blood not far away. I don't know whose blood, if the murderers dragged Gabrio there . . ." She shook her head. "If it was Ramon's blood . . ."

"The body was gone?"

"Some men came that night and said someone had found a body some distance away. By then I had been taken to a cave, and left with blankets and water and a woman to tend me. I was so sick I didn't know what was happening. We had been traveling with medicine, of course, but I had nothing with me when I escaped. I had a high fever. Every breath was like a knife. The next morning two villagers returned and told me that the dead man was Gabrio, and that the authorities claimed I had killed him. My gun was found beside him, and only my fingerprints were on it. The man who shot Gabrio had worn gloves, I think, although it all happened so quickly I could not swear to anything. But they said that I had been heard threatening Gabrio —"

"Because you said he seemed to think he would be better off dead than married to you?"

"Such a little thing at the time, a woman upset with her husband and hoping for reassurance. But that, the fact I had disappeared from the scene along with my brother, the gun . . . The car was found a week later near the Belize border. Even later there were stories I had withdrawn all our funds from our joint account, reports that I had caught Gabrio with a mistress. Lies, all of it. But I couldn't go home to defend myself."

He understood why. "Ramon?"

"Yes. By the time I had recovered enough to do anything, I knew if I returned to testify and Ramon was still alive, he would try to find his way back to me. And if he did, he would be killed. He was a witness that night, and he wouldn't be allowed to live long enough to tell the truth. Martin is a powerful man, far more powerful than I would ever be. His men had intended to kill all of us that night. Had we not fled, they would have made it look like a robbery. Once we ran, they could only make it look as if one or both of us had killed Gabrio."

"But surely there were friends, people in high places who could help you and protect your brother?"

"And which of our friends in Guatemala could be trusted to protect him? Who had told these men I kept a gun in my car? Who had told them where we were going and when we would be there? Who stole the money from our accounts, or falsely reported that my husband kept a mistress and that I wanted to kill him in revenge? Neither Ramon nor I was safe in our own country, and I knew I had no choice but to escape."

"And you've been on the run ever since." He wasn't even certain he wanted the answer to the next question, but he asked it anyway. "And Ramon? Do you know anything about him?"

"Can you imagine two people on the run, no contacts or plans, certainly no passports or identification, no one who can be trusted to help, terrified of being caught and killed? Two people with nothing, no money, no resources, not even photographs to show as they look for each other? Two people trying to disguise themselves with new hairstyles, sunglasses, taking new names and jobs they never trained to do?"

Sam couldn't. The fact she had gotten this far amazed him. "No, I can't."

"But there have been sightings."

Sam listened as she recounted incidents when Ramon might have been spotted, her own fruitless stays in both Manzanillo and Mexico City, and at last the phone call to Judy and the message that had been passed along to the caller. "And you think, if it *was* Ramon on the telephone, he would make the connection and come here?"

"This was the only place left I could think of to try. Ramon loved the stories my mother told of her life here. And I told him we would come here together. We spoke of it often. I know he would understand what Judy's husband said to him about wading in the brook. If it was Ramon . . ."

And that, of course, was the central question. Because Ramon might never have gotten more than a few hundred yards from the scene of Gabrio's murder. Ramon, like so many of the victims of military violence in Guatemala's highlands, might be buried in an unmarked grave on a mountainside.

Elisa's story explained so much. How she had come to this place in particular, why she had stayed. Why she had chosen to work at the church and the nursing home. Her future, though, was a mystery.

"I think if they had killed my brother that night," Elisa said, "they would have left his body with Gabrio's and tried to blame me for both murders. This gives me hope. But then I think, no, they would know better than to try to prove such a thing. My devotion to my brother was well known. . . ."

Her struggles broke his heart. "How long will you give him, Elisa? Or should I call you Alicia now?"

"I am Elisa. I learned to think of myself that way." She tried to smile. "My mother was an Elvis fan. My lullaby as a child was 'Are You Lonesome Tonight.' Alicia Maria? Does it sound familiar? Lisa Marie? She called me Lisa, and so did my father, but only at home. When I chose a new name, it was close enough to my own that I knew I would remember to answer."

He tried to smile, too. "American to the bone."

"As a matter of fact, yes. I am a U.S. citizen."

He let that settle for a moment. She nodded. "Yes, dual citizen of Guatemala and the United States. Recognized by both countries. I won't bore you with the way I came across the border. I did what thousands do each day, only I stole into my own country, and that's a twist on a familiar story, isn't it? If Ramon is here, he was forced to do the same."

"If you're a citizen, can't you appeal for help? You have rights."

"I am a fugitive. Others have asked questions for me, of attorneys who specialize in these issues. The answer is not good."

"What happens next?" It was the big question, and the one she had avoided answering.

"Soon I must go. I've made too many friends, raised too many questions. Years have passed, but someone from Guatemala could see me and make the connection. It is always a danger, but more so the longer I stay anywhere."

"And where will you look next?"

She was silent. At first he didn't understand; then, as the silence continued, he knew. "You're going back to Guatemala, aren't you?"

"I've run out of choices."

"But if you're in danger *here* . . ."

"Martin Avila Morales will soon begin a campaign to become president. There is opposition. Rumors of his past have begun to surface. Maybe I have a chance now of telling my story, of pointing the finger of suspicion . . . of finding out what happened to my brother."

"But Ramon —"

"Ramon has not come!" She took a deep, shaky breath. "And these sightings and rumblings I've held on to, these slivers of hope? He is not here! My brother is not here after weeks, and I have run out of options and places to look. I don't care what happens to me. I have never cared much about that. But I can no longer wait and hope that someday we will find each other, that I can keep him safe by my silence. It's time to step forward and speak the truth about what happened that night!"

"*I* care." He turned her to face him. She came reluctantly. "I'll help you. We'll find a way to keep you safe and find your brother."

"In the eyes of the law I'm a criminal. A woman wanted for murder. And you are a man who understands prison. Don't you know what will happen to you if you knowingly help me?"

He cupped her face in his hands. "Elisa, don't you know what will happen to me if I *don't?*"

Chapter Thirty-one

Elisa twisted away from Sam and got to her feet. The afghan pooled on the floor below, and she folded her arms as if to retain what she could of its warmth.

"Do you know — can you see — what you're letting yourself in for? Even if you weren't in danger of going to prison, what sort of future do we have? Let's say I turn myself in, talk to government officials and ask for their help. There is an extradition treaty in place. After I tell my story, the authorities will be forced to return me. And after I have been sent back to Guatemala, what do you think will happen then? Do you think I'll be easily vindicated, that I will come back to you so we can start a real life together?"

Sam tried to take her in his arms, but she moved away. He tried to calm her fears. "You said yourself there are rumors about Morales. Isn't it possible those who oppose him will protect you? Even more likely, isn't it possible that our government — and it *is* yours, because you're a U.S. citizen — will listen to what you have to say and keep you safe while they ferret out the truth?"

"You're an optimist, a man who believes that good prevails. I've seen it doesn't. My parents are dead because of Martin Avila Morales. My husband is dead. My brother . . ." She shook her head. "Do you think I want to lose you, as well?"

"So you'll be happier if we pretend nothing happened between us because it's inconvenient to be in love?"

"Inconvenient?" Her eyes flashed. "This is inconvenience? This hunt, this murderer's search to destroy me and everyone I have ever loved, is reduced to inconvenience?"

"Love comes when it comes, Elisa. It doesn't wait for the right time or place, for people who are prepared and waiting. I didn't intend to fall in love with you. You didn't —"

"I have never said I loved you!"

"Then say you don't! Say it right now. Not that it's going to make a difference to me. Because if you let me, I know I can make you love me."

"Oh, of this we can be sure? The world is in turmoil, my own world has spun off its axis, but we can be sure of this, that you can *make* me love you?"

"I'm sure because if you don't love me now, you're this close, aren't you?" He held out his hand, thumb and index finger nearly touching. "But you'll deny it to both of us, because you're afraid that loving you is a curse."

"It is." She was pale but resolute.

"Then I am well and truly cursed, and you know what? I don't care. Your life is not an inconvenience, it's a mess, a complete and utter disaster. I don't know how you've come this far, and I don't know how much further you have to go, but I'll take the crumbs, the disasters, the sadness and the whole package. I don't know where it will lead or where it will end, but I know *this*."

He reached for her and held her by the shoulders. "I want you. I want to marry you and, God willing, be the father of your children. I want whatever time we're allowed together. And I want to help. I know people, Elisa, people in the State Department. I know a representative or two. And

I know they'll be discreet and try to do whatever they can. Everything you've done and thought has revolved around your brother, and you've hardly begun to think about yourself and what might save you. Now it's time you did. It's time *we* did. Because I'm in this with you, whether you love me or not."

"I can't keep up. You want to marry me. You want to father my children. You want to perform miracles in the halls of the State Department, to consign a murderer to the flames of hell so we can live happily ever after? You want also to bring back the dead, Sam? There are so many dead to bring back."

"I just want to love you. And everything that comes with it." He gathered her to him. She resisted at first, but at last she relaxed against him. He held her close, stroking her hair, her back, whispering and murmuring.

"I love you," he said against her hair. "And the only miracle I've ever been part of was finding you."

"You can't love me."

"Can't isn't part of it."

"I should have gone away."

"And where would Tessa and her son be if you had? Where would I be? I can answer that. I'd be looking for you."

"You would feel at home in Guatemala. You are a man who is sure of *everything.*"

He tilted her chin so she had to look at him. "I'm not as sure as I want to be." He looked into her eyes, red-rimmed, blurred with tears, and yearning. "Tell me you love me. Or tell me you don't."

"You said it doesn't matter."

"I lied."

She gave a small shake of her head.

He lifted a brow in question. "The truth, please?"

"You will use it against me."

"We're getting closer to yes."

"It will give you power."

"It's not words that have the power."

"I'll bring disaster to your doorstep."

"We'll face it together."

"I didn't want to fall in love with you."

"And?"

"There are some things I could not protect myself against."

He kissed her then. The moment felt inevitable, as if everything that had come before had merely been a prelude. They had met, they had kissed, and everything between had happened in a heartbeat.

Her lips were so soft, the noises she made so sweet. The taste of her was a fire in his blood. The kiss deepened, and desire pounded through him.

"Marry me." His heart was beating so hard he was dizzied by it, but he pulled away just far enough to say the words. "Don't tell me you can't or won't. We don't have to tell the world. Just pledge yourself to me."

"I can't. There are so many reasons."

He wouldn't let her move away. "None that are good enough."

"I can't marry you as Elisa Martinez. I won't marry you as Alicia Santos. I can't, not without bringing the authorities to our doorstep. And what would marriage mean for you? They could send you right to jail. And by the time you got out, I would be gone, in prison myself — or worse."

When he would have answered, she placed a finger against his lips to silence him. "It's foolish to pretend otherwise, Sam. You know it is."

He took her hands and clasped them tight. "Marry me in the sight of God, then. Here, tonight. Just us. Make our vows a promise that whatever happens, we'll stand together. It doesn't matter what names we use, what papers we sign. This is between us and no one else, Elisa. Not the state, not the law."

"I won't let you tie yourself to me. Not in any way."

"I'm already tied to you."

"I'm yours tonight and as long as I can remain here. Let it be enough, Sam. It has to be enough."

He couldn't make choices for her. And his own? There would be no other woman for him, not as long as he knew she was alive. In his heart and soul he was as committed to her as he would have been at any altar. No, this was not enough, but it was too much to forfeit.

She lifted on tiptoes and kissed him again, and this time he was lost. He had dreamed of her, known how she would feel against him, remembered with all his senses their few brief moments of intimacy. None of it had been as glorious as this. Her skin rippled against his hands; the fragrance of her hair was intoxicating. With each movement, each time she touched him, he fell deeper into a vortex of sensation.

In his bedroom — and how they arrived there he could not have said — she removed the clip in her hair so it fell against her back in a dark, shining mass. He knew these were moments he should remember and treasure, but even as the thought flickered through his mind, they were un-dressing each other with little finesse and no hesitation to savor the moment. They were on his bed, on the spread, because they would not take the necessary seconds to pull it down. He could feel how beau-tiful she was, the perfect symmetry of her breasts and hips, the smooth length of her legs, the strength of her arms around him.

They were two, separated by a world gone crazy, by people who wanted to de-stroy her, by court decrees and dread. And then they were one.

He had never felt so greedy, so out of control, but some part of him registered Elisa's abandoned response and her own desire. She needed him as much as he needed her, not simply for this moment, but because she loved him. And that knowledge, that affirmation, sent him over the edge.

They lay together afterward without speaking. He didn't know what to say. He wanted nothing to separate them, nothing to tug at the truce that had brought them here. But he was aware, despite the deep satisfaction of his body, that making love had only intensified his need. There was nothing he would not give up for her, and nothing he could give up that would make a difference. He wondered where they could go to keep her safe, even as he realized she would not go into deep hiding unless and until she knew the truth about her brother.

"Dorie ran away," Elisa said, almost as if she'd read his thoughts. "Martha told me the end of the story, or as much as she remembers. Sarah woke up one morning, and Dorie was gone. She left to find Marie, and because she didn't want to put Sarah and Jeremiah in danger."

"Are you warning me?" He turned to his side and faced her, lifting a lock of hair that lay across her shoulder and twisting it around his finger. "Because you promised you wouldn't leave without telling me."

"I will keep my promise."

"I want to come with you. Wherever you go."

The room was dark; the only light was moonlight through dual windows, but he could see the emotion in her eyes. "You can't give up your life for me."

"I think you're too late. I think I've *given* you my life. You are my life now."

She touched his cheek; then she kissed him again, and this time, they moved as if in a dream, slowly drinking in each moment as if it might quench the thirst of a lifetime.

Just before dawn, Elisa, wrapped in a blanket, found Sam standing in the den gazing out on the winter-shrouded landscape. The December sun would not rise in a blaze of glory; rather it would gently highlight the horizon and slowly bring color into a world of elongated shadows. He wore jeans and a flannel shirt. His feet were bare; his hair was tumbled. Her heart squeezed painfully with love. For so many people, a moment like this one meant little. It was one of a lifetime of such moments, of careless intimacy, of comfort and ease taken for granted. But not for her and not for Sam, and that made it so much more poignant and important.

She watched him stare out the window, unaware that she was behind him. And she knew then that there was one thing she could give him in exchange for all he had given her — his faith in her, his devotion, even his very future, if she would let him.

"Sam?"

He turned, and his expression warmed at the sight of her. "What are you doing up? You'll freeze like that."

There was time to change her mind. She

was still torn, the desire to protect him warring with the need for the fortifying bonds of commitment. He couldn't protect her. He wanted nothing so much as that, but despite everything he had said, she knew he was a realist. Sam knew he could only love her and pledge himself to be beside her through everything that would come.

And she could give him that. It was so little, and still so much.

She went to stand beside him, looking out over the snow-blanketed trees. "This would be the moment to say our vows before God."

He turned her to face him. "You'll do that?"

"For you. For your God."

"Your God, too, Elisa."

She would not argue. Sam's faith was complex; he was not a man who believed in easy answers. But there was a deep, pure well inside him, an unshakeable belief that God surrounded him, that she did not share. It had little to do with words or theology, but she knew it was one of the things about him that she loved the most.

"For my God, too, then," she said. "For the God I would like to know."

His gaze was warm. He bent and kissed

her. "Here, like this?"

She touched his face. "You must promise that if we are separated too long, if there is no hope we will ever be together again, you will forget any vows we make today."

"This will be as real as any wedding."

"You are not an easy man to drive a bargain with."

"I'm just asking you for everything. What's so hard about that?"

She smiled. "Not here. I think outside, where the world looks as untouched as it probably did on the day it was created. Under a winter sky, with snow still falling."

"Where we will freeze."

"Together." She lifted his hands and kissed them. "Give me a few minutes?"

"Only a few. The sun's about to rise."

She showered quickly and slipped back into the clothes she had so swiftly abandoned last night. She left her hair down and went to find him again.

Sam was wearing boots and a snow-dotted sheepskin jacket. He held out her coat and Helen's rubber overshoes. "No bride will ever be more beautiful," he promised as he handed them to her.

Her doubts had resurfaced in the shower, but now the expression on his face chased them away. She had loved two special men in her life, and the second, standing before her now, deserved everything she could ever give him. He took her hand.

Outside, she saw that he had been busy as she dressed. He had shoveled a narrow path to the edge of the woods by his house. The sun was beginning to break through; the world was coming to life before their eyes.

"The snow has stopped," she said softly.

"It's performed its magic. The world is new and clean and pure."

The air was so cold it burned her lungs. Despite that, she felt exhilarated, born anew, and she turned to him and reached for his hands. "What do we do? What do we say?"

"Whatever we want." He laughed a little. "And quickly."

She was suddenly tongue-tied. As if he knew, he leaned down and kissed her.

"Alicia Maria Estrada de Santos —"

"How did you remember that?"

"From the first moment I saw you, I paid complete attention to everything you said and everything about you."

Whatever doubts she still had melted away. "And I to you."

His gaze chased away the cold. "You are my dearly beloved, the only witness I need today. I, Samuel Conner Kinkade, take you as my wife. I will hold you forever, in sickness and in health, in wealth and in poverty, in good times and bad, whether you are near or far. I will keep you in my heart even when you can't be in my arms. I will love, cherish and protect you with every breath I take. With God as my witness, I will never forsake you."

He kissed her left hand, where no ring could be placed. "And a passage I have excerpted in nearly every wedding I have presided over. From First Corinthians, 13.

" 'If I speak with the eloquence of men and of angels, but have no love, I become no more than blaring brass or crashing cymbal. If I have the gift of foretelling the future and hold in my mind all human knowledge, but have no love, I amount to nothing.

" 'This love of which I speak is slow to lose patience. It is not possessive: it is neither anxious to impose nor does it cherish inflated ideas of its own importance.

" 'Love does not keep account of evil or gloat over the wickedness of others. It is glad when truth prevails. Love knows no limit to its endurance, no end to its trust.

It is the one thing that still stands when all else has fallen.

" 'So faith, hope, love abide, these three; but the greatest of these is love.' "

He paused. "May our love be so," he finished.

Her throat closed. For a moment she couldn't speak. Then, from somewhere, she found her voice.

"Samuel Conner Kinkade, I, Alicia Santos, take you as my husband. Because, despite everything that can and will come between us, despite loving you so much I want only to protect you, I cannot forsake you. I will hold you in my heart forever, love and cherish you no matter what our future holds. With God as our only witness, I promise to remember this moment in all the moments to come."

She squeezed his hands. "I learned a poem in school as a girl, by a Spanish poet named Gustavo Adolfo Bécquer, and I've never forgotten it. May I recite it for you?"

"Please."

> *"Podrá nublarse el sol eternamente;*
> *podrá secarse en un instante el mar;*
> *podrá romperse el eje de la tierra*
> *como un débil cristal.*
> *¡Todo sucederá! Podrá la muerte*

cubrirme con su fúnebre crespón:
pero jamás en mí podrá apagarse
la llama de tu amor.

"Many things can happen," she translated. "The sun could cast nothing but shadows, the sea could evaporate and the axis of the earth could break like crystal. Death could cover me, but in the flame of your love, I will never die."

They gazed at each other as the world turned lighter. Then, as the sun broke free of clouds and sparkled on the unbroken cover of snow, they went inside, arm in arm.

Chapter
Thirty-two

The telephone rang at seven. Sam was making coffee, and he answered it with one hand while he ran water into the decanter with the other. Elisa watched him manage both and still use his toe to bring one of the dog's bowls closer so he could fill it once a hand was free. She was surprised he wasn't using his elbows, too.

He hung up after a brief conversation, but Elisa, who was taking inventory of his upper cabinets, already knew the upshot. "That was Gayle. She thinks we should cancel services today. I told her the road hasn't been plowed here, and she said the highway department's not making any promises to get as far as the church this morning. Early Meeks lives close enough that he can put a sign on the doors and a message on the answering machine.

Gayle's going to put the closing on the radio, and I'll call the staff and board. We have a phone tree for emergencies. Consider yourself notified." He shot her a grin.

"I imagine Gayle didn't expect notifying me to be so easy."

"I imagine Gayle would be pleased to know you're here. She likes you."

There was nothing to say to that. Elisa suspected Gayle would never find out. "Will some people try to come to services anyway?"

"With this kind of storm, most everyone will check the radio or call to be sure we're going to open our doors. But we've never canceled during my ministry. This caught everyone by surprise, including the snow removal crews."

"It's selfish, but I'm glad you don't have to be there. Not this morning."

"Ethically, I'm forbidden to say the same." He winked at her.

They had eaten all the bagels last night, and there was no bread. Elisa wasn't having any luck finding a substitute. "Do you have pancake mix?"

"That would require real cooking."

"Flour, baking powder?"

"Not likely."

"Eggs?"

"Yes."

She began to rummage through the lower cabinets. She found a box of blueberry muffin mix and held it out in triumph. "Breakfast!"

"I forgot about that. One of our families moved to Iowa and left me a grocery bag from their pantry. I also have canned salmon, Hamburger Helper and four jars of pickled beets. If you're interested."

"Maybe another day." She kissed his ear. "I'll be the cook, you can wash the dishes."

He gave her a one-armed bear hug. "Hey, you haven't tried my cooking."

"Which is why I'm alive to have this conversation." She laughed as he squeezed her harder. "I'll help you clean up. It won't be so bad."

They worked well together. While the muffins baked, she whipped eggs and grated cheese. Sam poured orange juice and set the table. The dogs, who had slept through most of the excitement that morning, romped through the kitchen, showing off for their guest. Just before the muffins came out, she made the omelet, finishing it off in the broiler as Sam poured the coffee. She was aware of every sweet, ordinary moment.

In the dining room, Sam pulled out her chair. "We won't have many Sunday mornings together. I'm always at church. This is a bonus."

He was so determined to point out that their marriage was real and somehow, despite everything, normal. *She* didn't point out they would probably never have Sunday mornings together, and not because Sam was a minister.

"We should have the *New York Times.* Reading it from one end to the other on Sunday morning, that's my fantasy. . . ." He grinned. "At least it's one of them. The other was having you sitting there across from me."

"I would settle for you and *El Periódico.* From Guatemala City."

"I'll really need to learn Spanish now, won't I? So when you're free to go home again, I can go with you and make myself understood."

"Sam . . ."

"It's not impossible. Don't say it is. First we're going to search for your brother. Then —"

They could not go on pretending. "My friends in Mexico? They hired an investigator, a good one. And my father's cousins in El Paso? They spend hours each week in places a boy like Ramon might go to find work, hoping they will spot him. There's a

645

lawyer in Guatemala City who has proved trustworthy. Judy sends him what money she can. His investigation there, in the city itself and in the Highlands, has cost him at least four times that much, although he doesn't think we know it. No one has found Ramon."

He gazed steadily at her over his coffee cup. "No one found you, either."

She frowned, not sure of his point.

"Come on, Elisa, you're sure people are looking," he went on. "They tried to kill you once and from everything you told me last night, you're a time bomb for Morales and his political future. If he's as influential as you say, he's most likely rich." He waited for her nod. "And if he's rich, he can hire people to find you. But have there been additional attempts on your life?"

"Not so far."

"Because you've hidden yourself well, and because you've trusted few people to help and chosen them wisely. So why believe your brother is different? You raised him. He was, what, fourteen when Gabrio died?"

"Fifteen."

"Then he's eighteen now?"

"I pray he is."

"Trust me, there's no wilier creature

than a boy that age. Speaking as someone who remembers. And by now, protecting himself will be a habit so deeply ingrained that the real problem will be taking chances at all. I lay awake last night and tried to put myself in his shoes. If it *was* Ramon who called your friend, then he's torn between coming here to find you and worrying it might be a trap. He didn't call back, did he?"

She shook her head.

"That might show he's afraid he gave himself away. So there's no chance you're going to find him waiting on Community's front steps one morning. When he gets to Virginia, he'll hang around the edges of things, listen without asking questions, hope he spots you. He won't know who to trust, so he won't trust anybody."

"Then what would you have me do?"

"Wait. Pray. Go to the places a new-comer might go to find a room or a job."

"I have done that, over and over."

"Have you asked your friends here to watch for him?"

"No."

"Could you do it without giving away who he is? Say he's a cousin of a friend who has run away? The more people who watch for him . . ."

"And what name would I tell them? Who would I tell them to watch for?"

"Tell them he probably won't be using his real name."

"So they would recognize him how?"

"A photograph."

"I didn't run into the night clutching our family album, Sam. I have only the school photograph the newspapers ran after Gabrio was killed that I got from the Internet. It is three years old. Never a good likeness to begin with."

"But better than nothing. Your friends would tell you if they suspected anybody might be the boy you were looking for."

"Ramon is a man now. My baby . . ." She hoped it was true.

He reached across the table and took her hand. "Make a list of the friends here you know you can trust. Tell them as much of the truth as you dare. What's your choice? Going back to Guatemala? Throwing yourself on the mercy of our government? You may have to do one or the other, but isn't it worth trying this first?"

She thought of Adoncia, of Patia and Inez. They were good friends, and each of them had contacts she lacked. She laced her fingers through his. "You want me to stay as long as I can, don't you?"

"I want you to stay forever. I never want to leave Toms Brook unless we've decided to move somewhere else because it's right for us. But the first step toward that goal is finding Ramon."

She said a prayer to the God she claimed not to believe in.

Mack arrived at three. Sam had spent part of the day on the phone with church members, part in bed with his wife. The plows had come just after noon, but Mack's was one of only a handful of cars to brave their road. Sam was glad to see him.

After he'd shaken the snow from his boots, Mack went straight to Elisa and pulled her into his arms for a hug. "I owe you everything," he told her.

She returned his hug before she stepped away. "The hospital refused to tell us anything. We called this morning and this afternoon."

"They're both doing well. Tessa could go home tomorrow morning, but they want to keep Ian an extra day, just to be sure."

"Ian?"

"Ian William MacRae. After both our fathers. He's doing great. Just shy of six pounds. The pediatrician says if he had been full-term they would have needed a tractor to haul him out."

She winced. "That's an image I would like to erase."

"He also said it was an incredible stroke of luck that you worked with a midwife in Mexico and knew exactly what to do. That one wrong move . . ."

She smiled. "That's what Tessa told him?"

"She spun a yarn you could knit a dozen baby blankets from. I had no idea she could lie so adeptly."

"Thank you."

"For what? For not telling the hospital a dangerous fugitive delivered our son and saved his life, and they should send the police to apprehend her?"

"Well, for that, yes. Particularly the last part."

"You have time to tell me the whole story?"

Elisa glanced at Sam. He nodded, glad she was willing. "I'll make another pot of coffee and warm the muffins. Tell him everything, Lisa Marie."

She narrowed her eyes. He escaped into the kitchen.

He could hear the low hum of conversation from the den as he took his time making coffee again. Mack was asking a lot of questions. By the time Sam joined them, Mack had a pad and pen and was jotting notes as they spoke.

Sam put mugs in front of them, and returned with cream and sugar. Mack was still jotting. Elisa had finished telling her story.

"You need to know," Sam said, "that Elisa and I are committed to each other, no matter what happens. I'm in this, too."

"What's one more complication?" Mack sipped a little coffee and didn't smile. "We have everything here. Murder, political intrigue, a fugitive, a missing person, false documents, a U.S. citizen escaping illegally into her own country." He lifted his shoulders, and they stayed there for a long moment. "That one's pretty unique. Romance . . ." He finished the shrug.

"Maybe you can impress on Sam how hopeless this is," Elisa said. "He is blinded by love."

"Not hopeless," Mack said. "Not at all. But tricky."

"Tricky?" Elisa clearly thought that was an understatement.

"Times ten." Mack put down the cup. "But not impossible. I'm going to have to pull every gambit I've ever heard of. But I've heard of plenty, and I know plenty of people who've heard more, including the best extradition lawyer in the United States."

"I can't afford to pay you," she said. "I'm certain everything Gabrio and I had must be gone now."

"Do you think I'd take a penny? I'll owe you for the rest of my life. We'll worry about my friend's fees later. He may do this *pro bono*. He likes the limelight."

"Limelight?"

He held up his hands. "Not right away. When it's necessary. But at some point you'll have to step forward and tell your story, and it's the kind of story that will hit the papers."

"And Ramon? What reason would Martin have not to find and kill my brother, who can back up what I've said?"

"First we have to find Ramon." Mack touched her hand. "Or we have to find out what happened to him."

Her eyes filled.

Sam looked away. "There's a woman I've been counseling, an investigative reporter for the *Post*. And her husband has the ear of some important people in the government. Could she help?"

"A reporter?" Elisa said. "Isn't she an unlikely ally? Her job is to tell the world everything she knows and hint at things she doesn't."

"Once your version of the murder is on record, Morales will have less reason to try to kill you. He would be the first suspect if anything happened to you, and he'll know it. Once we know about Ramon, it might be the right way to go."

Mack got to his feet. "Give me her name, and maybe when the time's right I'll get in touch with her. Right now I have to figure out exactly how to proceed. And I won't do a thing until I have your okay, Elisa. You can veto any idea I come up with. But I'm in this with you."

She stood, too, and held out her hands. He took them, leaned over and kissed her cheek. "Tessa wants you to be Ian's godmother." He glanced at Sam. "You'll do the christening?"

"With the greatest pleasure."

They watched as Mack patted the dogs goodbye, then made his way back to his car.

"Get used to this," Sam said. "You're not alone anymore."

"I am terrified."

He put his arms around her and pulled her close.

Chapter
Thirty-three

Elisa moved back to Helen's once the roads
were cleared, and although Sam understood why, he missed her even more than
he had expected — and he had expected to
miss her the way his lungs would miss oxygen. In the two weeks since the blizzard,
there had been another hard snow, but they
had managed to find time together, despite
the rigors of the holiday season and their
work schedules. Still, it was not the same as
coming home to find her there.

Today, just two days before Christmas,
there was no chance they would spend
time relaxing together. They *were* together, however. In the church social hall.
With sixty children, ranging from two to
fifteen.

Elisa clapped her hands. *"Damita,
camina más despacito, por favor.* Mary

would walk a little slower. Of course, if we can find a spare donkey you won't need to walk at all."

Adoncia, who was standing at the head of the ragtag procession with Fernando and Maria, swung her baby son into her arms. "No, then we will have to keep the donkey from stepping on San Jose. Now, everybody, remember, two by two. Walk very slowly. You are tired, and you are trying to find a place to spend the night. Then stand still when you get to the door and sing. This is the door. Pretend."

Two by two, the children of *La Casa* and the Sunday school began to march around the room. They had banded together to re-enact *Las Posadas* on Christmas Eve instead of the traditional nativity pageant. The Mexican celebration of Mary and Joseph's struggle to find shelter in Bethlehem had injected new life into the holiday. Instead of vying for the same old spots as shepherds or angels, the Sunday school children were learning Spanish songs. And for once the *La Casa* kids were teaching their language and performing starring roles, and they were making the most of it.

Sam saw a trouble spot just in front of him, and with heavy hands he weighted the shoulders of two particularly rambunctious little boys, one Virginia born, one from El Salvador. "Okay, guys, see if you can stay in character here."

Rory Brogan, the smaller of the two, locked his hands behind his back, a Pavlovian response Sam suspected his mother had engineered out of desperation. "Are we almost done? Angel and me want to play!"

"Do you know the songs?"

"I don't like to sing."

"Do you like parties?"

Rory was young, but not too young to know what came next. He chanted his response, as if he'd been called on to make it before. "If I sing and walk in line and co-op-er-ate, I get to hit the piñata."

"You got it, partner." Sam squeezed both boys' shoulders, dropped his hands and waited. The boys looked at each other as if to say, "Man, this guy is too much," but neither went back to the wrestling match. They continued the march.

"Okay, now we're at the last door. We're going to sing the song one more time," Adoncia said. "Then we have cookies and punch before *tus padres* come and take you home."

She turned to the boy Sam had once thought least likely to take a starring role in any production. "Miguel, *por favor?*"

Miguel, who had once been too depressed to speak, began to sing in a high, clear soprano, and the children joined him.

"En el nombre del cielo,
yo os pido posada,
pues no puede andar,
mi esposa amada."

The moment they finished, a little girl's hand shot up. She was about eight, and Sam recognized her as a chronic questioner. "What does that mean again?"

"In the name of heaven, I ask you for lodging for my dear wife, who cannot walk." Elisa translated for the umpteenth time.

"I don't think Joseph would have to ask," the girl said, shaking a head thick with blond curls. "Couldn't the man at the door see she needed a place to lie down? I mean, she's riding on a donkey and she's going to have a baby. When my mommy was going to have my little brother, she didn't even ride a bicycle."

"Just remember it's a story about the way we welcome strangers," Sam said, saving Elisa from trying to explain. "Sometimes we welcome them freely, even if we're a little frightened. We see they need help, so we help them. Sometimes we see they need help and we turn away, because we're afraid or just selfish and don't want to share. The people at the first few houses turned Mary and Joseph away, even though anyone could see they needed a place to stay."

"But Mr. Meeks would never turn anybody away," a boy about the same age said. "Once when my little brother skinned his knee in the parking lot, Mr. Meeks carried him back into the church and helped me find my mom."

Early Meeks, who lived just down the road, had agreed to let the children process to his door first. He had learned his part of the song, which he performed in an off-key baritone. He would refuse to let Mary and Joseph inside and shut the door in their faces so they would have to go to the next house, which belonged to another church member. Some of the children were still having trouble with this notion.

"Mr. Meeks is just pretending," Sam reminded them. "The same way you are. In real life, I promise he wouldn't shut the door." Aware he was losing his squirming audience, he took a shortcut. "But if he doesn't shut the door on Christmas Eve, then you won't get to come back here and have the party, right?"

That seemed to make enough sense that they were able to finish practicing their part of the songs.

With relief Sam watched as they finally disbanded and took off for the Sunday school chapel, where cookies and punch were waiting.

Sam corralled Adoncia before she could follow them to help several of the parents supervise. "I don't know what we would do without your help translating for some of *La Casa*'s kids."

She pulled a lock of her hair from Fernando's grasp. "I envy the way they pick up English. Some of them speak it better than I do now. Soon they will translate for me."

Elisa joined them, her hands over her ears. "I have never heard such noise!"

"You should be at Nana Garcia's house on Christmas morning," Adoncia said. "You think this is noise?"

"You're going to let the children open their presents on Christmas with her?" Elisa asked.

"You think I could hold them until the 6th, like we did at home? They will open some on Christmas and some then. They will have both days to look forward to."

"Do you have plans for Christmas evening?" Elisa's eyes flicked to Sam, then back to her friend. "I will be at Sam's. Could you come with Diego and the children for a little while? I have presents for all of you."

Adoncia hesitated; then she held out her hand. Sam didn't understand the significance, but Elisa did. "Diego's ring?"

"He found the beads you gave me. There was a fight."

"Donchita, I'm so sorry."

"It is not your fault we are no longer together."

Sam was sure this was the right moment to disappear downstairs with the children, but Adoncia finished quickly. "There could not be, as they say here, a meeting of our minds."

"I'm so sorry," Elisa said.

"It's best." Adoncia bit her lip. "I will take the children to Nana Garcia's after *Las Posadas* on Christmas Eve, then I will come here to your service before I go to Mass."

"Then we'll make plans for Christmas on Christmas Eve."

Maria galloped by, and Adoncia collared her. They left for the chapel together.

"He wanted children right away, and she didn't," Elisa explained. "It became a power struggle."

"It doesn't sound like anybody won."

"Maybe Diego will come to his senses. I tried to talk to him, but he refused to listen. I think Adoncia's had her fill of men who expect her to do things their way."

"It *was* a simpler system." When she glared at him, he held up his hands to show he was joking, then he smiled, leaned over and kissed her.

"Sam —"

He realized what he had done. It had seemed perfectly natural to kiss her here, perfectly right. Yet they were surrounded by people who didn't know why or when kissing her casually had become acceptable.

"I'd better get downstairs." She fled to the Sunday school chapel.

He wondered if anyone had noticed. He wondered how long he was going to be able to pretend Elisa was the church sexton and nothing more.

"Reverend Sam?"

He found himself face to face with Leon Jenkins.

"I didn't realize you were here," Sam told him. "I didn't see you with the others."

"I'm not here for any rehearsal." The boy sounded angry.

For a moment Sam thought Leon was upset because of the kiss, but immediately he abandoned that as the source. Leon was clearly too wrapped up in his own troubles to have noticed anything or anyone.

"My office," Sam said. "Come on."

In the privacy of his office, Sam motioned to the leather sofa that looked out on what had been his flourishing rose garden. Now it was a muddy patch of earth adorned with clumps of snow and skeletal bushes, waiting for the regeneration of spring.

"Okay, what's up?" Sam said.

Leon rolled back the sleeve of his sweatshirt. At the boy's first wince, Sam knew what was coming. As expected, in a moment he saw that Leon's arm was black and blue.

Sam reminded himself that anger was not the correct response. "How did that happen?"

"You know how it happened!"

"Your dad?"

The boy sniffed. Sam reached for the box of tissues he kept on a side table for parishioners who came in to unburden themselves or plan memorial services. He went through a lot of boxes every year. He held it out to Leon, who took several.

"What happened?" Sam asked gently.

"He's been drinking a lot more than . . . you know . . . he did."

Sam nodded.

"Last night —" Leon blew his nose. "I went to this Christmas party. Like, a friend invited me. Dad said I could go. But when I got home, he was passed out on the sofa, beer cans all over. A lot more beer cans than I saw at the party."

"It's not a good feeling to walk in on something like that."

"Most of the time I just leave him there. You know? It's easier than trying to get him into bed. But he was breathing funny. So after I cleaned up the cans, I shook him to see if he would wake up. I mean, I was worried he might be really sick from all that beer."

"That makes sense."

"At first he didn't know what was going on. Then he sat up, and that must have made him feel worse, because he put his head in his hands and his shoulders started to shake, like he was going to be sick."

Sam guessed that by now Leon was all too aware of the trajectory of his father's binges. He remained silent, letting the boy proceed at his own pace.

"He wasn't sick, he was mad. He lifted his head and started to shout. He said he'd been waiting up for me, that he didn't know where I'd gone. I told him I'd been at Jim's party and that he'd told me I could go, but he wouldn't listen. He said . . . I had betrayed him, that I was a bad son and I was growing up to be a . . . a loser."

Sam chose his words carefully. "Alcohol has a language all its own, Leon. Your father may be unhappy with some of the choices you've made, but he doesn't think you're a loser."

"And what's this?" Leon held up his arm. "Because when he got finished, he grabbed me and jerked me off my feet. Then he started to hit me. I bet I've got bruises on my back, too!"

"Your father was way out of line."

"I snuck out and walked all the way back to Jim's last night and slept on his couch. I'm not living with Dad another minute. I'm going to run away. I'm old enough. I can get a job. Anything would be better than living with him."

Sam made an effort to sound calm. "I'm going to find you another place to live. Don't worry about that. I think Gayle Fortman will take you in. You know her sons, don't you? You probably go to school with them, and they're in the youth group."

"Yeah." Leon wiped his eyes.

Sam knew that, as Leon's minister, he was not specifically required under Virginia law to report child abuse. But the law was murky enough that he could interpret it his own way.

"I'm going to talk to your dad and tell him what you've told me. Then I'm going to tell him he has to get counseling before I'll let you go home, and if he refuses, I'll explain I have to notify the authorities and ask them to take custody. And I will. But you've got to decide right now that's what you want me to do. Because if you change your mind or your story, my help is going to make things worse, not better. And things have to get better, Leon. You can't continue this way, and I can't let you."

"I'm not going to lie to anybody. And I'm not going home."

Sam could see that Leon meant his words, although he knew from experience that when emotion faded, resolve sometimes faded with it. "Let me call Gayle. You're okay with that?"

Leon gave a curt nod and sniffed once more.

Sam made the call. Gayle might not be a permanent solution, but nobody knew teenage boys better than she did, and, as Sam had expected, she agreed immediately. He hung up and recounted the conversation.

"She says you're very welcome to stay as long as you need to. But she recommended we not tell your dad where you're staying quite yet. Just that you're safe. If he goes to the police, we'll have to tell *them,* but we'll also report the abuse, and George will know that."

"I don't want Dad to know where I am. I don't want to see him!"

Sam knew that would change, but for the time being, this was best.

"I'll take you over there now and help you get settled. Then I'll go see your father."

Leon blew his nose before he stood. "Thanks. But I could have run away. I would have been okay on my own."

"You're a guy who can take care of himself," Sam said carefully. "But there's no reason to when you have friends. And you do. So you did the right thing by coming here."

The boy seemed to relax a little. "You ought to have kids. You know?"

Sam thought that under the circumstances, this was high praise indeed.

Jenkins Landscaping looked as bleak as Sam's rose garden. The driveway up to the parking lot was badly rutted, with ice forming in the hollows. The parking lot itself wasn't much better. Clearly Jenkins wasn't using his own equipment to grade his own property. Sam wondered if he was too busy elsewhere or just didn't care anymore.

Sam could hear voices in Spanish from the area beside the greenhouse where several trucks, at least one with a plow that would have made easy work of the driveway, were parked. Another snowfall was expected tonight, and he supposed Jenkins' workers were making plans how best to serve their regular customers. He started in that direction, but a shout from the house just above the office saved him the trip.

"What in the hell have you done with my boy!" Despite temperatures just above freezing, a coatless George came charging down from his porch. For the first time in his life, Sam wished he had listened to his father's advice and become a doctor, maybe a pathologist with no one to talk back to him.

"Shall we go inside?" Sam said, nodding to the office once George was just in front of him. "You're not dressed for the weather." His eyes drifted down the man's stout torso. George's short-sleeved shirt looked as if it had clung to his body for weeks. He smelled like beer.

"Where's my son?"

"I will talk to you inside. Take it or leave it."

George's scowl deepened. For a moment Sam was afraid he might throw a punch at him, but finally he stomped off toward the office. Sam followed.

The tiny reception area was neat but dusty. In contrast, the office just beyond was a mess. Papers were strewn on the desk, floor and sofa. Dirty coffee cups and heaped ashtrays decorated every surface not covered with papers. The trash can was brimming, and the room was cold. Without permission, Sam flipped on a space heater after clearing away the papers on top of it.

"Your life is out of control, George," he said with no preamble. He faced the other man. "And don't tell me how I know. I have eyes, and I've spoken to your son today. You're going to lose everything if you don't do something fast."

"Where's Leon?" The words weren't quite a shout, but they filled the small room.

"Safe. Safer than he was at home last night."

"I don't know what he told you —"

"He told me the truth," Sam said, cutting him off. "And he showed me the bruises. I could see marks from your fingers, so don't try to tell me he fell."

"What did you do with him?"

"I found him a place to stay. He'll be fine there. No one will get drunk and attack him."

The bellow became a whine. "I didn't know where he was. He went to a party without —"

"Leon says you gave him permission. You're blacking out, George. That happens to alcoholics. The gaps in your memory will get larger and longer. People will stop covering up for you. Your life will slide downhill so fast you won't be able to hang on for the ride. Is that what you want?"

"I'm not an alcoholic!" George ran a hand through his hair. "Maybe I did have too much to drink last night, but I was worried because —"

"You were worried because you're losing control. Look around." Sam kicked at the trash can, gestured to the desk piled with papers. "I remember coming in here at the beginning of my ministry. This place was spotless."

"My damned secretary quit!"

"Why?" Sam held his ground as the seconds ticked away. Finally he nodded. "Because she couldn't stand your abuse?"

"I just got tired of her incompetence."

"I bet she got tired of your tirades. Were you coming to work drunk? Are you drinking every morning just to get yourself out the front door? How many drinks have you had so far today?"

"What I do is none of your business!"

"Leon made it my business."

"I'm going to call the police and tell them you kidnapped my boy."

Sam gestured to the telephone. "I can't stop you. But right now the authorities aren't involved. I have discretion whether to report child abuse or not, and so far I've chosen not to report this. Leon's safe for the moment. But *you* won't be once that report is made."

George lowered himself to the sofa without moving the papers beneath. They crackled indignantly. "Child abuse?"

"No one would dispute it. I took photographs of Leon's arm and back before I came over."

"What, you're collecting evidence?"

"That's right."

"Why? So I'll leave you alone and stop trying to get the board to do what they should?"

Sam took a long time to release his next breath. "If you think this has *anything* to do with my ministry, then maybe you really are too far gone to help. If that's what this comes to, then we may need other professionals to intervene. But what accusations will you make against them? When do you stop blaming everybody else?"

George put his head in his hands. And then, taking Sam by surprise, he began to sob.

Sam knew better than to offer comfort. He stood quietly and waited for the flood to ebb. He wasn't sure whether it was the situation or early-morning booze that had precipitated the tears, but for the first time in a long time, a hint of compassion for George Jenkins returned.

When George began to gain control, Sam fished a box of tissues from beneath a pile of unopened mail and set the box beside him in the same way he had offered tissues to George's son earlier.

"My life's a God damned mess," George said at last.

"Mess, yes. God damned? No."

"I'm going to lose my business."

"If you keep on this way."

"No." George blew his nose. "I made some bad decisions, bought some land for expansion, then the bottom fell out of the economy and nobody was paying landscapers anymore. By the time things got better, I was in the hole big time and couldn't sell the land for what it was worth. Then I had to settle a lawsuit, and I wasn't insured for it. Got hit with taxes. Bad followed worse. I don't know how to tell Leon. If something doesn't change by spring, this place is history. And what will I do? Where will we go? How am I going to pay for his college education?"

None of this excused the abuse or the bullying, of course, but Sam finally understood some of what had been driving George. "It's a lot to handle alone," he said. "Have you tried talking to the bank or a specialist in debt management?"

"I handle things myself. Always have."

"You're not handling this, George. And I don't just mean the business. You're about to lose more than your company. You're about to lose your son. You're this close."

He demonstrated with his fingers. "And I'm not threatening you. This doesn't have anything to do with whether I report your behavior last night or not. Leon's about to give up on you."

"You're trying to steal him."

Sam didn't respond. He just kept his gaze steady and waited.

"I don't know what to do," George said at last, looking away. He slumped back against the sofa.

"There's an AA meeting every night of the week somewhere in the area. I know there are several every day in Winchester. There'll be one tomorrow night in Woodstock at the Methodist church."

"How do you know so much? You hit the bottle, too?"

"I have problems like anybody else, but that's not one of them. The good news is you're not alone. We've got other people in the church with the same struggle. I can call around and find one of them who will go with you tonight. If you'll let me."

"You'll hold this over my head, won't you? Keep me from seeing Leon until I go."

"Don't make this about me, okay? Don't even make it about Leon. Make it about you. That's the only way AA is going to help. Because you know you have to get your life back on track."

"Yeah, and everything will just come flocking back to me. My son, all the money I lost, my place in the community." He gave a snort.

"You might get your self-esteem back, George. Isn't it worth a try?"

George didn't answer.

"I'd like to pray with you," Sam said. "Will you let me?"

"I just want you to go away. Just go away."

Sam knew he had done and said what he could. The rest was up to the man in front of him, although he prayed silently for him as he left the office and started toward his SUV.

He had opened the car door when about half a dozen workers came around the corner of the greenhouse and began to pile into two trucks. He was lost in thought and didn't pay much attention until he realized that the man who was watching from the sidelines, short but powerfully built, was Diego Moreno, Adoncia's former fiancé. He remembered Elisa saying that Diego had gotten a job here as a foreman, and even though he'd only met Diego in passing, he recognized him. Sam realized that if everything George had said was accurate, all these men would lose their livelihood along with their boss.

He had one foot on the running board when he noticed a young man trailing behind the others. Sam was struck by how tall he was compared to the men in front of him. He was thin but wiry, with broad shoulders, not quite a man and not quite a boy. His hair was long, tied neatly at the nape of his neck, and his face was fine-boned, almost elegant and definitely striking.

Sam got in, slammed the door behind him and started the engine. He was nearly out of the parking lot when he realized why the young man had attracted his attention. Not because he was tall or particularly good-looking. Because he looked like Elisa.

He told himself not to get his hopes up, but there were two warring voices in his head. One counseled caution, the other prayed.

He stopped at the edge of the lot and got out, as if to check his tires. He kicked one as he waited for the men to finish getting into the trucks. The driver of the first truck slowed and rolled down his window.

"You need help?"

Sam waved a "no." "Just checking to be sure it's not going flat. It looks fine."

The man rolled his window up and continued down the driveway. Sam motioned for the second truck to pass him, noting that Diego was driving. He didn't see the young man, but once they'd passed, he saw that there were several workers sitting in the back.

He guessed they weren't going far. It was too cold outside to ride any distance that way, and also illegal. He got back in his SUV and followed at a distance. When the men pulled into the parking lot of a small cluster of businesses about a mile from Woodstock, he realized they'd probably arrived at their destination. Dirty snow was piled ineffectually, creating barriers to decent parking, and the ground had been churned by too many tires. The job looked as if it might last several hours.

Sam passed and went straight to Helen's. He took the steps to her porch two at a time and pounded on the door.

Helen answered, wiping her hands on a dishtowel. "From the racket you're making, I'd guess the world's ending and you want us to put on our Sunday best."

"Is Elisa here?"

Helen stepped back. "She's upstairs, working on her quilt."

He took those steps two at a time, as well, and found Elisa at the sewing machine in Helen's room.

"Put on your coat."

She pushed her chair back and got to her feet. "Sam, I thought you'd be gone all —"

"Do it quickly."

She searched his face; then she hurried past him and down the stairs. She got her coat and hat from the mudroom. He spent those moments apologizing to Helen. "I promise it's important," he told her. "I'll tell you later."

"Just so long as it don't include me putting these old feet into good shoes." She closed the door behind them with a bang.

"Now you'll explain," Elisa said when they were speeding down Fitch Crossing Road.

"I went to Jenkins Landscaping to talk to George about Leon."

"This is about Leon?"

He didn't know how to broach this, how

to warn her that he was probably wrong and the young man was not Ramon. He hesitated; then he reached out and tenderly cupped her neck for a moment.

"I love you."

"You got me out here to tell me this?"

"I —" He put his hand back on the wheel to turn a corner on to the main road that would take him to the parking lot. "Elisa, I saw a young man who looks so much like you I think it's possible he might be Ramon."

He couldn't take his eyes off the road, but he heard her draw a breath.

"He doesn't look that much like the newspaper photo," he continued. "He's young, but not quite a boy. It's the resemblance to you that's striking. Please don't be too disappointed if I've made a mistake here. But the only way I could tell was to bring you to see him. He's working for Jenkins, and Jenkins hires men by the hour. But they're just grading a parking lot, and I didn't know how long he'd be there."

He finally hazarded a glance. Her lips were pressed together, but she was nodding.

"Are you all right?" he asked.

"I have been disappointed many times. I will survive another."

She would survive, of this he had no doubt. But she would still be sad for days to come. He prayed silently the rest of the way.

The trucks were still there. He parked on the road, since the men had cordoned off the lot while they worked. Elisa got out, too, and he joined her on the passenger's side.

"Let's act like we're going into one of the stores. Just take your time." Sam spotted the young man over to one side, shovel in hand. He was filling potholes in the lot with gravel they'd brought in the first truck. No one paid attention to them.

"Let's go this way," Sam said, nudging Elisa toward the side closest to the young man. He glanced at her and saw she had already spotted him, but she said nothing. She was squinting since the sun was behind the building and the glare was noticeable. She shaded her eyes, then thought better of it.

"You see him?" Sam asked softly.

She didn't answer. She picked up the pace, moving closer quickly. Ten yards away she gasped.

Sam didn't know if the man heard the sound, as soft as it was, but he put his shovel down and turned to face them.

Sam wasn't sure which of them ran into the other's arms. The woman to the young man, the young man to the woman. He only knew that in a moment Ramon and Elisa were clasping each other as if no one would ever separate them again.

Chapter
Thirty-four

Shenandoah Community Church
Quilting Bee — December 17th

Despite the proximity to Christmas, everyone attended our meeting. Furthermore, we agreed to meet on Christmas Eve next Wednesday morning. I will read these minutes, we will open our Secret Santa gifts and share a potluck of our favorite foods, with extra to pack and take home to help with holiday meals.

There were no committee reports save one. Cathy Adams, our fund-raising committee chair, reported that we made a total of $746 on our Christmas quilt raffle. Furthermore, the winner, Hannah Grant, a relatively new member of Community's flock, burst into tears at the news. None of us are quite certain whether she was overwhelmed with joy or regret that she had purchased a ticket.

Show and Tell was remarkably understated. Once again we are piecing quilts to adorn La Casa, and we hope that this time they will not fall prey to vandals. Each member showed what project or another she is working on. Elisa Martinez brought her nearly completed Endless Chain quilt top for us to admire. Although it is bright enough to ward off slumber, we agreed that Elisa can be proud of her work. She plans to begin quilting it soon.

The meeting was adjourned after we were led in Christmas carols by Andy Jones, our choir director. Rory Brogan did an impromptu interpretive karate "kata" as we sang "Joy to the World." In the spirit of goodwill, several members recommended that Kate switch Rory to chess lessons in the new year.

Andy promised he will get a haircut before the Christmas Eve service. This *holiday gift to all of us was met with a round of applause.*

Sincerely,
Dovey K. Lanning, recording secretary

"How do you get back three lost years?" Elisa asked Sam. On Christmas Eve morning they were cuddled in front of Sam's fireplace sipping coffee. He had risen and built a fire, knowing Elisa would arrive early, even though she had departed well past midnight last night. Ramon was sleeping soundly in Sam's guest room and showed no signs of waking.

Sam had plugged in his tree lights for seasonal ambience. The lights were the discount store variety, nothing special, but the ornaments had all been made for him by Sunday-school children here and in Georgia. He treasured them, along with the three holiday lunch boxes parading across his mantel like a train pulled by a fleet of corny plastic reindeer.

He reclined a little more and pulled her between his legs to rest more comfortably. "You can't get the years back, but the two of you made a start on catching up last night. How do you find him? Different than you expected? More damaged by everything he's gone through? Less?"

"Less and more. He was always so open, so willing to talk about his feelings, his hopes and dreams. Now he thinks like an adult, but he hesitates before he says anything. Even to me."

"It makes sense," Sam said. "You were much the same way."

"Yes, and when you get used to not trusting anyone, it's hard to change back. I understand, but it's hard to watch."

"I like what I see. I'm looking forward to getting to know him once his guard is down a little."

"He's all grown up. All the things I had planned to tell him, he knows them already. And he's so handsome. If he hasn't yet broken hearts, he will soon."

"I guess it only makes sense that the two of you were in the same places but never at the same time. Not even close."

Ramon had told them his story in fits and starts as he consumed a meal of nearly everything Sam had on hand. They had discovered that after eluding their pursuers and hiding alone for two weeks deep in the mountains, Ramon had found his way to a rural hospital he and Gabrio had once visited.

A doctor there had kept him hidden for

a month while reporting what the newspapers were saying about Gabrio's murder and Elisa's disappearance. Then he had taken Ramon to stay with friends on the coast, who pretended he was a cousin from California visiting Guatemala to improve his Spanish. The select people who knew the truth had tried to help him learn Elisa's fate, but of course, no one had been able to.

Finally, almost a year later, when it was clear he would draw suspicion if he stayed in Guatemala any longer, he crossed the border into Mexico, using another boy's identification papers. No one had questioned him. From there he had followed his sister's route unknowingly, making detours, but stopping at the places he thought she might go.

As suspected, Ramon had waited in Manzanillo for their father's friends to return from Arizona, until he was afraid the police would question him if he stayed longer. The photograph from the funeral in Mexico City had been of someone else, but Ramon had been outside in the plaza listening and paying tribute.

The rest of the story was a saga of evasions and lies, of traveling from Agua Prieta in Mexico into ranch land in

Cochise County, Arizona, of being attacked by a gang on the border, of being badly beaten for refusing to carry drugs to pay his passage, of hunger and thirst, of the good luck of speaking such excellent English that no one questioned his increasingly complex stories, of traveling to Texas, where twice he was nearly picked up by police. And finally of finding Judy's telephone number on a library computer and making the call that had brought him across the country to Virginia.

He had been in the area for most of two weeks, watching the church without success for his sister. He had not traced Martha to the nursing home and had not known to check there. The money he had earned delivering flyers in Louisiana on the journey had run out, but he had managed to find several days' work at Jenkins Landscaping while he tried to figure out what to do next.

He was John Garcia, born in Brownsville, Texas, in 1983, and he had a driver's license to prove it, although Sam hoped he didn't try to buy alcohol once the license proclaimed he was twenty-one. Any good bartender would spot it as a fake.

"What did you tell Ramon about us?" Sam asked.

"I told him I love you. I think he understands that my love for you does nothing to dishonor my love for Gabrio. That I have been blessed with the hearts of two good men."

Sam was glad, but the next question was harder. "And the future? Did you talk?"

"There hasn't been time. It's enough now that he's here, alive, although much too thin."

"With that appetite, he'll fill out quickly."

"I had always planned that if we found each other, we would lose ourselves in New York or Los Angeles, take new identities and forget the past. I think that was a dream."

"And the reality?"

"After tomorrow, we can discuss alternatives. We have Christmas to celebrate together. The first in many years."

"Mack is free now to pull out all the stops, Elisa. Ramon is a witness, and he is here with you, and safe. He'll know how to keep you both that way."

"If it were only that easy."

He wove his fingers through hers. "Wait until the beginning of the year before you make any big decisions. You and Ramon deserve a little time together just to get to know each other again. Then we'll bring Mack in for a good discussion. But may I tell him Ramon is here?"

She considered. "It's a good plan . . . only —" She squirmed around to face him. "Our reunion was so public. I don't know what the men heard. . . ."

Elisa had tried to cover the emotional scene by telling the men closest to Ramon in the parking lot that Ramon was a friend of her family and she hadn't known he was living in Virginia. But Sam, too, wondered how much of the conversation between Ramon and his sister had been logged by Jenkins' crew before Elisa and Ramon remembered where they were.

"What reason would they have to report it?" He kissed her hand. "Wouldn't they have a natural distrust of the INS and sympathy for a fellow traveler, even if they suspect Ramon is here illegally?"

"Diego was not close enough to hear us. But he's angry at me because of Adoncia. He has already made threats. And if he suspects anything . . ."

"There's a lot of room between vague suspicion and a report to the authorities."

"I have come this far, and so has my brother, because we have struggled not to raise suspicions of any kind."

"It's not a skill you'll forget easily."

"Alicia?"

Elisa turned toward the doorway, and her face lit up. "Ramon, how did you sleep?"

Ramon, in an oversized T-shirt and sweatpants of Sam's, hair loose to his shoulders, smiled. "Without nightmares."

Trying anything new was always a challenge for a minister. For twenty years the Sunday school classes had held a traditional Christmas pageant. Former Josephs and Marys, grown up now, came back for the children's service at five to bask in remembered glory. Resistance to *Las Posadas* had been scattered but loud in some quarters. Conservative Shenandoah County sometimes viewed change with suspicion, and the church was a mirror.

Halfway through the procession down Old Miller Road, as the children turned back to the church, Sam thought that this idea, at least, had been a success. Apparently so did the parents who lined the route with cameras.

They had found a donkey for Damita, who was dressed as Mary, and Miguel, dressed as Joseph, walked beside her leading the docile beast. The other children were dressed as angels, shepherds or simply in their Sunday best. Walking slowly two by two with electric candles, they looked almost beatific. The sun set as they began the procession, and there was only the slightest sliver of a moon in the twilight sky. The sheriff's office had kindly agreed to reroute traffic for the brief duration of their walk, and the absence of cars made the event holier.

"It's beautiful, isn't it?" Elisa said.

He wondered if their children would ever be part of *Las Posadas.* With the demands of the Christmas season — one of a minister's busiest times of year — and with the arrival of Ramon, he'd had little time to contemplate the future. But he wondered if someday he would witness this event with a father's pride, Elisa at his side taking photographs or walking beside their children as an escort.

He put his arm around her for just a moment. "Very beautiful."

"And these are the same children who have been plotting how to divide up the spoils once the piñata is cracked. They learned important lessons from your last one."

The last piñata seemed very long ago. Sam realized how much his life had changed in a few short months.

With Ramon beside them, they followed the procession back to the church, where Andy, the choir director, would greet them at the door with the traditional response. This was the longest part of the performance, and as he neared the church, Sam could see that their audience had grown substantially. He was both surprised and gratified to see that many of the members who usually skipped the children's service and attended the traditional seven o'clock service had arrived to witness the procession.

He wondered how many were there to support the children and how many to support *La Casa* and all it encompassed. No matter. He was gratified his congregation had taken *Las Posadas* and all it stood for to heart. As he had told the children, this was a story of welcome, of overcoming fear to offer help to strangers. He was proud that this year Community Church had undertaken both.

At the church, he watched from the end of the line as Miguel knocked on the door and a scowling Andrew answered.

Then the children began their song, and at last this final innkeeper recognized Mary and Joseph and, with a smile, invited them to enter. All together, with Andrew, they sang:

"Entren Santos Peregrinos,
Peregrinos . . . Reciban este rincón,
que aunque es pobre la morada,
la morada . . .
os las doy de corazón."

"Enter Holy Pilgrims," Adoncia with her own children in tow, translated for the observers. "Receive this corner. This dwelling may be poor, but I offer it with all my heart."

Andrew threw open the door, and the children waited just long enough for "Mary" to slide off her donkey so that the animal could be led away by its owner. Then, with a whoop, they streamed inside.

"And the little angels turn back into children," Adoncia said.

The audience clapped loudly.

From inside, Mexican music filled the social hall.

"Everyone's invited for the party," Sam announced. "It will be short but sweet."

With another more solemn service coming up, and family celebrations still to be had at home, they had decided to serve only hot cider and cocoa. Sam was still

692

fairly certain a lot of Christmas Eve suppers would be untouched by the children who managed to scoop up their share of the piñata's spoils, as well as those who received plastic bags filled with extra goodies as consolation prizes.

"The older children have promised to let the little children have a chance before they charge in," Adoncia told him, as she passed. Her words were punctuated by a loud whack. Beyond her, one of the smaller girls, blindfolded and dressed as an angel, had managed a hit. He was glad to see that the piñata, a five-pointed star adorned with streamers, remained intact. The more children who took their turn with it, the better.

He circulated, accepting praise and good wishes from the adults and hugs from the children. Near the doorway into the hall he signalled Elisa, who was helping with the blindfolds.

"I'm going to my study to work on the next service," he told her. "If you need help, come get me."

"We'll be fine. Ramon has promised to help me clean up." Her smile was radiant. "It still seems a miracle."

"It's a season of miracles." He kissed her cheek and didn't care who saw him.

In his study, he lost himself immediately in preparations for the final Christmas Eve service. Although *Las Posadas* had been billed as the family service, the pre-teens and teens would participate in the next one as ushers and readers. The liturgical dancers would depict the nativity story as the choir sang a quartet of traditional Southern carols. A brass ensemble gathered from high-school band members and former musicians who had polished long-abandoned trumpets and French horns would provide the prelude and postlude.

He remembered the professional brass choir at The Savior's Church, made up of members of the Atlanta Symphony and professors from area universities. The towering floral arrangements and Christmas tree provided by one of the city's leading florists. The cantata written especially for the Chancel Choir — which accepted members by audition only.

Tonight the altar at Community would be adorned with fresh greens from Helen Henry's farm, and a blue spruce donated by another member and scattered with white lights and gaily colored origami ornaments made by the children. The choir was made up of anyone who liked to sing, some more apt to stay on key than others.

He felt such a wave of love, of knowing he was in the right place here, of gratitude for the gift of Elisa and Ramon in his life, that he bowed his head in a prayer of thanksgiving.

At six-thirty a knock sounded on his door; then Leon, in a suit and tie, came into the room before Sam could invite him.

"Reverend Sam?"

Sam didn't reproach him for walking right in. He didn't have to search Leon's face to see the boy was upset. He stood and came around his desk. "What's up?"

"I don't know. I'm . . . I'm not sure." Leon shrugged.

Sam glanced at the clock. There wasn't a lot of time before he needed to go to the sanctuary to make sure everything was ready. He had a meeting scheduled with the ushers in ten minutes. He needed to be certain the readers had their scripts. And his own reflections needed to be printed and put into a folder to use tonight.

"It's my dad," Leon said.

Sam focused on the boy. He wasn't surprised this was about George. "You know I talked to him, like I promised. And I had a friend from the congregation call to try to persuade him to go to an AA meeting this afternoon. He refused, but I don't think it's hopeless. I think your father realizes he has to make a change. We're going to keep after him as long as it seems helpful. We're just going to have to give him a little time."

Leon was fidgeting. "I talked to him, too. Not long ago. I . . . I called him from my cell phone. I just wanted . . . you know, to tell him I was okay."

"That makes sense. I know you miss him. Are you having second thoughts about not going home?"

"No!" Leon ran a hand through his hair. "No, he was drunk when I called. I —" He looked torn. "He, well, he tried to tell me all this was your fault."

Sam was sorry to hear that. Unfortunately, he could also hear the clock continuing to tick. "Let's talk after the service. You can stay, and we'll talk as long as you want, then I'll take you back to Mrs. Fortman's."

"I don't need to talk, but you need to listen."

"I am listening."

"He was making threats."

This did not surprise Sam, either. George had begun making threats early in Sam's ministry at Community. They had escalated steadily, but it only made sense that now, with Leon out of the house, George would be at his most desperate.

"He wants me out of the church," Sam said, with no desire to go into details. Most likely Leon had already been privy to most of them. "I guess he'll try to make his case with everybody who'll listen, at least until he gets himself under control. But this isn't something you need to worry about. People here care about your dad, but they also understand his life is in turmoil. They're going to discount a lot of what he says. Just take care of *yourself* now."

"It wasn't like that."

"What was it like?" Sam sounded more patient than he felt.

"He said stuff about having proof, about catching you good."

"He said something not long ago about folks not wanting anyone else to tell them how to raise their kids. And I'm sure that's true, but in this case I think people will understand why you're living somewhere else, don't you?"

Leon bit his lip. "I guess."

"I'll say it again. Take care of yourself. I promise I'll be fine. You look very nice, by the way. Are you going to usher with the Fortman boys?"

"I'm supposed to lead the little kids in to

light the candles. I get to carry the fire extinguisher."

Sam put his arm around Leon's shoulder and pulled him to his side in a rough hug. "You're going to get through this. I promise. I think your dad's going to come round. I think he'll go for help, but even if he doesn't, we'll see you through this. You're going to be okay."

"A lot of what he said didn't make sense, I guess," Leon said, as Sam walked him to the door.

"Alcoholism's a disease, and that's one of the symptoms."

"Yeah, I guess. He was talking about Diego, you know, his foreman? And something about Guatemala. It didn't mean anything to me. He was just talking crazy."

Chapter Thirty-five

Sam didn't need divine interpretation to understand what George's alcoholic rumblings had meant. Only moments ago he'd said a prayer of thanksgiving. Now, as he hurried through the building to find Elisa, he prayed again. Someone, one of Jenkins' crew, perhaps a Guatemalan himself, had viewed Elisa and Ramon together, had even heard her call her brother by his real name, and had made the connection. When Ramon left abruptly, the worker had told Diego, and Diego, seething because Adoncia had given him back his ring, had seen an opportunity for revenge.

Diego had gone to George Jenkins, whose need for vengeance was even deeper and more complex.

As he searched for Elisa, Sam was forced to greet members who were arriving for the service. He didn't want to appear upset, but he cut short conversations in a way he normally wouldn't have done. He managed to smile as he hurried on, but inside, he was in turmoil.

The church was large enough that it was possible for him to miss Elisa just by taking the wrong stairs or slipping into a room when she was in the hallway. He was aware of time passing quickly, of a need to be upstairs in the sanctuary, and still he searched.

He found her at last, downstairs in the Sunday school storage area. She was just coming out, and he nearly bumped into her. Ramon exited behind her.

"Sam? We were just coming up. The service is about to start. You don't even have your robe on."

Without preamble, he said, "I'm almost certain you've been recognized and reported to the police. You and Ramon need to get out of here right away. Go to Tessa's house, in Fairfax. Mack will know what you should do next."

In the dim basement light, her eyes widened. "But I don't know where she lives. I've never been there."

He fished in his pocket. "Doesn't matter. Take the keys to my SUV, in case they know what you've been driving. Just get in the car and get out on I-81 north, then 66. There should be a map in the glove compartment if you need one. Once you get close to Fairfax, find a motel or a restaurant if anything's open tonight, and sit tight. Take my cell phone." He put the keys and the phone in her hand, wrapping her fingers around them. "Do you need money?"

"I have money."

He felt her hand tremble, and for a moment, he held on. "I'll call as soon as the service is over and everybody's gone. I'll have directions for you by then, and I'll alert the MacRaes. If Mack wants you to go somewhere else, he'll tell me. Go. There are still people in the parking lot. You won't be noticed. Just get going now."

He pulled her to him and kissed her. Then he grabbed Ramon's shoulder and squeezed. "We'll work this out. I promise. Mack will know exactly what to do next."

"They're going to question you. They'll know you helped me escape."

"Doesn't matter," he repeated. "Listen, Elisa, this is no time to argue. What's done is done. We've got to make the best of this. Get going." He looked at Ramon. "Get her to the car, okay? I don't know how fast these things happen, but the police or the marshals could be on their way here. It's unlikely, but it's possible."

She cradled his face in her hands and kissed him; then she started down the hall. They were at the stairs before he realized he couldn't let them go out to the lot alone, not even if it meant he would be late starting the service. He ran up the stairs behind them, and once they were all in the hallway, he pointed to the side door closest to the staff parking spaces. With five minutes until the service, people in the holiday spirit were still milling around chatting, and Sam pretended he was seeing friends off for the holiday.

"You have a good trip," he said just loudly enough that anyone listening could hear him. "You deserve a break, Elisa. We'll manage fine without you. Enjoy time with your cousin."

He opened the side door just in time to see two dark sedans with flashing blue lights pull into the lot.

Elisa had always known it would come to this. From the moment she had escaped the men who killed her husband, from the moment she had sent her brother on a different path to save his life, from the moment she had paid for a passport and green card to enter a country of which she was already a citizen, she had known her flight would end this way. Perhaps not as publicly, certainly not with the man she loved standing beside her.

But she had known.

"We have a chance now," she said softly. "Ramon and I are together. We have the same story to tell. We can speak, knowing we will not endanger each other, that for the moment we are still safe. We can speak as one voice. There may be other people who know the truth and have enough courage to stand beside us."

Sam put his hand on her shoulder. "Go into the sanctuary, Elisa. Ramon, you, too. We're having a Christmas Eve service. That's where all of us should be."

She didn't want to cause any more problems for Sam. She stepped toward the door, but he anchored her where she was. "This is God's house," he reminded her.

"Sam . . ."

He was staring at the cars. Doors opened and men emerged. In the lone light at the edge of the grass, she could see that they wore identical blue jackets.

Sam spoke without taking his eyes off them. " 'Judge me, O God, and plead my cause against an ungodly nation: O deliver me from the deceitful and unjust man. For thou *art* the God of my strength: why dost thou cast me off? Why go I mourning because of the oppression of the enemy? O send out thy light and thy truth: let them lead me; let them bring me unto thy holy hill, and to thy tabernacles. Then will I go unto the altar of God, unto God my exceeding joy: yea, upon the harp will I praise thee, O God my God.' "

He turned to her. "We're having a Christmas Eve service. Tonight we'll go unto the altar and praise God, as the psalm says. We'll celebrate the birth of the greatest advocate of peace and goodwill the world's ever known. Come with me."

"They will come, too."

"So be it."

She understood then what he planned to do. He did not want the arrest to happen quietly in the dim light of the parking lot. He wanted the congregation to know. He wanted the world to know. Deceit and lies flourished in darkness and silence. And until now, because of her fear for Ramon, she had wrapped herself in both.

She thought of the other man she had loved. Gabrio had given his life to bring a horrible wrong in her country's past into the light. No matter the danger, her husband had never been silent. Her parents had spoken out, and they, too, had died because of it. Sharon Wisner, who had been baptized in this church. Roberto Estrada, who had raised his daughter and son to believe in the rights of all people.

If she gave in to the silence and the darkness now, she dishonored all of them.

She watched as Sam locked the door, then spun around. "Let's go."

One locked door would only delay the men. She turned to her brother and found he was no longer beside her. He was striding after Sam.

She was afraid for these two. She was not so afraid for herself. As she hesitated, she realized she would be more afraid for all of them if they simply let the struggle end so quietly.

She caught up and put her hand on Sam's arm. "Don't fight back," she said. "They are going to win. But they will not win without cost."

They turned into the hall leading to the sanctuary. She saw that the doors were open, that the ushers were in place, that the brass ensemble was in the front waiting for Sam and the choir to process.

Andy was the first to spot Sam, and he

hurried to meet him.

"You're late, for Pete's sake. The biggest service of the year, too. And where's your robe?" He glanced at Elisa and Ramon, and frowned.

Sam didn't answer. He stopped in the doorway and swept the sanctuary with his hand. "Elisa, Ramon, please go in and sit down." He finally turned his attention to his choir director. "There's been a change. Signal the ensemble, then begin the processional without me."

"Are you kidding? After all the rehearsing we did?"

"Not kidding. Do it. Now, please."

Andy shrugged, but he moved to the center of the doorway where the ensemble could see him and gave the signal. The choir assembled into two lines, waiting for the introduction to end.

Elisa and Ramon waited until he was done speaking. Tears in her eyes, she kissed Sam, then she took her brother's hand and went into the service.

The sanctuary was crowded, but she found two cramped spaces at the end of a pew in the middle of the room. She could smell pine and cedar and the melting wax of candles that had been set around the room. Frost adorned the windowpanes, which seemed to wobble under the power of trumpets, horns and voices raised in adoration.

The choir moved in slowly, singing "O Come All Ye Faithful." She had learned the carol in Spanish, of course, but she stood as they moved past her, along with the others in her row, and sang it that way, not caring that her words were different from those around her. She looked at Ramon, who was paler than she wanted to see him, but he was singing in Spanish, too.

When the carol finished, the choir was standing in front of the altar in rows. Sam was not there to tell the congregation to sit. But as everyone continued to stand, he walked up the aisle, not quite into the center of the room and held out his arms.

"And she brought forth her firstborn son and wrapped him in swaddling clothes and laid him in a manger because there was no room for them in the inn." He was silent for a moment. "Because there was no room at the inn. Can you imagine? No room for a mother about to give birth. No room for her husband, who wants only to make her comfortable. No room for a tiny baby.

"Our children imagined it this afternoon. Some of you were here for *Las Posadas*. Our children wanted to know why the Holy family was turned away time and time again. I told them it's a story of welcoming strangers into our midst, of providing for them, of giving comfort even when we are afraid.

"Of course, we don't know if that really happened, do we? We're relying on a man named Luke to tell us this story, and we know for a fact that he lived well after Jesus and got his information from other sources.

"But it's a good story nonetheless, isn't it? Even if it never happened quite this way. The Bible is filled with wonderful stories. Sometimes we get so caught up in proving they really happened, we forget their meaning. And let me tell you, as our children figured out, this particular story is heavy with meaning. A man, a woman, an unborn child. Turned away because there was no room. Room in the inn, room in our hearts . . ." He turned up his hands.

"Did you know that Luke was the only gospel author who told the story of Jesus's birth from Mary's point of view? He was also the narrator who acquainted us with Martha and a woman called Mary of Magdalene, who today some call the mystery woman of the New Testament. Through Luke we learned of Joanna, Susanna and other women he never mentions by name.

"He was a man who gave women their due in a time when few did. He was also a man with a joyous soul, our Luke, a man of poetry, a man filled with the Holy Spirit. Most likely he was a gentile, perhaps a doctor, certainly a man who believed in human rights. Only Luke tells us the story of the Good Samaritan. He showed us a Jesus who reached out to everybody, rich and poor, Jew and gentile, male and female. He tells us not kings but shepherds were the first to see the holy child after his birth."

There was a noise in the back of the room. Elisa closed her eyes.

"Luke wanted us to believe in a world filled with spirit, a world where the good we do is as important as the good we believe in. Luke, in his telling of the birth of Jesus, asked each of us to open our heart, to make room for strangers, to believe that the poor are as deserving as the rich."

"They're here," Ramon said softly beside her.

She took his hand. "Yes, I know."

"We learn from Luke that a humble stable was the home of God on that blessed night," Sam said.

Elisa opened her eyes and turned to watch him. He moved toward the back of the room. A buzzing began in the pews around her. Others were turning, too.

Sam stood at the double doors into the sanctuary. "On this blessed night," he said in a voice that carried to every corner of the room, *"this* is God's home. And we have room, we will *always* have room here, for anyone who needs us, but only for those who come in peace."

The room was suddenly so still that Elisa thought she could hear the candles flicker. A man stepped forward. Elisa could see that he wore a blue jacket. He kept his voice low, but his words penetrated the silence. "Pastor, finish your service. We'll wait."

Sam did not move away or turn. "These men are here to arrest two of our friends. Elisa, our sexton, who most of you know, and her brother, Ramon, are accused of a murder in Guatemala. Elisa's own husband was the victim, a man who spoke loudly and clearly for human rights. Gabrio Santos was killed for the terror he wanted to expose and the rights he espoused.

"They have only recently been reunited after searching for each other for three traumatic years. They were supposed to be victims themselves, but they escaped, and because they did, they are here with us tonight. Elisa and Ramon came to Toms Brook not by accident, but because they are the grandchildren of one of our former ministers, Alfred Wisner."

The buzz grew louder. Sam spoke above it. "I know Elisa is not a murderer. She is a physician, like Luke, a healer. I know Ramon is not a murderer. He was simply a child who experienced the horror of watching the man he loved like a father shot down in front of him."

He stepped closer and addressed the men standing there, pointing his finger. "I know that I can not permit you to enter this room and take them prisoner."

"It didn't have to be this way," the man in the blue jacket said. "We could have done this quietly. That was our intention."

"Yes, I know."

The other men moved forward. Elisa stood. Sam had made his statement. The story would be told now. She prepared to walk down the aisle to end this, but a man several rows in front of her now beat her to it.

Early Meeks, in Christmas suspenders, his bald head shining in the candlelight, joined Sam at the back of the room. He took Sam's hand. "This is the house of God," he told the men. "Step away."

Gayle Fortman got to her feet and joined them, taking Sam's other hand. "As president of this congregation, I'm asking you to leave. This is a house of God and a house of prayer. And we have given Elisa and Ramon sanctuary."

Others joined them, forming a chain, hand in hand, across the back of the church. Elisa hadn't realized Helen was there. She had grumbled about attending and looked for an excuse to skip the service. But now Elisa saw her trudging down the aisle along with Dovey and Gracie Barnhardt.

The human chain was spreading around the room. Young hands clasped in old. Dark hands clasped in light. She realized Adoncia was there, holding hands with Kate Brogan. Kendra Taylor stood between one of the Fortman boys and Leon Jenkins. The choir came down from the front and joined hands with the others. In only a minute's time the entire room was surrounded by an unbroken chain. A chain with no end and no beginning.

Andy began to sing in a high, light tenor. "Si-lent Night. Ho-ly Night."

The others took it up. Elisa knew she was crying. Ramon put his arms around her.

Then, as she watched from her brother's arms, one of the men in blue jackets stepped forward and wrenched Sam's hand free from Early's, doubled his arm behind his back and cuffed him.

Hand in hand, Elisa and Ramon stepped out into the aisle and waited their turn.

ℭhapter
Thirty-six

The meeting was called to order by Cathy Adams, our new president. For once we went straight to business, per-haps a sign for our future under the Adams administration? Cathy reported that together we have pieced a total of sixty twelve-inch blocks in red, white and blue prints, and from these we have assembled three sampler quilts — some more expertly than others. The quilting on the first two has been completed. The third is nearly done. We hope to raise as much as two thousand dollars auctioning the quilts at the annual Fourth of July picnic, and Andy Jones — whose haircut has much improved his appear-

*ance — is studying auctioneer tech-
niques to help us. The money will go to
help our minister and sexton with legal
expenses.*

*Helen reported that there might be
good news on the horizon, but that she
could not say more. We all agreed — a
rare moment indeed — that good news
would be very well received.*

*We completed the business meeting
with no interruptions for foolish items
like a treasurer's report or committee
notes. We set to work quilting our third
sampler. I must say, we were grateful
for the work and the companionship.*

*Sincerely,
Dovey K. Lanning, recording secretary*

Sam had not lost his appreciation for irony.
He had been arrested on Christmas Eve,
and he had reported to the Federal Correc-
tional Complex in Petersburg, Virginia, on
Good Friday. Had he believed he or any
man was important enough to be singled
out for a lesson by the Almighty, that might
have given him pause — particularly as he
was strip searched, photographed, finger-

printed and interviewed by a prison official with no sense of humor.

As it was, he had spent Easter Sunday in prison relearning the ropes. How not to touch another prisoner accidentally, how to wait to join a conversation, how not to make friends until it was clear which inmates were safe to approach. He had settled into the routine quickly, and that had bothered him almost as much as the three-month sentence, because it had implied a docility he did not feel.

The judge had not been moved by Sam's courtroom sermon on the historical role of churches as sanctuaries, beginning in medieval times and working up to the sanctuary movement of the 1980s that had aided Latin American refugees. Perhaps the dour old man might have been more inclined toward probation or house arrest had the political climate been different. But not only had Sam obstructed the work of a federal officer, he had already served time for civil disobedience. He had been lucky not to have been charged with harboring fugitives, too.

Sam was an annoyance, not a danger, and he had been sentenced to a low-security facility badly in need of renovation. The corrections officers had taken some getting used to again. Losing his freedom had taken more. For two weeks he awoke four or five times a night in a cold sweat, with the weight of the world pressing against his chest. Then, one morning in early May, he woke up in the coffinlike cubicle he shared with two other men and understood the truth he had refused to see.

Now it was June, and he was looking forward to a visit from Mack, who had told him he was bringing news of Elisa and Ramon. Their case had attracted widespread attention both in the U.S. and Guatemala. Kendra Taylor had written a detailed investigative piece for the *Washington Post* that had run in papers around the world. She had flown to Guatemala and, through an interpreter, interviewed residents who had found and helped Elisa and Ramon escape into Mexico. She had documented the abuses of Martin Avila Morales and his probable connection to the massacre in Wakk'an.

Others had come forward. Human rights advocates who had collected evidence on Gabrio's murder. Courageous government officials who had done investigations on their own and found that genuine evidence against Elisa and Ramon was nonexistent.

The U.S. government itself, unwilling to turn over two of its citizens unless the facts were in place, had, for the time being, declined to discuss extradition. Perceived to be flight risks, Elisa and Ramon had been placed in the Shenandoah County Jail until a decision could be made whether to move them into a federal facility. Until his own prison term began, Sam had been able to visit occasionally, sit behind a glass window and talk to them on visitation phones.

"Hey, Rev, you almost done with those weeds? We got to get this mulch spread all the way to China before we get to do any visiting."

Sam smiled at James, a young African-American who would not be so young after his sentence was served. Sam was assigned to the landscaping crew, and the hard physical labor helped him sleep better at night. He also found the work an interesting catalyst to conversation and reflection. One by one, although he had not suggested it, the other men were coming to him to discuss their spiritual concerns. As time passed, he had stopped being Sam. Now he was simply "Rev."

"I'll shovel, you spread." At James's side, Sam trekked to the mulch pile that steamed at the end of the parking lot and filled his wheelbarrow; then the two men trundled their loads back to the row of evergreens that was a demarcation, of sorts, of the prison boundaries.

"Who's coming to see you?" Sam asked as he shoveled the mulch into clumps under the evergreens so James could spread it.

"My girl. And she's bringing the baby."

"The baby have a name?"

"Taneesha. She's so fat we call her Roly Poly."

Sam wondered how long the baby's mother would continue to come and what James would do when the visits stopped. Because they probably would. Unless parole was once again introduced into the federal system, James, who had been convicted of conspiracy to distribute marijuana, would be a guest of Uncle Sam for the next eleven years.

"Baby girl needs a father," James said.

"Have you thought of ways you can be a father to her?" Sam asked. "While you're here?"

"I'm trying to get my diploma."

"That's a good start." Sam stood tall, stretched and, for this display of self-indulgence, earned a frown from the officer who was their supervisor.

He bent back to his task and shoveled mulch until his wheelbarrow was empty; then he started on the load James had brought. James stayed with him, patting and raking the shredded pine bark into submission as Sam dumped it. The guard passed on, satisfied Sam was earning his twenty-three cents an hour, the starting rate for prisoner labor. Had he been invited to stay in prison longer, he might have worked his way up to a dollar and some spare change.

"So what do you think I ought to do?" James demanded. "You got something in mind?"

Minutes had passed since the original question. "It's not what I think that matters," Sam said. "Getting the diploma is a great idea."

"What else can I do? I'm thinking I could sell my life story, you know, maybe to Spike Lee? Make me a million or two and save half for her. You thinking something like that?"

Sam knew James was joking, although grandiose thinking was the reason a lot of the inmates had ended up at Petersburg.

"I was thinking you might want to start writing letters to her," Sam said. "Get in the habit, you know? Ask your girl to keep them somewhere safe until she's old enough to read them. You can tell her your life story, at least the parts she should hear. Maybe you won't get a million for the letters, but they'd be worth more to Taneesha."

"Man, you always thinking about something other people need to do. You ever just unwind, kick back and do nothing at all?"

Sam tried to remember.

"I might write a letter or two," James said. "Nothing much to do at nights."

Sam had plenty to do with his. He spent his nights thinking about Elisa, and praying for her safety and Ramon's. When he wasn't praying, he was studying a Spanish textbook, dreaming and remembering.

They finished, cleaned up and went to lunch. In the cafeteria, he sat with James and two others in his unit. Mack was due at two, and Sam was anxious. He had hoped to be able to coordinate phone calls between the county jail and prison, but so far his petitions had not borne fruit. The letters he received were thoughtful and upbeat, but he needed to hear Elisa's voice to know how she was really feeling.

"Hey, Rev, aren't you going to bless the food?" Tyler asked as Sam picked up his fork. He was a squat man with no hair and the body of a weight lifter. He and Sam had ongoing conversations about the nature of God as they did push-ups together.

Sam looked down at his tray. A hamburger cooked so long it had shrunk to the size of a coat button. Rice glued kernel to kernel. Watery spinach that tinted the edges of the rice green. Half a slice of canned pineapple.

"Lord," he said, closing his eyes, "we ask that this food be given to those who truly deserve it, those prosecutors and judges who are far more worthy than we, your humblest of servants." Then, as the other men laughed, he smiled and began to eat.

Elisa was nervous. Mack had given her a long list of instructions about what to do and not to do before visiting Sam. She wore a knit dress that hung from a yoke just above her breasts and fell well below her knees. Tessa had bought it for her last week, while she was still in jail, and the subtle black-and-red check suited her without attracting attention.

The dress had short sleeves and revealed no cleavage, for which she could be turned away. Since there was always the possibility of a false positive with the drug detection machine, she had been careful not to wash her hands with perfumed soap or handle money after scrubbing them for the last time, or use hand lotion. She had made sure her bra had no underwire so she wouldn't set off the metal detector. She wore her hair loose to avoid a metal clip for the same reason — and because she knew Sam liked it that way.

She was ready.

"You're sure you don't want to come in with me?" she asked Mack, who had accompanied her to Petersburg. After six months in jail, she was a little shaky behind the wheel and hadn't wanted to drive.

"I'm not going to waste Sam's time today. I'll come with you tomorrow." Mack reached over and touched her arm. "Are you all right?"

"Yes, of course." She hesitated. "No. Of course not."

He laughed. "They aren't going to keep you. I promise."

"I think the worst prison in Virginia is probably better than what was waiting in Guatemala."

"I'm glad we'll never know."

She gave a short nod, along with a brief,

tense smile; then she waited as Mack thoughtfully got out to open her car door and walk her to the gates.

"You've got the coin purse and change?"

The coin purse, with money for the visiting room vending machines, had to be clear plastic, so she couldn't smuggle anything in. Tessa had found that for her, too. For months and months Tessa and Mack had done far more than their share to help her and her brother.

"And the folder," she said.

"There's no guarantee they'll let you give the folder to him. Nothing's ever a sure thing."

"I hope they will."

He kissed her cheek. "Good luck. I'll be waiting when they boot you out of there. Just remember, he only has another month. You'll make it."

She hugged him, then began her journey inside. It seemed to take forever. She filled out a form, removed her shoes, braved the metal detector and wiped her hands with a cloth pad when instructed so the pad could be checked for drug residue. She showed her brand-new ID — the first with her real name in more than three years — had her hand stamped, and finally waited to be ushered into the visiting room, minus the folder she had hoped to give Sam. She had made it, but the folder had not, and that saddened her.

The visiting room was much louder than she had expected. There were children and grandmothers and wives sitting at tables with men in tan trousers and short-sleeved shirts. There was a festive air, but beneath it she could feel an undercurrent of desperation. Each person was basking in this intimacy, while at the same time sadly contemplating its abrupt end and the return to separate lives.

She searched the room for Sam and saw him in the corner talking to another inmate, a young black man who gave her the once-over appreciatively before he returned to their conversation.

She pointed. "There he is." She tried a little humor. "The one in khaki."

The officer who had brought her in told her to wait, then went to get Sam. He was clearly annoyed that Sam hadn't come right to the door, but Elisa hadn't explained that her visit was a surprise. This was the kind of place where surprises were suspect.

She watched, breath held, as the officer tapped Sam on the shoulder and pointed in her direction. When elation animated

Sam's features, she released her breath slowly and smiled.

Almost immediately he was in front of her. He took her in his arms for a kiss that quickly became a tearful homecoming.

"Elisa . . ." He hugged her hard, then, regretfully, let her go. "One kiss now. And one at the end. There's a rule here for everything."

She smiled through her tears. "I was afraid I wouldn't even be allowed to touch you."

"The feds are so enlightened, you wouldn't believe it."

The officer motioned them to a table across the room with two chairs. Sam pulled hers out, then he pulled his beside her so their hips were touching.

"You're here." He took her hand. "I don't believe it. And I'm touching you. Am I dreaming?"

"They dropped the charges in Guatemala."

He closed his eyes. She thought he might be praying. When he opened them, they were suspiciously moist.

"Tell me," he said. "Everything."

"They haven't gone so far as to arrest anyone else. I don't know if they ever will, Sam. But under pressure they ruled there was no reliable evidence against me, and Morales has removed himself from the race for president and gone into seclusion. It's not enough, but perhaps it is something."

"Then you're free?"

She wasn't, not really. Although she was no longer wanted for Gabrio's murder, she knew that traveling back to the country of her birth was not, at least for the time being, safe. Her story had been documented, and so had her brother's. There was nothing to gain by their murder now, no information that could be suppressed. But retaliation was another matter, against her and anyone she embraced as a friend or tried to help.

"I am free here, in this country." She smiled when he touched her hair, pushing a lock over her shoulder. "I don't think I can go back to Guatemala to live. Not yet. Perhaps when the climate there is different, when we have new leaders who are serious about setting the past to rest at last. Perhaps even if Morales is arrested and tried for Gabrio's murder."

"And Ramon?"

"He missed three years of his education, but the year he spent hiding in Guatemala, he read every book his mentors could find for him. And his education was superior before. . . ." She lifted her hands. "He is passionate about going back to school, about becoming a doctor and specializing in public health to honor Gabrio. It's what Gabrio would have wanted. Ramon will find a way, and I'll be there to help him. For now we're living with Helen, and he is studying. When he is not playing with your dogs."

Helen, who didn't believe in "pets," had insisted that Sam's dogs needed a country vacation and made Zeke build them a large dog run in the back. Cissy, Zeke and Reese were home to stay, and now the old "Stoneburner Place" was alive with activity again.

Sam seemed pleased at that picture. "And you, Elisa?"

She was not ready to continue. She had waited too long for a real conversation, for details of his life. "No, first you. I know you still have a job. Helen tells me the board agreed unanimously not to accept your resignation. In her words, they would just appreciate you staying out of trouble in the future. If you're capable."

He grinned. "George Jenkins went into treatment and is off the board at last. That's the only reason the vote was unanimous."

"He'll be back," Elisa said. "Adoncia told me Diego is managing the business while he is away, better than he did himself. Diego came to see me in jail. He was sorry he told Leon's father who I was, genuinely sorry, I believe. It took courage to face me. He has had many talks since Christmas Eve with his priest."

"And he and Adoncia?"

She shrugged. "She is not yet ready to take him back, but if he proves he is sincere, she might. Still, he will have to jump through many hoops." She almost felt sorry for Diego.

"Jenkins will probably continue to cause trouble."

"Leon came to see me, too. I was the talk of the jail, with all my visitors."

"This has been difficult for him. I saw a lot of Leon before I surrendered."

"Even after his father returns, Gayle wants Leon to stay with her. Until he is absolutely sure it's a good idea to go back."

She realized suddenly that Sam hadn't said he planned to stay on as minister of the church. "I said you still have your job if you want it, but do you?"

He struggled with his answer. For a moment she was filled with apprehension that he had made plans that did not include her or a life with her. They had pledged themselves to each other, but so much had happened since, and months of separation had passed.

He looked up from their clasped hands. "Do you believe in revelation?"

She was surprised. She had not expected theology but something more alarming. "Mountaintops and stone tablets? Burning bushes?"

"No, I mean the kind that comes to each of us at quiet moments. The kind we probably don't even deserve. That moment when, zap, we understand exactly who we are and what we can do with our lives?"

"The day I decided to become a doctor."

"You do understand."

"And you have had this kind of revelation?"

"Elisa, I've struggled for years with the kind of ministry I want to do. And now I finally know. I'm going to begin a prison ministry."

She sat back and catalogued a new ease in his expression, a peace that hadn't been there before. "Yes," she said at last, "it only makes sense."

"I can't tell you if God put this in my path or if I've just finally made sense of random events in my life. It doesn't even matter. I do know that this is what I need to do, that it's the best way I can serve God." He smiled, almost as if he were embarrassed. "I'm thinking of these months as my internship, so to speak."

"Then you'll give up the church?"

"No, I'll talk to the board and see if they'll bring in an assistant pastor. The way we've grown, we need one anyway, and they can cut my salary if they need to, to make up the difference. I'll do the prison ministry part-time, at least at first, until I'm established. I feel sure I can work this out and do both. And I can bring lessons from one to the other, even involve Community if they're willing."

She could almost see his mind spinning, making plans, following the path he knew he was intended to pursue. "I know you'll find a way."

He leaned forward. He stroked her hair. "And you? What are you going to do, since you can't go back to Guatemala yet?"

A female officer as large and intimidating as any of the men came into the room and walked toward them. For a moment Elisa was afraid Sam was in trouble for touching her, but the officer dropped Elisa's folder on the table, turned and left.

"What's this?" Sam asked, reaching for it.

Pleased, Elisa slid the folder toward her instead. "Something I brought for you." She opened it and pulled out a dozen photocopied pages, and put them in front of Sam.

"What's this?"

"Letters from Sarah Miller to Amasa Stone."

"The letters Martha mentioned?"

"Yes. I don't know if she didn't want to tell me where they were because she wanted to be able to tell the story herself, or if she simply didn't remember. But when Martha went into the nursing home, she gave her most treasured belongings to Dovey. Dovey was too kindhearted to get rid of anything, just in case Martha ever asked for it. So she has boxes of Martha's stuff stored in her basement. When Dovey learned who I was, she decided I should have everything important, including Martha's old treadle sewing machine. It is a wonderful gift."

"Does Martha know who you are now?"

"After the arrest, Dovey decided not to tell her, in case . . ." Elisa knew he understood.

"And now?"

"Ramon and I went to see Martha the day after we were released. I told her who we are. I don't think she will remember, but during our visit, I think she understood. She even called me Alicia." She smiled, remembering. "It was a good moment, Sam."

"And the letters?"

"While I was detained, Dovey went through the boxes and separated the things she thought I should have. And she found them. These are copies. The originals will need to be preserved."

"I'll look forward to reading them. They're a real treasure."

Sam was hanging on every word and devouring her with his eyes. Elisa thought he would be only a little less enthused if she was describing the finest points of postpartum care. She felt the same way.

"They are more than a treasure," she continued. "They are the answer to a puzzle."

"Whether Sarah went on to rescue more slaves?"

"No, the puzzle of what happened to Dorie."

"But I thought Martha told you the end of that story?"

"Not quite, and I'm not sure why. I

think she probably didn't remember. But, Sam, it is . . . well, it's in the last two letters."

"Tell me. I'm sure not going to read it right now, not with you sitting right there looking so beautiful."

For a moment, gazing at him, she forgot what she'd been about to say. Then he clasped her hand, and she recovered.

"Jeremiah went to find Dorie. We will never know how exactly. Sarah does not give details, but she does tell Amasa that her brother has gone, and that Jeremiah has information he thinks will lead him to the right place."

"And that's all?"

"No, not quite." She removed the bottom letter from the stack. "She says it best. This is the last letter Dovey found. And now, you see, we would know, just from these letters, that Amasa went back to Toms Brook, because these were in Martha's possession. Amasa must have brought them back with him when he left Lynchburg to marry Sarah and take over the farm. That's the only way Martha would have had them."

"One happy ending, at least. And Dorie and Jeremiah?"

"Let me read a little."

She gazed down at the paper in front of her. "My dear Amasa. How I wish you were already here beside me. But I have news I believe will bring you faster. Today I received a letter from my brother."

She looked up. "That's even more proof that Sarah and Amasa were reunited. She says 'already here.' But there's more to come."

He played with a lock of her hair. "Go on."

She cleared her throat. "Jeremiah found Marie in Kentucky. Against everything we believe in, he paid for the child and her freedom, something he could not have done when Dorie was with us, because the trail would have led right to the child's mother.

"Now, with Marie at his side, he will continue on to Ohio, where he hopes to find Dorie. There are many places near Cincinnati where a woman might hide as she tries to discover news. He is confident that he will be able to trace her, if she indeed made the journey that far with success. And, Amasa, my beloved, if prayers gave Dorie's feet wings, if prayers kept her from discovery and capture, then she is safe in Ohio now."

Elisa looked up. There was a lump in her

throat. "This is difficult to read out loud."

"It's difficult to listen to."

"I will only read a little more." She looked down once more to finish.

"Jeremiah wishes us both God's grace, and he hopes that we will find happiness together. He counsels me to be strong, to think carefully before making decisions and to pray for him. But most important he says not to pray that he will ever return to Toms Brook. He asks me to pray that he will *not,* for if he does not, then he has made a new life in Canada."

She slid the letter under the pile in front of him and took a moment to compose herself. "After she read the letters, Dovey went to the courthouse and searched for information. The very next year after this letter was written, the farm was titled to a Sarah Stone, and Jeremiah's name was removed from the deed. And that's all we'll probably ever know."

Elisa saw that Sam understood what this final letter meant to her. She had given up on happy endings, certain from everything that had happened to her that they were not possible. Now, she was beginning to believe again. She would never know for certain that Jeremiah had found Dorie or, somehow, despite the odds, made a life with her. But now she believed it was possible. She could see that Sam, too, realized that the letters were about more than the lives of people long dead.

"What are *you* going to do now?" he asked. "Now that you're free?"

"There's work to do in the Valley. I want to find a way to help the Latina women I've met. To be licensed to practice medicine in Virginia, most likely I will need to do another residency." She made a face, trying to pretend this was of no importance. "Years of no sleep. I remember it well."

She realized she had averted her eyes. She made herself look at him and saw exactly what she hoped to see in his expression. "You could, perhaps, live with years of little sleep?"

"I expected little sleep once we had children. I'm resigned."

She laughed, because the only alternative was a return to grateful tears. And she had cried enough. "We could do that, as well. We can work out the timing."

"Elisa." He shook his head. "Did you think that the months apart had made any difference to me? Did you really doubt I still loved you?"

"I don't think a man or a woman can go

to prison and not come out changed."

"Yes, and I'm more sure after all this that I want to spend the rest of my life with you. I don't want to waste another day apart."

She saw he was waiting to hear the same. "This time a wedding ring? A church and people we love as witnesses?"

"It might be easier to explain than the way we did it before."

She smiled, wanting badly to kiss him, knowing they were probably being watched. "I will marry you again anywhere you say. Again and again if I have to."

"Once more should do the trick." He stole a kiss anyway. Quickly, but with promise.

"I have one more thing for you." She pulled a photograph from the folder.

He held the photo and stared at it. Ramon had taken it with Mack's digital camera, and Tessa had blown it up to a five-by-seven and printed this copy. Elisa was sitting on the front steps of *La Casa*, and spread across her lap was the colorful Endless Chain quilt. She had quilted it in jail using a lap hoop that Helen had brought for her. More than anything, finishing the quilt had helped her cope with her fears for the future.

"I wanted to bring it here for you," she said. "I wanted you to have it on your bed, to sleep under it knowing I had done the same. But it's not a gift I'm allowed to give you. So I'll sleep under it alone, every night, until you come home next month, Sam. But it's yours. My wedding gift to you."

He looked up from the photograph. *"Elisa, te amo con todo el corazón. Eres mi amada.* You are and always will be my beloved."

She didn't need to kiss him again. She didn't need to touch him. Looking into Sam's eyes she could envision the life that waited and all the promise it held. Promise was enough.

About the Author

Emilie Richards's many novels feature complex characterizations and in-depth explorations of social issues, a result of her training and experience as a family counselor, which contribute to her fascination with relationships of all kinds. Emilie, a mother of four, lives with her husband in northern Virginia, where she is currently working on *Lover's Knot*, the final book in her Shenandoah Album series.

Visit Emilie Richards's Web site at www.emilierichards.com